THE SPACE  _N

MAGGIE ROBBINS

Copyright © 2021 by Maggie Robbins. All Rights Reserved.

No part of this publication may be reproduced, distributed, or transmitted in any form or by any means, including photocopying, recording, or other electronic or mechanical methods, or by any information storage and retrieval system without the prior written permission of the publisher, except in the case of very brief quotations embodied in critical reviews and certain other noncommercial uses permitted by copyright law.

This is a work of fiction. Names, characters, businesses, places, events and incidents are either the products of the author's imagination or used in a fictitious manner. Any resemblance to actual persons, living or dead, or actual events is purely coincidental.

Maggie Robbins' Website
Find me on Twitter
Also, on Facebook
Documenting my life on Instagram

Join My Newsletter!

Developmental Edited by Lara Z Edits

Copy Edited by Jenna Bygall

Cover Design by LJ at Mayhem Cover Creations

I have a very long list of people to thank for making this book happen, and I probably will forget some people, but if you helped me, please know that it meant the world to me.

First and foremost, I would like to thank my British BFF Sarah, who was one of the first people to sit down with me once I had a draft done and really hash it out with me. I couldn't have done this without her, and truly, she is such a wonderful human being and a beautiful part of the lesfic community. Thank you for being such a great friend.

This book also wouldn't have been what it is without the help of Lara, who is truly a wonderful editor. I sent her my rough drafts and she graciously took them and tore them apart for me, so I could build them back up better and stronger than before. She helped so much in shaping the way this turned out, making me proud to say it's probably my favorite book I've ever written.

Another person who I owe a debt of gratitude to is my old friend Amanda, who I hope sees this book and reads this dedication, to at least know how grateful I am to her. Amanda was one of the people who believed in this story before it was even a story. She even sent me an International Space Station Lego set, that I still have sitting in my office. So, thank you, Amanda. You've always been someone who believed in my writing, even when I didn't, and I appreciate you.

Thank you to Cara Malone, who has been excited for this book for two years now, and to all those book club people who pestered me about getting it done.

To LJ, of Mayhem Cover Creations, who is by far the most fantastic cover artist I've ever met. The Space Between was the first cover she ever made for me, and I was in awe.

To all the fans that have stuck by me, thick and thin. The people who write me messages about how much they love my books, that they're excited for the next ones. The fans and even my colleagues that know me on a little more personable level and have reached out to me time and time again to make sure I was okay, to lend an ear and friendship. You mean the world.

And last, but certainly not least. To my favorite human in the entire universe, Jennifer. The person who gifts me with such wonderful inspiration to write about, who fills my days with unconditional love and compassion and hope. You're the best thing that ever happened to me. You're the reason I keep going every day, the reason I still have faith. I never want to live this life without you. You will always be the reason I write happily ever afters...

Thank you to everyone who made this book possible. I appreciate you all.

PART ONE
ACCELERATION

ONE

RUBY

"T minus sixty seconds and counting. All systems are go. We are about sixty seconds from the launch of Space Shuttle Discovery. Space Shuttle Discovery Flight Controllers listen up. Give me a go/no go for launch."

A torrent of voices filled the headset, dozens at Mission Control confirming systems checks one last time. The adrenaline flooded my system like it was on an intravenous drip – right into my blood at full pelt. I thought my heart would explode, and my eyes were wide and searching. Last-minute adjustments to my suit, ensuring the latches on my helmet were secure. My fingers danced across the grey and blue console in front of me. I'd memorized each of the several hundred controls in the cockpit thousands of times. Dozens of screens glowed in the early morning light, reporting on every single component of the shuttle.

"We are go for all-systems start. T minus seventeen seconds and counting."

I looked at my co-pilot on my right. Focused straight ahead, lost in thought.

"Ten... nine... eight... seven..."

A loud rumble signaled the ignition of the main engines. The entire orbiter rattled and shuddered like I imagined a skyscraper would in an earthquake. I had felt it before, but each time was just as intense as the last. I could hardly hear the final numbers being counted down until zero.

The massive kick in my back sent me jerking forward as the shuttle blasted off the pad and the solid rocket boosters ignited. The pounding exhaust from the twin boosters shook us continually as we sped up at 2.5 G's, ripping through the lower atmosphere under seven million pounds of thrust.

My body immediately felt the urge to break free of the restraints that were binding me to my seat. It felt constrictive in a very terrifying and real way. Trapped with no escape. The engines throttled back up to full thrust, while the spine-tingling scream of the slipstream outside of the cabin was clearly audible. It was the sound of immense power, unleashed in a barely controlled fury.

With the world burning around me, two minutes felt like a lifetime. But I knew when it hit by the loud bang of the empty boosters peeling off the external tank. In the last minute of the ride to orbit, all I could do was rehearse my duties once we were there. Praying for my safety, and for that of my crewmate.

Just like that, the primary engine was cut off. The pressure on my straps vanished, and all at once I was afloat, in a free fall at last. A flood of relief washed through me and the vastness of starry blackness engulfed us.

Every astronaut will tell you the first time you see your beautiful blue planet in the depths of space, it changes you. It's a view few will ever get to experience in person. It changes how you feel about your life, our species, and our place in the universe. It sneaks up on you, because you're busy and doing stuff. Your emotions almost end up behind you, because there's so many things happening all at once. You go through the launch and it's just chaos.

But then I got that moment. The entire universe paused, and it was just me and a panorama of brilliant deep blue ocean, shot with *shades of green and gray and white. Every mountain and ocean, every city. That little ball. That's where life was, where all the good stuff was...*

"COMMANDER PETERS, WHERE ARE WE?" My attention focused back to the classroom of students, and specifically the kid that was speaking, shaking my head clear of my thoughts.

The cupola surrounded us, a panorama of space. And above us, or below, depending on how you thought about it, the Earth. I could see the South Indian Ocean, the expanse of blue water stretched in every direction to the horizon.

"Okay, if you look closely, you can see we're passing over some icebergs. Isn't that cool?" I pushed my tablet against the round center window. My eyes scanned over a nearby computer console to confirm my suspicions. "It looks like we're somewhere between Africa and Antarctica." My attention turned back to my tablet camera and the little red light blinking in the corner. "Can anyone tell me how many times a day the International Space Station rotates around the Earth?"

Hands raised on the opposite end of the video call in a familiar classroom. One I'd grown up in. Someone shouted out the answer. "Sixteen?" I smiled and gave an enthusiastic nod.

"That's exactly right! Good job." I steadied myself against the computer console station that wrapped around the entire cupola. "Usually, we come up here to get a three-hundred-and-sixty-degree view of what's happening outside of the ISS. A lot of times we can watch shuttles dock or use the robotic arm." I tilted the tablet outward again and pointed toward the large titanium arm that extended from the station. "We use the Canadarm2, as it's called, to move supplies and equipment around in space and help the astronauts when they work outside. Nifty, huh?"

"Let's fly together and check out another one of my favorite spots on the ISS," I decided. I pushed off from the metallic blue support beam surrounding the computer consoles and headed back down into the heart of the station. It didn't look like much, just a bunch of aluminum and white plating. Across the walls were racks of electrical power and data. "We're back in Node 2 now and going to hang a left to head over to the Destiny module, where our research laboratory is housed." I pushed off toward the left, with a white room filled to the brim with electronic equipment and wires of all shapes and sizes. Once I'd reached the first computer station in the room, I turned the tablet to face me. Kids were already raising their hands.

"How about some questions?" I chuckled, nodding toward the screen. I ran fingers through my short curly black hair, a pixie cut to accommodate the job in space. I tucked a few loose strands behind my ear.

"Commander Peters," a young teenage girl in the front row of students spoke. I could barely make her out on the screen. "Is it true that the first civilian is coming on board the space station in a few weeks?"

I smiled and nodded. "The shuttle with our NASA scientist will arrive in just a few weeks, yes. We're helping with some research projects that study the effects of prolonged habitation in space on the human body."

In my peripheral, I saw a frame floating down Node 2, turning into Destiny with the same trajectory as I had. An unusually lanky, messy-haired brunette with a scruffy mustache made his way slowly toward me. I quickly spun the tablet around, and my colleague Daniel Richards gave me a dirty look before flashing a smile and a wave at the camera. "Hey there, kids. How goes it?"

"This is my fellow astronaut, Daniel Richards. He and Russian astronaut Adrik Ivanov have been up here with me for the past six months. Adrik and Daniel are headed back to Earth in a few weeks."

"Pleasure to meet you all." Daniel nodded, floating past me to another computer station.

"Daniel is working on robotics research himself. Before he joined NASA, he was an electrical and computer engineer." I explained, continuing to film him. "Smart cookie, that one." Daniel waved me off, turning his head over his shoulder to look back at the tablet.

"Stay in school, kids," he teased with another quirky smile.

I spun the tablet back around to face me. "Any more questions?"

"Commander Peters, is it true that you'll have been at the ISS longer than any other astronaut in history?"

"Ruby's a space monkey," Daniel called out into the room. "Adrik jokes that she's trying to outstay Valeri Polyakov." Valeri was a Russian astronaut who had accumulated twenty-two months of space experience, fourteen of which were spent at one time aboard a space station.

"I've been up here for a year, and I'm planning on staying a year and a half total," I explained, darting my eyes across the screen. Eighteen months in my career. Not quite twenty-two, but I wasn't against beating the record. "I've got time for one or two more questions before we need to get back to work up here. Anybody?"

When we'd wrapped up the tour, I spun the camera around to face a blonde-haired, blue-eyed woman who had her hair pulled up in a messy bun on top of her head. She was beaming at me, pushing her coke-bottle glasses up her nose. "Hi, sweetheart. Thanks for doing that." My aunt and I looked nothing alike. While I had black curly hair and brown eyes, my aunt's vibrant blonde hair and blue eyes were a striking contrast.

Still, she was the best pseudo-mother I could have ever asked for. After my father passed away, my mom passed me off to her sister to be taken care of. The pain of having to take care of a child without a father had been too much for her. "Hi, Mary," I replied, brushing that same strand of short, curly hair behind my ear. "No problem. Anytime, you know that."

"You look skinny," Mary noted, squinting at me. "Are you eating enough?"

"The same as I was last time we talked," I replied, looking down at my short, petite frame. While I was certainly small, I hadn't lost weight. They had us take meticulous notes about every aspect of our health when we were up here. My aunt just tended to worry. "I'm fine, I promise. Just staying busy."

"I can't believe you signed on for another six months." Mary shook her head. "I sent you a care package with the shuttle tomorrow. Some more crossword puzzles. Don't go through them too fast."

I laughed, looking over at the crossword puzzle book that was tied down next to my workstation. I'd barely been up here a few months and had already made my way through a dozen. "I'm not going to make any promises," I replied. Ever since I was a little kid, I'd loved puzzles. My record for the New York Times crossword was fifteen minutes, when I was just a teenager. I was still trying to beat it. Unfortunately, I didn't get a lot of NYT crosswords these days, being in space and all. But whenever I had a puzzle in my hands, I liked to solve it. "Listen Mary, I have to get going. We've got a lot to do before the shuttle gets here in a few days. Tell Eric I said hello when you go to lunch. Is he still liking his students?"

"He likes them well enough, but I don't think they'll like calculus, no matter how hard they try," Mary replied, smiling at me. "He's giving them a good college try, though."

"Just tell them they won't be astronauts until they learn about limits." My aunt laughed when I said it, and I gave her a wave. "Love you both."

"Love you more," she replied, switching off the tablet on her end. When the screen went black, I slipped the device behind a tie down next to my computer station. Afterwards, I turned my attention toward the plethora of emails in my inbox. I was the world's worst at checking emails, despite many meetings at headquarters where I was asked to be more diligent.

"I swear, if I get one more email chain about cleaning out the fridge at the KSC cafeteria... That's the third time this week." Daniel moaned behind me, clicking at his laptop loudly. The Kennedy Space Center employees were notorious for their chain emails that bombarded our inboxes. It was bad enough that I didn't check emails and made it a hundred times worse when there were a thousand to go through.

"They send it to everyone," I reminded him, finding the email buried in my inbox full of unopened messages. Before I clicked to delete it, I saw a message near the top that read "REMINDER: GALILEO BRIEFING MEETING SCHEDULED." It had been sent an hour ago, but the minute I saw the subject line I knew exactly what it was about. I had nearly forgotten about the meeting with the research staff at Johnson Space Center in Houston. When I clicked open the email, I decrypted the message into another window. The files opened across my laptop screen. At least a half dozen. I scanned over the briefing letter, which basically explained about the upcoming civilian mission to the International Space Station. NASA was sending a neurobiologist to come up and study the astronauts aboard the ISS for groundbreaking research.

"Did you see the briefing email?" I asked Daniel, scanning through the files.

"I was just looking at it," Daniel replied. "Damn, Peters. Check out your Dr. Carter."

The name immediately registered. I'd been reading about Dr. Daphne Carter for months. She was the head of the Occupational Health and Ergonomics division of the National Space Biomedical Research Institute. A medical doctor, she'd devoted nearly twenty years of her life to the study of spine health in astronauts. We'd helped her team with research in the past, but now she was making the journey as a civilian to the space station in a few weeks' time. I clicked on her resume, opening it.

There was a photo on the right-hand side. Daniel wasn't wrong. Piercing hazel eyes stared back at me behind square, black framed glasses. Her dirty blonde hair was pulled up tightly in a bun on her head. There was a fierce look on her angled face. She wore a fitted blue polo with the NASA emblem on the breast. And boy, was she ever beautiful. Every time I saw her, I found myself staring for a length amount of time, until I heard a laugh from behind me.

"I wasn't sure she'd be your type," Daniel chortled. "With that dark and brooding thing going on. Seems a little high strung."

He was right. She was a little high strung for my tastes, but if I had a resume like hers, I would likely be that way too. Her research and accomplishments were a mile long. She'd been doing groundbreaking research in collaboration with the National Aeronautics and Space Administration, NASA, nearly since she'd graduated her medical program.

"Meeting's about to start, Rubs," Daniel interrupted my train of thought. He'd come to float beside me, looking over my shoulder. I shook my head, closed out of the files I'd opened and went to start up the proprietary video conferencing software that NASA used for these "long distance" meetings with the ISS. Daniel and I chit-chatted about nothing for a few minutes, waiting for the other end to connect. Finally, a conference room filled the computer screen. There were at least a dozen people in the room, and only two that I recognized. One was Dr. William Hale, who was the director of the biology research division at NASA. We worked with him quite frequently with projects.

The other was Dr. Carter. She sat adjacent to Dr. Hale at the table, eyes focused on the screen. I'd never seen someone who looked so serious in my life, her lips pursed into a fine line, back straight in her chair. There were notes in front of her. I didn't even bother looking at the others in the room with them, too fixated on the doctor who'd be joining us in a few weeks.

"Good afternoon from Houston, Commander Peters, Mr. Richards," Dr. Hale said, offering a small smile and a head nod toward the camera. He was one of those people who very rarely smiled, so it looked a little odd on his face. I could make out a sunny blue sky through the picture window behind the group at the conference table. A gorgeous day in Texas. "Are you ready to discuss the project?"

"We were just looking over the briefing documents," Daniel

replied, before I was able to speak. "Pleasure to finally make your acquaintance, Dr. Carter."

The blonde-headed woman next to Dr. Hale nodded once, but still did not offer a smile. "You as well, Mr. Richards. Commander Peters, I assume you've gone over all the project materials that were sent over to you..." I nodded, opening my mouth to reply, but Dr. Carter beat me to the punch. "If you don't mind, I'd like to go over everything again, just to make sure we are all on the same page. I've decided to show you my funding presentation. I believe that will be the simplest way."

Again, before I could reply, the video of the conference room disappeared and Daniel and I were watching a screen capture with a PowerPoint presentation. *Lumbar Spine Paraspinal Muscle and Intervertebral Disc Height Changes in Astronauts after Long-Duration Spaceflight on the International Space Station.*

Dr. Carter went through the presentation for a good ten minutes or so, rehashing information that I'd already read a dozen times over. We'd been collaborating with this research since before I'd started on as an astronaut for NASA.

"I'll be conducting diagnostic testing while onboard the International Space Station, since this hasn't been completed yet by a medical physician in a microgravity environment. In addition, Commander Peters will be assisting me with my troponin activator drug trial testing on my research specimens. I assume that you've briefed yourself on the project and what you'll be assisting me with while I'm there and after I've left the station?"

My attention turned to Dr. Carter, whose hazel eyes were locked on me. I swallowed deeply before I replied, a little bit intimidated by her, to say the least. "I feel amply prepared," I replied, offering her a friendly smile to break her of her very rigid demeanor. "I've been over all the research materials and procedural documentation for months now. I don't think you'll be disappointed."

"I should certainly hope not," Dr. Carter replied, looking completely unfazed by my attempt to be friendly toward her. "We only have a limited amount of time together, after all, and this is ground-breaking research, Commander. Research I've spent nearly two decades working on. I expect only the best from you."

There were a few moments I felt annoyed with her and her questioning of my abilities. But I shook it off, replying swiftly. "Your research will be my primary focus for the upcoming months, I assure you."

"All of us are happy to help you with anything you need," Daniel added.

Dr. Carter looked skeptical, to say the least. She was still staring straight at me, and her eyes made a shiver rip down my spine. Even with how serious she looked; she was beautiful. Ageless, looking nothing like a woman in her forties. "Commander Peters, might I ask you a couple of questions regarding the troponin activator drug trial, since you'll be assisting?"

Apparently, my reassurances hadn't been enough. "Of course," I replied.

She looked down at her notes briefly, then back up at me. "Explain to me what the drug is meant to do."

She was pitching a soft ball. "The drug amplifies the response to motor neuron input, increases muscle power, and improves muscle fatigability." Dr. Carter nodded, taking notes on the paper in front of her. I wondered, briefly, what she could possibly be writing. Instead of waiting for another question, I continued. "The drug has been shown to improve function with amyotrophic lateral sclerosis. And the intent of this drug trial is to, in addition to other supplements and exercise regimens, potentially help muscle wasting diseases and atrophy that occurs with prolonged space travel."

Dr. Carter opened her mouth to reply, but this time I beat her to the punch. "Previous MRI scans of ISS astronauts have indicated significant atrophy of the paraspinal lean muscle mass during their time in space. The goal of the drug trial is to help reverse damage to muscle structures and alleviate back issues post-missions." I paused briefly, and then nodded to the rest of the room. "And since your research is presently being funded by a very well-known private space exploration company, I'm assuming finding ways to mitigate muscle wasting would be extremely beneficial for longer space missions. Say, to Mars, for example."

In that moment, I noticed a tiny change in Dr. Carter's facial expression. There had been a hint of a smirk on her lips for just a half of a second, before it disappeared. She nodded, finishing up the notes she'd been taking. When her attention turned back to me, I noticed that her gaze had softened just slightly. "Rather impressive, Commander Peters." I couldn't help but shrug and offer a small smile back in return. It felt good to impress her, for some reason.

"I think it's about time we let Mr. Richards and Commander Peters get back to their duties on the station. Thank you for your time."

Daniel and I said brief goodbyes to a responsive Dr. Hale. When I glanced at Dr. Carter, she still had her eyes on me, until we'd disconnected from the video call. The minute we had, Daniel let out a very amused laugh into the room.

"Well, looks like you got your hands full, kid," Daniel was grinning at me when I turned to look at him. "She's going to be all over your ass if you do something wrong." Luckily, I wasn't the type that made mistakes. At least very rarely. It was the reason I'd gotten where I was, I was thorough. I liked to know exactly what I was doing. And while Dr. Carter was an enigma and hard to read at times, I intended to prove my worth to her, however I could.

WHEN DANIEL and Adrik went to rest for a few hours, I found myself back at the cupola. It was my favorite place on the station, and for good reason. I loved working with the view, even if it made it hard to focus sometimes. The planet just glowed. I remembered trying to explain it to my mother one time, what it was like looking at it. "The simplest way I can think of is just, take a lightbulb—the brightest lightbulb you could ever possibly imagine—and just paint it all the colors you know the Earth to be, and turn it on, and be blinded by it." Because day, night, sunrise, or sunset, it was just glowing all those colors.

I didn't expect it to be like that. I remember thinking it would be pretty, but I didn't expect it to feel like you could almost reach into it. I couldn't deny that it was a planet. That we lived on a planet. For the first few days that I'd arrived on the ISS, I kept looking out the window, expecting to see Florida and my home. But after a few days, my feelings shifted, and I started to develop this feeling of interconnectivity. I still wanted to see Florida, but Florida had just become this piece of a bigger picture. And that bigger picture was Earth.

Every time I looked at it, it was the most beautiful thing I had ever seen.

Except for maybe Dr. Carter, who was on my mind a lot more than I expected that evening. The way she had been looking at me when the video call had disconnected. Those hazel eyes were as vivid in my mind as if she'd been right there staring at me on the station itself. I shifted through her dozens of research papers on one of the laptops in the cupola, feeling my body floating effortlessly as I worked.

Floating.

I remembered when I'd first arrived, my instincts were constantly trying to take over, my brain telling me that I was falling and that I needed to try and catch myself. Then over time, I started understanding. If I was in rational control of my movements, microgravity was just like the realization of a dream, either floating or flying through space.

Right now, I barely noticed. I was too engrossed in language that was almost outside the scope of my vocabulary, trying my best to absorb twenty years of research in which Dr. Carter had been studying the effects of microgravity on the spine. It was fascinating, to say the least. When I could understand what she was saying, anyway.

I clicked back to Dr. Carter's resume, studying her face again.

Imagining what she might be like in person and dreading the idea of disappointing her. Finally, I clicked out, deciding to check my social media sites. I scrolled through pictures of babies and new houses and summer vacations, all on a planet I was nearly three hundred miles away from. Catching up on nearly a week's worth of people's lives, that I barely stayed in touch with anymore, outside of the occasional like or comment on a photo or two.

Before I could stop myself, I searched for her name. It had been several months now since the last time I'd checked up on her. When Amber Ray's profile filled my screen, her new picture caught my eye. She'd cut her hair shorter, cropped across her face. Sitting in her lap was her one-year-old son Bennett, who looked the spitting image of his mother. Next to her was Peggy, her wife. They looked happy, and as much as it hurt, I was happy for them too. Even if the longing for my ex-friend was still awful at points. She'd moved on, and so had I.

I pulled out the crossword puzzle book from behind a white tie-down next to the computer. Flipped it open to an empty crossword near the end of my book. I liked my life. I loved the career and the path I'd chosen.

Even if, at times, it was a very lonely one.

TWO

DAPHNE

The world spun in streaks of blurry white and grey. All I could focus on was the pressure on my chest as we moved, like an elephant was crushing me and making it hard to breathe. As the vessel slowed reality started to take shape around me. The pressure on my chest relaxed, but all at once there was a pounding in my head and a churning in my stomach.

This hadn't been my first ride in the simulator. In fact, it had been one of several in the past month in preparation for our launch in a few weeks to the International Space Station.

I tried not to think about it.

As we came to an abrupt halt, the room continued to move. I reached for the white container that was in front of me, strapped to the console. I struggled to breathe as I retched into the bag. The odor was strong, and only made my nausea that much worse. When I was finally able to regain my composure, I sat up properly and wiped my mouth with the back of the sleeve of my jacket. "I don't think I'm ever going to get used to this."

One of the astronauts that would be accompanying me to the International Space Station sat to my left in the simulator. She forced a polite smile, though she looked quite ill from what she'd just witnessed. Her short brown hair was frazzled from the intense ride. "Luckily it doesn't last that long." I wasn't quite sure if she was trying to reassure herself as much as she was me. I believed it was her first trip up, so she likely was as nervous as me.

"I'm meant for research," I muttered, unstrapping myself from the seat as the hatch door to the simulator opened. "All this flying nonsense was for you astronauts. The ones who are masochistic enough to enjoy it."

"They wouldn't go through all this trouble if you weren't important to have up there." Mason Evans, a thick haired brunette in his late thirties with eyebrows as bushy as his hair, and a scruffy beard to match, appeared in the doorway. He wore a black and red plaid shirt and smiled through his mustache hair. The man was right, this mission was crucial for my decades of research, and I had absolutely no choice but to go. "It reeks in here."

Both the young astronaut and Mason looked like they wanted to flee the room as quickly as possible. I frowned, watching as the two weaved their way back out of the simulator while I followed shortly behind. I disposed of the white barf bag in the nearest trash bin once I'd reached the bottom of the metal staircase. After, I fiddled with a piece of my shoulder length blonde hair that was flying in every direction, trying to flatten it down against my head.

"In just a few weeks, you'll have gotten all this over with, Daph," Mason assured me, giving my shoulder a squeeze. "Trust me. It'll all be worth it when you get out there." I wanted to say, "And you know this how?" but I refrained, offering a reluctant nod instead. "Though I'm curious how your rats are going to handle it."

"They'll be just fine," I replied. If I could make it, so could they. Ten specimens had been specially prepared for the trip to the International Space Station and were being used to assist in the next phase of our drug trial, in addition to the physical research I'd be doing with the astronauts aboard the station. My pedigree and background with this project had been the main reason I'd been asked to come. The project had been years in the works, only waiting for certain components of the space station to be completed before we sent them up. Now everything was ready to go, and hopefully would be successful, so long as the astronauts didn't screw it up.

Ruby "named for the coding language" Peters had been the top of her graduate class at MIT and had received many accolades in her time serving in the Air Force. Even still, her background did not instill confidence in me. In fact, it made me more nervous. Handing my research over to an aeronautical engineer to assist me was not what I had envisioned. She'd minored in biology in her undergraduate years, but that had been a while ago now, and she'd since devoted her time and energy to other things. It took a delicate hand to maintain research specimens, and an even more meticulous hand with my drug trial. In fact, I wasn't quite sure there was anyone else on the planet I'd trust with this project, but I wasn't about to spend more time on that space station than I was forced to.

To say I wasn't thrilled about the situation was an understatement. At least she had seemed relatively prepared at our meeting a few days prior. She'd answered every question I'd asked quite thoroughly and had surprised me. There weren't very many people who stayed ahead of me on my knowledge about my work, but she seemed to be right on par, which had been rather impressive. I liked the idea of another woman who worked in our field to be as headstrong and passionate as I felt I was. For whatever reason, she'd been on my mind a lot since that call.

Before I could follow the astronaut down the hallway back toward the temporary research lab I'd been working in, Mason stopped me. We were in front of a large picture window that overlooked the courtyard in front of the Kennedy Space Center Operations Support Building. The sun was just starting to set for the evening. Towering in the distance was the vehicle assembly building, with the official NASA logo and American flag painted along the side. The Space Shuttle Galileo sat inside, which would be making its second trip this year to the International Space Station, with a few new crew members, and myself. I got lost in the view for a few moments, admiring the Florida palm trees swaying in the wind outside.

"Dr. Hale wants to talk to you," Mason's voice brought my attention back inside. As soon as I heard his name, I knew what the conversation was most likely going to be about. I frowned, turning to look at my coworker. My friend. "I know you aren't happy about it, but you have to humor him anyway." An arm wrapped around my shoulders and started to lead me down a different hallway.

We walked into an open conference room that overlooked much of the KSC campus. It was a room full of windows and glass, very attractive for board meetings and impressing big wigs that happened to come on site. I'd only been in the room once since I was here for my orientation and was surprised to be back again. Once we'd sat, Mason pulled a container of Altoids from his pocket and slid them across the table.

"Figured you could use one." He was grinning at me underneath all that fur on his face.

Even while rolling my eyes, I graciously took one of the mints, plopping it into my mouth. The taste and smell overrode everything, much to my relief. I slid the container back to Mason just as the doors to the conference room swung open. Outside, I could hear voices as a slew of people entered. Mostly it was garble, unimportant, except for one voice that I found distinctively familiar. A voice that sent a chill racing down my spine.

Dr. William Hale entered the room first. Though his face was covered in wrinkles, his eyes themselves were a lively shade of blue and seemed to be full of energy. He'd been working alongside the National Space Biomedical Research Institute nearly as long as I'd been there. We'd come to know each other quite well over the past few decades. And I was rather good at predicting what he was about to say or do most times, without much thought.

"Dr. Carter," he greeted me with a small smile that stretched the lines around his lips. It was strange to see him smile. He didn't do it much. It gave me an unsettled feeling.

Before I could get in a word of reply, a final body entered the room. His presence made time stand still. I could hear chatter around me, but it didn't matter. Mason had said my name, but I was no longer paying attention to him. All I could do was stare at the man in the doorway, feeling the room starting to spin, and voices fading out of my mind, replaced by ringing.

Michael hadn't changed much in two decades. The same wispy brunette hair was now dusted with grey. Round glasses accentuated his brown eyes. Still twiggy and thin as he always was. And that familiar pleasant smile that misled so many people into thinking he was a good guy. The truth was, he had been a poisonous snake in the grass for me my entire career.

All I could hear in my mind was the last words he'd spoken to me.

"It's a shame, Daph. All that time and effort. For it to come to this..."

And then I'd signed my name on the final page of divorce papers and had walked out of the lawyer's office without so much as another word from him. I wanted him out of my life for good; to never have to see his face or hear his name ever again. Unfortunately, as closely related as our research projects were, he was always looming around. I'd been lucky not to run into him since our last meeting, however. Not until today.

It didn't take but a few moments for Michael to spot me across the room. That deceptive smile of his widened, and I watched him wander into the room and around the table, until he'd approached me. I'd risen from my seat at some point, likely startled to see him there. Before I had an opportunity to stop him, he wrapped his arms around me, hugging me gently. The hug felt oddly familiar, even after all these years. The hugs that used to comfort me on long days in college and medical school. The arms that had held me at our junior prom, or when we'd danced at our wedding.

The hug felt hollow now, as if I was being squeezed by a corpse of a human.

"Daph, it's been *forever*," Michael said when he released me from his grasp. Somehow, I found my breath again, even if it was shaky. That horrendous nickname of his that I used to tolerate. The only person who was allowed to call me that nowadays was Mason. My heart was beating so furiously that it was threatening to rip itself from my chest. "You look gorgeous, as always. Haven't aged a day. I'm so happy to see you're well. I follow your research constantly. Very impressed with the work you've been doing with NASA."

I watched my ex-husband trail around the conference table and come to sit adjacent to Dr. Hale. My eyes couldn't leave him the entire time, in disbelief that he was in the room with me, after I'd spent all these years hoping I'd never have to be in his presence again.

Why is he here?

My attention turned to Dr. Hale, trying to formulate words to speak. "Dr. Hale," I said, falling back into my seat and watching him as he got settled in his own chair across from me. I did my best to ignore the fact that Michael was even in the room with us at this point. "Is there a reason you've decided to invite Dr. Riddler to this meeting? The last I checked, he doesn't work for NASA or the Biomedical Research Institute..."

"I was recently promoted to the Chief of Physical Medicine and Rehabilitation Service position at UC San Diego and still teach in the residency program..." My fists clenched when he mentioned this fact. It had been a long time since I'd thought about my days in San Diego, but there had been good reason for it. "I also was inaugurated onto the Board of Directors for the International Society for Gravitational Physiology last month. And our research department has been collaborating with the Biomedical Research Institute for a few years now."

This was news to me. Perhaps it was because I tried very hard not to follow Michael and his endeavors, especially after everything that had transpired between us. Surely someone would have mentioned that he was working with the same institute. Especially Dr. Hale, who had been aware of Dr. Riddler and the tumultuous past we shared.

"Daphne." My attention turned back to Dr. Hale, who met my gaze. There was an unreadable expression on his face. He very rarely ever called me by my given name, especially in front of our colleagues. It made my blood run cold. "I'm afraid we're going to have to pull you from the ISS mission and overseeing the troponin activator drug trial."

My ears began to ring again, in complete disbelief of what I was hearing. "Pardon?"

"Clearly you aren't physically capable to handle the demands of space travel," Dr. Hale said, simply. I'd guessed the meeting was going to be about that fact, but the last thing I had expected him to do was pull me from the mission all together. It was ludicrous. I was the only person remotely prepared enough to carry out the necessary functions while onboard. "There's a lot of money going into this project, you know as well as I do. We can't have issues like this arising."

"You're planning to scrub the trial all together? What happens to the funding then?" I wasn't quite sure where he was going with this. Certainly, the organizations giving us our project money weren't going to like the idea that we were discontinuing it.

"No," Dr. Hale corrected me. "We need someone focused, trained in your research, and physically able to carry out the role of the instigator of this drug trial."

Someone to carry out the job.

My eyes landed on Michael, whose attention was on me. We watched each other a moment, and I could tell by the look on his face what was coming. I hoped desperately in my mind that it wasn't true, trying to defend myself. "Dr. Hale, I can assure you... I'm getting better with the simulator. There's still several weeks until launch. I fully anticipate being ready by that time. I just need a little longer—"

"I'm afraid this is non-negotiable, Daphne." Again, he spoke my first name, but I assumed this time it was to be kind, knowing how much this news would devastate me. Even just the idea of being pulled from the project at the ISS itself was unimaginable. But Michael, too.

Before I was even consciously aware of doing it, I'd stood up from my seat at the table, glaring back at Dr. Hale. "It's one thing to pull me from the project I've spent my entire career focused on. The most groundbreaking project we've attempted. But for you to—" I had to take a breath to try and steady myself. "*Michael?*"

"Could Dr. Carter and I have the room?" Dr. Hale announced this to the entire conference room. There wasn't any debate, everyone filed out rather quickly, including my ex-husband who caught my gaze for a few seconds before he disappeared out the door. When we were alone, Dr. Hale turned his attention back on me. "Given Dr. Riddler's background, and the recent work he's been doing that ties closely with the spinal research and the drug trial, he was one of the best options to replace you. He leads the research division at UC San Diego..."

"I know very well where Dr. Riddler works, Bill." I knew most of it anyway, outside of his more recent collaborations with the Biomedical Research Institute. The work that everyone had neglected to tell me about. "If you do recall, we both went to medical school there and completed our residencies in San Diego together." I realized that I had spoken Dr. Hale's given name, but I was pissed. "I worked on the same research projects as him, in fact."

"Daphne, I'm not about to get into an argument about your messy history with your ex-husband. You want to know why we didn't inform you that Dr. Riddler had been collaborating with us? We knew you wouldn't be able to work together, given your history. It's been two decades, Dr. Carter. I need this drama to be water under the bridge."

Water under the bridge.

"Michael Riddler blatantly *stole* that job from me. He took sole credit for major parts of research we collaborated on together, and I watched my cohort and dozens of faculty and staff let him, without so much as a blink of an eye. An entire life I should have been living. I was nearly discredited from the department because of the lies he spread. It took every effort I had to get on board with the Biomedical Research Institute and NASA..."

I sucked in a deep breath of air and let it roll out of my nose. "I worked my way up from *nothing*, Bill. In a male dominated field, where there are very few leadership roles for women, I now run an entire department of one of the largest research programs in the entire country. I spent two decades working to prove to myself that no matter what that horrendous excuse of a human being took from me, I could survive and flourish regardless. And yet here I am again, my job, my work, threatened by blatant sexism..."

"I assure you that this has nothing to do with you being a *woman*, Dr. Carter. Don't be ridiculous."

"Like hell it doesn't—"

Dr. Hale held up a hand to silence me and I snapped my mouth shut. Regardless of how incredibly furious I was at him in those moments, he was still in charge. "Dr. Riddler is one of the top scholars in the field. He's been following the same research you've been working on for years now, collaborating with the Biomedical Research Institute and NASA. There is a lot of overlap between you both. The only reason we haven't approached him sooner is out of respect for you. And I'm afraid it's about time you reconciled your differences and moved on."

I stared at him, in disbelief of what he was asking of me. And certainly not buying that it wasn't a sexist power move by a variety of my male superiors. I dreaded what was coming next. Didn't believe it could be possible, not until I heard him speak the words. Words that I had desperately hoping would not come out of his mouth after seeing Michael.

"Dr. Riddler has volunteered to carry out the drug trial project..."

"This is *my* research," I reminded Dr. Hale, my tone as dark as my face must have looked in those moments. "Twenty years that I've invested and poured every ounce of my life into. If you think I'm going to let that lying, manipulative, traitorous bastard come anywhere near my work ever again, you are sorely mistaken."

Bill looked dissatisfied, but I couldn't have cared less. I was seconds from turning and leaving the room, but he got in a few last words.

"I'm afraid Dr. Riddler is going to be taking your place," Dr. Hale warned me. "I know this isn't what you want to hear, Daphne, but it's what's been decided. And I suggest you start singing a different and more cooperative tune, for everyone's sake."

I didn't reply, only glared at him. "Is that all, Dr. Hale?"

Bill turned his attention toward the door, nodding. "Mr. Evans will likely be waiting for you to escort you to the laboratory where the research specimens are being stored. I'd like you to check that everything is together and make up a briefing for Dr. Riddler, with everything you've prepared. Please have it done by tomorrow."

Instead of replying, I turned away from him and shoved open the conference room doors. The group that had been in with us earlier was still collected outside, including Michael, who was making small talk with some of them. He eyed me briefly, but I turned my attention toward Mason, who was at the end of the hallway.

"Dr. Hale said you're taking me to the rats?" I asked Mason, once I'd reached him.

Mason nodded, and the two of us began the walk toward the laboratories. "Are you alright?"

"No, I'm not alright!" I snapped. My voice was louder than I had expected it to be. I felt on the verge of tears, which was exceedingly rare for me. There hadn't been a time I remembered crying in front of another person. I wasn't about to now. Instead, I did my best to calm my racing heart and steady myself.

"I swore, when he betrayed me all those years ago, that I would never let him near any of my research ever again. That everything I did from there on out was my own doing, and that I didn't need anyone else's help. I worked my ass off to get where I am now." I sucked in a deep breath of air, shaking my head. "These last two decades have been *my* doing, Mason. This is my work, my blood and sweat and tears. If that lying son-of-a-bitch thinks he's taking more away from me..." I paused in the middle of the hallway, unable to move, my head spinning and ears ringing loudly.

There was a hand on my shoulder. "Breathe, Daph." I listened to him, as much as I didn't want to at that moment and took in a few deep breaths. When I'd settled a little, he squeezed my shoulder before releasing it. "This isn't your medical school program," he gently reminded me. "You both are older now. People can change."

I let out a bitter laugh, looking at Mason. Trying my best not to snap at him, since he was one of the very few of my colleagues I considered a trusted friend, and who tolerated being around me. I did my best to be polite. "There is no universe in which I will ever trust my ex-husband ever again."

"Well, it looks like you might not have a choice," Mason noted. And the very idea that his words were even remotely true was destroying me.

AFTER A SHORT TREK across the Kennedy Space Center campus, we reached a research building by the vehicle assembly building, where most of the equipment for the mission to the International Space Station was being stored. Mason led me inside a windowless door and through a very white fluorescent lit hallway, and into a room toward the center.

A large picture window sat on the far side of the open space. Racks of equipment lined the walls, and to my satisfaction, my ten rats and their housing stacked in their rig. Before I headed over, I felt Mason's hand on my shoulder. I turned to look toward him. There was a thoughtful look on his face, along with a slight hint of a smile.

"What?" I said, my tone a little more annoyed than I'd meant it. I was *very* on edge.

"I read an article not too long ago about something called

hydroseen... hydrodine..." Mason scratched his beard, apparently stumped on the name. "It's an antinausea medicine. Have you heard about it?"

"Hyoscine," I corrected him, knowing almost instantly what he was referring to.

"Yeah, that," Mason nodded. "They were trialing it on some of the newer astronaut recruits, I think. Helps with the motion-sickness of launch. I was just wondering why they hadn't suggested that for you. But I guess maybe it's still in trial phases, so maybe it's not ready yet."

Anti-nausea medication. My head spun at the mention of it. I'd read some of these articles before in passing. I knew what he'd been talking about. Why it hadn't occurred to me until Mason had mentioned it, I had no earthly idea. "Yes, I know what you're talking about. They've been combining it with dexamphetamine to counteract the sedating effect. The trials have been fairly successful, from what I remember."

"Maybe you could pitch the idea to Dr. Hale," Mason said, with a shrug. "I know it hasn't been 'officially' approved yet, but with all the success of the studies, he might still go for it. You never know."

"If I was the type of person who kissed people, I'd kiss you for that," I said, feeling a rush of excitement. "I'll get started on it immediately. Thank you, Mason. Genuinely." Mason smiled at me, nodding appreciatively.

"I'll let you get to it," he said, giving me a polite wave and turning toward the door. He glanced over his shoulder briefly. "Have a good night, Daph."

And then he left me, disappearing behind the door we'd come from a minute earlier, without another word. I didn't linger too long, walking over to the equipment on the far side of the room, and the rig that had been specially designed to house the ten rats that were going to the space station. Most of them were awake since they were nocturnal creatures.

I watched them for a few minutes and checked the housing structure and the other equipment that was going on the space shuttle, while I booted up my laptop. Then I opened the several pieces of software we used to input research data. After I'd made some brief notes about the research specimen, I checked my emails. Nothing new of note, some emails briefing us about the mission, an annoying chain email about leaving food in the KSC refrigerator. Things I didn't care about or had already read too much about.

My body felt too wired and anxious to return to my hotel to sleep, for a variety of reasons, mostly because I was wanting to get started preparing an argument for Dr. Hale about the hyoscine trials and its potential usage for this mission. I spent hours working, going over every shred of research with a fine-tooth comb. I prepared every possible response to the arguments that I planned on Dr. Hale making. By the time I'd finally finished, it was nearly two in the morning. I doubted I'd sleep that night.

I thought of making some tea, so I wandered down the hall to the small cafeteria in search of some. I was sorely disappointed to find there was only green available, much preferring the floral taste of Earl Grey.

When I sat back down with my tea a few minutes later, I pulled up NASA's website and clicked through to the various pages until I found the International Space Station's website. Every few days they'd update the page with new videos. I'd been following most of them ever since I'd found out I'd be taking a trip up there, and even sometimes before then. Today, a new one had been posted, talking about the view of Earth from space. I would have been less enthusiastic about the topic and such a simple video, one that I'd seen and heard about dozens and dozens of times, but a face caught my eye. Short, raven black hair, and deep brown eyes.

Commander Ruby Peters.

I clicked on the video. It was dark when it started to play. Ruby glowed in a distant light. By the background, it appeared that she was in the cupola, an observation module on board the space station. The woman's glowing white smile lit up the screen as she looked upward.

"This is why we call this the 'best seat in the house,'" Ruby said. She had a hint of a lisp when she spoke, something I'd noticed in the many videos I'd watched that featured her, and in our meeting the other day. I very rarely noticed when people spoke. They all tended to sound the same. But she'd been different. The camera tilted upward, so that Earth was in view behind her.

The glowing blue, green and white orb filled the entire length of the screen. Even I, who had read so many articles and seen so many videos about the view, still found it mesmerizing. Ruby glanced upward, and flecks of golden brown from her eyes caught the light of the Earth, illuminating them, along with her smile. For some reason, she was even more captivating than the view itself was, her fascination and child-like pleasure she took in watching, alluring. To her, that view was everything. It was who she was to her very core.

We had that in common, she and I. Things that defined us as human beings. For me, it was the research that I was about to entrust with her. Nearly twenty years of work that I hadn't trusted my closest colleagues with. That I didn't think I would ever trust another person with, ever again. Yet here she was, this unfamiliar woman, in an unfamiliar place, who I was bestowing the most important research I'd ever done.

As much as she loved her work and everything she did up there, she would have to learn to love my work all the same. Everything depended on it. On her. That mysterious, enchanting black haired, brown eyed woman who was occupying my thoughts.

And I hoped, too, that it would be me there with her in a few short weeks.

THREE

RUBY

In... out... in... out...

The weirdest thing I had ever experienced was hearing the sounds my body made.

In the real world, everything you did was drowned out by background noise. The creaks and pops and rumbles that came from everything you did, disappeared. Until you found yourself in the quietness of space. Suddenly, you could hear the saliva bubbles in your throat when you swallowed, or the low and constant tinnitus buzz in your ears. It was almost terrifying in a way. It brought you to a new place that you never imagined existed.

Which was why I focused on the steady rhythm of my breathing.

"Alright, Peters. Let us know when you make it."

Two years ago, when I had completed my first spacewalk at the ISS, the new sounds I was hearing nearly made me lose my mind. Now, it was almost meditative in a way. It caused me to focus on my breath and what I was doing at that moment. Instead of focusing on the sounds, I stared out at the bright, glowing Earth below me. We were above a cloudy Europe now, and it almost felt like if I were to let go of the titanium I was hoisting myself onto, I'd fall straight down.

Maybe I'd land in Italy. I'd always wanted to go to Rome.

My attention turned back toward the station as I finished my travels. While the technical term was a "spacewalk," it tended to be more like a "space ballet on fingertips." Adrik often said it should be called "*space working*." Everything you did, from propelling yourself to stopping yourself and holding on to things, was with your fingertips. It was precise and carefully measured and methodical. There was no "walking" about it. Legs just mostly got in the way.

Meanwhile, my mic was still hot. There was radio silence now. I assumed my colleagues at Mission Control and the ones onboard the ISS were waiting for my signal.

"I've reached the RMS," I announced. The Remote Manipulator System, also known as the Canadarm2, was a series of robotic arms that were used to deploy, maneuver, and capture payloads. I'd been asked to do some minor repairs to the plating system before *Galileo*'s arrival in a few hours. Any excuse to be outside was always welcome. It didn't come so often anymore.

"Alright, Peters. Let us know when you've repaired the elbow joint, like we talked about." This time it was Mason Evans, a NASA engineer, who was on the other end of the line. Somewhere at a desk down at Kennedy, several thousand miles and an atmosphere away now. Likely chugging down a vanilla coke while he was typing furiously at his mechanical keyboard, headset strapped across his head. "Daniel, you with me?"

"Affirmative," Daniel's voice echoed into the headset loudly, and a squeal of feedback followed. There was a scuffle of movement and Daniel spoke again. "Sorry about that."

"How about some music?" I asked, while I situated the drill that was attached to the carabiner on the outside of my suit. "Something peppy this time, Richards. From the playlist." Daniel chuckled in my ear, and I heard puttering for a minute before the cheerful drumbeat filled the soundless background. When Katrina's "ow" came at the beginning of the song, I laughed. "I think I'm about ninety-two million miles short of walking on sunshine," I replied as I got to work, listening to Katrina and the Waves' "Walking on Sunshine" in the background.

While I inspected the RMS, I awkwardly "danced" around it while floating, enjoying the beat of the song. I could hear Mason laughing in my ears. "You're on live feed right now, Commander."

"Well aware," I replied. "Space dance. Feel free to join in, Mason."

"I don't have any rhythm," Mason admitted. "But I'll live vicariously through you."

While I worked, I sang along, much to my colleague's displeasure. I wasn't gifted with the world's best singing voice, but it hadn't stopped me in my twenty-five years of living.

"Harmony, Daniel!" I shouted, over the chorus.

Daniel laughed. "No thanks, Peters. Don't forget to check the end effector while you're out there. You've got an hour until your meeting with Dr. Carter."

"Will do," I replied, turning my focus toward the device. While I hummed along I flipped open the panel, inspecting the inner workings. The song eventually faded, replaced by a more mellow James Taylor song. "Everything looks good."

"Speaking of Dr. Carter," Mason said, having been silent for a few minutes while I had been working. "I'm afraid she got pulled from the mission last minute. She's been having a difficult time physically handling the space travel, so Dr. Hale had to bring in a substitute. I haven't had a chance to speak with him yet, but he's supposedly very well versed in the research that Daphne was doing."

I was surprised that Mason had called her by her first name, but then I'd recalled that he'd mentioned on one or two occasions that they had been friends and former colleagues when he'd been at Johnson. My thoughts about his very informal name-calling were very short-lived, however, more focused on the fact that Dr. Carter was no longer coming to the ISS.

"Who's the new guy, then?" I asked, curiously.

. . .

ABOUT TWENTY MINUTES before my scheduled meeting with Dr. Michael Riddler, I was busy looking him up on the laptop I'd be using for the video conference. He was all over the internet. A professor at UC San Diego, Chief of Physical Medicine and Rehabilitation Service, and one of the foremost experts in orthopedic medicine for astronauts. He'd been working for decades doing research very similar to Daphne's. The similarities were almost unreal, to the point that I thought perhaps they were working together.

Then I'd found an article, buried several pages back in the searches I'd been making. It was two decades old. A small newspaper from Seattle that I didn't recognize. I might have gone back to my search if it hadn't been for the photograph on top, that I saw before I had even read the headline of the article. It was a photograph of a man and a woman in front of a large University of Washington sign, dressed in lab coats. The man was Dr. Riddler, I'd known this only from the other pictures I'd seen of him on various other websites. The woman... I had to stare at it for a great length of time to even believe it.

The woman was Daphne Carter.

My eyes finally dropped down to the title of the article. "*Former professor dismissed from UC San Diego research program after falsely representing data.*" I continued to read, wondering how this could possibly tie to Daphne, and was surprised to find that it had been she who had been let go from the program on accusations that she'd been inaccurately portraying findings. The attempt to get her removed from the program had been by Dr. Riddler, who I discovered had not only been her research partner, but also her ex-husband. He had gone on to continue the research they'd been working on, and pursuing the career that they both wanted, while Dr. Carter had been forced to find work elsewhere.

I read the article twice, in disbelief that after everything I'd read about Dr. Carter and her two decades worth of groundbreaking research, that she would have ever done something so outlandish as falsifying research. There would have been no way that NASA would have hired her on if that had been the case. And yet they'd brought on Dr. Riddler as her replacement? I could only imagine what Dr. Carter had felt about that situation.

A ringing interrupted my thoughts. There was an incoming video call from the Kennedy Space Center in Florida. Dr. Riddler, I assumed, calling for our meeting together to continue preparing for what would now be his arrival instead of Daphne's. There was a weird feeling in my stomach as I stared at the blinking box, signaling the video call that was waiting for me. It took me a few long moments before I managed to click on the button to answer.

The window opened across the entire length of the laptop screen. On the other side was a brown-haired man with round glasses that reminded me of my mother's. He was twiggy and thin and had speckles of grey in his hair. Unlike Dr. Carter in our first interaction a few days prior, Dr. Riddler was smiling at me.

"Good morning, ah—Commander Peters," he said, glancing down at notes on his desk. Had he not even known my name? Eventually, he looked back up at me again. "I'm sure you've been made aware that I'll be replacing Daphne for the ISS trip." I nodded, feeling a weird sense of anxiousness at this idea. He continued. "Good, good. Let's get started, shall we? I wanted to make sure you were up to speed before my arrival."

"I've been over a lot of this with Dr. Carter," I explained, glancing at him briefly, before I turned my attention toward notes that were strapped down to the desk from the last meeting I'd had. "I'm sure the protocol isn't going to change, right?"

"Ah, Ruby," Dr. Riddler continued to smile at me, and the longer he did, the more I didn't like the way it looked on his face. "Can I call you Ruby? You'll find that Daphne and I have *very* different ways of handling things. I want to make sure that you and I are on the same page, too."

It was strange hearing him call Dr. Carter by her first name. I liked her name, truth be told, but I wouldn't dare address colleagues like that. It was too informal. And again, it made that weird feeling that Dr. Riddler was giving me, that much worse. "Sure," I replied, somewhat late to answering his question.

"So, I see that you graduated from the Massachusetts Institute of Technology with a degree in aerospace engineering... Top of your class, in the Air Force... Graduated young, too. One of the youngest to join the astronaut training program. Quite impressive..."

"Thank you—"

"You've been up on the ISS for eighteen months. Trying to break the record, I see." Michael flashed another smile at me and then pushed his glasses up his nose and continued before I was able to reply. "And you have a minor in biology. Good, good. I'll need your assistance in various aspects of the drug trial. You'll oversee the research specimens upon my departure from the station..."

"Dr. Carter has gone over all of this with me," I reminded him, trying to stay pleasant.

Michael seemed unfazed by my comment, continuing to talk almost as if I wasn't there. "Tirasemtiv is a fast skeletal troponin activator that sensitizes—"

"The sarcomere to calcium, which amplifies the response of muscle to neuromuscular input, producing greater force when nerve input is reduced. It's a means to increase muscle strength." I'd read at least a dozen articles on the troponin activator drug trials that were being conducted. None had been explicitly tested in a microgravity environment for use with astronauts and long-duration spaceflight civilians. This was a groundbreaking trial. A trial that was supposed to be Daphne Carter's.

"You've been reading the research materials." When I expected to find Dr. Riddler impressed with my dedication and proactiveness regarding the trial, he instead looked somewhat annoyed with me, but somehow maintained that friendly demeanor. "I do realize that you are a high-ranking military officer and a leadership position with NASA and aboard the ISS. However, Ruby, regarding the National Space Biomedical Institute's research program, you are not in an authoritative position. I am. I will be conducting the drug trial and monitoring your activities for the spinal studies. This is not your project, so I expect you to act under my instruction."

I stared at him, mouth hanging slightly open, having not expected him to very openly talk down to me. There was still a pleasant look on his face, but it had darkened a little. For a few seconds, I tried to formulate some sort of reply. Then it hit me.

"Last I checked, you aren't really in an authoritative position at the Biomedical Institute either," I made strong eye contact with him, trying to maintain a neutral expression. "Didn't I read that you're a professor at UC San Diego? I see you dabble in a little bit of university funded research, but I think Dr. Carter was the authoritative figure with this project at the BI. Not you."

Dr. Riddler's smile disappeared completely. He stared at me, probably in disbelief that I'd challenged him at all. I shouldn't have, but there was something about him that was really getting under my skin. "Last I checked, Commander Peters, Daphne is no longer a part of this leg of the project. I suppose I will have to do." He paused for a moment, looking like he was regaining his composure. "And since we'll be working closely together in a few weeks, I suggest you start warming up to the idea of working under my...guidance."

While I had tried to keep a steady look on my face, I was certain I was frowning a little. I forced a compliant nod, deciding not to argue. There was a limit to the amount of headbutting with the civilian scientists that I was allowed. It happened from time to time. We lived such different lives; it was hard to relate to certain things. But there was only so much I could do before I'd hear about it from my colleagues and supervisors.

"Good, I'm assuming that's a sign you're going to listen." Michael was smiling again, and it was all I could do not to interject another snarky comment. Somehow, I managed not to. "Let's go over the drug trial protocols, while I have you here."

THE DAY of *Galileo*'s arrival, the three astronauts on the ISS were lost in games of poker. "Adrik, you can't win *every* game," Daniel scoffed, as he shuffled a deck of cards in his hand. Unfortunately, it was Adrik's favorite game, and he had a habit of beating Daniel and me. The cards floated in the air momentarily, spinning in a circle, before Daniel reached for them again and dealt out another hand. "Damn if I couldn't go for a good Cuban right about now."

A favorite pastime of Daniel Richards was his expensive Cuban cigars. I had spent an evening or two with him before at his Cocoa Beach house, out on his patio, smelling the rich scent of tobacco in the air. With a cigar and a glass of scotch, he was about as content as any man could be. "Six more months and you'll be able to have one again."

"Damn, I can't believe it's still that long," Daniel said, studying his cards before he shuffled a couple of them back into the deck and drew new ones. Adrik passed along a few cards as well, and then me. "I've been missing Elle and the boys. I don't know how you can stay up here so long, Peters. Don't you get homesick?"

"A little," I admitted, squinting at my new cards, feeling rather disappointed. There was no way I was going to win this round either. Adrik, on the other hand, looked pleased, as he usually did. He showed us his hand.

"Flush," he grinned widely, his very light accent rolling out. I laughed and Daniel scowled, not even showing his hand. "I win again?"

"You win again," I smiled, shuffling my hand back into the deck, and then reaching for Adrik's and Daniel's hands. Just as I'd finished, there was a noise over the radio. An alert sounded, and when I turned to look at the monitors behind us, it showed *Galileo* within distance.

"About time," Daniel said, pushing off against one side of the wall until he had made his way around me and to a computer station. I backed out of the center of the room. Daniel called out over the radio to the shuttle that was approaching. "*Galileo* this is the ISS. We've got eyes on your approach. Waiting for all clear from Mission Control."

"ISS, this is Commander James Mertz of *Galileo*. It's good to hear your voice, Daniel."

"You too," Daniel replied. Commander James Mertz was a friend of Daniel's from a small town in Canada called Chetwynd, and someone I had only interacted with a handful of times, but he seemed nice enough. Somehow, they'd both ended up working at NASA together.

The entire docking process took a while. We watched on screen as the shuttle's alignment was fine-tuned with the docking target. Once Mission Control had cleared a list of requirements, including checking the external parts of the ISS, it closed in with the docking ring. The node we were in rumbled to life, as a series of hooks engaged to lock the shuttle into the docking station.

For the next few hours, while we waited for the passage between *Galileo* and the ISS to pressurize, we worked on preparations for the crew's arrival. Daniel chatted with James a bit, but the rest of the people onboard were radio silent. My anxiousness was starting to get the best of me, worried about having to interact with Dr. Riddler in a short time. How I was going to last three weeks around him, I wasn't quite certain.

When the pressurization was complete, James was the first to head out into the node of the ISS. With his helmet off, I recognized him immediately. He was a tall, slender man, in his early thirties. He had short, spiky black hair and green eyes, along with a very sharp jawline. We'd worked together a bit, and although he was quiet, he was a nice guy.

"Welcome aboard, Commander," Daniel greeted him first, with a giant smile, and the two shook hands. James looked about as wired as anyone who had ever flown a shuttle for days straight. It had to be especially nerve-wracking carrying civilians to the space station. When the two broke their handshake, they both turned to look toward the hatch leading to *Galileo*. James grabbed a hold of one of the metallic blue support beams that the rest of us held onto.

It wasn't too long until the remainder of the three astronaut crew members exited the shuttle. We all took turns greeting them. Andrea Bratcher and Tony Reynolds. Andrea was a seasoned astronaut that had been up to the station before. Tony, however, had never been before and seemed in awe of everything.

"Welcome to the ISS, Tony," Daniel said. He was floating alongside me, smiling pleasantly under his mustache hair.

"Quite a trip being weightless, huh?" I called out to Tony. He was still smiling nervously, looking rather overwhelmed. It was natural and expected after a space flight like he'd just undergone. Even the most trained astronauts had those moments. He nodded, while James helped lead him into the room, with the help of support beams.

Once Tony had made it successfully inside, my attention turned back toward the hatch. For a few minutes, there was no movement. Michael Riddler was the final face we had yet to see. I thought briefly to make my way inside to check on his status, but James beat me to the punch.

"Maybe they need some help," James said, thoughtfully. He turned back to the hatch and made his way back inside. We waited for a few minutes until James reappeared in the hatch entryway. And when he moved back into the node, there was a figure behind him, still with their helmet on. James assisted getting them moved into the node.

I approached, deciding to offer my own help, even though the last thing I wanted was to do anything for Dr. Riddler. "Let me help you take this off..." A gloved hand reached up to swat at me, attempting to help remove the helmet. I frowned slightly, using the metallic support beam to move away from him a bit. After a minute of fiddling with the helmet, it was unlocked.

And I could barely believe what I was seeing.

FOUR
DAPHNE

Mere days before the launch of the space shuttle *Galileo*, I found myself waiting outside of the very same conference room at the Kennedy Space Center where I'd found out that Michael would replace me on the ISS mission. I paced up and down the hallway, looking at notes on flashcards that I'd prepared and trying to take deep breaths to calm myself.

Mason leaned against the wall by the door. Every time I glanced at him, his eyes were following my movements. He looked contemplative, but also peaceful. The exact opposite of what I was feeling in those moments. But then again, he wasn't about to give a career-altering presentation to a room full of people.

"Can you not stare? It's rather rude, Mason." My voice came out kind of snippy, and I imagined I was glaring a little at him.

Somehow, Mason appeared unfazed by my attempt at being menacing. Instead, he let out a little chuckle and shrugged. "You need to relax a little, Daphne. I'm sure it's going to go fine. You've been working really hard on this for weeks."

"I have *one* chance of getting it right," I replied. "One. That's it. If this falls through... I don't know what I'm going to do." Truthfully, if this didn't go well, there would be nothing that I *could* do, whether I liked it or not.

"Well then tell yourself it isn't going to fall through," Mason argued.

I sighed loudly, looking back at my notecards. Still continuing to pace. It was the only thing I could think to do that would keep me relaxed enough to stay focused. I was about to make another comment to Mason, when the door to the conference room opened. Dr. Hale was on the other side and made quick eye contact with me. Behind him, I saw the entire room filled with people. It didn't help calm my nerves.

"We're ready for you, Dr. Carter," Dr. Hale said, nodding at me. Mason looked as though he wanted to enter the room, but he was stopped quickly. "I'm afraid there's not enough space in here for an audience today, Mr. Evans. Dr. Carter will have to enlighten you about the presentation later."

Mason looked a little disappointed but nodded. I felt his hand reach out and squeeze my shoulder affectionately. "Remember, you got this."

"I've got this," I repeated, swallowing deeply before I entered the room.

As I made my way to where the projector had been pointed at a large white wall, I glanced around the room. Some faces I recognized. Employees at NASA and the Biomedical Research Institute. A few employees from the National Science Foundation and the National Institutes of Health, two major funders for the spinal research and drug trials we were about begin. Two employees from the bioscience company who had designed the Tirasemtiv troponin activator drug that would be used in the drug trials. Dr. Hale, and Michael. And a few others, I didn't recognize.

I stood at the computer that was connected to the projector in the room, opening the PowerPoint presentation I'd created for the meeting. My nerves were starting to get the best of me again, after seeing the number of people in the room. I'd expected half a dozen, not nearly four times that much.

The presentation flickered onto the projected screen against the wall. *Hyoscine in the Treatment of Motion Sickness related to Spaceflight*. Dr. Hale had come back to his seat, just as I'd gotten set up. I looked out into the room, trying my best to offer a pleasant smile. Smiling did not come naturally to me. I very rarely did.

"Good afternoon," I projected my voice across the room, after I'd cleared my throat. "I have had the pleasure of meeting with a handful of you before, but for those of you who don't know me, my name is Dr. Daphne Carter. I am the Director of Occupational Health and Ergonomics department for the National Space Biomedical Research Institute. My primary focus of research for the past two decades has been on spinal health with long-duration spaceflights."

I flipped through the first couple of slides that detailed my curriculum vitae, including my educational background and all my research endeavors since I'd graduated. "I won't bore you with my qualifications, suffice to say that I am one of the foremost scientists in this field. The civilian ISS mission that we have planned has been a project I've been preparing for years."

"Both the Institute and NASA's goals in this specific endeavor are to study ways of alleviating spinal injuries and pain in our astronauts. Back pain is common during prolonged missions, with more than half of crew members reporting spinal pain. Astronauts are also at increased risk of spinal disc herniation in the months after returning from spaceflight—about four times higher than in matched controls." I clicked through slides again. Most of this information was familiar to a few in the room, but I wanted to establish a background regardless.

"While this study and drug trial is important in altering the way we handle occupational health and ergonomics regarding our astronauts, it also is of interest for future projects that may eventually lead humans further into space than we have ever been—Mars, for example." I continued, just grazing over this topic, as I knew most in the room understood the intentions of the work that we were doing.

"Perhaps you'd like to get on to the reason for this meeting, Dr. Carter." Dr. Hale was staring at me from across the conference room table. I blinked, surprised at his interruption of my presentation.

Instead of arguing, I just nodded, flipping through a few more extraneous slides that I had prepared, until I'd stopped on the research I'd conducted about the hyoscine drug.

"Some of you may be familiar, but for those of you who aren't, hyoscine is an antinausea medication that is currently being trialed for use with astronauts who suffer from motion-sickness due to spaceflight." I clicked through another few slides detailing some of the background of the research that had been done. "The trials have been very successful, and while it is still not an approved method for astronauts just yet, I believe this project is special circumstance and that I should be considered for a waiver to utilize this drug for the ISS mission."

There were murmurs around the room. One of the National Science Foundation employees raised a hand. I called on her, and she nodded before speaking.

"Dr. Carter, how do you expect to get approval for emergency use of the hyoscine drug in such a short amount of time? *Galileo* is set to launch in just a few days. Not to mention that you haven't been preparing for the mission itself in weeks, given you were replaced."

It was the first question, out of several questions, that I was expecting. I swallowed deeply, glancing at Dr. Hale before I answered her. "After my initial inquiry about the drug, I spoke with the FDA about applying for an emergency waiver. I'm pleased to say that it was approved just a few days ago."

"—I didn't authorize this," Dr. Hale stared at me, looking rather shocked.

"I may have bypassed a few steps," I replied, trying to be as nonchalant as possible. "The goal was to be as efficient as possible, with the hope that I could maintain my role for this mission." Dr.

Hale was glaring at me, which didn't make me very hopeful, but I continued anyway. I had many other people to convince to be on my side for this.

"Dr. Hale, wasn't there someone who wanted to speak about Dr. Carter? One of the astronauts at the International Space Station, I believe." This time, it was a staff member at the Johnson Space Center. One of Dr. Hale's several assistants. I barely interacted with him, but I recognized his face almost instantly. "They're on a video call right now."

There was a moment of silence, where Dr. Hale looked as though he was pondering over the assistant's suggestion. Then he nodded at me. "Dr. Carter, if you'll pull up the conferencing software on the computer, we can connect to them." I nodded, walking back over to the computer and doing as I was instructed. All the while, I wondered who could possibly be wanting to talk about me. And I hoped, desperately, that it wasn't to my disadvantage.

The software loaded quickly and began to connect to the ISS feed. A couple seconds later, a video screen popped up on the computer and was then projected onto the wall. If I hadn't been so wound up and nervous, I might have made a noise of surprise. Instead, I just stared, mouth slightly hanging open.

Ruby Peters' brown eyes were staring out into the room. By the looks of it, she was in the cupola, but there was only a sliver of an image of the Earth behind her. I wouldn't have noticed or cared, anyway, too surprised to see her.

"Commander Peters," Dr. Hale said, staring at her on the wall. "It's a pleasure to speak with you again. To what do we owe the pleasure?"

"The same to you, Dr. Hale," Commander Peters replied, flashing a friendly smile. "I see you have a full house there today."

"A lot of people have a vested interested in this project," Dr. Hale replied, matter-of-factly. "Including Dr. Carter here, who is presenting us with some information about an anti-nausea drug..."

"Hyoscine," Ruby replied, swiftly. I hadn't spoken a word of this to her. We hadn't communicated since our meeting before I was kicked off the mission. How she knew anything about what I was doing, I wasn't sure. "They've had a lot of success with the trials for that drug, isn't that right?"

Dr. Hale's eyes narrowed slightly. "We were just discussing this with Dr. Carter, who informed us that she decided to bypass the chain of command here and apply for a waiver from the FDA for its usage."

"I may have helped with that," Commander Peters replied. My heart jumped in my chest, still staring at her in disbelief. What had she done exactly? How on earth had she pushed along the approval for the emergency waiver with the FDA? I didn't think it was common of them to interact with astronauts. "I spoke with one of the individuals overseeing the drug trials for the hyoscine drug. She was rather supportive of pushing the emergency waiver through and getting Dr. Carter on this mission."

"And why do you have such a vested interest in Dr. Carter's involvement with this mission? Is there something I'm missing?" Dr. Hale took a sideways glance at me, and I shook my head, completely oblivious to what Commander Peters was doing.

"Because I've done nothing but learn about Dr. Carter for months," Commander Peters said, matter-of-factly. I swallowed deeply at the comment. While I knew many people who took interest in me and my research, for some reason the idea of Commander Peters doing so surprised and intrigued me. "She's a pioneer in her field, as I'm sure you're aware. Two decades dedicated to occupational health, and more specifically to spinal research. Dr. Carter started with the National Space Biomedical Research Institute as a research assistant. For a woman with a medical degree, that's a big step down. But, as I'm sure you are aware Dr. Hale, Dr. Carter has more ambition and drive than I've seen from just about anyone involved with the space programs. She spent her whole career working her way to where she is now."

"I don't believe I'm understanding your point to all of this,

Commander," Dr. Hale looked unimpressed by her speech, drumming his fingers on the top of the conference room table. "There's a lot of important people in this room right now, who have things to do and don't need their time wasted."

"I'm aware," Commander Peters replied. "This isn't a waste of their time, I assure you. My point is, Dr. Hale, I *know* Dr. Carter. I've done nothing but get to know Dr. Carter for a while now. And seeing that this is a multi-billion-dollar project at stake, I don't think you're taking pulling her from this mission seriously enough. She and I are working together, as a team, for the drug trial. We've all gotten to know her up here as a scientist who will be doing work with us. The point is, we *know* her. And while I certainly think that Dr. Riddler is a very competent scientist, I feel very strongly that he's not a suitable replacement for Dr. Carter."

The room erupted into murmurs again. There was a discussion between the employees that had come from the company for the Tirasemtiv troponin activator drug that would be trialed aboard the space station. The NIH employees and National Science Foundation were also conversing. Commander Peters had brought up the massive funding that was going into the project, which even I hadn't thought of using as an argument in my defense.

"Well, Commander," Dr. Hale finally spoke, looking at her. "You certainly have given us a bit to think about." He was taking glances at the others in the room, who still were conversing amongst themselves. I hadn't seen him look as panicked as he did in the history of my knowing him. "Thank you for your time." Commander Peters nodded, and then disconnected from the video call without another word.

When she did, I turned my attention back to Dr. Hale. "Shall I continue?"

Dr. Hale gave a dismissive wave of his hand to silence me. "Dr. Carter, I need to excuse you from the room while I have a discussion with our colleagues."

"If the discussion is about me, I'd like to be present," I argued.

"I'll find you later," Dr. Hale said, in a tone that screamed that my exit was non-debatable. His eyes fell on the door of the room. After picking up my notes by the computer, I made a swift leave, finding Mason outside of the room waiting for me.

"Did Commander Peters show?" he asked almost immediately when I appeared.

I stared blankly at him for a moment and then the realization hit me how she must have known about the research I'd been doing and the meeting. Mason had been in communications with her. I wasn't sure what to think about it, but I nodded regardless.

"Do you think she helped?"

"I have no idea," I admitted, wondering the same exact thing myself.

MASON WALKED with me back to my temporary office and left me a few minutes after. I wasn't quite sure what to do with myself, filled with too many nerves about what had just gone down at the conference room. Unsure if Ruby's appearance had somehow lessened the likelihood that my presentation had been successful. I hadn't even gotten to finish it.

The more I stewed, the more annoyed I started to become. Until I found myself clicking away at my computer, opening the video conference software and attempting to connect back with the ISS. Surprisingly, it was Commander Peters who answered the call.

"Dr. Carter," her voice sounded relatively surprised to see me. "I expected you to still be in your meeting." This time it was obvious she was in the cupola. I could make out the Earth clearly behind her, bright as day. It distracted me for a moment.

Finally, I came back to reality. "I was dismissed after your little appearance," I replied, realizing after that my voice had come out a little snippy. Once I'd cleared my throat, I continued. "Which you had no right interfering without my permission, even if you were in cahoots with Mr. Evans."

"Mason came to *me*, if we're going to point fingers," Commander Peters replied. "Which I certainly hope you won't, because we both were on your side of this. My intention wasn't to sabotage your presentation, Dr. Carter. I was trying to help."

"And you very well might have ruined my chances now," I said, feeling rather frustrated. I didn't like being kept in the dark about things. I hated surprises, which made this situation particularly annoying.

"I think I deserve a thank you, not to be berated, Dr. Carter." Commander Peters' facial expression remained neutral and calm, despite all the emotions that were racing through me. "And I'll admit, my help was partially self-serving. I didn't want to work with Dr. Riddler. Like I said, I've spent months trying to understand your research and getting to know you. I didn't want a stranger to work with me on such a ground-breaking project. Especially after what he did to you..."

What he did to you. Did she know? "What he did to me...?" I couldn't *not* ask.

"I may have stumbled upon some articles about the allegations from your medical school years. When you two were still married and doing research together." Commander Peters was staring at me intensely, but her eyes had softened a little. Like she was doing her best to try and understand.

"And you didn't believe them?" I replied, in somewhat disbelief. Those allegations had followed me everywhere, and still haunted me from time to time. So many people had taken Michael's side, I nearly always assumed that was the case. Commander Peters had taken me by surprise.

"Of course not," Commander Peters said. "And anyone that knows you well enough should know better, too. I know with absolute certainty that was all a bunch of lies."

"Commander Peters, I haven't even met you before. For you to say you know me..." I shook my head. "You don't know me."

"Try me. I can recite your resume for you, practically by heart.

Summarize every research article you've ever published. Hell, I probably can name them all. I know every facet of your spinal research, down to the minute details regarding this mission..."

"I'm impressed with your knowledge of my career and my research," I admitted, though she wasn't the only person I'd met to know this much information about me. "I'm afraid that still doesn't mean you *know* me, Commander. Whether you have the right to judge about my integrity, my reasons for doing what I do. Certainly not enough to formulate opinions about what transpired between Dr. Riddler and myself."

"I know you prefer Earl Grey tea over coffee," Ruby responded without a second of hesitation, and now there was a small smile on her face. "That your favorite food is chicken tikka masala and saag paneer from an Indian place by your home in Houston. Your favorite book is *The Martian* by Andy Weir, which you supposedly read at least twice every year. By the look of every picture you've ever been in, your favorite color must be grey, because that's the only color clothes I think is in your closet..." I stared at her, slightly flabbergasted by all the things she seemed to know about me. Most she probably found in articles, but she'd remembered them all the same. "Your favorite quote is a quote by Marie Curie – 'Nothing in life is to be feared, it is only to be understood. Now is the time to understand more, so that we may fear less.'"

"Apparently I have quite the follower," I said, still trying to process my feelings on her abundance of knowledge of me and what exactly it meant. Part of me was flattered that someone had taken so much time to understand me, but on the same token it also left me unsettled.

"My point is, Dr. Carter," Commander Peters said, bringing my focus back to her and less on my wandering thoughts of this conversation. "As a woman who has spent her entire life in pursuit of a dream and a career that is, even still, dominated by men, I can't *not* understand and relate to another passionate, career-driven woman, who fights the same fight as me, every day. Working from the ground up, building your entire life, working twice as hard as any of your male colleagues to get where you are, to be respected and understood. Dr. Carter, we're one in the same in many ways. More so than you realize. And it's not because we both love Tikka Masala. That Marie Curie quote is all I needed to know you're a genuine woman with integrity."

"All from a Marie Curie quote?" For the first time in a while, I felt the smallest hint of a genuine smile crossing my face. While I was certainly still a little annoyed with her, this had been one of the first times in my career I'd ever felt as if I'd related to one of my colleagues. Commander Peters understood on a level that most everyone else I worked with didn't. Couldn't.

"She was the first woman to win a Nobel Prize, after all," Ruby was smiling back at me. "And if you remember right, her father couldn't afford her to go to university, and higher education wasn't available to women in Poland."

"But she went on to get her doctorate anyway," I added.

"And if I remember right, she took part clandestinely in the nationalist 'free university,' by reading in Polish to women workers. And funded her sister's medical studies."

"She wanted other women to succeed, as much as her." There was still a lingering smile on my face. I appreciated how much Commander Peters understood about Marie Curie's background, and surprisingly, why her life had such a profound impact on my own. Apparently, it was something she connected with me on, on a deep level.

"That's why I said something," Commander Peters explained. "That's why I know that the allegations of Dr. Riddler's weren't true. Because you're a woman of science, in a man's world. A woman who dedicated her life to the pursuit of knowledge that would better humanity. And I honestly saw it as a disservice to Marie Curie herself not to help another woman succeed. Especially someone like you."

The small smile lingered on my lips for a few more seconds, as I stared at her. It was funny, looking at her then. I'd always noticed she was a pretty woman, with soft facial features and alluring short curly black hair that demanded my attention. Eyes that were so expansive and expressive that it was hard to look away from her. But now, there was something different about her. Something different in the way I saw her, that filled me with weird sensations I hadn't felt in the longest time. My stomach was flipping, my palms felt slightly sweaty. My pulse faster.

"Thank you, Commander Peters. I appreciate your confidence in my work."

"Well, I also did it because Dr. Riddler seems like a smug ass," Commander Peters added, still smiling when she shrugged. A laugh escaped me. One that shook my belly and warmed my body. I hadn't laughed like that in ages, and it felt and sounded so foreign. "I only hope it was enough to help." Ruby stared at me deeply, with those enchanting brown eyes.

"I do too," I replied, the warmth in me fading away, replaced with worry.

FIVE

RUBY

Dr. Daphne Carter.

The tiny blonde-haired woman, engulfed in a large flight suit, was standing right in front of me, in the flesh. Bits of her hair were floating around her angelically. Those hazel eyes of hers had lost their intensity, and instead seemed somewhat distant and glazed over. It took me only a matter of seconds before I realized why.

"She's going to pass out," I warned Adrik, and the two of us pushed off from the wall, floating toward her as quickly as we could in the microgravity environment. Just as we'd reached her, the woman went limp. We wrapped arms on either side of her, and I couldn't help but laugh, even through my concern. "Welcome to the International Space Station, Dr. Carter."

Meanwhile, in the background, I could hear Daniel communicating with Mission Control, even amidst the chatter between all the astronauts. "Yeah, she's out of the shuttle. Looks like she might have lost consciousness... I'll let you know when she comes to."

"Let's get her somewhere to recover," I looked at Adrik and he nodded.

The two of us made our way through the winding nodes, until we came to a vacant "sleep station," as we called them. Personal sleep compartments for the astronauts aboard the station, that were the size of telephone booths. Adrik and I fastened Dr. Carter half into a sleeping bag within the compartment, to keep her localized. Once we had her secured, Adrik left me in the room, at a computer station.

Dr. Carter stayed unconscious for a good thirty minutes, while I occupied my time catching up on the plethora of emails I had yet to open. When I heard her start to rustle in the bag, I closed out of the computer and pushed off the wall toward her sleep station. By the time I peeked my head inside, Dr. Carter's hazel eyes were peering out at me. Truthfully, she looked rather adorable wrapped up in a cocoon of sleeping bag. But the expression on her face read that she was *not* in the mood for hearing that.

"You're strapped in," I explained, even though it was obvious that Dr. Carter realized this. "Can't have you floating away in all the microgravity." I watched her eyes blink a few times, likely trying to adjust to the glowing whiteness and artificial lighting of the node. She took in her surroundings before I added. "Welcome to your sleeping quarters, Dr. Carter. I don't usually like to take a woman to bed the first time I see her, but I made an exception for you."

It was a joke, clearly, but Dr. Carter seemed to not want anything to do with it. I watched her start to try to clumsily remove herself from the sleeping bag. "Here, let me help," I offered, reaching in to try and pull one of the straps away. When I did, Dr. Carter batted my eager hands away, and continued to awkwardly help herself.

"I've got it, Commander," Dr. Carter replied, sounding somewhat on edge. Once she'd relieved herself from the final strap, she began to float slowly forward, toward me. I watched, without speaking, having gripped on to one of the nearby metallic blue railings along the wall. Dr. Carter floated helplessly forward and up, looking unsure of what to do with herself.

I outstretched a hand again toward her, and despite her initial reservations, Dr. Carter took it, firmly. She seemed to notice that we'd relieved her of her flight suit, glancing down at herself briefly. We floated together, hand in hand, as Dr. Carter started to try to acclimate herself. She looked miserable, to say the least.

"It takes a little bit of getting used to," I assured her. "You'll acclimate. Let's go find the rest of the crew." Dr. Carter looked as though she was going to protest for about a half second, then she closed her mouth. I moved us along the railing in the module, using my fingertips to propel us forward. The doctor seemed overwhelmed by her environment, so I let her try to take it all in as we moved. We passed walls filled with equipment, strapped down. "This is Node 2," I explained, as we veered into an adjoining room. "It connects with Destiny, our research laboratory."

"And my rats?" Dr. Carter asked, seeming rather abruptly alarmed.

"Safe and sound in the laboratory, from my understanding," I assured her, giving her hand that was latched on to mine the tiniest squeeze. We made a sharp turn to the left. "And this in front of us is Destiny. Where we'll be spending most of our time for the next few weeks. I'm sure you recognize a few of the folks in here."

Most of the crew had gathered in this room. Daniel, Adrik, James, and Andrea. Tony, who had been a bundle of nerves upon arriving, had gone to rest in a sleeping station for a few hours. Daniel was the first to see us as we made our way inside. He gave a small wave, smiling under his bushy mustache. "I see the doc has woken up," he said.

When I turned my attention toward Dr. Carter, I realized she was looking a little off again. This time, it looked as though she was feeling sick. "Dr. Carter, are you feeling alright?"

Daniel seemed to have realized this before I did. He'd come over to meet us, toting a white barf bag, which Dr. Carter frantically grabbed from him the minute he arrived. She spent a good minute awkwardly heaving into the bag. The entire room went quiet, I assumed everyone must have felt bad for her. When she finally relaxed, Daniel took the bag away from her to dispose.

"I think this might help," Daniel said, exchanging the barf bag with Dr. Carter and handing her medications and a pouch of water. Once he had, he left us again, likely to dispose of the result of Daphne's motion sickness. She took the meds and water eagerly, and I watched her for a moment trying to figure out how the pouch worked.

"Would you like some help?" I offered, and Dr. Carter's nostrils flared. If I could have taken a step back from her, I would have. Instead, I remained suspended in front of her, patiently waiting for her to figure it out. Surprisingly, she did, taking the pills she'd been offered and then sucking the water pouch into her mouth. She took a rather large drink. When it slipped from between her rosy lips, a dribble of water floated into the air.

Dr. Carter watched in fascination as the water floated in a perfect circle into the room. I smiled and reached for her wrist, without even a moment's thought, and brought her hand to the water. It clung to her skin, dancing around her palm.

Before I could explain, she spoke what I had been thinking. "Because of the surface tension," she breathed, rotating her hand a bit so she could see more clearly. Those hazel eyes had grown wider.

"Even I still play with it from time to time," I admitted. "We aren't really supposed to." I trailed off, distracted when Dr. Carter pressed her lips to the curve of her hand and sucked at her skin, letting the water fall into her mouth. The image caused a lump to form in my throat, to the point I was unable to formulate words for a minute. For a woman in her forties, she had a very youthful looking face. Soft skin, nearly untouched by wrinkles, full lips that would be killer when she smiled.

It *was* killer when she smiled.

I remembered the conversation we'd had a few weeks prior, when she had let herself be happy for a few moments. That uptight, no-nonsense version of her had faded away just for a bit. The day she'd presented about the *hyoscine* drug, and I'd spoke for her. She'd been so surprised by my appearance, by my unwavering support. Her smile, her laugh, it had been so genuine and real. And now, there was a child-like innocence about her curiosity.

Unfortunately, it didn't last long. Daniel interrupted her fascinated haze, reappearing beside me. "Dr. Daphne Carter," he said, outstretching a hand to her. "Daniel Richards. Pleasure to finally make your acquaintance. Folks back on Earth said you might have missed your dose of hyoscine before the launch…"

"I did, in fact," Dr. Carter replied, nodding. She took his hand, firmly, and gave it a shake, the other hand still wrapped around the metallic support beam. "Nice to meet you, Mr. Richards. I've heard good things."

"And I'm Ruby, obviously," I said, when Dr. Carter had turned her attention back on me. I offered a friendly smile, to which she didn't return. Instead, she was sizing me up and down. I held out a hand to her, shaking it firmly when it was received. The kind of shake I appreciated in a woman, that oozed confidence and security in herself. "But you knew that already."

"Yes, Commander Peters," Dr. Carter replied, looking at me again. "I know all about you." When my attention drifted to Daniel, he had raised a brow, but I ignored it. We both needed to know about one another, for the sake of the research. The two of us were partners, after all. If we didn't know each other well enough, if we couldn't trust each other, then her lifelong work might fall through the cracks once she left the station.

"How about a quick tour?" Daniel offered. "We've just been chatting, but I'm sure you're interested in seeing everything."

Dr. Carter didn't even hesitate before replying. "I'm afraid I've got work to do, Mr. Richards. I'm here for three weeks. This isn't a vacation, not by a longshot." Her eyes came back to mine. "If you don't mind, I'd like to see my rats."

"Down here," I said, nodding toward the far end of the module. A blue rack of cages and equipment had just been inserted into the wall, next to a computer station. I floated off down the stretch of room, looking back to see Dr. Carter following behind me. I couldn't help but smirk, looking at Dr. Carter's white-knuckled hands.

"Is there a problem, Commander?" While Dr. Carter looked completely overwhelmed by her environment, she also was casting a very annoyed look toward me.

"You might want to loosen your grip on the railing there, Doctor." I nodded toward her white hands. "Use your fingers to propel you. It shouldn't take a lot of effort."

When she loosened her grip a bit, the white knuckles disappeared. Dr. Carter glanced up at me, and we continued moving back toward the far end of the module. "Does it always feel like you're falling?" Daphne seemed to be trying to convince herself she wasn't. "It's dreadful."

"Just give it a little time," I assured her, stopping in front of the computer station adjacent to the rat enclosures. "And wait for the *hyoscine* to kick in. I'm sure that's not helping." Dr. Carter nodded, and then her attention turned to the rats, which she'd landed in front of. Ten, each inside their own compartments, all exposed to the microgravity. Most of them were sleeping, I assumed worn out from having to adjust to a change in their environment.

"I assume you received their latest vital information, prior to launch?" Dr. Carter asked.

"That they're in perfect health?" I replied, nodding. "I've been keeping up."

"Good," Dr. Carter replied, still scanning over each of them. "The procedure will be the same here, as it was on Earth. In addition to administering the drug daily, we'll be keeping regular data on their vitals, as well as regular magnetic resonance images of their spinal health."

"I'm aware," I replied, coming to float right beside her at the enclosures. "Dr. Carter, I've been very religiously following your work, as I mentioned several times before." She seemed rather unimpressed, her attention still on the research specimen. I wasn't even sure if she was entirely listening to me at all, or mostly just talking to herself. "I noticed through your logs, for instance, that Bob appears to be a voracious eater."

"Bob?" That seemed to get Dr. Carter's attention. She looked at me, a perplexed look on her face, like she was unsure if she really wanted to know the reason that her research specimen had a common name, and not a letter designation. I tapped on the enclosure for the second rat, Rat B, and Dr. Carter's face seemed to eventually figure out what I meant.

"I was reading some research recently that giving laboratory animals proper names helps with their stress levels. I know their designations are A to J, so I just decided to give them names off their letter. Bob, obviously is—"

"Rat B," Dr. Carter mused, a hint of irritation in her tone. I couldn't quite tell what she thought of it, but it seemed that she wasn't a fan. "If you must give them names, all I ask is that you refer to them by their designated letters in your reports. For consistency's sake."

"For consistency's sake," I echoed, nodding. "Can do. So long as you designate my proper name in your research reports, and not 'Astronaut R' or something like that." Dr. Carter blinked at me, apparently caught off guard at my attempt to make a joke again.

"If you're done humoring yourself, Commander, I suggest we get started. We have a lot of work to do."

I FLOATED LAZILY around the corner a few hours later, food in hand. Dr. Carter had been working non-stop at a computer station in the Destiny module, since she'd arrived. The rest of the crew had evacuated the room, finding various other tasks to do. Some had gone to sleep for a few hours. I probably should have too, but I was much more interested in Dr. Carter's doings.

"Still at it?" I asked, as I pushed along the wall of the room, holding on to my food with the other hand. It was contained in disposable packaging. Coffee and a trail mix bar. My favorite breakfast on the station, but it also made a good snack.

I landed next to Daphne at the adjacent computer station and peeked to see what she'd been up to. It looked as though she was buried in data about the troponin activator drug for the trials. She was wearing a pair of black glasses that I'd never imagined her wearing. Where she'd retrieved them from, I had no idea. The look caught me off guard, and I found myself staring and admiring how they accentuated her hazel eyes.

"Are you done gawking, Commander Peters?" Dr. Carter sassed, though I could tell by the tone of her voice that she wasn't quite as annoyed as she was acting.

I pried my attention from her and focused back on my food, ripping open the soft container of coffee and slipping it onto my mouth. I sucked some of the liquid out, feeling instantly more alert when I did. Sometimes, I missed the taste of drinking a fresh pot of hot coffee like I had on Earth, but this was as good of a substitute as any. It worked all the same.

"I've been working on the preliminary setup for the drug trial," Dr. Carter explained, clearly nose deep in whatever she was working on and not wanting to be disturbed. By the looks of whatever she was reading, I hadn't seen some of it and likely would have to ask to later.

"Can I bring you something to eat? Are you sure you don't want to rest for a few hours before getting into this?" I offered, taking another swallow of coffee. After, I ripped open the packaging to my trail mix bar, taking a rather ravenous bite.

Dr. Carter did not seem enthused with me when her eyes drifted upward and landed on my mouth. "Can you chew any louder, Commander Peters?"

I swallowed the bite and offered a smile. "You can call me Ruby, you know." I paused for a second before continuing. "I apologize about my eating. My mom always called me a voracious eater." Dr. Carter nodded once, turning back to her work, eyes glazed over looking at the screen. "You sure I can't bring you something?"

"I'd prefer a little peace and quiet," she said, rather coolly. "If that isn't too much trouble for you. I'll need your help in another hour or so, but for now I have reading to finish."

Instead of arguing, I simply nodded and turned my focus to the computer station I was at. I disposed of my garbage in a container beside it, before waking up the console. I was feeling rather sleepy myself, doubting I could go very much longer without a little sleep. How Dr. Carter was managing, I had no idea.

I got lost in what I was working on, until I noticed the feeling of eyes on the back of my head. In a slow motion, I turned to look over my shoulder, finding Dr. Carter's intense stare on me. She cleared her throat. "Perhaps I could use a little food after all," she replied. "Whatever you're eating. But no coffee, please. I can smell that wretched stink from across the room."

"I'm sorry we don't have some Earl Grey for you," I replied, reminding her that I was aware of her beverage preferences. Instead of inquiring further, I moved out of the room again, disappearing around the corner, on the hunt for some food. When I returned minutes later, Dr. Carter was inspecting some of the other equipment in the room. I floated over to her, handing her a pouch of water and the trail mix bar. "I can show you some of this other equipment, if you'd like..."

"Perhaps another time, Commander Peters," Daphne said, taking the food from me. Our hands lingered for a fraction of a second. Perhaps it was the lack of human contact lately. The fact that the last person I'd touched without a space suit on had been my aunt and uncle months ago, when I'd hugged them goodbye. But something about her skin against my fingertips, even for a moment, sent a jolt through my spine, the likes of which I hadn't recalled feeling in years, if ever.

I shook my head free of the thoughts, and turned my attention to Dr. Carter, who had ripped open the trail mix bar, her focus back on the computer. I watched her as she nibbled at it, almost like a chipmunk in a way, delicate and hardly eating. How she wasn't as thin as paper, I wasn't quite sure. If my mother saw her, she'd have had something to say about it.

"Let's take vitals," Dr. Carter decided, breaking my train of thought. She'd turned her attention toward me then. "I assume you know how to do that much, and I can use your assistance to make things faster and more efficient."

Together, we worked to obtain the measurements from all the rats, one at a time. While Dr. Carter worked with Alfred, I handled Bob. As soon as I'd fetched Delilah, she squirmed in my hand nervously, rather alarmed.

"Rat D has always been a bit more skittish," Dr. Carter explained.

"Shush," I said to the rat, trailing a finger down her back. "It's okay Delilah." I heard a sound to my right, where Dr. Carter was. Without looking, I couldn't have been certain, but I imagined it had been the blonde giving me an annoyed huff. I ignored it, focusing my attention on the rat as I quickly ran through the list of things I needed to check. When I'd finished, I returned her to the enclosure.

"I hope that during your tenure at MIT, they taught you the importance of multiple trials," Dr. Carter mused from beside me. "Data isn't necessarily valid just because some minute trial in some inconsequential laboratory at a public university said it was."

I realized, during her speech, that she was referring to the research I'd mentioned to her earlier regarding naming the research specimen. It was funny how aggravated it seemed to make her. Some small part of me gathered a little satisfaction from that fact, especially since she was starting to question me at every turn.

"Dr. Carter," I said calmly, placing Harold back into his compartment once I'd finished checking over him. "I'll do whatever necessary to ensure the comfort of your research subjects while they're aboard the station. If that means I call them by proper names, because some 'Podunk' university, after one trial, said it might help, I'll do it anyway. You're entrusting me with their care after you leave. Assigning them names isn't subjecting them to any harm, and perhaps it might be doing some good. And if it helps me care for your research to the best of my ability, I'm going to continue to do it." I paused for a half second, then added. "So, I suggest you get over it."

It had been a long time since I'd felt so inclined to argue with someone, but she'd gotten under my skin a little more than I had anticipated. My attention turned to her briefly, and I could tell by her body language that she was stewing over my answer. I wondered if she'd make a snide reply, but instead she kept her mouth shut, until we'd finished all the rats.

Daphne clicked through screens on the computer she'd been using and cleared her throat. "This screen will hold all of the specimens' vitals information. You'll want to make sure to back it up twice, and submit it to NASA, the Biomedical Research Institute, and the drug company for review."

I nodded and watched as the data transfer completed, eyeing over the numbers. "It looks like Delilah and Jeffery both are having some weird readings..."

"Anxiety, likely due to their new environment," Dr. Carter replied. "Let's give them a bit to acclimate and see if it improves." Her eyes scanned through the screen, examining all the data carefully. I watched as she handed me her half-eaten bar that she'd left strapped under her computer console. We didn't waste on the ISS. I didn't argue with her about it and instead chose to eat the rest of it. If Dr. Carter wanted to starve, so be it. I wasn't going to stop her.

"Now that vitals are squared away, I'd like for you to read over this information about the Tirasemtiv troponin activator drug. It's important you understand this if you're assisting me. And since you don't have a medical background, like I would have preferred, I need to know that you're capable of learning this information..."

I stared at the literature she had open. "Dr. Carter, I've already looked over all of this—"

"And I'm asking you to read it again," Dr. Carter snapped, seeming a little annoyed with me. I felt an equal surge of displeasure with her. "While I'm standing here beside you, Commander. I want you to know this information backwards and forwards." I wanted to argue with her. Which part did she want to know about? What side effect was she concerned with? What results did she need to be elaborated upon?

"I can look over this in my sleep station," I suggested, glancing at her. "It's getting about time for a few hours of rest, don't you think Dr. Carter?" Did she ever rest?

Dr. Carter stared at me, unwavering. Apparently, she did not agree. So instead, I dove into reading the article, focusing as best I could. Trying my best to not think about the fact that Dr. Carter was looming over my shoulder. Occasionally, I'd glance to see her nose sticking out and her lips pursed, but I did my best to ignore her.

That was until I heard a soft, rhythmic sound filling my ears. My attention turned back on Dr. Carter. Her eyes were closed, mouth open just a fraction. She was snoring. And it was a little cute, even. A quiet chuckle escaped me. Stubborn as she was, her biology couldn't escape her. The woman had exhausted herself, no doubt about it.

And for the first time since she'd arrived, she seemed a little more human.

SIX

DAPHNE

For the second time since I'd arrived, I awoke cocooned in a vertical sleeping bag, in what was supposedly my "sleep station." It was a tiny room, barely bigger than a phone booth, that housed a sleeping bag, pillow, lamp, a computer strapped to a wall, and an area for personal effects. I stared out at the white room beyond the hole I was tucked in, trying to acclimate myself to my surroundings. Usually I was a morning person, but since there were no "mornings" in space, I wasn't quite sure what I was here.

I realized I felt well rested and much less sick than I'd been earlier. The idea I'd been enclosed in this tiny space again, likely by Commander Peters herself, annoyed me. I could barely remember what had happened before I'd fallen asleep. The Destiny Module came to mind, and watching Ruby read at the computer. Vague memories of fading in and out of consciousness as Ruby drug me through the station and back to this place.

As carefully as I could, I unraveled myself from the sleeping bag cocoon and floated away and out of the sleep station. The fact that I was floating would still take some getting used to, despite the numerous simulations on Earth. I wasn't even sure if I *would* get used to it by the time I left. It was a little too surreal for my liking.

My attention focused back on the room, and I realized I was not alone in it. The Russian astronaut, who I only knew through my research, was working at a computer station on the far side of the module. He was watching me as I made my way out and offered a friendly smile. "Did you sleep well, Dr. Carter?" I was surprised to find that the man's accent was very light.

"Well enough, I suppose," I replied, refusing to admit that the rest had done me good. "You must be Adrik Ivanov, from St. Petersburg. Graduate of the Yuri Gagarin Cosmonaut Training Center. Top of your class. You wrote a paper in your university years about lunar research. I believe it's what they've been saying has sparked the 'renaissance of Russian space science,' correct?"

Adrik grinned at me. "Yes, yes. The Cosmonaut from St. Petersburg. That I am." He paused for a moment, thoughtfully. "I've always been very interested in lunar research. But I admit, I've been hoping to be involved with the joint mission with NASA to reach Venus."

"That's years away," I said, raising a brow at him. "And still hypothetical."

"I like big dreams," Adrik replied, swiftly. He studied me for a moment, and then spoke again. "If you're looking for Ruby, I think she may be in the cupola." I stared at him a moment, surprised that he would assume I wanted to see her. There must have still been a confused look on my face when I finally nodded, and it made him laugh. "Ah, it's easy to get a little lost in this place, yes? I'll show you the way."

Getting "a little lost" was an understatement. Even paying careful attention, I wasn't quite sure I could find my way back to where I needed to be without assistance. Being in a microgravity environment made it very easy to get disoriented. When we made a final turn, I was looking up into a familiar rounded hub. One that I'd seen in videos many times now. The cupola.

Commander Peters was working at a computer. My mind flashed

back to the conversation we'd had after my meeting, when I'd seen her in the same location. Behind her, the Earth shone in clear view. I couldn't make out where we were from the distance I was at, but I wasn't looking at the Earth. Instead, I was watching Ruby's short curly raven hair, floating around her, catching bits and pieces of the light from the planet. Admiring the flecks of gold in her brown eyes, and the way the light illuminated her soft skin. She was mesmerizing.

I didn't get an opportunity to stare long. Adrik's voice cut through my thoughts. "Ruby, Dr. Carter needed to see you."

"I didn't need to—" I stared feeling caught off-guard. I wasn't *looking* for her. At least I would tell myself I wasn't. Somehow, she still felt like a tether in this place. A sort of comfort that I wasn't expecting her to be. Like she'd never steer me wrong. A haven in a foreign land. I fumbled for a reasonable excuse as to why I was there but failed. "Commander Peters."

"Call me Ruby," Ruby reminded me from above. She was looking down now, having twisted herself slightly in position.

"—Ruby," I tried to keep my tone flecked with as little annoyance as possible. It felt strange to call her by her first name. Casual. I wasn't sure if I liked it or not, but I rather liked the sound of it regardless. "I was just looking to see if you were ready to resume working."

"You never stop, do you?" Ruby replied, laughing. "I mean, unless you literally pass out..." I tried my best to continue to remain unannoyed and forced a very small smile at her rude attempt at a joke. "How about we work up here for now?"

"Have fun, ladies," Adrik said, and then turned and moved away from us, disappearing back around the corner. I returned my focus back to Ruby, who was waving at me to join her. I realized I was floating somewhat in the middle of the room and had nothing to grab on to. Ruby seemed to come to the same conclusion as me, sliding down a bit to offer me a hand. She pulled me upward, sending me into the small cupola space, where I grasped hold of a metallic blue handle to steady myself. Once I had, Ruby released from me.

I still found myself thinking about the feeling of her hand against my own. I couldn't remember the last time I'd felt another woman's touch, and Ruby had made physical contact with me numerous times since my arrival. In Houston, I was surrounded by male colleagues. I shook hands often, but not with other women. Ruby's touch, while full of confidence, was also warm and inviting. Something I wasn't quite used to and didn't know how to interpret.

"Welcome to the best seat in the house," Ruby announced, having taken a spot at a different console outside of the cupola space. For a second, I thought to explain to her that it hadn't been necessary for her to give up her spot. But then I looked upward, basking in the glow of the Earth above us, or below us, I wasn't sure which. It glowed so radiantly; it was as if it demanded my entire attention. I had no idea how one could even remotely focus when they were in this space, especially if they were new to it. "Pretty, huh?"

My eyes drifted down to meet Ruby's. She was staring at me a few feet away at one of the computer stations just outside the cupola. A broad, bright smile stretched across her face. In my mind, she could have meant that in several ways. Her curly hair was still floating around her, and the pearl white glow of her teeth was hard to break away from. The glow of the Earth accentuated the curves of her face and the shine of her small lips.

What was I doing?

I cleared my throat. "This computer is available?"

Ruby nodded. I turned my attention to the screen, fingers flying across the keyboard as I punched in my login credentials. I brought up my emails, searching through several dozen that had been sent to me since I last checked. "How long was I asleep?" I wondered aloud, surprised I'd received so much correspondence.

"About ten hours," Ruby said. I felt a wave of shock ripple through me. There wasn't a time in recent memory I'd slept for that long. Generally, I slept six at the most, sometimes seven. I must have been more mentally and physically fatigued than I was admitting to myself. "Can I call you Daphne, or do you insist I call you Dr. Carter?"

The sound of my name on Ruby's lips struck me like I'd heard a beautiful piece of music. It was like she'd sung it, and it wrapped around me unlike anything I'd felt in a long time. The sound was so distracting, that I lost myself in it for far longer than I realized. Eventually, I noticed Ruby staring at me, a puzzled expression on her face. I shook my head. "I suppose that would be fine."

"Daphne," Ruby said, thoughtfully. "It's a very pretty name."

Outside of a few acquaintances outside of work, I was rarely called by my first name. And seeing as my life revolved around my work, it was what I was almost always doing, so it had been a while since I'd heard "Daphne" aloud. There was something sweet about the sound when Ruby spoke it, with that lisp in her voice that intrigued me.

"I was named after my mother," I admitted, a fact not many people knew about me. My mother, like myself, had been a woman of medicine. While she hadn't obtained the prestigious career, I'd ended up having, she'd worked hard and devoted her life to her craft. I had always admired her, up until the day she'd died.

"Oh," Ruby said, and I could sense by her tone of voice she'd gathered my mother had passed. I hadn't meant to be so open, but it felt rather comfortable and normal. "That's really lovely. She must have been quite a woman to raise such a revolutionary of a child."

I raised a quizzical brow at her comment but nodded. "She very much was."

"My aunt and uncle adopted me when I was a baby. I don't know if you knew this, but my dad died while my mom was pregnant with me. She couldn't handle raising me after what happened. You might have heard of him..."

"Commander Jeffery Peters," I interrupted her train of thought. I knew more about her background than she probably realized. "One of the seven crew members aboard the *Eclipse* space shuttle when it exploded. I remember that day, vividly." The facial expression on Ruby's face had changed slightly, and I knew that the subject must have always pained her, even if she'd never known him. "I always assumed it was the reason you were so headstrong. It was in your genes."

"—If you're implying that I used my father as a way to get ahead," Ruby started to argue with me, her eyes having narrowed slightly.

I raised a hand to her, stopping her mid thought. "Not at all, Comman—Ruby. Jeffery was an extraordinary astronaut, with a tremendous work ethic and dedication. I only have fond memories of him, even though I only met him once, when he spoke at a conference months before the explosion. I assumed he was the reason for your passion and drive, your motivation for the work that you do. Contrary to what you may believe, I'm very aware of how hard you worked to get where you are. We're 'one in the same,' remember?"

Ruby stared at me blankly for a few seconds, processing what I had said. Eventually her facial expression softened, and she met my eyes. "Can you tell me about meeting him? My dad? What was he like?"

We watched each other while my mind tried to replay the old memory in my head. "It was years ago, now," I said, trying to recall anything about my time at that conference. "The two things I really remember about him, were that I thought he must have been a very kind person. I always saw him holding doors for people at the conference and answering questions." When I looked at Ruby, I realized she struck me as someone who would do similarly. "And something he said at his presentation always stuck with me, too."

"What was that?" Ruby asked, brown eyes wide.

"That curiosity is the essence of our existence," I replied, thoughtfully. "Admittedly I always looked at you astronauts as 'space junkies,' in it for the high and thrill of the adventure, not the joy and necessity of the discovery of science. Your father made me realize that in essence, we're all in it for the joy of discovery, in our own ways. And that in and of itself is a grand adventure, regardless of what path you chose to take, what life you live."

Ruby was smiling softly at my words, and I studied her for a minute while she ruminated on them. When her focus turned back on me, she spoke again. "Well, anyway," she shook her head. "My aunt and uncle ended up naming me after—"

"The programming language," I replied, having heard this a dozen times by now. It was a fact she seemed rather proud of, regardless. "I'm aware."

My comment made Ruby grow quiet. Instead of continuing, she turned her attention back to the work she'd been doing. By the looks of it, she was reading more published papers on spinal studies in astronauts. I recognized bits and pieces of it that I could see from the distance I was at. I was impressed how focused and dedicated she seemed. I returned my attention back to emails and enjoying the silence between us.

Occasionally, I found myself looking up at the Earth above us. It was hard not to, given how bright and magnificent it was. I realized, when I'd focused well enough, that I was looking at an upside down, familiar looking continent.

"We're over the United States," Ruby seemed to read my mind. I glanced at her, noticing she was pointing, and focused my eyes toward where her finger had landed. "There's Texas."

It was a little hard to identify, given that we were in an unusual direction, but I noticed the familiar curve of where the gulf ran along the coast. I couldn't help but smile slightly. The state felt so small up here. Almost insignificant that it was a state at all. Even the country itself felt oddly like a small piece of a bigger whole.

There was a planet down there. Something I hadn't thought about in much detail before.

"Pretty surreal, right?" Ruby asked me. I nodded, watching as the world spun by us. "Hard to believe we pass by it sixteen times a day. I forget about that sometimes."

I pondered on the idea, feeling rather small in that moment, in the depths of space. It was a humbling thought, how minute our planet was in the grand scheme of the universe. I didn't really think about it much. Space. The universe. My mind had always been so focused on my work and ambitions on Earth. Now it seemed so miniscule. So distant from me...

NEARLY AN HOUR HAD PASSED when I finally looked up from my work, noticing that the room had begun to grow darker. When my eyes scanned outside, I noticed the Earth was disappearing into blackness. Ruby had noticed my attention had drifted and spoke from below me. It had been so quiet, I barely remembered she was there with me.

"Sunset," Ruby's voice was soft and calm. Obviously, I'd assumed this, but I didn't say anything in reply. "Just wait until you see all the lights."

Though I had been engrossed in a journal article, I forgot all about it while watching the Earth as it spun above us. The rest of it began to disappear, until there was only a thin sliver of horizon. As we moved, lights began to glow below us.

"We're above the Philippine Sea. China is to your right, and Japan, to your left."

We were still upside down, but it didn't matter. I couldn't make out the countries anyway, only the brilliant array of lights that spanned across them. It hadn't occurred to me how many you would be able to see from so far away. "I love watching during the day, but there's just something else about the night..."

"How often do you work up here?" I felt somewhat curious. It seemed like it could get rather distracting, and Ruby herself was a rather distracting person, so it took twice the effort to focus on anything at all.

"Adrik and Daniel joke that I hog it. My colleagues the previous two times I've been up here said the same thing. I just can't get enough of it, you know?" Ruby was still staring upward, watching as we flew in what seemed to be slow motion, across the sky. In reality, we were moving at nearly five miles per second. "How amazing it is that everything we know is on that planet. Our entire lives."

"Your life seems very much on this station," I noted, and watched as Ruby turned toward me. She was smiling, ear to ear, that very distracting, glowing white smile that I was finding myself unable to look away from.

"It is," Ruby agreed. "I do love being up here. I'm in love with my work, not unlike yourself." Her words surprised me, although I'd heard it many times before. "Isn't it nice just to get wrapped up in something you're so passionate about, you lose track of everything else?"

I found I'd been focused on her intently, and it took a second to process what she'd asked. I blinked, and then nodded. "Most of the time," I thought, aloud, realizing that while I certainly enjoyed my work and what I did, there were times I missed the smaller things in life. Ruby seemed to be having a similar thought as me.

"I see all my friends, my old classmates from college, all on social media. How they have houses now, and families, and are traveling and seeing the world, and living on that planet up there...down there..." She paused for a moment. "But then I think, look at how I get to see the world. I'm one of the very few that get to see it this way." Ruby shrugged. "Sometimes I get a little sad considering the ways my life could have gone if I stayed on Earth. But then I remember that I'm really lucky to get to do this for a living."

"Indeed you are," I agreed, my eyes returning to the glow of lights on the Earth above us.

FOR THE FIRST time since I'd arrived on the station, I was surrounded by a whirlwind of activity. Three US astronauts were gathered in the same module, at the same time, all participating in the mandatory exercise routines that were required of them while they were on mission. Now that I'd arrived, their normal activities would change to suit the needs of my research. And as such, it was important that I monitored their progress while I was on board.

The current program emphasized the maintenance of bone mineral density, aerobic/anaerobic capacity, and muscle strength/power, primarily focusing on the large muscles of the proximal hips and shoulders, and endurance. My goal was to continue significant lumbar strengthening, in hopes that it may aid in reducing back muscle and disk changes post-spaceflight.

Presently, my attention was on Daniel Richards, who was pedaling on what was affectionately named the "space bike," because Cycle Ergometer with Vibration Isolation Stabilization, or the CEVIS, was a complicated mouthful. Not like a variety of other men I associated with, he was particularly stubborn, and not very fond of doctors.

"Mr. Richards," I said, working at the computer station next to where the bike was. "Your pulse is borderline high. Might I suggest slowing down a bit. It's not a race..."

"James and I have a bet going on who can get the furthest distance on this thing in one session," Daniel replied in pants, continuing with his rapid pace.

"Daniel is the reason they had the world's foremost engineers fixing these things," Andrea said beside him, on the treadmill, with the same complicated name as the bicycle. She wasn't wrong. The Vibration Isolation Stabilization portion of the names came from the engineering that went into the exercise equipment. When they had first been installed on the ISS, it was quickly realized that when in use, they were *moving* the space station and messing with some of the equipment on board. Since then, they'd been redesigned to eliminate the problem, hence the complicated names.

Andrea's teasing seemed to get to Daniel, who slowed his pace a bit on the machine. His breath returned steady, and the vitals I'd been measuring, a little more normal. "Thank you," I said, glancing at Andrea, and she nodded back at me.

Once I'd finished adding some notes into the software I'd been using, I made my way across the module, leaving Andrea and Daniel behind. It was getting a little easier to navigate myself through the station, but I still found it difficult not to want to cling to the handrails everywhere I went.

I turned a corner, spotting Tony Reynolds on the Advanced Resistive Exercise Device, or the ARED, which was basically meant to simulate weight training for the astronauts. There was no computer station nearby, so I was forced to take written notes and data on what he was doing. Tony looked as though he was still getting used to the equipment, working rather timidly. It was his first time on the station, after all.

"Everything alright, Mr. Reynolds?" I asked, floating in the doorway by the machine.

Tony, who was strapped into the machine, hands around the robotic arms that were used to bench weight, glanced over at me. "Just getting acclimated to this thing," Tony said, matter-of-factly. "It's taking some getting used to."

"Need some help, buddy?" Daniel's voice rang out beside me, and I saw him looming in the doorway opposite of where I was. Tony nodded, and Daniel floated into the nook, checking out what the newbie astronaut had been doing. While he was explaining things, I took a few more notes, before I decided I'd done enough between the three of them.

"Does anyone know where Commander Peters is?" I asked, feeling a small surge of annoyance that she hadn't joined the rest of her colleagues.

"Probably where she always is," Daniel said, matter-of-factly.

I left the men at the resistance machine, returning to the computer station I'd been working at. Before I typed up the rest of the notes that I'd handwritten, I attempted to contact Ruby over the radio. "Commander Peters," I said, trying to keep my voice as neutral as possible, despite my annoyance with her. "Is there a reason you aren't with your colleagues during your *mandatory* exercise time?"

There was a bout of silence, and I assumed she wasn't going to answer. Then static. "Sorry about that, Dr. Carter. I'm in Destiny.

Checking up on your rat babies. I can come right now if you want." Surprisingly, she hadn't been in the cupola after all.

"Stay there," I replied, quickly. "I'll be right over." Once I'd answered her, I set to work typing in the last bit of notes I had to enter, and then closed out of the software and the computer. By the time I had, Daniel had come over to meet me, clearly having finished helping Tony with his resistance training.

"Need some help getting over there?" Daniel asked, smiling under his scruffy mustache hair. Somehow, he'd known that I was going to have issues otherwise. I nodded, graciously. "Alright then, Dr. Carter. Let's roll." He outstretched a hand, and I took it. It felt nothing like when I held Ruby's hand. Just ordinary, like any other man's hand I'd ever shook or held before. But Daniel was friendly enough, and I appreciated his help regardless.

We made our way out of the module with the exercise equipment, turning around a bend. While Daniel moved us gracefully along the support beams, I watched as everything passed us by, a blur of white and florescent lighting. "I don't believe I'll ever find my way around this place," I admitted, as we moved.

"Honestly, I got lost for months my first time up here," Daniel agreed with me. I saw him glance back at me, and did my best to offer a small, polite smile. "It's a bit confusing when everything all looks the same, no matter where you go. And then there's no real "up" or "down" on top of it..." He trailed off, focusing on turning us again in another direction.

"A bit like hamsters in a plastic ball," I noted, which got a chuckle out of Daniel.

"A titanium, Kevlar, and steel ball," he corrected me, just as we'd floated into Destiny.

On the far side of the room, where the rack of enclosures for the rats had been stowed, Ruby was working intensely at a computer station. She hadn't even looked up when we'd arrived, clearly very focused on what she was doing.

"Thank you for the assistance, Mr. Richards," I said, offering another small smile again. There hadn't been a time in recent memory I'd remembered smiling as much as I had since I'd arrived here. Daniel nodded at me, and then turned to leave Ruby and I in the Destiny module alone. When he turned the corner, Ruby finally looked in my direction.

"Sorry about missing exercise," Ruby said, her brown eyes on mine. "I was in here working and noticed that Jeffery was still acting strange. I'm not really sure what's wrong with him..." As she was speaking, I made my way across the module, using the handrails as best I could to assist me. "It was just a little worrisome, so I wanted to make note of it."

I reached her at the computer station and looked over her shoulder at what she'd been working on. The software used to input information regarding the drug trial was open, and by the looks of it, Ruby had added extensive notes about Rat J's observable state, and his present vitals. For a moment, I thought to reprimand her for working on anything related to the drug trial without my assistance, but at the same time, I appreciated her care of my work, and her attention to detail regarding the research specimen.

"These are the vitals you just took?" I asked, pointing over her shoulder at the notes on the screen. Ruby nodded, and I spent a good minute going over everything she'd analyzed, and the extra notes she'd added. "Commander—"

"Ruby," Ruby corrected me nearly instantly.

"...Ruby," I replied, glancing sideways to look at her briefly. "While this is something that is good to take note of, and I appreciate your initiative, I want to give him a few more days to acclimate to the new environment, before it's cause for concern."

"Right," Ruby replied, as she finished typing a sentence. Then she saved the data and closed out of the software without another word. Once she had, she turned to face me. "Sorry for making you come all the way over here then. If it's nothing. I didn't mean to worry you."

"Like I said, I appreciate your help," I replied. "It was good to make sure and to document everything. The 'money' likes to know every minute detail." Money, of course, was our funders for the drug trial. Ruby seemed to understand and nodded. "Besides, since we're both here, I should do your initial medical examination."

"It's going to be weird not having a real bonafide doctor do my ME up here, and not Daniel," Ruby said, thoughtfully. "I suppose you need to know where all our equipment is then." While I'd been instructed about this during my preparations for the mission, there had been so much I needed to know, that the location of equipment wasn't high on my priorities. I nodded and watched as Ruby floated across Destiny to a storage compartment. "Anything specific?"

I rattled off a list of things for her, and she pointed out the location of the X-ray equipment, and the portable MRI machine that had been adapted for the ISS and brought with my arrival. When she returned a few minutes later, we worked together to strap down the things I didn't need.

While I was certainly used to the mundane routine of medical examinations on Earth, it would be a wildly different experience on the space station, in a microgravity environment. When Ruby handed me my stethoscope, I floated in place, one hand on the metallic blue support beams along the wall, the other wrapped around the stethoscope.

Before I even knew what was happening, Ruby had looped her fingers into the belt loops of the khaki pants I'd been wearing. Suddenly I was being tugged forward, closer to her. My breath hitched in my throat and I felt a tumbling in my stomach.

"Commander Peters, what are you doing?" I blinked. The stethoscope had released from my grip momentarily, until I realized and snatched it back as it was floating beside me.

"I usually hold on to Daniel while he does these routine checks," Ruby explained. "Don't want you floating all over the place while you're trying to work." She offered a small smile, trying to ease my sudden wave of panic at her actions. It was still hard not to think about, but I took a deep breath and then nodded.

"Cardiopulmonary testing first," I said, trying to keep my voice steady when I looked her in the eyes again. Ruby was wearing stereotypical attire for the astronauts here, a navy-blue t-shirt and a pair of cargo shorts. I released my grip from the handrail, kept in place only by Ruby's grip around my pants. Once I'd placed the earpieces, I retrieved the chest piece, at the end of the tubing, and then looked at Ruby again.

My hand pressed against her chest with the stethoscope. The steady rhythm of Ruby's heart filled my ears, along with the rhythm of her breathing. And then her voice. "I think this is the first time I've had a woman doctor since I joined the—"

Before I realized what I was doing, my free hand instinctively went up to Ruby's face, placing a finger to her moving lips. She stopped speaking abruptly, and I too, froze in place. I could feel the heat of her breath against my skin, and the dampness of her lips which indicated she must have just licked them. The imagery flashed through my mind and caused a shiver to rip down my spine, violently. I pulled my finger away abruptly and met her eyes.

"I'm trying to *listen*," I said calmly, holding up the metal end of the stethoscope.

"Sorry," Ruby mouthed, offering a small smile to me. I could barely look at her, considering the random fleeting thoughts I'd just had, and instead returned to what I'd been doing. I placed the stethoscope chest piece back against her and returned to checking all four valves of her heart. A little faster than normal, but acceptable.

"Your heart sounds healthy," I said, unable to look her in the eyes still. "I'm going to check for bowel sounds now. No talking." In my peripheral, I saw Ruby nod. I moved the stethoscope down onto her clothed stomach. I pressed down firmly, listening for sounds of bowel obstructions or paralytic ileus. Instead, I was greeted with loud gurgling sounds, ones that were usually ignored on physical examinations.

Ruby seemed to realize her stomach was making excessive noise. When my eyes focused on hers, her face had reddened slightly. "I guess I'm a little hungry." Something told me that with the way Ruby Peters ate, she was almost *always* hungry.

"A 'voracious eater,' right?" I realized I was smirking just slightly when I said it. Ruby's embarrassment turned back into a small, pleasant smile at the realization that I'd remembered her comment from earlier. She nodded. "Everything sounds normal. Turn around."

Ruby released her grip on my pants loop, once I had a hold on the railing again. When she did, I felt the ability to breathe easier. She spun herself around, back facing me then, and I replaced the stethoscope, this time listening to her breathing. Again, it sounded perfectly normal.

"Blood pressure," I said, and Ruby turned back to face me again. She wrapped her fingers around my belt loop again, without even a moment's hesitation. My stomach tumbled for a second, and then I released the handrail, fetching the blood pressure cuff that I'd stowed. Once I'd fixed it to her arm, I reminded her to keep quiet again, with a quick draw of my finger to my mouth. Once again, the imagery of Ruby's tongue drawing across her delicate lips flickered in my mind, but I forced it away, instead focusing on getting a good reading.

When I'd finished, and released the cuff from her arm, I stowed it back in its place. "Everything sounds normal. Let me just take notes of all of this and we'll continue." Ruby let go of me once again, and I moved myself back to the computer station to work. I spent the next few minutes typing up relatively standard ME notes, while Ruby hoovered along the wall beside me.

"You know, I noticed that you bite your lip just slightly when you're really focused," Ruby's voice interrupted my thoughts as I was working. I glanced over at her, meeting those curious, big and expressive brown eyes head on. "You've done it several times now, since you got here."

The sudden realization of a habit I had, made me feel rather self-conscious. "I didn't realize," I replied, immediately focusing on making my mouth as neutral as possible.

"It's cute, Daphne," Ruby replied, swiftly, as if she knew she'd caused me a bit of anxiety about it. My attention on my work drifted, suddenly focused on the fact that she'd said some little extraneous quirk of mine was cute, and the idea that she'd been watching me work so closely to have noticed at all...

"Perhaps your focus would be better served if it was on the ground-breaking research, you're assisting me on," I reminded her, returning my gaze to my computer. After I'd taken a breath, I continued writing my notes, while Ruby had gone quiet beside me. I wondered if I'd offended her by not appreciating her flattery more. Truthfully, I had appreciated it, and it was all I could do not to think about it. But I was here for three weeks, on a multi-billion-dollar assignment, in charge of *two* different research projects. Ruby was here to assist me, as my colleague. She wasn't a stranger, flirting with me at a bar, even though it had certainly felt a little like she'd been flirting with me. We were partners. There was work to be done.

"I'd like to run the MRI next, then a brief optometry and audiological examination, then some bloodwork, and then I'll let you be on your way." I nodded toward where the MRI machine was and headed in that direction. Ruby followed alongside me, across the room, until both of us had reached the handrail on the opposite side.

"Only a few things then, Dr. Carter?" I was busy fiddling with the MRI machine when Ruby had said it, and it caused me to glance up at her again. She was smiling at me playfully. "Are you sure I can't interest you in one of my kidneys? An appendectomy maybe?"

"Supposedly you have a manual around here somewhere instructing you how to do an appy, so I assume you can do that on your own time." Surprisingly, I returned her smile, after my comment. The ISS astronauts did have a manual for explaining specific medical procedures, since there was very rarely a medical doctor on board. My comment got a hearty laugh from Ruby, whose smile widened further.

"I really hope I never see the day I have to remove an appendix," Ruby said, matter-of-factly. "I'm not great with blood and guts. I love biology, but that's pretty much it. No medical school for me. And definitely not surgery..."

"I believe you picked the right profession," I replied, and then nodded to the MRI. "This should only take a little while, and then you can resume your normal routine." Ruby had come next to where the machine had been placed. Beside it was a vertical examination table that sat against the wall. Unlike my other tests, an MRI required patients to be quiet and still.

Once Ruby had aligned herself on the table, back against it, she met eyes with me. "I think you're going to have to strap me down now, doctor." She winked at me playfully with those expansive brown eyes of hers, and I stared back at her for a moment, unable to interpret what her intentions were exactly. Unsure if I even wanted to ruminate on that thought.

Colleagues, I reminded myself, trying my best to ignore her. I cleared my throat, and released myself from the metallic blue railing momentarily, to retrieve the several Velcro straps that would keep her in position for the scans. I fastened one around her waist, tightly, so she was firmly against the table.

"Wow, you *really* don't want me going anywhere, do you?" Ruby wasn't even a foot away from me as I worked to secure her. When I glanced up at her, she had that same playful look in her eyes from before.

I frowned. "Commander Peters—"

"Ruby," she corrected me.

"*Ruby*," I replied, somewhat annoyed. "This test requires you to be *perfectly* still and *perfectly* quiet. I don't suppose you could manage that?" Honestly, I wondered how long Ruby could be quiet in the first place, it seemed as if she liked to talk a great deal. "I know it might be difficult for you, but I need you to try, please."

We were still looking at each other when I finished speaking. Ruby's playful expression went more neutral, and she nodded at me. Once she'd settled, I resumed fastening her in place on the table, securing her arms and her legs.

As I'd politely asked, Ruby went very quiet for the duration of the MRI. Occasionally, I'd glance over at her while I was working. She'd closed her eyes, breathing rhythmically. I wondered if she'd fallen asleep.

While the images populated on the computer that was connected to the MRI, I released Ruby from the examination table. When I reached her to unfasten the Velcro straps, her eyes fluttered open, and she met my gaze.

"Done already?" I nodded, just as I'd finished, and Ruby reached out a hand to grasp hold of the metallic blue railing beside her. The two of us floated together, barely separated, and still staring at one another. Once again, I was momentarily fixated on the way Ruby's short curly hair floated around her head, and the softness of her pale skin. Eventually, she interrupted my wandering thoughts. "How long do the MRI scans take to process?"

I shook my head, turning my attention toward the computer. "Not long," I replied, and then pushed off the railing back to the station, checking on the status of the images. They still hadn't come up yet. When I turned my attention back to Ruby, she'd floated around behind me to situate herself at an adjacent computer, a little to my left.

The minute she'd settled, typing in her login information, the MRI scans populated on my screen in my peripheral. My attention returned to my work, my eyes narrowing at the results I was seeing. Before I continued, I searched through NASA's medical research database for Ruby's pre-flight ME records and her MRI results, and the records from her previous two excursions to the ISS.

As was usually the case with nearly all the ISS astronauts, and the reason for the desperate need of research and treatment for it, Ruby had significant atrophy of her paraspinal lean muscle mass. It seemed to worsen over the course of her stay on the station, then resolve somewhat during her recovery and stay on Earth. However, unlike some of her colleagues in earlier years, since there had been improvement in the regulation of orthopedic health in astronauts during long-duration spaceflight over the past decade, she hadn't shown very much change in the height of her spinal intervertebral discs.

That was, until the scans today. Not only had Ruby's lean muscle decreased since she'd been on this latest mission, but her disc height had also changed substantially. "Ruby," I glanced over at her working at another computer. "Your personal logs since you arrived here indicate you haven't had any reports of back pain, correct? Even your medical records seem to show this has never been a problem."

"I was surprised too," Ruby said, looking up so her attention was on me. "Something like half of individuals who have been on long-term spaceflight report back pain, at least that's what I think I remember reading..."

"Right," I replied, nodding. My attention turned back to my computer, clicking back to the new scans. The change in her spinal column was significant and a little worrisome. How she hadn't reported any pain, I had no idea.

Ruby seemed to sense my sudden alarm, and I felt her eyes on me. "Is everything alright, Daphne?" When I looked up, there was genuine concern on her face.

It was pointless to worry her, not until I had more information at least. Such a significant change in her spinal health could mean a million different things. "Everything is fine," I replied, even though the idea of possibly ending Ruby Peters career was anything but.

SEVEN

RUBY

The first week of Dr. Carter's arrival seemed to go by faster than I had anticipated. Time was a funny thing on the space station. It was so cut and dry on Earth, days, nights, hours, minutes... There were no "real" night and days in the florescent white box we lived in, flying through space. Time still existed, as a human created concept, an Earthly concept. But in reality... if we didn't have deadlines and strict schedules, if there weren't things for us to do, reasons to occupy our time, time might cease to have any meaning at all. Entirely irrelevant.

Except all I could think about was time passing while Daphne was here. The days, the hours, the seconds, until she'd be gone again. Our work relationship had seemed to develop perfectly, and without much effort. Despite her callous exterior, truthfully, Daphne was rather pleasant to work with. Smart, witty, charming even.

The only real flaw I could really find in her, after we'd spent some time working together, was that it seemed as though she *never* stopped working. Which bothered me more than I cared to admit. Especially when it was Scrabble night.

Anyone at NASA would say—there was no one on Earth, or in

the galaxy, that was more intense about a word game with a bunch of wooden tiles, than the astronauts aboard the ISS.

"Damnit, Ruby, cacophony is not a word," Daniel was busy shuffling through a dictionary, trying his best to prove me wrong. I laughed, studying the remaining pieces I had, enjoying the fact that I'd received a Q and an X, which were golden letters in a hardcore game of Scrabble. My colleagues were in for a rude awakening. It was just the four US astronauts this time. James was asleep, and Adrik was off in the cupola. I had been told I needed to share, at some point.

Daniel's face dropped and I knew he'd found the word.

"Your voice is a cacophony," I grinned, and Daniel chucked the book at me. It floated aimlessly in the space above the board, and I laughed loudly.

"Go, Andrea," Daniel said, and I watched her steal the spot I had been planning to take next, spelling out "Qui." It had earned her triple points. I glared at her playfully, and she smiled.

"You must have had the X," Andrea teased me, and as much as I wanted to keep a straight face, I couldn't help but grin again.

"You both are a pair of cheaters," Daniel grumbled, placing down his tiles. Once he had, our attention turned to Tony, who looked as though he was still deciding what to do. He was still new to our regular games and hadn't had much practice yet. He'd get there.

There was a noise behind me, which prompted the group of us to look. Daphne was floating in the doorway of the Destiny module, which was around the corner from where we were playing at. She was glaring at us menacingly.

Daniel waved at her. "Dr. Carter, you should come join us for a game or two. Andrea was just about to beat us again anyway." I watched Daphne rotate a little in her position, trying to keep steady against the wall. She still was struggling to adjust to her environment, even after a week. Sometimes it took some people longer than others, I supposed.

"Unlike the rest of your noisy group, I was busy working, Mr. Richards," Daphne explained, trying to keep her voice neutral, despite the very annoyed look on her face. "I don't suppose it would be too much to ask for you to keep your enthusiastic chatter down to an acceptable decibel level."

"We like to relax when we can, Dr. Carter. You should consider it too. I haven't seen you stop the entire time you've been here." Daniel said the words I had been thinking.

Daphne did not look any less amused. "There's a lot to be done, Mr. Richards. I don't expect you to understand the pressure of having multiple billion-dollar projects at stake, but I don't have time to waste. In fact, Commander Peters should be in here with me."

Ruby, I thought to myself, but didn't say it.

Instead, I decided to argue with her. "I like to have a day off every once in a while, Daphne." I explained. "Haven't you ever read about the importance of 'play' in all that research you like to drown yourself in? It's good for you. And that's a proven fact, based on countless studies, not just some random find from some 'Podunk' university." The recollection of her rude remark about my other suggestions a few days prior made me grin, but it caused Daphne's glare to darken. I decided not to tease her further. "You should really take a break. It would be good for you."

Ignoring me, Daphne spun around and disappeared back around the corner and into the Destiny lab. Her bitter mood left a bad taste in my mouth, but I shrugged it off for the time being, continuing to play.

Even still, during our next few games, I couldn't stop thinking about her. I was feeling rather agitated that she was so hell-bent on a schedule and working until she was blue in the face. And then even more frustrated that I was letting it get to me in the first place. The woman barely slept, barely ate. She lived and breathed her work. And even I, who thought I was dedicated and passionate about my work, couldn't keep up with her.

After we'd wrapped up our fourth game, we disbanded, and I went across the station to put up the Scrabble game. As soon as I had, I spotted the old chess set that had been onboard the ISS since the very first module was brought into space. Chess was a classic astronaut favorite. And it gave me the perfect idea. I snagged it from the storage container and shut it behind me. Figuring Dr. Carter was in the research lab still, I headed in that direction.

Sure enough, Daphne was busy working at a computer station by her rat specimen. And appeared to be eating a trail mix bar, by some stretch of a miracle. I watched her briefly, adorned in those very attractive, black-framed glasses, hoovering over her computer screen. Before I knew it, she'd turned her head in my direction.

"Staring is rather rude, Commander Peters."

"*Ruby*," I mumbled, pushing myself off the wall I'd been floating by, and then headed down the entryway into Destiny. Once I'd made it to Daphne's computer station, I grasped a hold of the nearby metallic blue railing and stared at her. "How are the rats?"

"Well," Daphne replied, eyes still focused on her computer screen, beneath those glasses. "Which you would have known, had you been working with me. We have two weeks, Commander. I realize most of this effort is on me, but I expect your continual support with the project once I'm gone. And I don't feel very confident in leaving this multi-billion-dollar research—"

"Multi-billion-dollar research project—" I echoed her, and by the time we'd both finished speaking, Daphne snapped her mouth shut and glared at me. "I don't care right now. Right now, you're going to take a break. Just for a little bit."

Daphne scoffed at me, continuing to read whatever it was she had pulled up on the computer. I placed a hand on the desk in front of the computer and forced a more serious tone. "I'm not joking, Dr. Carter. Put your research away for a half hour. We're going to play."

"Commander—" Dr. Carter started, until I glared at her, then she corrected herself. "*Ruby*... I don't take *orders*."

I had her outplayed now. "See, that's where you're wrong, Dr. Carter." I inched closer to her, pulling myself toward her side of the desk she was standing in front of. Daphne backed up until she'd landed against the wall. There was no place for her to go as I approached. "Right now, on this station, I'm the highest-ranking officer. Even for a NASA civilian, or a contract employee such as yourself. Ask all my colleagues here with me. I'm the one in charge." Finally, I paused, inches between us then, and somehow still maintained my authoritative tone. "I am not *asking you*. I'm *telling you*. You are going to take a break and play a game of chess with me. Are we understood?"

A visible shiver ripped from Daphne Carter then, her hazel eyes wide and staring straight at me behind those glasses. Her mouth hung slightly open in surprise. Despite my annoyance with her in that moment, my heart had begun to race in my chest. My body felt like it had all been thrown into a fire, which I had chalked up to my anger, but now was questioning if that was really it at all. It was like an invisible string was tugging me closer to her.

Suddenly, all I could focus on was those perfect, full lips. Wondering what would happen if I closed the gap between us all the way, pinned her to the wall and planted our lips together. Kissed her domineering, bossy mouth into submission...

"Well, yes ma'am," Daphne cooed, and I swore there was the tiniest hint of a smirk. I realized then, when I comprehended what she had said to me, that I must have been staring straight at her mouth in a lusty haze and wondered if she had any idea what I'd been thinking.

Daphne drew herself from the wall, leaning in toward me. I felt dizzy, thinking for certain she knew exactly what I wanted. She was so close, hovering. I could feel the heat from her mouth against my own, watched as she drew up by the side of my face, until I could almost feel her lips tickling my earlobe. And then she whispered to me. "Though I do hope you enjoy losing, Commander Peters. I'm *very* good at chess."

It was my turn to shiver. The older blonde snatched the chess board away from my hands and pushed off the wall around me. I watched her move to the other side of the room, where we'd have space to play. When I finally approached her, she was already unpacking the board, setting up the pieces.

"Let me see if I remember... President of the Chess Club in high school, right?" I raised a surprise brow at her comment, and even though Daphne didn't look up, she smiled. "You aren't the only one who can do a stalker amount of research."

"When have you had time to be reading up on me?" I asked, situating on the other side of the board and gawking at her. "All you do is work. I thought you didn't have time for 'free time.'"

"Learning about my research assistant isn't a hobby activity, Ruby. I can't leave my life's work in the hands of just *anyone*." Daphne continued laying out the remainder of her pieces, which she'd taken the white ones, not surprisingly. White pieces traditionally always made the first move, and Dr. Carter wasn't the type to dilly dally. She acted. However, I hadn't minded her going first, since it was almost always my preference to have a minute to think.

Once we both set up, Daphne looked up briefly at me to see if I was ready, and after a confirming nod, she moved a pawn two spaces forward. I followed, mimicking her move. We made several turns in silence, and rather quickly, before one of us spoke again.

It was Daphne who cleared the silence. "Is this the original set?"

I would have been more surprised that she had known that fact, but Daphne was a smart woman, and it wasn't the world's most uncommon knowledge. "It's been here since the beginning, yes," I replied. The look on Dr. Carter's face seemed amused, and I wasn't sure why until she spoke again.

"Like you, I suppose." A joke. Had the woman just uttered a joke? It vanished in an instant, not unlike her amused smile. "Your turn." We played a few more rounds, silently focused on what we were doing. Finally, Daphne spoke again. "Tell me about the lumbopelvic muscle changes article you were reading yesterday."

When I looked up, she was watching me. My eyes narrowed. "Daphne," I replied, keeping my tone calm and collected. "We're playing chess right now. Not working."

Daphne looked slightly annoyed. She'd been testing me, it seemed, but I hadn't been fooled as she'd hoped. Eventually she nodded, and then moved her knight, which overtook a pawn of my own. "Be careful, Commander Peters. You're getting close to losing."

"Not yet," I replied, countering her move by moving with my rook and taking one of her own knights. "I still have some moves left."

Another hint of a smirk crossed Daphne's lips. I wasn't quite sure if she was surprised by my move, or she had anticipated it. Likely the latter. We each took another turn, moving pawns, before I decided to speak again.

"Are you always so all-work-no-play, even in Houston?" When I looked up, she was busy scrutinizing the board. I wondered if she was worried, I had her figured out. By my guess, she only had a few more moves before I'd put her King into check.

Once she moved a piece, Daphne looked up at me. "What do you think?"

"You don't have any hobbies?" I inquired, knowing she had to at least have something she enjoyed outside of the confines of the Johnson Space Center. "Gardening? Reading? A boyfriend?" Dr. Carter raised a brow at me, nodding for me to take my turn. I moved my knight again. "Check."

For a minute, Daphne focused on the game again. It didn't take her long to make her next move. Another pawn slid forward on the board. "I have a Chinese Evergreen at my condo," she admitted. "I read plenty for work. And no, Commander Peters, I don't have time for dating." I understood. Neither did I, really. There weren't very many people who understood the rigorous lifestyle an astronaut had, and still had the willingness to date someone that was three hundred miles above them, in another world entirely.

I moved a pawn forward, and Daphne moved quickly after. "Check."

My eyebrows narrowed, and I focused on the board. How had she managed a check? I realized I'd lost my focus a little, and now I was unsure if I could recover. When I turned to Daphne, there was a smug look on her face. I wanted to argue how she'd caught me off-guard, but I had no excuses. She'd made an excellent move that I hadn't predicted. I moved my King.

Daphne followed suit. "Check," she repeated. Then I felt her eyes back on me, and I looked back at her. "I doodle from time to time. And I do like to bake a bit, in my spare time. Mostly simple things, like banana bread and pumpkin muffins in the wintertime, if I'm feeling festive." I smiled, surprised she'd added that small little detail about the holidays.

When I moved another pawn forward, trying to block her from continuing to check me, I realized I'd been cornered. It hadn't mattered what I did at that point. The idea that Daphne had opened a little to me, had held my attention far more than winning the game.

"Checkmate," Daphne said. "I told you, Commander Peters. I've had a lot of practice."

Truthfully, she probably hadn't played as much as I had, as recently as I had. The likelihood that I should have lost that game was miniscule, but I blamed it on distraction. Daphne Carter was proving to be exceedingly good at being distracting. And I hadn't minded, even if it meant I lost a chess game and would likely never hear the end of it.

"That was fun," I said, offering a small smile. Daphne didn't verbally agree with me, but the look on her face seemed to indicate she'd relaxed quite a bit. "Thanks for playing with me." She nodded, and I picked up the pieces from off the board, stowing them away. "I'll put this up and then we can work for a bit."

"Take your time, Ruby," Daphne said. I was caught off guard by the sudden utterance of my name. She glanced at me for a moment, and then turned away, pushing off the wall to head back to the computer station she'd been working at before I'd interrupted her.

I started to head out of the room, toting the game under my arm. Just as I'd started to round the corner into Node 2, I turned back to look at her. "Daphne?"

"Hm?" Daphne turned in my direction, hazel eyes wide under her glasses.

"Maybe I can try your pumpkin muffins sometime," I said, thoughtfully. "Pumpkin and the holidays are my favorite."

Daphne hesitated, pondering on what I'd said for a moment. I thought for certain she'd ignore me and go back to what she was doing. Deny that I'd said anything at all. Her attention turned back to her computer, and I almost knew for certain. I'd just about made it around the corner when I heard her speak again.

"Perhaps," Daphne replied, quietly, as if she thought nothing of it. And even if she had already been out of view, and I had no idea of truly knowing, I could almost hear the smile that was on her lips when she'd said it.

EIGHT
DAPHNE

"I'll only be a few hours," Ruby promised me, as we floated in Node 2. I'd been trying to hunt her down for the last thirty minutes, with a slew of trial-related duties that needed to be done. When I had, she was halfway suited up, Daniel following behind her with the rest of the gear. "It's just a quick fix on the robotic arm. It's been having some issues lately."

I frowned. While I certainly wasn't about to get in the way of the duties that were required of Ruby aboard the station, we still had so much work ahead of us, and so little time left to do it. Half our time was already over.

"Be quick, Commander. I'll want to run some tests once you've returned."

"Back in a jiffy," Ruby promised. While her eccentric little remarks had annoyed me when I'd first arrived, I was starting to get used to them. It felt normal. Perhaps I even enjoyed it a little. "You should go watch. It's pretty neat to see."

While the idea sounded somewhat appealing, there was too much work to be done. "I've got things to catch up on, tests to run. I'll have a whole list of things to do once you return."

"Well, there's always the cupola computers, if you need a change of space," she argued. "But do what you'd like, Dr. Carter." As soon as she'd said it, she turned away from me, and I watched her follow Daniel out of Node 2 and turn into another part of the station.

My first instinct was to return to Destiny, where I'd been working before. Instead, I found myself headed in the opposite direction, up toward the cupola. Andrea and Tony were nearby, working at other computers. They both looked surprised to see me.

"Come to watch Ruby?" Andrea asked me.

"I needed a change of space," I replied, echoing what Ruby had said minutes earlier. I slid up into the small area of the cupola and logged into the computer.

Nearly an hour had passed before I finally heard Daniel speaking over the radio system onboard. I realized, once I'd adjusted my focus, that he was guiding Ruby outside. My eyes scanned out the cupola windows, as a white suit came into view from afar. She'd come out a nearby airlock, attached to a tether and an oxygen system, and slowly making her way out of the station.

"Where's my music?" Ruby asked, over the radio.

Dear God, there was music? It was hard enough to focus as it was. I'd made a terrible decision coming up here to work, that was for certain.

"I've got it," Tony said, and I glanced down, watching him working at his computer. Did they all need to encourage her? "Your normal playlist, right?"

"The *only* playlist," Ruby confirmed. There were a few seconds of silence, and then a song belted out of the radio speakers across the station. It was one I recognized, but wouldn't have listened to normally, preferring classical music, like the New York Philharmonic, whose Christmas shows I adored around the holidays. However, I found myself more interested in the Whitney Houston classic, "Dance with Somebody," than I expected myself to be. Likely because Ruby was singing along with the chorus.

I watched her glide along the outside of the station, until she'd come up near the cupola windows. Suddenly, Ruby's face was staring right at me, through the glass of the window and the visor of her helmet. Brown eyes twinkling from the glow of the Earth behind her.

"Well, look who decided to join us after all," Ruby smiled at me, during a break in the lyrics. I shrugged, looking back down at my work and tried to focus. That was until I saw her bobbing her head along to the music, out of the corner of my eye. "Space dance, Daphne!"

There was a chorus of chuckling over the radio, from the various crew aboard the ISS, and some from Mission Control. I tried my best to ignore Ruby and all the incessant noise, but for whatever reason I couldn't keep myself from looking up. She was still there, that glowing smile still filling her face. Ruby was watching me.

"Get to work, Commander," I said, nodding toward the direction of the Canadarm2, the robotic arm she was repairing. She nodded and then moved slowly from the window, making her way along the station, in the blackness of space. The view of Earth filling the sky behind her. I could only imagine what it would be like to be out in that environment. Likely terrifying, I assumed. I'd nearly given up entirely on working, too transfixed on Ruby and what she was doing.

"Grapple fixture shaft," Daniel said over the radio.

"Got it," Ruby replied, once she'd reached the robotic arm. I watched her open a panel and begin to adjust some of the components inside. Meanwhile, Whitney Houston had faded into a classic Beatles melody. "Looks like it might be just a few wires that need adjusting. Should be an easy fix."

While Ruby worked, I attempted, once more, to return my focus back to my computer. I managed for a little while, until Ruby had wrapped up what she was doing and was returning to the station. When she reached the cupola window again, her gloved hand knocked lightly on it. I looked upward again at her.

"Hey, Dr. Carter," Ruby said, locking eyes with me.

I stared back at her, curious as to what she could possibly have wanted. "Yes, Commander?"

"Would you like to come outside for a few minutes?" Ruby asked. "I'm supposed to be doing some training with Tony so he can take over repairs when I leave, but I could just show both of you together."

"Commander, I'm swamped with work right now," Tony piped up over the radio. "I'm going to have to take a rain check on the spacewalk."

There was a significant amount of chatter from Mission Control, that was very quickly turned down, Daniel speaking over top of them. "Rubs, you know that isn't gonna fly. She hasn't had the proper training or experience." Faintly, I could hear Mission Control's explicit disagreements against Ruby's plan, too.

Even I had my own reservations. "Mr. Richards, I do have to correct you in saying that I was in fact trained about space walks. I have absolutely no intention in ever doing one myself. I have work to do, Commander Peters. Work that involves you too, and our limited amount of time together."

Then Ruby said something I hadn't expected. "What about that interview of yours?"

Had she been talking to me? "What interview?" I asked, staring out the window at her. "I've done hundreds of interviews, Commander. You need to be more specific than that."

"Back when you first started at the Biomedical Research Institute. The one where they asked you if you could do anything else with your life, what would you do?" I stared at her blankly, trying to remember what she was talking about. "It was the one with your old med school friend, I can't remember his name—"

Then I realized what she'd been referring to. My first year at the Biomedical Research Institute. Fresh out of medical school, months after a grueling battle with my ex-husband and an equally devastating divorce. It had been a radio interview that I'd done in my office. I remembered the question exactly, as it had come from my old friend's mouth.

"Patrick had asked me if I hadn't become a doctor, what other career would I have chosen," I replied to Ruby, feeling a small smile breech my face. "And I told him, I'd never have the courage to survive a shuttle launch, or the stomach to withstand the G-forces, but I would give up my entire career to be able to see the Earth from astronaut's eyes." The memory was so vivid, I could recall how I'd been staring up at the large poster of the Earth from space, framed above my desk.

"And look at you now," Ruby was smiling back at me. "Funny how things go."

"Funny indeed," I replied.

"Still ain't gonna happen," Daniel argued, returning us both to the matter at hand. "I'm not hearing it from corporate later about how we spent a shit ton of government allocated funds to let a civilian out for a 'fun' spacewalk."

"—Mr. Richards, I actually had an argument *for* the space walk," I said, surprising myself when I did. "I have only a small amount of data on the effects of spacewalks on the spine. I have intentions of examining scans of Commander Peters' spine after this adventure, but I realized now, that I could be used as a control in this situation."

There was a bunch of chatter on the end of the radio that was transmitting from Earth, but it was inaudible. Daniel turned it down the rest of the way, and then I heard him speak. "Commander, you're in charge here. You're gonna be the one to take the heat from this, not me."

"Thirty minutes, tops," Ruby promised, and then nodded at me. "What do you say, Dr. Carter? Care for a little adventure outside?"

It would likely be the only opportunity I'd ever have. Even still, even with the small amount of training I'd had, the aspirations I'd had when I was younger, the idea itself was terrifying. Any number of things could go wrong in those minutes, and I wasn't quite sure if I was brave enough to try it. But when I looked back at Ruby and saw the way she was looking at me, I realized that she'd wanted me to say yes, desperately. And truthfully, I'd wanted to for my own benefit, but mostly I wanted to do it for her. To see the joy flow from her again.

"If you insist, Commander," I replied, shrugging. Ruby's smile widened, just as I turned my attention away from her to close out of the computer I'd been working on.

"Meet me at the airlock. Daniel will get you suited up."

A short while later, with the help of Daniel and Ruby, I'd been fitted into an extravehicular mobility unit, or an EMU, which was a full-equipped space suit meant specifically for space walks. I'd worn one a few times in training but had forgotten how bulky they were. It consisted of a pressure garment and a life support system. The pressure garment protected the body and enabled mobility, and a cooling garment, to regulate body temperature. The life support system included a backpack that contained oxygen, electricity, and a regulator for keeping the correct pressure. Ruby fit the communications cap on my head last, which contained earphones and microphones that connected to the ISS radio system, and to the other astronauts.

Ruby smiled at me once she'd fitted the cap onto my head, brushing some of my blonde hair under it. I'd felt so bulky and awkward in the giant suit, that I would have had trouble doing it myself.

"There you go," she said, matter-of-factly. "I'm going to glove up again and let Daniel handle your helmet." Ruby gloved me delicately, while I watched Daniel secure my helmet, immediately triggering the oxygen system inside the suit. Ruby's voice echoed in my ears through the speaker system. "Oxygen flowing?" I nodded.

Once I'd been suited up, Daniel assisted us through the airlock, where we would depart and head out. When he closed the door behind us, I felt my nerves starting to get the best of me. Ruby seemed to notice my heavy breathing over the hot microphone in my suit, speaking calmly into my ears. "I'll be there the entire time," she replied. Before I could say otherwise, she'd taken my gloved hand in her own and squeezed it. I barely felt it through the thickness of the glove, but it was still reassuring. "We'll be out for just a little bit. Remember your interview."

I'd give up my entire career to see Earth from an astronaut's eyes.

A great deal of time passed with the airlock pressurizing so we were able to head outside. Ruby and I made small talk over the radio. I imagined she was trying to keep me distracted and my nerves at bay, and it helped, a little. When I glanced at her at one point, she was smiling at me through her visor.

"What?" I asked, feeling somewhat uncomfortable by the attention.

"Oh, nothing," Ruby shrugged, still smiling. "You just look like a real, bonafide astronaut right now. It's rather cute, to be honest, despite that terrified look on your face. You'll be okay, I promise. I've got you." Ruby reached out and placed a hand on my shoulder.

Eventually Daniel's voice came over the radio again. "Alright ladies, all ready to go on my end," he said. The two of us waited momentarily, until the hatch began to open.

"I'll be there the whole time," Ruby reminded me, and when I looked at her, she gave me another one of her soft, reassuring smiles, and I imagined in that moment there was no one in the entire universe I could have trusted more than her. "Trust me, it'll be worth it. I promise."

All at once there was a sea of speckled blackness in front of me. A sea of space and stars. I took a deep breath, holding on to Ruby as she pushed off, leading us out into it. While we were floating freely, there were tethers attached to us, keeping us attached near the station.

The world around me became overwhelming. I realized, the only thing between me and the rest of the universe, seeing the whole cosmos of creation, is the glass faceplate of my visor on my helmet. My entire body floated outward. If it had felt like I was falling all the time inside the station, it was a whole new experience out here. I didn't really know what my body was doing, whether I was floating or flying, or what was happening. My senses were overstimulated, and I could do was look everywhere as we floated alongside the station, just a short distance from the airlock door we'd come out of. It was hard to focus on anything at all. Just Ruby's hand, still on my own, as we started to turn in a circle, away from the space station.

"Daphne," Ruby said into the speakers against my ears. "Welcome to my favorite spot."

"Favorite spot?" I echoed, and Ruby nodded.

"Look down."

And there it was. The Earth, in all its glory, straight below us. Big and bright and beautiful as ever. I could barely breathe, looking at it. Seeing the Earth framed through the shuttle's small windows versus seeing it from outside was like the difference between looking at a fish in an aquarium versus scuba diving on the Great Barrier Reef. I wasn't constrained by any frame. The glass of my helmet was polished crystal clear, and every direction I looked, there was nothing around me but the infinity of the universe. I was out there, floating in it, swimming in it. I felt like a real astronaut.

"Quite a view, huh?" Ruby said, and her voice brought me back to look toward her. She was smiling again and nodded back down at the Earth. When I looked back down again, I had the strangest sensation, that if I let go of Ruby's hand, I could fall straight through the atmosphere and down to the world below. I wondered where we were floating above now, trying to discern our location amidst a large covering of clouds.

"That's Cape Town below us," Ruby seemed to read my thoughts. "Have you ever been to Africa?"

"Never," I replied. Outside of a few conferences in Europe and Canada, I hadn't been to many other places in my lifetime. There wasn't much time for travel when you worked as much as I did.

"Me either," Ruby agreed. "It's pretty from up here, though." I could only agree, nodding my head. Ruby was still holding on to the space station, and to me. My head turned toward her for a moment, admiring her looking down toward the Earth. She looked so serene and peaceful. At home where she was. I realized in that moment, that my nerves had vanished. It was calm out here, and in the silence, all I could hear was my slow and steady breathing.

And then a jarring alarm echoed into my helmet and jerked me back to reality.

"Commander, I'm getting a faulty reading from Dr. Carter's oxygen tank," Daniel said, over the speakers. A wave of panic washed over me, and I sucked in a large breath of air, finding myself still able to breathe. At least for now.

"*What?*" I said, my voice coming out higher pitched and squeaking.

Ruby's hand tightened on mine, though I could still barely feel it. "Alright. Stay calm, Daphne. We're going to go back inside." She spoke over the intimidating beeping coming from my suit. Still in panic mode, I was sucking in deep breaths of air, praying that there was something wrong with the monitoring system on the suit, and not the actual oxygen system itself.

I hadn't realized I'd been hyperventilating. "Daphne," Ruby called out to me. I barely heard her over my panicked breathing. She squeezed my hand, and I felt myself rotating in space. "Daphne. I need you to take slow, gentle breaths. Can you do that?" While we turned, I continued panicking, unable to calm myself. Ruby's hand shook me a bit. "Daphne. Listen to me. I need you to stay calm and breathe. We're going back inside. I promise, everything is going to be okay. You'll be okay, but you need to conserve your oxygen, just in case."

I managed to hear her voice clearly enough through my rapid breathing and anxiety ridden state. I nodded and tried as hard as I could to slow my breathing. It took a minute or two, but eventually I managed. Meanwhile, Ruby had turned us around back toward the door to the airlock, just as Daniel had opened it.

I just needed enough oxygen to get through the pressurizing stage inside the airlock. Then I'd be back onboard and able to get rid of this god forsaken suit. "Just a few minutes, Dr. Carter. Everything is going to be okay." Ruby's voice spoke calmly in my ear, as the hatch closed behind us and the electronic mechanisms of the room began working.

"Hang in there, ladies," Daniel said, over the speaker in my suit. I felt myself sweating profusely under the thick fabric, even though my breathing had steadied somewhat. My pulse was still skyrocketing, and I imagined my blood pressure, too. I just needed out of this suit. Back into the safety of the station.

"We're almost there," Ruby said, looking at me. I looked back at her, realizing my vision was starting to blur as I made contact with her warm, brown eyes. And then the world faded into darkness around me.

I AWOKE what was only a few minutes later after we'd gotten back inside the space station. The Russian astronaut, Adrik, and Ruby, had removed me from the suit, just as I'd started to come to. I'd never been more relieved to be somewhere in my entire life.

The rest of the day, I was shook. Even though we'd made it unscathed, the thought of suffocating in the vastness of space had been terrifying. Yet, Ruby had been right. She'd gotten me back to safety, as promised. And the longer I had to calm myself from the frightening events, the more I was able to remember how utterly amazing the small adventure had been.

Work had been barely holding my attention, though it hadn't been entirely because of my thoughts about the spacewalk. Ruby had been fidgety and unruly the entire time, which made it very easy for me to take out my residual stress from the experience out on her.

"Commander, I'd appreciate it if you could actually *focus* on something." My voice came out annoyed and snippy. "We have a lot of things to cover."

"Sorry," Ruby replied. "Spacewalks always give me an adrenaline rush, and it's hard to come down from it. And today was a little exciting..." She trailed off for a second, and then her attention focused on me. "Speaking of that, are you doing alright? I'm sure that probably ruined the whole experience for you, that suit glitch. I'm really sorry."

Surprisingly, the more I had a chance to relax, the less the situation bothered me and the more I was grateful I'd gotten to go out at all. "It was a bit frightening there at the end," I admitted, even though that was a gross understatement. "But I appreciated the opportunity, Commander. It was quite the experience."

Ruby's face broke into a smile, and it warmed me a little. "I'm glad," she said, simply. There were a few minutes of silence between us as the MRI collected scans of my spine post-spacewalk. I'd already done Ruby, but as I'd decided to be a control, I needed my own data. "All finished, she finally said, and then removed the restraints holding me to the exam table. "What are we doing now?"

"While we wait for all the scans to develop, let's check on Rat J," I instructed her. "His vitals are off again today. I want to see what's going on with him internally." Ruby nodded and moved across the room to the rat housing. As I made my way over to the adjacent computer station, I saw her unhousing the rat.

"Hey there, Jeffery," Ruby said, once she'd retrieved him. "I hear you're still feeling a little under the weather. Let's get you checked out, okay? Don't be worried. It'll be okay."

By now I'd memorized all of Ruby's pet names for the rats, and grown used to her random conversations with them, which, truth be told, had become rather endearing. Once Rat J was sedated, he was moved into the compartment for the portable x-ray machine.

It took a while for the scans to complete, so we waited patiently. Ruby continued to be as fidgety as ever, spinning in place off to the side of the Destiny module, doing flips in the microgravity. I wondered how she was managing not making herself sick. I watched her wordlessly, admiring her carefree spirit, even though she was making me rather nauseous, even with the anti-nausea medication. "Are you bored, Commander?"

"Just like to keep myself busy," Ruby replied. I watched her for a minute more, until the computer finally signaled that the x-ray had completed, and the scans came up. Much to my surprise, the rat looked completely normal. "That's weird," Ruby said from beside me.

"It is," I replied. "Let's take him back to his compartment for now." Ruby tucked the rat, who would remain sedated for another hour or so, away in his nesting spot. Then we both turned our attention toward the computer. "Well keep watch on him for a few days. Hopefully he improves and this was all just a fluke."

Ruby nodded. Meanwhile, I clicked through the remainder of the data on the rest of the rats. Everything else seemed relatively normal.

"Alright, Commander," I said, breaking the silence. "I have some work to do with the MRI scans from the spacewalk. I suppose you can get your other duties done for the time being. I'll come find you if I need you." Ruby smiled at me and nodded, and I watched her float over to another nearby computer console. Meanwhile, I returned to the console by the MRI machine and pulled up the scans.

My attention focused on my work for quite a while. The scans had shown minimal changes in my spine, nothing dramatic. However, Ruby's scans had looked just as discerning as they had been the few other times that I'd checked her. How she hadn't been in pain from what I was seeing, I had no earthly idea.

I was just finishing up with my records and note keeping for the spinal project, when I heard Ruby speak from across the room, interrupting my train of thought. My hyperactive brain must have still been on overdrive.

"What do your parents think about you being up here on the space station?" It was a random question that had caught me off guard. "My parents always worry. They think I'm a little bit space crazy."

They weren't wrong in that assumption. She most certainly was. But it was an endearing quality about her that I very much liked and related to. "My mother passed away about ten years ago," I said, truthfully. "And my father and I haven't spoken in a long time. I imagine he wouldn't be that impressed, even with this venture into space. But my mother would have been, having been a woman of science and passionate about her work."

Ruby went quiet, like she was thinking about what I had said, and trying to process it. I'd spoke about my mother before, and had vaguely implied that she'd passed away, but now I'd confirmed it.

"You're a civilian on the ISS after all," she finally noted. "It's a pretty big deal."

"I realize," I replied. I was very aware of what a "big deal" this experience was, and how important my time here was. "That's why I've been so diligent about this work. About your involvement. It's important we get as much done before I leave as possible. I'm entrusting you with something that I've spent nearly two decades of my life on. If you knew how unbelievably rare my trust is with people, you'd understand why I'm so adamant about every detail being right. This is a multi—"

"—Multi-billion-dollar project," Ruby interrupted me. My eyes narrowed at her, somewhat annoyed. "You don't have to keep saying that, Daphne. I get it. It's very important. And I understand about your trust issues. After everything that Dr. Riddler did to you all those years ago. I don't understand how other people couldn't see that, too. He sounds like a real piece of work. And with how protective you've been about your research… I just assume it's because of that. It's understandable. I don't know how I could trust anyone with my work if that had happened to me…"

I couldn't find the words to say. It was all I could do just to nod.

Ruby's face broke into a small smile, the kind she'd given a lot to me over the past few weeks, that reassured me when I was feeling doubtful. "Well, I know it's only my word, but I would like to think I'm a pretty decent human being," she said, simply. "And I swear to you, it will mean just as much to me. I'll take care of it. Of them." Ruby glanced at the rats, briefly.

Somehow, a smile breached my lips, too. "I don't doubt you will," I admitted. "And to be honest, I'm still terrified of that at every moment." I paused for a second, until Ruby's attention had completely turned back on me. "But I don't think I could have picked a better person to help me, that is for certain. At least I have a lot more confidence than I did when I first met you."

The smile on Ruby's face widened. She shrugged. "Appearances can be deceiving."

We went back to work for a while, staying mostly silent. While Ruby worked on inputting data and read over charts, I found myself distracted from my drug trial work. Instead, I was doodling on a notepad at the computer station. Before I knew it, I'd drawn an outline of Ruby's portrait from across the room.

My mind had gotten so wrapped up in filling in the little details about Ruby, I hadn't noticed when she'd come up behind me. I lifted my pen from the page, briefly, and found her reaching down to snatch up the paper from me.

I panicked. "Commander Peters, that wasn't for you to take—"

"*Ruby*," she reminded me, admiring what I had drawn. "You're really good at that. I didn't think you'd be *this* good. You missed your calling to pursue art instead of research." I wasn't quite sure whether to be flattered or annoyed with her comment. Eventually, I decided to be gracious and nodded.

"It's just a hobby," I replied. My instinct to take the paper back from her had lessened, and I watched her eyes as she looked up and down the page. "It was just a concept sketch. I didn't mean anything by it, and it isn't even that good..." I found myself rambling, trying to come up with any excuse for doing what I'd done.

"You took some creative liberties," Ruby noted.

"What do you mean?" I asked, raising a brow. I looked back down at the sketch, upside down for me, and then back up at her.

"Well, I'm certainly not *that* pretty," Ruby said, looking down at the page. It had been a good thing. She'd missed the hint of a smile that lingered on my lips for a few seconds.

"I was only drawing what I saw," I replied, and the comment made Ruby's face flush a light shade of pink. She avoided looking back up at me.

"Can I keep this?" she asked, and finally her attention came back to my face. "I mean, only if you're okay with it." I nodded without hesitation, and Ruby folded it and put it in her pocket. She smiled at me, and I found myself smiling back, a warmth spreading through me from head to toe. "You really surprise me sometimes," she said, matter-of-factly.

"I surprise you?" I repeated, finding her comment curious. "How so?"

"You're just a lot softer than I expected you to be," Ruby replied, still smiling. "I was worried before I met you that we'd never get along. And yet, the more I'm around you, the more I think you're the first person that I've ever met who seems to really get me on a level that most people don't, you know?"

"I completely understand," I replied, nodding. "The feeling is very much mutual."

We stared at one another, floating in that space in front of the computer station. I couldn't take my eyes from her, and it seemed she felt the same way. The way she was looking at me was making it hard for me to breathe. I couldn't remember the last time anyone had looked at me that way, with an affection so deep and pure and real, an affection I equally felt for her.

Some part of me wished in that moment that I had been brave enough to close the space between us. That I had the courage to put my hands on the side of her soft cheeks, and let my fingers get tangled in her hair. To tell her that I couldn't stop thinking about her, and that besides the research I'd been doing, she was on my mind constantly. And then, surprisingly, as I'd never had any sort of feelings like this for a woman in my entire life, I wondered what it would have been like to kiss those small pink lips with my own.

Finally, I cleared my throat, breaking the little trance between us. "I think it's about time I get a few hours of sleep," I replied, feeling a wave of exhaustion hit me.

"It's been a long day," Ruby agreed. There was a strange hint of disappointment or sadness in her eyes, and I couldn't explain why. "We'll get back to work first thing. Have a good night, Dr. Carter."

I blinked, and nodded, watching as she turned away from me and started heading out of the Destiny module. Suddenly, I was feeling rather terrible that I'd ruined the moment between us and wished desperately that I could have rewound time and said something different. Just as Ruby had reached the entrance to the module, she turned back to look at me.

"Thanks for the drawing," she said, offering a small smile. And then she disappeared without another word.

NINE
RUBY

While everyone on board the station had been sleeping for a few hours, except for Adrik, who was busying himself doing his own research for the Russian astronaut program, I was working in the cupola, alone. Another week had passed with Daphne Carter onboard. The days seemed to be blurring by, and the reality that she was only here for a few more days was starting to hit me. And it was hitting me harder than I'd expected it to. I tried not to think about it, instead working on a crossword puzzle, as Earth glowed above me. I'd never get sick of the view, no matter how many times I got to see it.

I had barely gotten started on the crossword when I heard a rustle beneath me. When I looked down, I saw Daphne making her way through the entryway, up into the space directly below me. I rotated myself a little bit and pushed out of the cupola space, so that I had joined her in the more open area of the room, still holding on to my crossword.

"I thought you'd gone to sleep," I told her, and she settled beside me, logging into a computer.

"I couldn't sleep," Daphne admitted. Which hadn't really been a surprise. The woman didn't sleep much at all, constantly busy working. She was a machine most days. "And I wondered where you were."

The comment caught me off-guard. *Wondering where I was?* I shook my head and offered a small smile. "I couldn't sleep either," I replied.

"What are you doing?" Daphne asked me, studying the book in my hand.

"A crossword," I replied, showing her the barely started puzzle. Daphne glanced at it, looking rather impressed.

"I was never any good at crosswords," she admitted. "I prefer a good game of Sudoku."

"And I'm the opposite," I laughed. "I could never figure out those puzzles. Even with studying calculus and differential equations for years."

"It takes a certain type of brain power," Daphne agreed. "Though it's the same with crosswords too, I'd imagine." I nodded in agreement. "Do you do them often?"

"A little every day, if I can." I was surprised she hadn't noticed me working on one before, but then again, she'd been so immersed in her own research while she'd been here, it was understandable that she hadn't. "My mom just sent me a new shipment with your shuttle. I have to be slow about it, otherwise I run out quick. Sometimes I do them on the computer, too." I nodded toward the computer station she'd logged into. "I like puzzles. I don't like leaving one unfinished, if I can help it. It drives me mad."

"You do seem like the type to love puzzles," Daphne agreed. "Mind if I help you on this one? I'm curious if I can guess any of the answers." I smiled again and nodded, and Daphne rotated herself so she was closer to me while I opened the book again. She glanced over my shoulder; body lightly pressed into my side. It made it somewhat difficult to focus on what I was doing, with her in such proximity. I found I really enjoyed her being there. It certainly beat being up here all by myself.

Daphne studied the puzzle, and I watched her out of the corner of my eye as she scanned the page, pondering. Eventually, I heard her voice, breath against the side of my face. The warmth hitting me like a brick wall. "Twelve down is onomatopoeia?" I glanced at the book and was surprised she'd gotten the right answer. "And three across...Caracas?"

I found myself laughing. "I thought you said you weren't good at crosswords?" Daphne shrugged, and I couldn't help but continue to smile. "Thanks. I was stuck on twelve for a while."

"Teamwork," Daphne said. I watched her eyes look in front of me, into the cupola, where my computer remained open on what I'd been looking at before I'd started the crossword. I'd forgotten what I'd been doing. Daphne stared for quite a while, until I glanced over my shoulder. My social media had been left open, on Amber Ray's page again. I pushed off the metallic blue railing into the cupola, and closed out of the computer, quickly.

Still, it seemed to be on Daphne's mind anyway. "A friend of yours?"

I found myself hesitating, briefly. My focus attempted to return to the crossword, but I was already feeling a mix of emotions running through me. "Used to be," I admitted, even though I wasn't sure why.

"Used to be?" Daphne echoed.

"We kind of had a falling out," I said, and my mind wandered back to Amber Ray. My heart sank into my chest a little. "It was a complicated situation." I tried to leave it at that, hoping Daphne wouldn't press me about it further.

She ignored my attempt to drop the conversation. "Difference in opinions?"

"You could say that," I said. I went quiet, focusing back on the puzzle. After I filled in another answer, my attention turned back on Daphne. For whatever reason, I found myself admitting more about the situation than I anticipated I ever would, to anyone. I'd never talked about it, not even to my parents. And the word vomiting almost felt like a relief.

"Her name is Amber," I started, and watched Daphne's eyes land on mine. "I used to have feelings for her a long time ago." I paused for a second and took a small breath in, then continued. "She was married and had kids. It was a stupid situation that got out of control, and to be honest I think she kind of led me on, even if it was an accident. I didn't mean for it to happen, but it did. We just couldn't stay friends after that. It was too hard."

After I'd said my piece, I worried if Daphne had thought I'd said too much. If I had overshared by accident, and it made her think less of me for some reason. The idea was terrifying. But then she surprised me.

"I had a falling out with my father, too," she replied. "Right after my mother passed. It's tough letting the people you love go. I still check on him from time to time, myself."

"Really?" I asked, surprised she'd admitted such a detail. "I feel guilty wondering how she's doing. Like I should have let it go by now. But I miss her more than I thought I would."

"How long ago?" Daphne asked me.

"It's been a few years now," I admitted. "Since we last talked. I still haven't completely gotten over it, but it's getting easier." My voice cracked a little as I spoke, realizing it was hitting me again, harder than I expected it to. Still, it felt less painful than I expected it to be. Perhaps I owed that in part to Daphne, who had been a great distraction.

We went quiet for a minute, until Daphne's hand reached out to wrap around my own. She held it for only a few seconds, giving it a gentle squeeze, before she released it.

"It gets easier," she promised me. "It won't go away completely, but you'll find it less difficult the more time goes on." I nodded, unsure of what else to say. We both focused on the crossword puzzle again, and I filled in an answer while I was silent.

Eventually, I said what was on my mind. "You've been a great distraction from everything," I said, without hesitancy. "It's been a long time since I've had someone around who makes me feel less alone. I love Daniel and the rest of my colleagues, but..."

"It's not the same," Daphne agreed, glancing at me for a moment. I nodded in agreement, and the woman's face broke into a soft smile. I was really enjoying seeing it more and more often now and appreciated that she'd relaxed a lot around me. "I could say the same thing about you. It's been years since I've felt this way about someone."

Since I've felt this way about someone.

There was a silence between us again. I hesitated, wanting desperately to ask what she'd meant by that. If, perhaps, she was feeling the same sorts of things that I had been, feelings that were constantly evolving and changing the more I had gotten to know her. The more I had gotten to understand her, a NASA colleague, who was all-work and no-play, and who could come across as cold and heartless and empty. Except she wasn't, not in the least. There were more layers and complexities and depth to Daphne Carter than I could have ever imagined there to be, and I was lost in them all. Every single part of her.

"Eleven across is 'fortification,'" Daphne said, breaking my train of thought. I shook my head, coming back to the room with her. Away from those fleeting words that I found myself too afraid to speak, in fear that she couldn't possibly feel the same.

A HANDFUL of hours before the preparations for Daphne's return to Earth, my mind was a thousand miles away. I'd been busy doing my normal routine of duties on the station, cleaning and helping Andrea and Tony with system checks. When the two had retired for the evening, I first started to head toward the cupola, something I would normally do. Midway there, I thought of Daphne, realizing I hadn't seen her all evening, and I'd strongly noticed her absence.

I tried not to think about her not being around after tomorrow. That in a few days, I'd be a whole atmosphere and miles above her. Her company and presence aboard the station had been a welcomed treat for me. While I'd certainly bonded with my colleagues, something about my relationship with Daphne over the past few weeks, had been deeper and more meaningful than I had ever expected it to be. Perhaps that was a good thing, since I'd be taking care of her research.

When I reached Node 2, instead of heading in the direction of the cupola, I took a turn, deciding instead to visit Destiny. I was quite sure that Daphne wasn't asleep yet. Especially since this was her last night aboard the station. She was probably working away.

Sure enough, when I made the turn into the doorway, Daphne was across the room, working at a computer station. She hadn't noticed my arrival, so I floated there silently, watching her working.

I heard her speaking from afar, and it took me a moment to realize what she was saying.

"That's a good girl, Delilah," Daphne spoke, softly. I realized she was holding on to a rat, carefully placing her back in her compartment. Once she'd closed it, she leaned down, getting eye level with her. "I'm certain Ruby will take excellent care of all of you. I don't doubt it."

Daphne was talking to the rats. Calling them by the common names I'd dubbed them. A warm feeling radiated throughout me, and I couldn't help but smile watching her. She made conversation with them for a while, and I stayed as motionless as I could in the doorway. Eventually, she turned her focus away from the research area, and caught a glance of me. Her body went rigid, and her face straightened.

"Commander Peters," Daphne said, looking me up and down, clearly a little startled. "How long have you been watching me?"

"I wish you'd call me Ruby," I replied, a smile stretched on my face. I decided not to elaborate on how I'd been watching her talk to the rats. "Just a minute or two. I was wondering what you were up to."

"As if you didn't already know," Daphne broke into a small smile, eyes on me. "Did you finish all of your chores?"

"All done for the evening," I replied, starting to make my way into the room. "And I think mostly everyone is asleep for a few hours. It's just me and you." Just Daphne and I. Something I'd very much enjoyed over the past few weeks with her. "How about you? Getting some last-minute work in before you leave?" I could barely believe it. Only a few hours left.

"I'm also done for the evening," Daphne replied, looking at her computer and logging off. Once she had, she glanced over at me, as I made my way across the room, using the metallic blue railings along the walls. "I've gotten my last MRI scans. Everything has been written up and sent back to Earth for me to look over later. The rest of this is in your hands now, I suppose."

"I'll take good care of your research," I promised, slowly coming to a halt once I'd reached her.

"I don't doubt you will," Daphne replied, that small smile still on her face. Bits of her blonde hair, most of which had been pulled up into a small ponytail, floated around her face. It made her look angelic and soft, which most people would have never pegged her as, if they didn't know her. But she was different to me now. Behind that fiery exterior was a kind and gentle human that I'd been grateful to get to know.

Daphne was looking at me rather intensely, like she was trying to read what I was thinking. Truthfully, I didn't really know what I was thinking. There had been so many thoughts in my mind these last few weeks, it was a confusing mess of emotions. They just lingered there, unspoken and distracting.

"Fancy a game or two of chess before I go?" Daphne asked me, clearing the silent air.

"You just want to beat me one more time," I laughed. We'd played at least a dozen times in the past three weeks, and I hadn't won once. Daphne shrugged, still smiling, and I held up a finger. "Give me a minute. I'll go grab it."

A short while later, we'd set up and started in the middle of the Destiny module. We played through several games, and not surprisingly, Daphne beat me every time. Admittedly, I wasn't very focused.

I could barely keep my attention from her, wishing desperately that she was staying a few more weeks. Feeling like somehow, when she left, she'd be gone forever, even though we'd be working together closely from afar.

The feeling I'd felt looking at the Earth, following my friends and family on social media; that distance I felt... it already felt stronger with Daphne, and she hadn't even left yet. It was overwhelming me, more than I ever anticipated that it would. I tried to understand what I was feeling exactly, and realized it was sadness. That I'd miss her company and companionship onboard. She was already feeling so distant, and she hadn't even left me yet.

"Are you alright?" Daphne asked me, and when I turned my attention back to her, I found she was staring at me intensely, with those beautiful hazel eyes of hers. "You seem rather distracted." I watched her moved a pawn and then she nodded at me to take my turn.

I shook my head, trying to keep my face pleasant. "I'm fine," I replied, as I moved my knight on the board. I wasn't sure how many moves I had until Daphne would beat me again. I'd completely lost track.

Daphne pondered over the board for a minute, before she spoke again. "Ruby, I realize we've only known each other for a few weeks," she said, moving her rook. "But I'm quite sure you aren't 'fine.'" I moved again with my knight, and Daphne moved quickly after. "Check."

I realized she'd been waiting for me to make that move. I sighed, softly. "I suppose I'm just a little distracted." I moved my King, hoping that I could finagle my way out of losing such a short game. When I looked up at Daphne, she was smiling at me again. I couldn't help but offer a small smile in return. The look she was giving me was holding me captive.

That was until she made another move, barely giving the board a glance. "Focus, Commander." I looked down, realizing she'd cornered me yet again. "Check." I made another move with my King. She followed my move, and when she did, I realized I'd been beaten. "Checkmate."

Before I could stop, I found myself admitting what I'd been feeling. "I'm going to miss you," I said, my eyes slowly looking up to meet hers. "I've really enjoyed your company."

Daphne smiled again. "You're not alone in that feeling," she replied. "It's been a while since I've been in such good company. Especially with another woman."

The way she'd phrased it felt strange. Once again, I found it difficult to interpret what she'd meant. If she'd meant it deeper than it had come across. I studied her for a long while, trying to gauge what she was thinking by the expression on her face. It was hard to tell.

"I'll miss you kicking my ass at chess," I finally said, laughing. "I thought for sure I was going to beat you at least once while you were here, but boy did you prove me wrong."

"You'll beat me next time," Daphne promised, in a decided way. It was as if she had already assumed there would be a next time. Even if that was over six months from now, which was starting to feel like an eternity.

"Next time," I replied, starting to pick up the pieces from the board and stowing them. "I wish you didn't have to leave." I couldn't look up at her when I said it, too afraid that her expression would indicate that she didn't feel the same, or at least not the way I did.

When I finally had the courage to meet her eyes, after we'd been in silence a while and I'd finished putting up the pieces, Daphne's mouth had twisted. She was studying me, a strange look on her face. "I'm sorry," I apologized. "I didn't mean to make things weird between us. I just really needed to say that."

"I'm going to miss you too, Ruby," Daphne said, softly.

All at once I found myself fighting the urge to close the distance between us. A sense of urgency drove me. I realized, in that moment, I wanted to be near her. To touch her, in case I didn't have the opportunity again. I pushed off against the wall, drawing closer. Daphne's attention was laser focused on me. Her breathing had slowed. I could barely see her chest moving.

Daphne had moved against the wall, hands gripped onto the metallic blue railing. I fell into her gently, letting our bodies collide together. I swept her, weightless, into my arms, holding her snugly. I buried my face against her chest, feeling her slowed, rhythmic breathing. I felt her arms wind around me, sinking into my cushioning embrace. We stayed like that a while, holding one another.

When I finally moved away, I felt her breath, warm and damp against my face, and my heart raced. Daphne's soft hazel eyes had met mine, and after a few seconds, I couldn't stop myself. It looked as though Daphne was about to say something, when my lips fell on hers, gently covering her mouth with my own. The kiss sang through my veins and left my mouth burning. She returned my kiss with reckless abandon, like she had the same burning desire, the same aching need, for more.

There was a dreamy intimacy to that moment. Daphne moved her hands up to hold the sides of my face, her fingers running into my curly hair. I wrapped myself in her, my body tingling from the contact, and having no desire to back out of her embrace.

Finally, our lips parted. Daphne was panting softly as her hands fell to her sides. "Ruby," she whispered, those soft lips forming the sounds of my name, and it felt as though she was electrocuting me. My hands released her, and reached up to cup her face, like she'd done to me, feeling her soft, warm cheeks, against the skin of my palms. "I don't know what this is. This thing between us."

"I don't either," I said, breathlessly, the tug of my body so strong I couldn't resist it any longer. The want, the desire, was consuming me. I wanted her—needed her. "I think—"

A voice echoed around the corner of the doorway, in the adjoining Node. "Hey Rubs." It was Daniel, calling my name. In one swift motion, I pushed away from the wall, floating backwards away from Daphne. Our attention was still on one another, but the distance between us was agonizing and painful. It felt as if I had been ripped from a tether that I was clinging desperately to. When I finally looked over my shoulder, Daniel was floating in the doorway.

"We should get the shuttle prepped and ready to go," he said, glancing at us both.

My attention turned back to Daphne for just a moment, and I could tell by the look on her face that she was feeling something as deeply as I was in that moment. I nodded to Daniel, and he turned out of the room and headed back in the opposite direction he'd come from. I watched Daphne's hand outstretched in front of her, and I found my own reaching for hers. Our fingertips touched lightly together, and I let out the softest of sighs. The touch lasted just for a second, before I turned away from her and headed out the doorway.

A few hours later, the shuttle had left us, returning to Earth with Daphne and Adrik. And all I could think about was the last words that Daphne uttered to me, tucked away in her space suit, as she floated in the hatch doorway that led out to the shuttle.

"Take care of yourself, Commander Peters," she'd said, a softness to her voice. I stared at her deeply, trying to memorize the contours of her face. The sound of her voice. The way her eyes were looking at me. I wished desperately that I could have had even just a few more moments to know what her lips had felt like against my own. That I'd had a second longer to hold her against me. "I'll talk to you soon."

"Talk to you soon," I replied, hardly able to speak. She nodded at me, and then turned back, heading into the doorway and on to the shuttle. I watched until she'd disappeared behind the door.

And I hoped, desperately, that I'd see her again.

PART TWO
SEPARATION

TEN

DAPHNE

The soft puttering of rain outside my office window held my attention. I found myself staring out into the courtyard at the Johnson Space Center campus in Houston, watching the steady shower and the occasional flash of lightning. It had been nearly a week since my return to Earth from the ISS, and the weather had been about as dreary as my mood.

There was a knock at my door, and my intern assistant Jenny stuck her head inside my office. "Dr. Carter," she said, offering me her usual cheerful smile. "Dr. Hale and Dr. Scott want to meet with you in a half hour."

I stared at her, knowing full well that there was only one reason my supervisor and the head of the Biomedical Research Institute were requesting a meeting with me at the same time. The one person that I had graciously avoided thinking about for the last few weeks was about to demand my entire attention, once again. I frowned at the idea, but then nodded to Jenny. "I'll make myself available."

Jenny nodded and then left me alone. I had been busy working on a draft of a new research paper, documenting my findings about the astronauts at the ISS. My mind had not been focused at all on the task at hand, and hadn't really been actively back from my trip, even though I'd been home for days now. Instead, my thoughts had been constantly on Ruby Peters, and my trip to space. Surprisingly, I found myself wishing I was still there. A thought I wouldn't have ever expected myself to have.

Across my computer monitor, on my desktop background, was a picture of Ruby floating in front of the cupola window aboard the ISS, with the Earth behind her. It was a shot that one of her colleagues had taken the first time she'd ever gone to space. I'd found it when I'd been perusing the ISS website the day before. The sight of Ruby every now and then, and that special place aboard the station that she loved so dearly, brought me a sense of comfort.

Just as I had finally drawn my attention back to my work, there was a ringing from my computer. When I looked, it was an incoming video call from the ISS. A small smile breached my lips. It was the second time I'd spoke to Ruby since I'd arrived back home. Even though our conversation had been brief, she'd been a welcome sight.

I answered the call and was greeted by a dark view of Ruby in the cupola.

"I can barely see you," I noted, though I could make out bits and pieces of her black hair floating around, and the warm flecks of brown in her eyes at certain angles.

"I just wanted to check on you," Ruby said, quickly. "Everyone is sleeping. I figured I'd see how you were doing."

Not really a business call, like the last chat had been. While I was rather flattered at the idea, she was calling to check on me, I was very much aware at that moment that Mission Control and a variety of our colleagues, not to mention anyone watching live feeds of the ISS, were listening in on our conversation. It was the middle of the day here, so there were likely a lot of eyes on us. "How are you doing, Commander?"

"About the same," Ruby said, though I could tell by the tone of her voice that there was something on her mind. She didn't speak of it, however. "Staying busy. Your rats are good, by the way. Jeffery seems to be doing a lot better than he had been."

I smiled softly. "I'm glad to hear it."

"How are things on Earth?" Ruby asked, rather nonchalantly. I stared at the computer screen, wishing I could make her out more clearly at that moment. I had only communicated with her via telephone the last time we'd spoken, so it had been nearly a week since I'd seen her.

"About the same," I replied. It was difficult not to elaborate further. To tell her that she'd been on my mind almost constantly since she'd left. I missed her and our conversations. Our chess games. Being in that place with her, suspended above the Earth in our own little bubble, had been almost like a dream. I hadn't felt so comfortable with another human being in a very long time, and I missed it terribly. "Where are you now?"

I nodded to the Earth behind her, a tiny sliver of light. I could make out some of the lights below, but it was nearly impossible to know where she was. It still baffled me that somehow, now, she was high above me, racing by, passing me sixteen times a day. Perhaps that she was above me sometimes, should have been a comfort. Maybe it was a little. But I still missed her.

"Somewhere in the South Pacific," Ruby replied. I watched her flip a light on beside her, illuminating her face and her raven black hair. It was refreshing to finally get to see her again. I found it difficult not to tell her this, but somehow, I managed. I was still very much aware that we weren't alone, even if it felt like we were. "Are you still working on drafting your paper?"

I nodded, hating being unable to tell her what I was thinking in those moments. Instead, we were just making small talk. "I'll need your help with the drug trial data eventually. I'm still working on the spinal study side of things."

"Of course," Ruby nodded. "I'm here when you need me." When I looked at her again, she was staring straight at me, her gaze unwavering. We exchanged pleasant smiles, and I wondered what she was thinking about in those moments.

"You'll call me tomorrow to go over data for the week?" I asked, trying to clear my head of all the thoughts that were racing through it. She nodded, without speaking. "Good. Take care, Commander Peters."

Ruby's facial expression was unreadable. "Take care, Dr. Carter."

The video cut off and I stared at my computer for a few moments, before I forced myself to return my attention back to my paper. When I finally glanced at the clock again, I realized it was already close to my meeting time. The conversation I was dreading. It was a short walk to Dr. Evan Scott's office, so I decided to leave.

I wove my way through the large office building, reaching Dr. Scott's office with only a few minutes to spare. I wasn't one to be late, but my desire to avoid this meeting was overwhelming. When I knocked, I heard Dr. Hale's voice calling me to enter. I opened the door, stepping inside. My eyes scanned the room, until they landed on the far side of a large desk, focused on the man I had hoped I wouldn't have to share a room with ever again.

Michael glanced up at me through his round glasses, offering a deceptive smile. "Daphne," he stood up from his desk. The look he was giving me was making me uneasy. It felt so disingenuous and sinister. He knew what he was doing, without a shadow of a doubt. This wasn't an innocent desire to pursue research. This was a hostile invasion of the life I'd built over the past two decades. The life I'd created without him in it, without threat of him ripping it away from me.

Except here he was. Threatening to take everything away.

"Dr. Riddler," I said curtly, making my way into the room. He watched me sit at the opposite side of Dr. Scott's desk, picking the seat furthest away from him as humanly possible. The more separated I felt from him, the better. His very presence in this room was nauseating beyond belief. It took everything I had in me to speak his name after everything he'd done to me, but I'd managed, somehow.

The moment I sat down, the door opened again and Dr. Scott and Dr. Hale made their way inside, with two others I didn't recognize. Likely some of our funders for the research I was working on. I felt smaller in that room than I had in a very long time, suffocated by the suits, my supervisors, and that cockroach of a man across from me, staring me down.

"Good," Dr. Scott spoke, as he seated himself at the long desk. The others followed suit. "I'm glad you were both able to make it."

"As you might have guessed, Dr. Carter," Dr. Hale spoke then, and I turned my attention toward him. "We're going to discuss Dr. Riddler's involvement with our research projects." I barely managed to hold my tongue, feeling a surge of anger ripple through me. It was as much *their* research as this facility was mine. Everything for the past few decades had been my doing. My blood, sweat, and tears. Perhaps, with the assistance of other researchers, some interns now and then, and the supervision of Dr. Hale and Dr. Scott and others at NASA and the Biomedical Research Institute. But the work itself? The hours upon hours of dedication... that had been me.

"Dr. Hale, if I could interject," I began, but Dr. Hale silenced me with a wave of his hand. I swallowed, deeply, and found I couldn't argue with him, even if I wanted to. Instead, I sulked back into my seat.

"Daphne, if you're here to argue, I'm afraid you'll find it's futile at this point," Dr. Scott spoke then, leaning forward to rest his arms against the wooden top of the desk. "This decision was above your pay grade, I'm afraid."

"I'm sure if you give it a little while, you'll find this was an appropriate decision, given Dr. Riddler's background and expertise." Dr. Hale spoke again, and I held back a glare. Of course, Michael had expertise in the field, his entire start to his career had been both our doing, despite the fact that he'd ultimately claimed our research as his own. "Given he's the head of the research department at UC San Diego, and on the Board of Directors for the International Society for Gravitational Physiology I'm certain he'll be a tremendous asset to your team. I don't know why you're fighting us so hard on this. It looks good for everyone."

Why I'm fighting so hard? The idea that he wasn't even considering our past together was ludicrous. I wanted to yell. Better yet, I almost found myself storming across the room, just to punch my ex-husband square in the face. Somehow, I managed to remain stoic, taking long, deep breaths from my nose. Trying to rationalize with myself how this decision wasn't disastrous for me, but every outcome I could fathom just involved Michael screwing me over, yet again.

"Perhaps she just needs a little time to warm up to the idea," Michael interjected, and my blood boiled at the sound of his voice. "We made such a good team back in the day, Daphne. We can do it again with this. I'm sure you'll find my input useful."

I swallowed, deeply. Took another breath, and then got up from my seat. "Was this the whole intent of this meeting?" I was looking at Dr. Hale then. "Couldn't you have sent me this in an email?" They could have not made a show of it. Given me an excuse to avoid having to be in the same room, breathing the same air, as Michael Riddler.

"We have some details to discuss, Dr. Carter. I just wanted to make myself very clear about how this was going to go before we started." Dr. Hale leaned back in his seat, staring at me. "Please sit back down."

It took everything in my power not to storm from the conference room. I sat back down in my seat, taking a few deep breaths again. When I glanced at Michael across the desk from me, he was staring back, that devious smile stretched across his face.

"I took the liberty of getting acquainted with Ruby Peters earlier this morning," Michael explained, and my ears rang a little at the news. He'd been talking to Ruby? Why hadn't she mentioned this during our conversation? Did it not strike her as something I would have wanted to know? Especially since she knew all about our past together. "She seemed very well versed in the drug trial. I do think we'll all work well together, Daphne. Just give it a little time."

A little time. The last thing I wanted was any time spent with Michael, however brief. But it seemed as though he'd already finagled his way into my life again, into my work, whether I liked it or not. And now he was forcing himself into Ruby's life as well, like a wedge between us. As much as I hated his presence around me, I found it bothered me even more that he was anywhere near Ruby. It was as if I was more concerned that he'd do something to jeopardize my relationship with her, than how he would impact my research. Which was a very strange thought to have, considering how attached to my work I was. But things had been very strange the past few weeks. A lot had changed since my trip to the ISS.

"Let's get started," Dr. Scott said, and my mind came back to the conference room and away from Ruby, miles above me. Preparing for my entire world to be turned on its axis, by the presence of just a single man in my life.

THE BUILDING WAS quiet late that evening, most of the employees having left for the day. I'd worked far past what I had initially intended to, but the meeting with Michael, Dr. Hale, Dr. Scott, and the suits had taken far more time from my schedule than I'd anticipated. I hadn't minded working late. I enjoyed the peace and quiet, and the soft sounds of the light rain dancing on the window outside.

I was working on organizing the data from the drug trial, in preparation to send to Ruby so she could update it with more results since I'd left the station. Unfortunately, now that Michael had come aboard the team, he'd also be overseeing all of this and likely would have to have a say before Ruby or I did anything.

Occasionally, my attention would drift to the desktop background of Ruby and the cupola. My thoughts would go back to being up there, lost in space, away from the confines of this building, this state, the entire world. Michael. Everything had been different there.

Reality was cold and relentless now, especially given how my circumstances had changed.

In my last few minutes of compiling all the data, my cell buzzed on my desk, alerting me of a message. My first instinct was to ignore it, especially in my desire to finish my work and get home for the evening. But something caused me to check anyway. The message was from Ruby. An email, from her personal account. Something that likely wasn't so closely monitored by Mission Control, just to give the astronauts some semblance of privacy.

I opened the email, which contained no subject. It was just one line, and I hadn't been quite sure what to expect. But it stirred something inside me so ferociously that I could barely contain my heart in my chest when I read the words.

I miss you.

Before I could think, I'd hit reply, my fingers flying across my phone screen faster than I'd ever typed before. *I miss you too. You've been on my mind since I left you.* I hesitated after I'd typed the message. My mind wandered to Michael, who I could only imagine was looming over my shoulder at every moment. Reading every correspondence between us. Embedding himself in my life again, whether I liked it or not.

I pondered for a long time what to do, letting the message hang there on my phone, my fingers just paused. The words read repeatedly in my mind, and every time were followed by Michael's voice in my head.

I'd almost lost my control of this research to him once, when he'd tried to take over the mission to the ISS. There was no universe in which I would let that man take anything from me ever again. He could try. Weave his way as much as he could, into every faucet of my research. But ultimately, I was still in control. This was my life. My projects.

I couldn't give him any fodder for the fire. No reason for my superiors to take my work away from me and send it into the greedy hands of my ex-husband. And that meant, that even if it was the most difficult thing in the world for me to do, I couldn't reply. That this thing between Ruby and I, what had happened on that station, couldn't exist any longer. It wouldn't exist. Not so long as my research was on the line.

It took a few long moments, but I finally hit delete. And before I left for the evening, I changed my wallpaper back to a generic one. I stared at Ruby for a few seconds more before I did, wishing desperately that there was any other way around this. But there wasn't, not really.

Ruby was my colleague. That was all she would ever be.

ELEVEN

RUBY

The whir of pedals spinning on the space bike filled the small quarters. I was alone, tearing into the machine as hard as I could, my heart thudding loudly in my chest, sweat running down my forehead. This was the most intense I'd worked out in a long time, even though I used this machine frequently. My mind was all over the place. Mostly focused on the stupid email I'd sent the previous evening to Daphne. And the fact that I hadn't heard back from her about it.

I thought, perhaps, that she might not have seen it yet. That it was still sitting in her inbox, unopened. But that thought was just as awful as the idea that she'd blatantly ignored me. If it was still there, waiting to be read. I felt mortified. I never should have said a word. The small exchange between us when she had been on board the station had been a mistake. We were colleagues, working on important, career altering research. There wasn't time for trying to navigate feelings that shouldn't have existed in the first place.

Except she was all I could think about. All the time. And it was driving me mad.

And so, I did what little I could do to keep the thoughts at bay.

I pushed harder on the bike, feeling my heart ripping through my chest. Hoping that working this hard would tear the thoughts from my mind. Thoughts that were keeping me from being completely focused on my duties aboard the station. On my duties as an assistant to Daphne Carter's decades' worth of research.

"You're going to break that damn machine." I heard a voice from behind me. When I looked over my shoulder, slowing my pace a little, Daniel was floating in the doorway of the room. I had no earthly idea how long he'd been there watching me. "You okay?"

I turned my attention back to the bike, knowing there was no way I'd admit to him what was going on with me. My thoughts about Daphne Carter. That I was beyond distracted. Before I knew it, he'd come beside me, hanging on lightly to the metallic blue support beam against the wall. His eyes softened a little bit. "You've been out of sorts for the past few days. Since *Galileo* left. It's not like you at all."

There was no way I could look at him. Not without giving myself away. I continued looking down at the bike, still pedaling slowly, without response. "It must have been nice having another woman on board," Daniel said thoughtfully. When he said it, my eyes diverted up to meet his just for a moment. "Seemed like you two had a good rapport going. Dare I say maybe even becoming friends, maybe..."

Had Daphne and I become friends? It appeared as if we'd bonded more than just on a colleague level, at least while she'd been on board. Now, I had no idea what she was thinking. If she cared about me at all, outside of helping her with her research. Not that it mattered anymore. We were in two entirely different worlds.

"I think we got along well enough," I finally replied, shrugging. My pace picked up a little on the bike again, but not so much that the whirring of the machine prevented me from hearing what Daniel was saying to me. "It's good we got along. We'll be working together for a while. It would be best if she didn't hate me."

"Rubs, anyone with eyes could see the woman didn't hate you. You're impossible to hate. Maybe a little high energy sometimes..." I rolled my eyes and Daniel grinned underneath his mustache hair. "The point is, it seems like you miss her. And it's understandable."

"Sometimes it's impossible not to feel alone up here," I said, simply. At that point, I'd slowed the bike down completely and sat motionless. "I mean, I wouldn't trade it for anything, you know that..." Daniel nodded. "But sometimes it just feels like everything is so far away." I wasn't sure what I'd meant by that. Mostly, I had meant it about Daphne, but every aspect of my life on Earth felt that way, at one point or another. It was hard not to, when you were up here.

"Keep your chin up, Commander," Daniel said, and I felt his hand squeeze my shoulder gently. "The trick is to keep yourself busy. You're up here for a reason. You get to do what almost no one else gets to, and it'll be gone before you know it. Try and make the best of things. It's not all that bad."

"I know," I replied, offering a small smile of gratitude. He was right, and for the most part I felt that way, too. It had just felt exponentially more difficult since Daphne had left. And even worse worrying that I'd made myself vulnerable to her and she'd blatantly ignored it. But Daniel was right. My life was up here, on this station. For six more months at least. And it was a privilege to be here, to get to do what I did for a living.

So, I'd do everything I could to make the best of it.

DANIEL LEFT me shortly after to sleep for a few hours. James had taken up residence in the cupola, so I stayed in the laboratory in the Destiny module, working at one of the computer stations near the rat enclosures. Instead of working, I decided to attempt a new crossword puzzle from the books my mother had sent along with *Galileo*.

The thought occurred to me once I'd opened the book and flipped to the first puzzle, that the last crossword I'd finished was the one that Daphne had helped me with before she'd left. It left me feeling melancholy all over again that she wasn't there to help me. Being alone hadn't bothered me as much as it was bothering me now.

My computer at the workstation I floated in front of dinged. I unlocked it and pulled up my emails. At the top of the inbox was a new message from Daphne, and I could feel my heart fall deep into my chest and pick up speed.

Had she answered me?

I finally found the courage to open the email. Inside was a single line of text.

SEND the vitals data for this week as soon as you are able. - D

I STARED at it for a few moments, unblinking. Read it twice over. And then the realization hit me that she had to have received my email from the previous night. She'd chosen not to respond to it. The thought sent a flurry of emotions through me, and I couldn't decide whether to be sad or angry or hurt or what exactly I felt about it. So instead, rather mechanically, I hit reply and typed up the most cordial response I could think of.

WORKING on it now. - R

FOR A MINUTE I just stared at my message. Wondering if I should say anything more to her. Then I pushed the thought from my mind, hitting send and closing out of my emails. The best thing I could do now was to distract myself as best as I could.

Which meant I needed to take the morning vitals of all the rats.

Like every other day I'd done this routine, I sort of fell into the motions. Set up the sensors that needed adjusting. Prepared each of the specimens, one at a time. Populated all the data into the record keeping system we'd been using. It was mindless work really, routine. But I made sure to make conversations with the rats as I worked with them, like I usually did. I felt like it always calmed them a little when I talked to them.

Jeffery was always the last on the list to check. I nearly always went in alphabetical order, for consistency's sake. I'd pulled up the last chart to auto-populate and then went to fetch the rat from his enclosure. Like I did on any other normal day.

Except Jeffery was motionless when I retrieved him. I could just barely make out the faint rise and fall of his chest. The rat could hardly open his eyes. For a minute I talked to him softly, running my fingers along his back. Trying to get a response from him, but he remained limp and lethargic.

My mind went to panic. Even still, I ran through my normal motions, setting up the monitoring equipment to take his vitals. Populating them into the software. When I finished, I returned my focus to the rat, trying desperately to get a response out of him. He didn't look good. Not at all. *Had he been like this yesterday?* Surely, I would have noticed, if he had. The vitals had all checked out.

Somehow, I could have still missed something. I was admittedly very distracted for days now. There could have been evidence right in front of me. And now there was something *very* wrong with Jeffery.

Instead of filling out the remainder of the paperwork to send to Daphne, which included the vitals of the rats, I saved the draft of the information and closed out the document. All I could think of in those moments was that somehow my lack of focus had potentially ruined Dr. Carter's research. And if she still had any little bit of feelings toward me, if she still thought of me as more of a colleague, if we had been friends... If I went to her with this... If she'd entrusted me with something so incredibly important to her and I'd ruined it...

She'd never forgive me. I would never forgive myself.

Trying to resist the urge to panic more, until I absolutely had to, I searched on the internet about caring for sick rodents. Everything I did on these computers was monitored by NASA employees. I just hoped with every fiber of my being, it was being glazed over. That nothing would get back to Daphne. Not unless it had to. For now, I tried to have some expectation that there was something I could do to fix this.

I spent the next few hours trying every suggestion that I could find, which was only helpful to a point, until it said that I needed to contact a veterinarian. A vet would do me little good when I was separated from them by an entire atmosphere. Even after everything I did, Jeffery was still listless. I'd begun giving up hope when my computer that I'd been working at in Destiny rang, signaling an incoming call. When I checked, the call was from Houston. Likely Daphne at this point, wondering where the data I was supposed to send hours ago was.

Somehow, I managed to answer, while nearly on the brink of tears.

Daphne's face appeared on the screen, and I felt my chest aching. It was wonderful to see her again, all those ageless features of her face and her enchanting hazel eyes. She'd even been wearing those black framed glasses that accentuated her face so well. I swallowed deeply at the look she was giving me. It was as daunting and as fierce as the first time we'd met.

"Is there a reason you've taken hours to get me the vitals data? When I said send it, Commander Peters, I didn't mean tomorrow." Her stern gaze didn't waver, and the tone she was using with me made my mouth fall open a fraction.

"I was working on it—" I started to speak, trying desperately to maintain my composure, despite the extreme amount of stress I was starting to feel, and the anxiety of having to explain to her about Jeremy at any moment. It was looking inevitable at this point.

"What is taking so long, then?" Daphne asked.

Once again, I barely managed to speak. "Dap— I mean, Dr. Carter... I need to tell you something—" Before I could get it all out, there was an instant message that popped up on the computer, over top of the video chat. It was from Mason Evans, who I knew from Mission Control at Kennedy.

Give me a call before you talk to Daphne.

I blinked. Read the message again, and then closed out of the IM, turning my attention back to Daphne then. "I'll have to call you back in a minute—"

"Commander Peters!" Daphne started, but before she could get another word in, I'd disconnected from the video chat. I would probably regret that later, but I'd decided to take Mason's advice. Almost the second I'd turned my attention to my phone, it was ringing. A private number. I assumed it was Mason and answered promptly.

"Hello?"

Mason's voice echoed on the other end of the phone call, with a slight delay. "Ruby, this is Mason. I have Dr. Miranda Pulitzer from the University of Florida on the line with me. She's a veterinary professor. Knows quite a lot about research rodents, specifically. Figured you might want her help."

My colleagues had been monitoring what I'd been doing after all. The idea that they had been stressed me out a bit, even though I knew it happened often, but at the same time, I was grateful that Mason had been paying attention. And grateful for any help I could get at this point that might save me from having to tell Daphne I'd killed one of her rats.

"Hello from Florida, Commander Peters." I assumed the woman's voice that had come through over the call was Miranda's. "I have to say, it's pretty cool to talk to an astronaut on the International Space Station. That sort of thing doesn't happen every day."

"Am I glad to talk to you," I breathed in reply.

"Let's try to figure this out, shall we?" Miranda said, and there wasn't a time in my life I felt more grateful to hear someone say words than those, in that moment.

I WORKED with Miranda for nearly an hour, trying to diagnose what was wrong with Jeffery. While we talked, Mason had promised to distract Daphne so she wouldn't harass me further via video chat or email about the reports that were long overdue. By the end of our conversation, neither of us had come to any real conclusions, but I'd managed to send over blood work information for Miranda to look at. She'd promised to have ideas the following day.

Still, that meant I had nothing for Daphne except for bad news. And Mason could only distract her for so long. When I hung up from the call with the veterinarian, I spent a few minutes trying to collect myself. I'd done everything I possibly could to try and solve this, and it was out of my control at this point, until I had more information.

Daphne needed to know. She had to assume something was wrong since I'd avoided sending her the data at all today. It hadn't been fair of me to keep her in the dark this long about her research, even if it was the last thing I wanted to tell her.

I pulled her name up on the instant messaging system. Typed out a short message.

Can we talk?

Then I stared at it, for what felt like ages. Debating sending it at all, even though it was inevitable at this point. I clicked send.

And then I waited, eyes glazed over the computer screen. *What time was it there?* She was likely still working, even if it was after hours. I assumed she'd been diligently checking her work computer for an email with the testing results for the day, which I'd still neglected to send.

The computer rang, and I jumped in surprise, even though I'd been expecting it. I sucked in a deep breath of air, letting it roll back out of my nose. And then I answered the video chat.

It was growing dark in Houston. The window behind Daphne showed beautiful pinkish colored fluffy clouds that filled the sky. There was a small desk lamp in the office Daphne was working in, that illuminated her face somewhat, but the main light in the office was off. She was glancing in another direction for a few seconds, looking as though she was finishing up working on something. Eventually her attention turned back to me.

"I still don't have the data from this morning, Commander Peters."

I swallowed deeply. Her eyes were stern, but her facial expression itself was unreadable otherwise. She just looked hyper focused on me. "Daphne," I spoke her name calmly, trying once again to steady myself. "I need to talk to you about something…"

There was a slight shift in the doctor's facial expression. "What is it?"

"I—" I didn't think I had it in me to tell her, but somehow, eventually, I managed. "Something is wrong with Jeffery. Rat J. He's been lethargic and unresponsive all day. I've been working with a veterinarian at the University of Florida to try and diagnose him, but we haven't figured out what's wrong yet."

Daphne's face was still looking concerned, at least for a few seconds more, then it turned slightly angry looking. "You couldn't have informed me of this earlier?"

I didn't have a response for that. Not really. I could have told her earlier. I probably *should* have told her earlier. But my fear of disappointing her had outweighed my desire to clue her in on the fact that I'd quite possibly jeopardized her drug trial. "I was going to but—"

"But *what*, Commander Peters? You decided to evade me all day, to blatantly keep important information about *my* research from me… Why? Are you just that ignorant?" My mouth dropped open again at her words, and just when I thought she'd stop, she continued. "Or perhaps your ego got the best of you. That somehow you, with your aerospace engineering background, could somehow magically diagnose the problem."

"I wasn't trying to imply that—" I tried to speak again but was jarringly interrupted by Daphne's *very* pissed off tone of voice, talking right over top of me.

"I hate to inform you, Commander Peters, but your fancy MIT degree means nothing to me. Your career as an astronaut means nothing to me. You mean nothing to me. You're assisting me with my research endeavors. I didn't expect to have to hold your hand and coddle you through this entire process, but clearly I was mistaken."

I barely heard the words she'd spoken after "*You mean nothing to me.*" She'd been cruel the entire time, but that? Those five words had felt like she was stabbing me in the chest with a knife and twisting. Like she was purposefully wanting to hurt me. And she'd gotten her way. She had most certainly done that. "Dr. Carter, I'm so sorry I put your work in jeopardy. I promise you it was an honest mistake."

"I should have never trusted you with any of this," Daphne said, almost as if she was talking to herself at this point, instead of me. "You're clearly about as competent as a college intern." The blows kept coming. I didn't think I could handle them much longer. But Daphne had quickly lost interest in talking to me, too. "Have the veterinarian contact me immediately with any results she has. And send me the vital information for the research specimens you *didn't* kill."

And then she hung up, without so much as a goodbye. Daphne hadn't even been looking at me in the end, clearly missing that I'd been in tears. I very rarely cried about anything, but she'd managed to chip away at me enough to bring me to that point. Before I closed out of the computer, I emailed Daphne the vital information I'd taken earlier. And then I retreated through the station to my sleeping quarters, hoping with every fiber of my being that no one would bother me before I got there.

Luckily, I'd gotten tucked away inside my nook, with my sleeping bag without an interruption. It wasn't until I'd gotten settled that my personal computer inside of my space, attached to the wall across from me, began to ring. At first, I thought it was Daphne again, calling to yell at me more, or to tell me I'd done the vital testing wrong, or something. Instead, it was my aunts's account calling.

While I didn't feel in the mood to talk, I wiped my face again and decided to answer anyway.

"I thought we might catch you," Mary said, smiling brightly at me. My uncle was sitting beside her. They looked like they were home, in bed. Both had their readers on, and I could barely make out a book open on my uncle's lap. Most likely a murder mystery, if I had to take a guess. "We haven't heard from you in a few weeks. Just wanted to check in and see how you were doing. Eric watches your new videos on the website, but we missed seeing you."

I offered a fragile smile, trying my best to hide the extreme emotions I was feeling at that moment. My aunt and uncle were a comforting sight, even amidst all of what just had transpired. "I'm doing okay," I replied, tugging the monitor a little bit off the wall so it was closer to me. "I've just been really busy with work."

"How was the visit with the doctor?" My uncle asked me, adjusting the glasses on his face. My aunt had tilted the tablet they were using toward him a bit. "He wasn't too bossy, was he? Did you get along?"

"It was a she, Eric," I corrected. Then I hesitated, not wanting to talk about Daphne Carter now, but I supposed I didn't have much of a choice. "She was actually pleasant, for the most part. We got a lot of work done. She left a few days ago." It had felt like she'd left months ago now, even though it had only been a few days. And I had missed her, quite a lot. Until just a little while ago, when she'd been so cold and cruel toward me. Now I didn't have any idea what I felt toward her, if anything at all. "Sorry I haven't called."

"We knew you were busy," Mary said. "We just wanted to see your cute face for a few minutes." My mother's face grew closer to the screen. "You look tired. Are you doing alright?"

The last thing I wanted to do was to talk to my family about what had transpired between Daphne and I, both when she'd been aboard the station, and then now, this past evening. So, I said the best thing that I could. "I've just got a lot of things on my mind, I guess."

"You're eating enough?" My aunt asked, and I couldn't help but smile at the question. She asked every time, constantly concerned about this. I had always been a small person, even when I hadn't been living aboard the space station.

"I'm eating enough, I promise," I reassured her, and then tried to change topics. "What are you all doing this week?"

"We're going to the beach market on Friday," my uncle said. "I wanted to go fishing on Saturday at the pier, but the weather folks are projecting that hurricane to be hitting us after all." The hurricane? I realized I'd forgotten all about my mother's email mentioning it a few days prior. "They say it's going to be a Category 4."

"Hurricane Kevin?" I asked, and I saw my aunt nod. My face twisted a little, suddenly worried and distraught for an entirely different reason than I had been moments earlier. "Mary, you all are right on the water. You need to go more inland, or up to Georgia or something. You shouldn't stay there this weekend. It's dangerous."

"The neighbors are going to help me put up the storm shutters," my uncle said. "And your mom and I are stocking up on food. We've got the generator too—"

"Eric, I'm serious," I interrupted him. "A Category 4 hurricane can be catastrophic. I know you and mom love the house, but we've lived in Florida our entire lives. You two know better than to stay there."

My aunt's attention had drifted from the video chat, and I heard the very muffled sound of the television in the background. She turned back to me. "Honey, my show just came on. I'm going to let you go."

"Mary—"

"I'll call you soon," my aunt said, blowing a kiss to the camera. And before I could get another word in edgewise, she'd hung up the phone, leaving me alone in my quarters. Staring at a screen that had gone black. Trying my best to breathe.

And for the first time in my career, I wished I was anywhere but on that station.

TWELVE
DAPHNE

The wheels of the Gulfstream jet bounced and rumbled on the asphalt ground of the runway as it touched down at the Cape Canaveral Space Force Station. It was one of the longest runways in the entire world, stretching almost fifteen thousand feet. A short plane ride from Houston to Cocoa Beach certainly was less eventful than the shuttle ride to the ISS. Even if I wasn't exactly thrilled to be back at the Kennedy Space Center for a few days. Especially when a massive hurricane was approaching the state.

But when major funding was on the line for my research, I would just about do anything. Securing funding meant that I could continue to pursue my projects without fear of being shut down prematurely.

Usually I did these presentations alone, but today I had unwelcomed company tagging along today, and wasn't the least bit thrilled about it.

"I just love the KSC campus," Michael said, his head tilted to peer out of one of the circular jet windows. I watched him ogle for a few moments, then focused straight ahead, trying not to engage him as much as humanly possible. "Beautiful place, huh, Daph?"

I cringed, hating the fact that he'd called me that pet name. For a moment I thought to correct him, but then decided it wasn't worth the effort. "It is," I replied.

The jet pulled up to the stairway where we would depart from. Once the pilot had parked, I unbuckled myself from the seat and got up promptly, fetching my carry-on bag from the storage area. I didn't wait for Michael, and instead made my way out of the aircraft, wanting fresh air and some space.

At the bottom of the stairwell, there was a town car waiting. There were two NASA employees standing outside of the car, one who opened the back door to let Dr. Hale out. His hair blew in the balmy Florida breeze. I couldn't make out his eyes under his well-tinted sunglasses, but his facial expression was much like it usually was, expressionless and straight.

"Dr. Carter," Dr. Hale gave me a nod. I caught Michael coming to stand next to me. A little closer than I would have liked. I took a sidestep away from him. "Dr. Riddler. Glad to see you could join us."

"I wouldn't have it any other way," Michael replied, and I felt my face twitch at his response. Every fiber of my being wanted him as far away as humanly possible. "Are we headed straight to the meeting?"

Dr. Hale nodded, while the NASA employee opened the town car door again for us. "They're waiting for us now." He disappeared inside of the car, Michael following behind him and then me last. As much as I didn't want to, I sat across from Dr. Hale and next to my ex-husband but tried desperately to get as much space between us as possible. The two NASA employees sat in the front, and within a minute we were off.

A half hour later, Michael, Bill, and I were standing outside of the reserved conference room, waiting to be let in for our meeting with the client that was potentially going to help fund our research. Dr. Hale was adjusting his tie, while Michael was reading notes off of some papers, he'd brought with him. Meanwhile, my attention was turned outside one of the large picture windows by the conference room, staring at the center of the Kennedy Space Center campus. I made out the Vehicle Assembly Building in the far distance, where

Galileo was likely being housed. I couldn't help but think briefly about the ISS, and then my mind wandered to Ruby...

I hadn't spoken with her since yesterday, when she'd delivered the news about Rat J's status. Since then, she and a veterinarian from the University of Florida had been working to resolve his issues, but I hadn't checked in on them today. I had been so stressed from this last-minute excursion to Florida and the fact that Michael would be accommodating me, that the news of the status of my research specimens had been more than I could handle at that moment.

Perhaps I shouldn't have been quite as cold to her as I had been. I'd been thinking about it quite a lot since yesterday, wondering if I should contact her to apologize. But the presentation and the short trip had occupied my time, so I had decided I would attempt to speak with her in the evening, if I could. Hopefully Ruby and the vet had come to some solution. The fact that I hadn't heard anything was a bit concerning, but I didn't have much time to think about it.

The door to the conference room squeaked open, and my attention turned from the window. Dr. Hale shuffled his way inside the room, followed by Michael, and then lastly, me. There were a half dozen people in the room. The "suits," as most of the research at NASA liked to call them. I'd had so many meetings with the suits over the years, they hardly intimidated me anymore. My presentation was memorized nearly verbatim. Dr. Hale would introduce the project, and then I'd speak about the research.

Simple, really. We'd be done and out within the hour, hopefully with funding secured for a few more years at least.

"Good afternoon," Dr. Hale said, stepping in front of a large projector screen that was already loaded up with the usual slide show we presented. "Thank you all for your patience with our arrival. I trust our interns got you some beverages while you waited." There were coffee cups and bottled waters on the table, so I assumed that they'd been taken care of. "If you're ready, we can get started..."

The group's heads all bobbed around the table, and I stepped up toward the projector screen. As soon as I did, however, Michael followed suit. "Michael, if you don't mind giving them a bit of an overview—" When I looked at Bill, he was focused on Michael instead of me, who still had the collection of papers in his hands.

"I thought I was supposed to—" I started, in protest, but was quickly interrupted by Dr. Hale's hand coming into the air. My mouth snapped shut.

"We decided to let Dr. Riddler have a chance to do the presentation," Bill said quietly, when he came to stand beside me. "It will give him an opportunity to get up to speed. Handle some of the logistics and such. I don't think you'd mind a break, would you, Daphne?"

The idea of Michael presenting research that I'd overseen for nearly two decades, with very little experience, when I had it memorized exactly, was nauseating. Somehow, I managed a nod. Dr. Hale gave a wave of his hand for Michael to begin, and I stood silently, watching as he gave the presentation that I'd been giving for years. And much to my disappointment, he was rather good at it. He'd known far more than I'd anticipated him to, and even managed to slide in some information in places I wouldn't have thought to do. Michael hadn't changed much since our college years. He was still as charismatic as he always was, and a great public speaker. Better than I ever was, but I'd never admit that to him. Truthfully, he did an excellent job. I hated every second of it.

As soon as the meeting had ended, I separated from Dr. Hale and Michael Riddler, finding Mason Evans waiting for me in the halls outside the conference room. I'd completely forgotten about our promised coffee and tea date, to catch up with one another. We didn't speak as often since he'd moved from Johnson to Kennedy and had interacted the most we had in years when I'd been training for and visiting the ISS.

"You look murderous, Daph," Mason's eyebrow raised at me once I'd spotted him in the hallway and approached. "Was the presentation that bad?"

"If by bad you mean that I didn't give a presentation *at all*, then yes. It was very bad." I supposed I must have been scowling, but I was certain it was only made worse by the mention of me being kicked off my own presentation. "Michael did all the talking, I'm afraid. But at least we secured our funding for another five years."

"That's excellent," Mason said, as we began making our way toward the building's cafeteria. "I mean, about the funding. Not about Dr. Riddler stealing your thunder."

"It's not that he stole my thunder," I argued, as we made a turn. Mason gave me a look that said that I was lying when I'd said that, so I paused a moment before continuing. "All right, it is about the fact that he stole my thunder, at least in part. I've been doing that presentation for over a decade, Mason. But that wasn't the point..."

Mason glanced at me, grabbing a hold of the cafeteria door and pulling it open to let me inside. "What's the point then?"

"Thank you," I said graciously, sliding around him. As soon as I had, I stopped and looked back at him, standing in the doorway. "The point is, he was *better* than me at it." And that was, truthfully, what bothered me more than anything.

AFTER I'D FETCHED myself some Earl Grey tea, and Mason had gotten a very large and very black cup of coffee that I could smell from across the table we'd chosen to sit at, we continued our conversation. Mostly it was chit chat about work related things. We were friends, but a lot of it was work that bonded us.

"I think Ruby and Miranda diagnosed your rat," Mason said, in the middle of our conversation. "I guess you've been busy all morning and haven't heard yet. He's going to be just fine in a few days."

While the research had been the topic of discussion for the last hour during the meeting, I'd been busy stewing for most of it, and hadn't thought too deeply about Ruby and the sick rat aboard the ISS. Or the fact that I'd been so belligerent to her the afternoon prior.

"That's good news," I replied, taking a sip of my tea.

"You should probably apologize for being such an ass, you know," Mason said, after he too had taken a drink of his coffee. I tried to keep my face from showing the disgust I had for his beverage choice. "That rat getting sick was out of her control."

I frowned at him then, having forgotten how much of the interactions between employees aboard the ISS and at headquarters were monitored. Mason was someone who was often one of the ones monitoring it, since he was in a managerial type of position.

"I was planning on speaking with her this evening, once I got settled," I replied. I didn't elaborate on my annoyance with him that he'd been snooping on our conversation, but he wasn't exactly wrong. I had been rather cruel toward her. The stress of a last-minute flight to Florida with Michael and worrying about something happening to my research when I was so far away had gotten the best of me. I had intentions of apologizing to her, without Mason needing to remind me of it, or what I had done.

"Good. She's been a little stressed out today, so I'm sure she could use it." Mason scratched at his bearded face for a moment.

"Stressed about what, exactly?" I asked, drumming my fingers against the side of the paper cup that my tea was in, eyeing my friend. "Jeffery? I thought you said he was going to be on the mend?" I'd realized, after I'd said it that I'd used Ruby's common name she'd given the rat, instead of its research designation. The idea I had made her linger in my mind for a moment.

"Her family lives in Port St. Lucie, right on the water." Mason explained, after finishing off the remainder of his coffee in one giant swig.

"Isn't that where Kevin is supposed to hit?" I said, referring to the Category 4 hurricane that was headed toward Florida the upcoming weekend, and Mason nodded.

"They aren't leaving either," he replied. "The Coast Guard has been recommending everyone to evacuate but I guess her uncle is being pretty stubborn about the whole thing and Ruby is understandably worried."

I sipped on my tea for a minute, leaning back in my chair. While I wouldn't have known what it felt like to be Ruby in those moments, both because of the absence of both of my own parents, and the fact that I wasn't on the ISS with everything on Earth out of my reach, I still found myself empathizing with her. The idea of being that far out of reach from something, to watch it unfold and be unable to do anything at all... It must have been terrifying.

When the thought hit me, I looked back up at Mason, after finishing off my drink. "You wouldn't happen to be able to get me their names, would you?"

A FEW HOURS and a quick trip to a local rental car facility later, I had left the Kennedy Space Center, my colleagues, and Mason behind. Traveling south, down the highway, toward Port St. Lucie. All I had was an address that we'd managed to look up from the names Mason had on file. I didn't even have a telephone number to get in touch with them.

I drove in silence, as I often did, the entire time arguing in my head that I was crazy for doing something so ridiculously out of character for me. I didn't know either of these people. They were strangers. The only tie I had to them was through Ruby, who likely hated my very existence after how I'd behaved, and I'd still yet to apologize to her. Still, there I was, planning to show up at her family's doorstep with no invitation, in the hopes that they'd evacuate their home that they were too stubborn to leave, all to bring some sort of comfort to Ruby, who had absolutely no way of reaching them otherwise.

I was still insistent upon believing that I could convince myself that she meant nothing to me. That the moments we'd shared when I'd been up there, aboard the space station, had been fleeting and unimportant. Except, she was always on my mind. Far more than anything else, except for my research. And not thoughts about her just as a colleague. They were thoughts that I'd never had about another woman before, or about anyone in years and years now, but they lingered constantly. I found that I was almost pining for her, and

I couldn't discern if I was frustrated about it because there was nothing I could do, or because it was inappropriate, and I shouldn't be.

I'd never done this sort of thing for anyone. Ever. I was lying to myself if I said she was just helping me with my research endeavors. That she meant nothing more.

"You must really have a thing for her," Mason had said, when I'd tucked myself away in the rental car.

"I don't have any idea what you're talking about," I argued, turning up the air conditioning in the car to try and ease the wave of heat from outside. "She's a colleague. A research assistant. I'm just doing her a favor, is all."

"A favor she *didn't* ask you to do," Mason noted. "And, for the record, I've never once seen you trying to do anyone a favor, for as long as I've known you. No offense, Daphne, but you're rather self-centered most of the time, whether you want to believe me or not."

I believed him. And he hadn't been wrong. This entire idea was completely out of character for me, and something I would have never considered doing for anyone else I knew. "Do me a favor and don't mention where I'm going. And tell Bill that I'm finding my own way back to Houston."

"I'll do my best," Mason replied, patting the car a few times and then taking a step back. "You know Bill with his questions… Drive safe, Daph. Text me when you get there."

When I'd made the few turns off the highway in which it took to get to Ruby's parents' neighborhood, I spent a few minutes trailing up and down the road in the SUV I'd rented, trying to pinpoint the house. The address was tucked away in a weird location over the front doorstep, and I eventually managed to spot it.

There were two cars in the driveway, which gave me hope that they were at home. I parked the car behind them and then hopped out. The sun was setting to the west, casting a beautiful array of colors into the sky. I admired it briefly, as I made my way up the pathway to the front door of the house.

Did I really want to do this? Was I being ludicrous? I'd driven two hours to get there. It was late, and every hour the hurricane was getting closer to landfall. It wasn't like I had all the time in the world.

I'd been standing in the doorway, debating what on earth I was going to do, when the front door opened, and my fate was decided for me. A blonde-haired woman with blue eyes and coke bottle framed glasses answered. She was dressed in her pajamas, hair pinned up on top of her head. And she was staring at me, perplexed, without speaking at first. The look in her eyes seemed as though she was trying to place who I was exactly.

"Who's at the door, Mary?" A man's voice called from inside the house.

Then her expression lit up, and a smile breached her face. "It's the scientist friend of Ruby's, honey. The one that was up on the space station with her... "

"Daphne Carter," I said, extending a hand toward her and offering a small but pleasant smile. "I'm sorry to bother you so late. I hope it's alright."

"What on earth brings you to Port St. Lucie?" The woman, Mary, asked me. I hoped that somehow, some way, I could do what Ruby hadn't, even if it seemed impossible. That they'd listen to me, and I could offer Ruby this small favor, after everything she'd done for me. And that if I did, it would stay between us without word getting out to my colleagues. Because this, my being here and doing this for Ruby, wasn't just an act of random kindness. It wasn't a favor for a colleague.

I had feelings for her, without a shadow of a doubt.

THIRTEEN
RUBY

Although I'd stayed constantly busy the remainder of the week and into the weekend, it also seemed to pass impossibly slow. Miranda and I had eventually figured out a solution to help Jeffery, and by Friday he was already seeming much better than he had been. It had certainly eased my mind a little bit, but only a little. I hadn't heard from Daphne in several days, since she'd been so angry with me over our video call. Nor had I had contact with my parents. Even Mason had been no use in helping me get in contact with Daphne.

So, I was up in the cupola alone, sending more data to a radio silent Daphne, wondering if she was ever going to speak to me again. Surely Mason had told her the good news about Jeffery. She had no reason to be worried anymore, everything was getting back to normal. Yet I'd heard nothing, except the occasional regular updates from Mission Control and my colleagues aboard the space station.

Above me, we were starting to pass by North America. It was daylight, Saturday by the computers that kept track of the time differences. And there, on the east coast of the continent, a terrifying cyclone that was starting to envelope Florida. Its eye was nearly as wide as the entire state. I'd been up here and witnessed things like this before, major storm systems, other hurricanes. But never had I been aboard the station when a hurricane was hitting so close to my home. So close to my family.

My parents were down there, in the middle of it, and I had no idea if they were safe. All I could do was watch it all unfold below me, without any ability to do anything at all. It was out of my control. And I hated every second. I couldn't focus on anything else, and wouldn't, for the next hour and a half as we passed over. And even when it disappeared from my view, it would still be on my mind. Until I knew my parents were safe.

"Damn that's a big storm," a familiar voice spoke from below me, beyond the entrance to the cupola. When I looked down, Daniel was floating nearby, hanging on to one of the metallic blue support beams. There was a hint of concern in his eyes. "Still no word from your folks, huh?"

I shook my head, trying to force myself not to constantly stare at the hurricane, but I couldn't fight it. My eyes stared up anyway. "I've been up here a lot and I don't think I've ever not wanted to be up here, until I found out about that. I would give *anything* not to be up here."

"Your folks are going to be okay, Rubs. They'll get in touch with you soon. I'm sure they're just buckled down right now. I haven't heard much from my family either since they evacuated…"

"At least they evacuated," I said, feeling my facial expression drop. Why had my parents been so stubborn? We'd lived in Florida since I was born. They'd been there nearly their entire lives too. When the coast guard told you to evacuate because of a hurricane, you evacuated. Even if the house had been my childhood home, it hadn't been worth their safety. And had I been there, able to go to them, I wouldn't have taken no for an answer.

But there was nothing I could do. Not three miles above them, separated by atmosphere and space. Hopelessly floating in this tin can that was only capable of viewing their fate.

"Don't worry until you have to, alright?" I felt Daniel's hand reach around my foot and give it a squeeze. It was the only thing within reach now. When I looked down at him, I smiled softly, appreciative of the affectionate gesture. "Feel like playing some Scrabble? We all were itching to play a few games."

"Give me a few minutes to finish all this up and I will," I replied. As much as I wasn't really in the mood to play a game, the distraction would probably be a good thing at this point. I finished sending off the data I'd gathered so far that day and my notes I'd taken, and then closed out things on the computer. I was just about to log off entirely, when the speakers began to ring, and a video call alert popped up on the screen.

The call was from Mason, at Kennedy Space Center. One of the several people I'd been trying to get in touch with over the past few days. I wasn't sure whether I should feel relieved or anxious about seeing him calling me, but I didn't give myself too long to think about it.

"Mason?" I asked, as his picture came across my screen. He wasn't in his office at the space center. It looked like he was in a bedroom.

"Hey there Commander Peters. Some of us are working from home today because of the hurricane," he explained, answering my questions about his location. "Wanted to give you a call and see how things were going up on the ISS."

"They'd be better if I could get a hold of Daphne or anyone on the research team," I replied. "She's been out of the office, and I keep getting Michael's answering machine. And the interns have been no help. They said Daphne hasn't been in the office in a few days. What's going on?"

"Just had some urgent matters come up that she needed to take care of," Mason said. There was a strange expression on his face, like he was looking a little too intensely at me for some reason. "She should be sending you an email with some work stuff shortly. Wanted me to make sure you read over it thoroughly. And to give her a call if you have any questions."

Daphne had some nerve, not even speaking to me herself or remotely trying to apologize for her brash behavior the other day, and just sending me work to do. I nodded anyway. "I'll look over it as soon as I get it." The minute I'd spoken, my email dinged, and sure enough it was an email from Daphne. Oddly enough, from a personal email rather than a work email. I wondered if she'd used it due to being out of the office because of the hurricane.

"I got it," I let Mason know. "Thanks for getting in touch with me. Stay safe down there."

"We'll be in touch soon," Mason replied, giving me a smile before he disconnected from me. When the video call ended, I turned my attention toward my email, opening the message Daphne had sent. It wasn't extraordinarily long, and when I started reading it, I realized it was all mundane information about her research project I'd already read before. It looked like notes for a presentation, even. Why she'd sent me such a random document, I had no idea.

I'd gotten about done with the reading when I noticed a random out of place line. *"If you have any questions while I'm out of the office, I can be reached at this number. Please call with your personal cell."* It wasn't local, the area code looked completely unfamiliar. I stared at it and wondered whether I should call. If I really wanted to talk to Daphne now, after everything that had happened. But she'd sent this weird email, with mundane information I already knew and no context, and had asked me to call a random telephone number with my personal phone, that I normally only used to contact family or friends when needed. Or sometimes I would use it for social media.

For a while I did nothing. Reread the email over again. Watched the hurricane above me, now enveloping Florida entirely, just as we were drawing close to it disappearing. Then I stared at the telephone number again and fished my phone from the pocket of my khaki pants. I typed the number in and hit the call button before I thought about it too much longer.

The phone rang once, twice.

"Ruby?"

Never in my entire life had I ever been more shocked and simultaneously relieved to hear my aunt's voice. It warmed me from head to toe and I savored it for a few seconds before I managed to speak. "Mary? Why are you— what is going on? Where are you?"

"We're at a hotel just south of Atlanta," my aunt replied, and I gripped onto the metallic blue railing around the perimeter of the cupola. The biggest sigh of relief escaped me. "We got here a few hours ago." I had so many questions running through my mind at an impossible speed, I couldn't keep up. All I could think about at that moment was that my parents were safe in Georgia. That they weren't in the middle of the terrifying storm I had been watching.

"How did you— Why did Daphne give me this number?" I finally managed to formulate some semblance of a question to ask her.

"Daphne was the one that came to get us," my aunt explained, and my ears rang a little bit at the words she spoke. I was in disbelief. Daphne had come to get my parents in Port St. Lucie? How? She'd gone all the way from Texas to Florida just to help them? Why? "She was at Kennedy for some sort of meeting and came down. I'm not quite sure how she convinced your uncle to leave the house, but she did." My aunt laughed into the phone. "You didn't know? I thought you put her up to the whole thing."

"I had no idea—" There were so many emotions tumbling around inside of me all at once, I wasn't sure what I was feeling. Relief, that was for certain, but also confusion and disbelief that Daphne would have ever done such a thing for me. Especially after how things had ended between us a few days prior. I assumed she'd hated me at that point. "Is she there with you? Can I talk to her?"

"Just a second, sweetheart. Glad you called us. Love you."

"Glad you're safe. I love you, too." I replied. My mother's voice disappeared, and I heard a brief, inaudible conversation, and then the rustling of the phone.

Daphne's voice came through the speaker. "Ruby?" My heart skipped a beat at the sound of her speaking my name to me, in such a delicate way. It wasn't ordering me around about research work as Commander Peters. It wasn't brash and straightforward, like it usually was. Her tone was soft, and affectionate, even. Taking great care when she spoke my name to me.

"You went and got my aunt and uncle?" I asked her, unable to think of anything else to say because of how much I was still in disbelief at what she'd done. "Why would you do that?"

"I was in town briefly for a presentation, and Mason might have mentioned in passing that they were— ah— being a bit *stubborn* about leaving in the wake of the hurricane." Daphne explained to me, her tone still soft and warm. "I knew you must have been worried about them, so I thought I'd try to help if I could."

"And you drove them all the way to Georgia?" I asked, baffled. "Daphne, I— Why? I don't understand..." I didn't know what to say to her for a few seconds, still trying to process it all. And still so grateful that my parents were okay. That Daphne was okay. "I honestly thought you hated me after our last conversation. I haven't heard from you in days, I just assumed I'd have to work with Michael or someone else from now on...That you were done with me."

"I don't think there's a world in which that could be possible," Daphne replied, gently. I heard a door shut in the background. Then she continued. "I'm sorry for my behavior the other day. It was completely unacceptable, regardless of my reasoning. I should have never treated you that way... I won't ever treat you that way again, I can assure you."

"You were worried," I replied, my voice having grown as soft as hers. While I knew I was alone now, I still had a strange feeling that my colleagues might appear at any moment and overhear, even if we were saying nothing wrong. "I know Dr. Riddler's involvement with the research has stressed you out, and believe me, I know how much this project means to you. I kind of let you down a little, and I'm sorry for that."

"Mason told me that Jeffery is doing better," Daphne replied, and I could swear by the tone of her voice she was smiling. "I was glad to hear it." She'd called Rat J by the name I'd given him, and once again I felt a warm flutter through me. A feeling that I hadn't experienced since she'd left the station. "And Ruby, despite everything, I know you'd take care of my research. It's *our* research now, really. Like you said before."

"I was joking when I said that," I noted, but her comment made me smile a little.

"Well, I wasn't," Daphne replied, simply. "I couldn't do this without you. Even if I may have said otherwise, I didn't mean it. I hope you know that."

"Water under the bridge," I replied, still smiling.

"Would you like to talk to your aunt and uncle again?" Daphne asked me then. "I think they wanted to talk to you before I let you go."

"I would like that a lot, actually." I hesitated for a moment, listening to the sounds of Daphne opening a door again and then hearing my parents talking in the background. "Hey, Daphne. Before you go..."

"Mm?" Daphne said, and I hesitated. The last time I'd opened myself up to her, she'd rejected me. Part of me feared if I tried again, it might happen again. But after this, after what she'd done for my parents...

"I was wondering if you'd watch *Back to the Future* with me. Have you seen it before? None of the crew are big fans of sci fi movies, believe it or not, and I'm itching to watch it."

There was hesitation on the line, and I wished at that moment that I could have seen her facial reaction and knew what she was thinking. Eventually she spoke. "I haven't," she said, simply. Then another second of hesitation. "I'd love to. I can't recall the last time I've watched a movie."

Somehow, that fact didn't surprise me in the least. "This weekend? Eight your time?"

This time, Daphne didn't hesitate, a warmth in her tone. "Sounds perfect."

"It's a date," I said, matter-of-factly.

Daphne didn't reply to what I'd said, but there was a brief silence on the line before she spoke again. "Alright, I'll give you back to your mother now."

"Thank you, Daphne. Truly." I said, hearing the phone rustle. I'd thought she'd handed the phone over for a second, but she surprised me when she spoke one last time.

"Oh, and Ruby?"

"Yes?" I asked, leaning into the phone as my eyes turned up toward the Earth above me in the cupola. Even as the US began to disappear, I felt far more at ease than I had about it. Like everything was going to be okay.

"I miss you too."

FOURTEEN
DAPHNE

As much as I hadn't wanted to, I decided for one of the few times in the history of my career at NASA, to join some of my colleagues for dinner upon my return to Houston a few days later. It had been a very impromptu and casual retirement party for a fellow researcher, a biological engineer named Edward. Most of my entire research division had come along, it was a group of a dozen of us or so. Unlike my friendship with Mason, I wasn't close to most of these people. I didn't know Edward very well, but he'd always been a kind person.

We'd ended up at a small restaurant on the beach on Galveston Island. A place I avoided as often as possible, due to its touristy nature. The party had started late into the evening, the sun already setting, streaking the sky with pinks and oranges that reflected off the water. The light pollution, while less here on the island than in downtown Houston, still made it difficult to make out as many stars as I would have liked. Nothing had remotely compared to the view onboard the ISS, so it hadn't mattered much.

I did my best to focus on the random conversations at the table. I had sat next to my intern, and two female colleagues, Stephanie and Kelly. On the far end of the table, where Edward had been sitting,

Dr. Hale sat, with my ex-husband beside him. Michael hadn't been in Houston long, yet somehow, he'd made friends with nearly everyone. His charismatic personality was infectious, so I wasn't completely surprised. But still, it bothered me.

"How's your research going?" Kelly asked me, and it brought my focus back to the people around me, which I was grateful for. "Dr. Hale told us that you managed to secure more funding for the project."

The mention of the securing of the funding had me thinking of Michael all over again. That hadn't been my doing this time, unfortunately. "Actually, it was Dr. Riddler that gave the presentation," I replied, hating having to give the man any sort of credit at all, but I wasn't a liar. I wouldn't take credit where it wasn't due, unlike him. "And he did quite well, to be honest."

"Commander Peters is doing well, too?" Stephanie asked. "It must be interesting working so closely with an astronaut aboard the ISS." The comment was most likely harmless, just casual conversation, but the mention of our "closeness" and our working relationship gave an uncomfortable tumble in my stomach. No one knew about what I had done in Florida a few days prior. No one knew of the things I had admitted to Ruby that had indicated that I was far more invested in her than purely work colleagues.

And no one was going to find out, I hoped. "She's been very helpful," I decided to say, taking a sip of my water and a bite of my food to try and distract myself from speaking any further on the matter.

"How is it going with Michael assisting you? He must be pretty helpful if he was the one that managed to secure the funding for the research..." It was Kelly that spoke then. I resisted the urge to let my displeasure with that fact show on my face, even though I was grateful for the change of topics from Ruby. "He's working with Ruby now too, right?"

"Well enough, I suppose," I replied, though in reality I expected the other shoe to drop at any moment. And the idea of him having anything to do with Ruby was maddening beyond belief, both that I wanted him as far away from her as possible, but also because every second he was around her gave him more of a chance to figure out that there was something going on between us. The idea terrified me beyond belief, that he could use it against me somehow. That the nightmare I'd endured two decades ago would unfold all over again.

There was a clinking at the far end of the table. One of our other colleagues, whose name escaped me in that moment, stood up from his seat. "Let's raise our glasses to Edward." He gave a short speech that I only half paid attention to. Toward the end, I heard someone else interrupt him from down the table, and realized it was Michael.

"Isn't that the space station passing over?" The entire table turned toward the sky, including myself. Sure enough, there was a small streak of light moving across the sky. Too slow to be a shooting star. The trajectory and speed made it obvious.

I stood up, following it. Not taking my eyes from it for a second. Right now, Ruby was high above me. Two hundred and twenty miles separating us. Quickly, I pulled my phone from my pocket and snapped a photo. A selfie of myself, with the sky behind me. Perhaps I'd gotten the space station in the shot, perhaps not. It didn't matter. I watched the craft blaze across the sky, keeping my eye on it until it had disappeared into the horizon. And then for a long minute afterward, I just stood there.

When my focus came back to the table, our food was arriving. Before I sat down to eat, I pulled open my email, composing a message to Ruby and attaching the photo. Trying to find words that were as innocent as possible yet conveyed what I had felt in that moment.

HELLO FROM THREE hundred miles below you. My eyes were on you tonight. - D

. . .

WHEN I RETURNED HOME for the evening, after the excursion to Galveston Island, I couldn't focus on anything. My condo was only a few blocks away from the space center, but I didn't feel like going back to work. Instead, I found myself at the end of the block at the small family-owned grocery store, gathering an arm basket full of baking supplies. I rarely had anything in the house to eat and couldn't remember the last time I'd had things to bake. Years, probably.

For whatever reason, banana bread with chocolate chips sounded delicious at that moment. A staple I'd made in my undergraduate years. I rarely ate sweets nowadays, but my mind kept lingering on Ruby to an exhausting point, and I needed a distraction. Something that didn't involve work, which would continue to make me think about her. Perhaps the baking would do me some good.

As soon as I'd placed the unbaked loaf into the oven, my attention turned to my personal phone that was buzzing on the counter. A video call, from a number I didn't recognize. It was a Florida area code, Cape Canaveral and Cocoa Beach area. Perhaps it had been Mason, for some reason, but why he'd be calling me so late I had no idea.

I answered, and surprisingly it was Ruby Peters face that appeared on the other side of the screen. This time, she was in the Destiny research lab with the rats, not in her usual spot at the cupola. She smiled at me.

"The babies wanted to say hi," Ruby explained, panning down on the rats in their containers. "Say hi, everyone." I heard her squeaking loudly in the background, imitating what the rats might have sounded like saying hello to me in various voices.

A laugh came out of me, that shook my belly. Her goofiness was certainly infectious, and just the kind of thing I needed right in that moment. Eventually the camera turned back to face her, and she spoke again. "And I guess I wanted to say hi too," she shrugged.

"Are you working?" I asked, leaning back against the kitchen counter.

"A little," Ruby admitted, and when I glanced at the computer screen behind her, I could see that she'd been taking vitals of the rats, most likely. "Mostly distracted thinking about you."

There was an uncomfortable stirring in my stomach then, worrying who was watching our correspondence. There was no privacy aboard that station, not for the astronauts. Which meant that there was no privacy between us now. Everything we were saying could be watched, by God knew how many others.

Somehow, Ruby knew exactly what I'd been thinking. "Mason's helping me give us a little privacy," she admitted. "It's just you and me right now, I promise." Mason was helping us. While it still made me nervous that even he knew of my feelings, the idea that he was going out of his way to protect me was comforting. He was a good friend. "Are you at home?"

Ruby's question brought me back to her. I nodded. "My condo. I just got home from a retirement party at Galveston Beach with some colleagues. It was dreadful."

"I got your message," Ruby said, matter-of-factly. "I was sad I wasn't in the cupola to see us pass over you. I've been trying to get some work done. Stay on schedule and all of that."

She made me smile again. "I appreciate your diligence."

"You should give me a little tour of your place," Ruby suggested, nodding behind me. Had it been any other person, I might not have been so inclined to humor them. Perhaps even laughed at the idea. Very few people had ever come to my condo. Maybe Mason a handful of times when he'd lived here. A date or two, many years ago. Mostly it had just been me.

Instead, I found myself rather flattered that she'd wanted to see where I lived, as boring and simple as it was. I flipped the camera around on my phone, so it no longer faced me, but went into the room, and began to walk around, lighting each room and panning around.

It was very clear by the state of the condo, that I very rarely "lived" there, outside of my bedroom and parts of my kitchen. The bed was still unmade when I walked into the room, but I showed her anyway. Something felt so intimate about showing her the place where I'd slept. As few people who had visited my home in the past, even fewer had seen this room. But then again, Ruby and I had slept only feet from one another for several weeks, so for some reason it didn't feel as strange as I thought it would.

When I returned to my kitchen, I flipped the camera back around to face me. Ruby's face was glowing with a smile. "It's a nice little place," she said. "Though it's very obvious you're a workaholic." I couldn't help but laugh warmly again and nodded in agreement.

"It's that obvious?" I replied, though I knew the answer.

"Very," Ruby replied, still smiling. "What are you doing right now? Did I see cooking supplies on your counter? The oven was on?"

"Baking," I admitted, impressed by her keen observational skills, walking over to check on the bread. It was slowly rising in the pan but would need another twenty minutes or so by the timer I'd set. I panned the camera on the food inside, so she could see.

"What is that?"

"Banana bread," I said. "I used to make it all the time in college. It's been ages since I've had it, and for whatever reason I felt the urge tonight."

"With chocolate chips?!" Ruby sighed loudly, as I turned the camera back on myself, so I could see her on the phone again. "I'm so jealous right now, I can't even see straight."

"Perhaps I can make some for you when I see you again," I replied. We paused for a moment, neither of us speaking. Just looking at one another in a deep way, a way I hadn't looked at another person in years. The way we'd been looking at one another on the space station in those moments before I'd left her.

I wished so badly that I could touch her again. Kiss her. I'd never kissed a woman before, hadn't even entertained the idea, really. But I had wanted to kiss Ruby Peters. It had been the most wonderful feeling. And I felt that way again, now, staring at her.

"Did you really mean what you said?" Ruby finally asked me,

breaking me from the thoughts that had me distracted from her momentarily. "Did you miss me?"

"I miss you constantly," I admitted, without hesitation. Hoping that Ruby and Mason's efforts had in fact been true, because that simple admittance was threatening everything. "You're always on my mind. Not because of research, not because you're my colleague..." I trailed off.

"I understand," Ruby replied, a soft smile on her lips.

"This is complicated, Ruby," I replied to her, my facial expression somewhat serious. "This. Us. Whatever this is. It threatens our livelihood. And with Michael working with us now... I feel like I can't risk it, as much as I want to. I desperately want to."

"He could take it away from you," Ruby said, understanding. "I know. I don't want that either," she admitted. "I wouldn't put you in jeopardy like that, ever. I promise."

I wondered then, if she and I were coming to the same, impossible conclusion. That this thing between us, these feelings we had, we couldn't. Not with so much riding on the line. Instead, when Ruby continued speaking, she surprised me. "So, we lay low then," she replied, simply. "We're colleagues, for now. For the time being. And maybe, when I come home—"

"Six months from now..." I said, the number agonizing to hear aloud.

"Six months from now," Ruby repeated, and I could tell by her facial expression that it pained her just as badly. "Maybe this can be more. We can be more."

And with every fiber of my being, I desperately hoped so.

THE NEXT MORNING, I was tucked away in my office at Johnson Space Center before the sun had even risen. I worked at my desk with just a small lamp on, illuminating my workspace, and the soft glow of my computer monitors. Everything was blissfully quiet.

There were a few wanderers up and down the halls, but over in the research facility, most of the staff wouldn't be in for an hour or two more.

Surprisingly, for one of the first times since I'd arrived back from my mission to the ISS, I found that I was able to focus. Perhaps it had been the lack of commotion from a busy building, or the hopeful conversation that Ruby and I had the previous evening, or our plans tonight. My mind felt calm, my body relaxed, which was exactly what I had needed in order to tackle the extraordinary amount of work required of me with my two projects I was overseeing.

Just as the sky was lightening, in beautiful shades of purple and pinks, there was a knock at my door. I glanced upward, intending to invite whoever was on the opposite side of my door inside, but I didn't have a chance to. The door swung abruptly open. The moment I saw Michael standing there, I felt the calmness that my entire body had felt dissipate within a matter of seconds, my heart beginning to pound in my chest, my jaw clenching.

"I thought I saw a light on in here," Michael flashed me his signature smile. Why he was trying to keep up appearances when it was just the two of us, I had no idea. I wouldn't be fooled by his attempt at kindness, no matter if it had been even slightly genuine at all. He made his way into the room, closing the door gently behind him. I thought briefly to demand that he keep it open, but found I said nothing.

He walked over to my desk, sitting down two white paper coffee cups, with black lids. The strong smell of stout black coffee filled my nostrils and made the sickening feeling in my stomach that much worse. Once he'd set the drinks down, Michael drug the other chair in my office from the opposite side of my desk to the side I'd been sitting on, in front of the computer.

"I don't suppose you've started sifting through all the results from your in-person studies for the lumbar research, and the troponin activator drug trial?" I glanced toward Michael then, watching as he drew the coffee cup to his lips, took a long drink, and then sat it back on the desk. "I brought you an Earl Grey tea. It's still your drink of choice, right? Didn't turn into a coffee drinker on me after all these years?"

While in any normal circumstance I might have found it impressive and somewhat flattering that someone would have remembered my drink preferences after two decades, I couldn't help but question if every single word that came out of my ex-husband's mouth was disingenuous. Even still, I did my best to muster up the smallest of gracious smiles.

"It is," I replied, nodding. And then somehow, I managed to add a thank you.

"Of course, Daph," Michael replied, still smiling that smile of his. To most, that smile was one of the things he was remembered for. He did have a very nice, very charismatic smile, I would give him that much. But for those who knew him well enough, they might not have found it quite so endearing. I certainly didn't. Not anymore.

Michael focused his attention on what I'd been working on at my computer. It was obvious that he'd been right, a lot of the data from the lumbar studies on the astronauts was open. At that very moment, I'd been going over the data I'd collected on Ruby Peters, specifically the MRI scans and the notes and work related to them.

When I realized what I had up on my computer, I felt a small sense of dread overcome me. The scans open on the computer were very apparent of the intervertebral disc shifts that I'd tried to underplay to Ruby while I'd been aboard. The startling findings with her were concerning to say the least, and I still hadn't decided how I would discuss the topic with our superiors, and to Ruby herself. I hadn't had the heart to worry her about the possibility of it putting her into early retirement, until I absolutely had to.

Which meant I had intended to lay low and evaluate all my options before I acted. The idea that Michael had access to this information now plummeted me into a well of panic, the likes of which I hadn't experienced in a long time. Thoughts rapid fired in my mind. Perhaps trying to close out of the tabs I had open on my computer.

Distract him with something, *anything* else that didn't have to do with Ruby.

Instead, I just froze, watching Michael's brown eyes, which were dull and lifeless comparatively to the dazzling warmth of Ruby's. He'd grown rather focused, leaning forward in his chair, looking over the scans I had open, which were the very last ones I had taken before I had returned home to Earth.

"These are Commander Peters?" Michael asked, using a finger to shove his sliding round glasses back up his nose. He looked at me briefly, and as much as I hadn't wanted to, I nodded. It was futile to even attempt distracting him now. He'd woven his way in, with these few bits of information. Like a dangerous parasite, invading everything I'd worked for. And now, he not only threatened me, but Ruby's life and career as well.

Michael took control of my computer mouse without even so much as a single word asking for permission to do so. I shouldn't have been even remotely surprised, but still I found myself having to bite my tongue. There were other, more pressing things to be concerned with now outside of Michael's incessant need to be in control. I watched him, clicking through screens, opening every single file on Ruby I had since I'd arrived back. Studying over every MRI scan, all the clinical notes I'd written. My heart, which had not slowed since Michael had invaded my office, was a frantic mess inside my chest.

"This doesn't look good for Ruby at all," Michael clicked his tongue and I watched him scratch at his chin momentarily, deep in thought. "I'm surprised you didn't think this more urgent to emphasize to her superiors at Kennedy, Daph. Truthfully, she should have been on that shuttle coming home with you, not staying another six months in that station. Look at these results. And no spinal pain? If there was this much shifting in this last trip for her to the ISS, I don't see how she's going to come back home and not have massive pain now. This could potentially cripple her. How you thought this ethical as a physician, I have no idea."

As much as I hated my ex-husband, for so many reasons it

became hard to count at times, he wasn't wrong in what he was saying. It was concerning, to say the least, and I had been dreading approaching the topic with both my superiors and Ruby's. Yes, the impacts on her spine may very well be crippling, but it too would be absolutely crippling to her career as well. It had been my intention to stall as much as possible, hoping for an alternative way to resolve the issue, without threatening to end Ruby's career entirely, and her dreams of breaking records. I knew, with the career and ambitions that I had, how much hers meant to her. We were one in the same, in that regard.

I had come up with some semblance of a plan, but it was still brewing. The thought to pitch it to anyone else hadn't been on my mind yet. There were still kinks, and a moderate probability of it failing entirely. But I had kept a sliver a hope.

And before I knew it, I found myself explaining it to Michael. Mostly to dampen the severity of the situation and to provide some sort of solution, or at least a distraction. "I was aware of the gravity of the situation, Michael," I replied, finding it strange that I'd called him by his first name. It felt bitter on my tongue, reminding me of the time I'd tried an unripe persimmon off a tree when I'd been young, and it had made my mouth fuzzy and uncomfortable. Nothing like the way it had felt speaking Ruby's name aloud. "However, I think I might have come up with a solution for the issue that you might be interested in..."

Michael had turned his focus on me then, seeming genuinely curious. "Really?"

"I've contacted Cytokinetics and the FDA about acquiring an emergency waiver to utilize the troponin activator drug for Ruby," I explained, calmly. Cytokinetics was the company that made Reldesemtiv, the drug, and the FDA was overseeing the drug trial, and would ultimately have the final say in its use. "It's been done from time to time for various reasons, and I feel, given the severity of the situation, it might be an advisable approach. The results from the studies on the research specimen at the station were very promising."

It looked as though Michael had become intrigued by the idea, and I watched him ponder for a few moments. When he focused on me again, there was a curious expression on his face that gave me a very uncomfortable lurch in my stomach. "You really must like the woman for you to have let all of these findings slide, Daph." His words were terrifying threats to my already violently beating heart. I felt my hands becoming clammy, and the overwhelming urge to flee the room without another word.

Then he finished his thought. "That is a very promising idea, however. No word from the FDA yet, I presume?" I shook my head, and Michael nodded. "I'd like to be involved with this correspondence from here on out. We're a team now, Daph. It's important you realize this." My emotions were all over the place. Relieved for his open-mindedness of my plan, dread at the possibility that he had any inkling of the relationship between Ruby and myself, and a nearly impossible to ignore urge to punch the man in the face for even remotely suggesting that we were a team.

Unfortunately, I lost the battle with my attempt to stay quiet over his last few words. "Dr. Riddler," I said, trying to keep my voice calm. "Let me make myself *very* clear. There is no universe in which I will ever consider you a colleague of mine ever again. You may have every other sexist member of this research staff blinded by your..." I tried to find the word but found I couldn't. "Well, *you*," I said, finding my eyes narrowing at him. "But that will never be the case with us, no matter how deeply you try to twist yourself into my work. I may have given up and left with my tail between my legs in San Diego, but I promise you, I will be relentless now."

Michael seemed genuinely surprised by my words, and I watched him shift in the chair he'd been sitting in, so his entire body had turned toward me. The strange look on his face, which still held his very convincing allure of patience and kindness but was also laced with hints of malice and threat toward me.

"Twenty years later and you're still stewing over some misunderstanding," Michael shook his head, like he was disappointed in me for having any emotions at all. It was astounding, to the point I felt as though I was starting to ignite into flames right there at my desk. "Really, Daphne, it's doing you no good. You're just taking years off your life about something that's so far in the past now, it's irrelevant. Look at your life. The career you made for yourself—"

"No thanks to you," I cut him off, finally unable to hold my tongue. "And for you to even begin to gaslight me about my feelings about that situation speaks volumes about your integrity. You may fool a lot of people with your bullshit, Michael, but not me. Ever again."

I'd hit a nerve; I could see it on his face. We'd been together long enough, even if it had been decades ago now, I still recognized those subtle body expressions he made. Michael got up from his seat, snatching his coffee and towering over me. Clearly trying to appear as threatening as he possibly could in this situation, however futile of an attempt it might have been. His eyes narrowed, lips drawing in a very thin line.

We were locked in a stare down for what felt like an eternity, and then he finally spoke. "Regardless of what you might think of me, Dr. Carter," Michael began, and the fact that he'd used my work title on me for the first time since we'd been in contact with one another again had a surprising effect on me. It sent a chill down my spine. There was no façade of pleasantries any longer. He was serious and threatening and real. "I'm involved with this research for the foreseeable future. And, if I might quote Dr. Hale, it would behoove you to start singing a more cooperative tune about this, or else, you might find yourself in a very similar position as you were in at UC San Diego. I would truly hate for that to become the case."

My insides were screaming. I fought every urge to become violent in those moments. I wasn't a violent person, and even in my attempts to be focused and rigid regarding my work life, I very rarely found myself even a *mean* person. But Michael Riddler was drawing it out of me, buried deep, and making it look obscenely easy.

I'd opened my mouth to speak, watching him as he weaved his

way around the desk after he'd spoke and made his way to the door. There were no words I wanted to say. Nothing that would even matter if I did. He'd gotten so far as to open the door, before he turned toward me a final time, and offered another smile. This time it was forced, not even an attempt to be pleasant with me or make peace. It was a threatening smile that screamed all the ways he intended to ruin me yet again.

"I expect to be involved with every detail from here on out, Daphne," Michael said, not even a hint of leniency in his tone or body language. "Or else you may find yourself in a very difficult situation, or worse, impact your newfound friend on the ISS." The way he said it twisted my insides so hard, I thought I might vomit. My mind was racing at the idea that he had any inclination about her and me. That he was on to us more than he was leading me to believe.

But I wouldn't even attempt to try and find that out. Not now, not with him like this. I nodded, feeling sickly obedient in those moments, but also like I had no other option. Once I had, Michael stepped out the door. "Have a good morning."

The moment he'd left, I snatched the untouched and tainted tea from my desk and watched as I made it crash into my empty trash bin. While it certainly wasn't as satisfying as the punch that I'd wanted to give Michael's face since he'd arrived, it helped a little.

WHEN I ARRIVED BACK at my condo for the weekend, it was the very first time in as long as I could remember that I was *glad* I didn't have to be at work. After the terrible morning that I'd endured, the day seemed to be agonizingly long. Briefly, I'd dabbled on the idea to cancel my plans with Ruby that evening but found that no matter how many times I tried to rationalize that it might be for the best, I couldn't. Honestly, it was what I needed in those moments.

I'd even arrived a little earlier than normal. There were things to be done, and I only had a short window to do them. The first being, to set up my unused living room and couch in an orderly fashion.

During the week, I had a new television delivered. The first one I'd ever owned since moving into the condo. I situated it on a brand-new television stand. I'd done my research to find the appropriate streaming service for the movie that Ruby had wanted to watch later. I'd even bought an oversized soft blanket for my couch, which hadn't been sat on but a handful of times since I'd bought it years and years ago.

Before I settled down, I fetched a "movie snack" that Ruby had insisted upon. I'd finished off the banana bread earlier in the week, but I'd been told that it was "tradition" to have a snack when you watched movies, so I humored her. Chocolate covered pretzels. I'd never tried them before, but Ruby had told me that they were delicious, so I'd bought some. Nearly the exact moment I'd settled onto the couch, my personal phone rang on my side table. Sure enough, Ruby was calling.

"Are you ready?" she asked when I'd answered, not skipping a beat. "Got your pretzels?"

"Yes, on both accounts," I replied, holding up the pretzels to show her, before I opened them. I put the phone on speaker. The phone beeped at me just as I had, and I realized she'd attempted to connect me to video chat. "I thought we were talking on the phone?"

"I want to see your reaction to things," Ruby explained, and I raised a curious brow at her. She smiled at me, shaking her head. "Just do it. Please."

"Fine," I replied, accepting the video call. Admittedly, it was nice to see her. She was nestled in her sleeping quarters, bundled in the strange sleeping bag, and staring back at me. Admittedly, she was unbelievably adorable to look at, and I found myself momentarily distracted by her, but I wouldn't speak those words aloud. Not when we weren't sure who was watching us. When I'd managed to focus again, I glanced at my television, the movie paused at the beginning. "Are you ready?"

Ruby nodded. "Play on three... One, two, three... go!" Ruby announced, and then I hit play on the remote. "I can't remember what year this movie was made."

"1985," I replied, having seen it earlier when I'd done my research.

Ruby looked rather pleased that I'd known this fact. "I wasn't even born yet." The very brief mention of her age made me realize what a difference it was between us. Yet even still, it hadn't felt like it mattered much. We'd bonded so fiercely on so many things, it felt like just a number to me.

"That's a lot of clocks," I noted, as the opening credits played.

"My mom likes to collect clocks," Ruby said, and I glanced at her briefly on the video chat. She was busy watching the movie on her end, eyes slightly diverted away from the camera. My eyes lingered on her, admiring her soft smile and intense gaze on the screen. Her brown eyes were so beautiful... "The ticking used to drive me crazy."

I remembered that detail about her mother, when I'd visited their home in St. Luce. There had been a lot of clocks. "I noticed," I replied, and Ruby glanced at me briefly, a strange look on her face.

"I guess the guys at Mission Control are getting to listen to the movie with us. I know there's a handful that really like this movie, Mason included. I've heard him with a few Marty McFly quotes before..."

Her comment made me realize why she'd been staring at me so oddly. I'd very nearly said what I'd been doing in St. Luce the previous week, with her parents. A fact that no one knew about, and most certainly couldn't know. I was gracious for the reminder. "I didn't realize Mason liked this movie," I admitted, staying on topic with Ruby. She nodded, and it seemed as though she was grateful. I'd gotten the hint.

For a while after that, we just watched the movie. Perhaps the fact that we weren't alone had dampened the mood a bit, but we both made the best of it. "Ah, so this is why the DeLorean is so popular," I realized, a little later into the movie. "I always wondered why there was such a craze with it. I thought it was just a car fanatic thing."

Ruby was smiling again when I looked at her. "You didn't know about the DeLorean?" I shook my head. "Oh, Daphne. We're going to have to break you in, then."

"We could do this every Friday," I suggested, rather fond of the idea of spending time with her outside of work, at any capacity. And even if I was going to be watching a movie with who knows how many others, I still wouldn't have minded if I also got to watch it with Ruby. "The pretzels were good, by the way." I'd eaten nearly half of them, which was quite surprising.

"I know," Ruby replied. "I could tell by the way you looked when you were eating them." She'd been watching me eat? "You get this cute blissful look in your eyes, and they close for just a few seconds while you're chewing." I could feel a little burning in my cheeks and tried to fight it off. "It's endearing really." There were a few moments of silence, in which we both seemed to realize we'd gone more off track than we should have about things.

Ruby finally replied to me. "I'd love to watch some movies on Fridays."

We settled it then, without taking things any further. As much as I'd wanted to inquire more about her watching me eat. Or to tell her how difficult it had been to watch the movie at points, for being so distracted with her on the other end of the call. Or how I'd wished we'd been together, her beside me on this couch...

Ruby's gaze softened on me, for just a moment. Mine did too, in return. Both of us smiled and then Ruby's attention turned back toward the movie without a second thought. "Pay attention, you don't want to miss the end." We watched the last few minutes in silence, and I did my best to just watch the movie then and not focus on her, as much as I wanted to. When the credits began to roll, I finally picked up my phone and turned my attention to her again.

"Did you like it?" Ruby asked, those brown eyes flickering with the light of the ending credits across from her in the sleeping quarters. "It seemed like you did."

"I did," I replied, smiling. "And I didn't mind the company, either." It was an innocent enough thing to say, but I hoped she'd understood how deeply I'd meant it. I leaned back into the couch, still snuggled underneath the soft blanket I'd bought myself. "What are you going to do now?"

"I think I'll read for a little bit, before I go to bed. Maybe work on a crossword..." Ruby said, thoughtfully.

"I do miss doing the crossword," I replied, remembering that time with us together, fondly. It had been one of many things I'd enjoyed up on the station. "It was more entertaining than I expected it to be."

Ruby's eyes lit up then, and I watched her hold a finger up to me. "Hang on just a second, will you? You gave me an idea." I had no earthly idea what she was up to, but I nodded. And then I watched her as she went clicking through screens on her computer, her attention focused elsewhere.

A minute later, my phone rang with an email message to my personal account. When I checked, I noticed an invitation to an online crossword puzzle site. While I was looking over it, Ruby spoke again. "I thought maybe we could do them together. I forgot that these shared ones even existed, to be honest. Not until you said that."

I smiled, clicking through the site to sign up for it, while I had her on the video chat still. "I'm signing up now. Thanks." By the time I'd finished speaking, I'd returned to the video chat. Ruby was busy clicking away at the computer again. A few seconds later, she turned to look at me again, and smiled.

"I'll let you go then," I decided, feeling myself getting rather tired, and suddenly feeling like we were doing too much with too many eyes on us. "Thanks for the invite to the site."

Ruby nodded. "It's your turn," she replied. And then the video chat disconnected.

When I found myself tucked away in bed a few minutes later, I pulled up the crossword puzzle, studying over the different clues until I'd found one that I knew the answer to. I filled it in. S-*i-e-n-n-a*. Once I had, I noticed an alert on the page. A message, in a small chat box beside the game.

What are you doing now? I didn't ask. Ruby had written. I wondered for a moment if I should even reply with anything at all, still fearing that someone might be watching us, even with something as innocent as this.

I made this private, just us. Mason may have helped me again. Ruby answered me without knowing what I was thinking. The small message made me smile and let out a small sigh of relief. *We can talk freely at least, without worrying if someone will see.*

I'm lying in bed. I replied, and as soon as I'd sent the message, Ruby had filled in another answer on the crossword. It was my turn again. I sat pondering over the clues, trying to pick one that I knew, but before I could decide Ruby had said something again.

You took me to bed with you. I could almost hear her saying the words aloud, and they made me laugh into the room. Another belly laugh that rarely happened and filled me with warmth. I smiled and returned my focus back to the clues so I could fill in another answer. Once I had, I returned to the chat box. She'd typed another message to me. *I used to watch you sleep. For being so high strung, you sleep like a baby.*

I was still smiling, reading her words. I replied. *I've been told that before. It was very strange, sleeping while floating. I don't think I could get used to it. I'm not sure how you do.*

Ruby had sent another answer. I looked at it, and then the clues again. Seconds later, she replied to me. *I miss sleeping in a real bed. I was envious when I saw your bed earlier. It looked so cozy.*

For a few moments, I studied her words. Without thinking, I typed back and sent it. *I wish you were lying here with me.* It felt strange to admit, when I first read it back to myself, but I hadn't regretted saying it. It was meant more innocently than anything, just to be in her physical presence again was all I wanted. Though admittedly, the idea of her lying in my bed gave me a pleasant stirring in places I hadn't expected it to.

I would love to watch you sleep again. Ruby replied to me, while I was busy filling in another answer.

Maybe one day. I typed back.

And I waited for a few minutes, to see if she'd say anything more. But nothing came, and before long I found myself drifting. Imagining the sound of Ruby's voice beside me in my bed, talking to me. Letting her follow me into my dreams.

FIFTEEN

RUBY

"Okay, we're rolling," Daniel said, after he'd adjusted the video camera he was holding, panning it over to James, Andrea, Tony, and me across Node 2 from him. He gave us a nod, and I adjusted myself on the metallic blue railing I was holding onto, so I had a good view of the camera. The rest seemed to be waiting on me.

"Greetings from the International Space Station," I said, giving the camera a bit of a wave. I'd been filmed so many times since I'd first started coming up to the station, that this was nothing to me anymore. To James, who was a bit more introverted than me, it probably was a bigger deal. So, I didn't mind talking. "We're live right now and presently above Beijing, China. Is that right?" I looked over at Daniel, who was holding the camera in my direction.

"That's right, Commander. Just flew over a few minutes ago, actually."

I smiled, looking back at the camera. "We don't stay put long. For those of you who don't know, the space station travels at about 5 miles per second. We make about sixteen trips around the Earth every twenty-four hours. Give us an hour and a half and we'll be back over China." I paused for a second, looking at James, who nodded at me.

Then I looked back at the camera. "My name is Commander Ruby Peters, and my colleagues here with me are Commander James Mertz, Andrea Bratcher, and Tony Reynolds. And filming with the camera, we have Daniel Richards." I watched Daniel turn the camera around to offer a smile beneath his bushy mustache, and then he returned it back on me.

"We tend to do tours of the space station about once a month, but we've been busy, so we haven't in a while. The crew and I thought you were overdue to see what has been happening aboard. So, let's get started, shall we? Follow me over to the US research laboratory, Destiny, and I'll give you a little presentation about the projects I've been assisting on."

The group of us made the small turn into the module. The rest stayed behind a bit, while I headed over to the familiar back corner of the room, where Daphne's rats were housed and where I'd been working every day for a while now. I paused in front of the computer station, and then turned back. Daniel had kept pace with me, floating near the wall, a few feet away.

"As you're aware, we recently had a civilian guest, Dr. Daphne Carter, aboard the station. The NASA employee was here to engage in some very important research. Now that she's returned to Earth, both Daniel and I have been maintaining her projects aboard the station, in collaboration with her back on Earth."

"I believe we have Dr. Carter on our feed now, Commander," Daniel said, nodding to the computer I was standing next to. It was already logged in and had the web link up for the conference call that our camera was feeding into. I clicked through a few screens and pulled it up. Sure enough, there was Daphne on the other end. And much to my unwelcomed surprise, Dr. Michael Riddler beside her.

There was an uncomfortable lurch in my stomach seeing him there. He and I had spoken on a few occasions now, since he'd joined the research team. Mostly just pleasantries and small talk. As much as Daphne didn't like him, I didn't either, and it wasn't just because I was biased. He seemed to have a bit of an ego about him that didn't sit right with me.

"Dr. Carter, Dr. Riddler, you're on live," Daniel said, standing next to the computer station where I was at. When I paid attention to the screen, Daphne's eyes were straight ahead, looking into the camera or the computer or whatever it was they were situated in front of. I wonder if she could see me on her end or not.

"Greetings from Earth," Michael spoke before the rest of them, giving a wave. "Thanks for having us on to talk about our research." *Daphne's research*, I thought bitterly, staring at him. "We're glad to be able to clue everyone in a bit about what we've been working on."

I managed a nod. "We're looking forward to it. Thank you Dr. Riddler." My attention turned to Daphne then, and then to the camera. "Dr. Carter was aboard the space station for a few weeks to conduct research with us. She worked with me on two different projects. Her spinal research, which studies the effects of long-term spaceflight on the lumbar spine paraspinal muscle and the intervertebral discs. The other project was a drug trial for a troponin activator drug, used to help reverse the adverse effects from spaceflight on astronauts' spines." When I'd finished, I glanced at Daphne, who looked rather impressed.

I waved for Daniel to pan around me to the compartments where the research rats were held, and he did what I asked and filmed it for a few seconds while I spoke. "Behind me are the ten rats that we've been using for Daphne's drug trial." I realized, a second after I'd said it, that I had spoken her first name instead of her professional title, but I tried my best to ignore it and move on. "Dr. Carter and I measure vitals and other important data daily. Our hope is to keep track of them over an extended period, to be able to measure the long-term effects of the drug. We had very promising results over the course of her visit."

Daphne looked as though she was about to open her mouth to speak, but Michael beat her to the punch. "Ruby is correct. We've been gathering a lot of exciting data that we're looking forward to sharing with you. The goal of our research is to hopefully find ways to make space travel less negatively impactful on our astronauts. This will be helpful for longer missions, to Mars, for example. It's exciting times at the Biomedical Research Institute, and NASA."

I stared at Michael until he'd finished speaking. *Our* research. He'd spoken like he'd been involved with this project for a long time. The audacity he had to just speak over Daphne like he was, was astounding. I could tell by Daphne's body language that she was seconds from turning and punching the man in the face, but she was showing amazing self-restraint.

"Daphne should tell us a little bit about her experience up on the ISS. I don't think she's had an opportunity to speak at length about it, and I'm sure the viewers are curious." I found a small window where Michael had paused and decided to take it.

There was a moment where Daphne was trying to keep up with what I'd been saying, perhaps it was a short delay in the audio feed back to Earth, but then she nodded, and I could tell by her facial expression that she was gracious for the opportunity to get Michael to shut the hell up. She spent a few minutes explaining about her time on the space station and the variety of things we'd done together when she'd been here.

Listening to her made me miss her terribly. There were still several months before I'd have a chance to see her. And even then, our relationship seemed next to impossible given our present circumstances. Our present circumstances being the man who blatantly interrupted Daphne before she'd finished, yet again.

"I don't suppose Ruby knows about the exciting news we just received?" Michael's attention focused on the camera again, while Daphne looked completely dazed beside him. "In fact, I'm not sure that even Daphne knows about this yet." Both Daphne and I were staring at him blankly, neither of with any idea of what was in store.

Michael looked as though he was clicking through something on the computer, they'd both been sitting in front of. There were a few moments of silence, in which I watched Daphne's facial expression go from annoyance to near horror. Whatever Michael had up his sleeve had been something she'd been entirely unaware of, it seemed.

"I don't suppose Daphne shared with you the MRI data she collected from you while onboard the ISS?" It took me a moment to realize that Michael had been speaking to me, and when my attention landed on him again, he'd also been looking at the computer screen, presumably at me. "She had some rather interesting findings." Daphne couldn't have looked more uncomfortable if she tried, and the sight of her squirming in her chair miserably was giving me the worst feeling imaginable.

I managed to formulate words, despite my concerns. "I'm afraid I didn't get to see any of the MRI data that Daphne had gathered while she was here, Dr. Riddler. That project was mostly left up to her, she was here doing an in-person study, and we all did our best to accommodate her as best we could."

"I'm sure you did," Dr. Riddler nodded. A second later, he and Daphne had disappeared from the screen, and an MRI scan appeared, visible to all of us on the station, and to everyone who had been watching. While I had no experience with reading MRI's and only a very limited biology background, I still had an inkling of an idea what I was looking at.

Michael wasted no time to clarify my assumptions. "This is the first MRI scan Dr. Carter took of Commander Peters after she arrived on the station. One of the reasons for the spinal research we are conducting, is because commonly, there is significant impact on astronauts post long-duration spaceflights, lasting longer than a few months. For those of you watching who may not know, over half of astronauts on these extended missions report significant back pain upon their return to Earth and to the effects of gravity. This is largely due to a phenomenon that seems to occur with long-term exposure to microgravity environments, in which the intervertebral disk height changes, quite dramatically. In many cases, we see astronauts return to Earth having grown a few inches taller as a result."

I'd been listening to Michael speak, not focused on the MRI, but after he'd said the last little bit, I was studying it over again. While I had absolutely no understanding of medical science or any inclination of how to read an MRI, there was something obviously strange about what I was looking at on my scans.

Michael interrupted my thoughts. "Now, Ruby, it's my understanding that you have, surprisingly, after what will be a year and a half total aboard the ISS in just a few short months, never experienced any significant shift in your disks or spinal structure, nor experienced any post-spaceflight back pains, correct?"

Even though I couldn't see Michael now, still looking at the scans on my screen, I nodded regardless. "That's true. Several of the physicians and therapists who work with the astronaut program had even mentioned to me how unusual it was."

"Practically unheard of," Michael agreed with me. "Interestingly enough, your present trip to the ISS has impacted your spine substantially, as clearly evident by these scans." Michael took a few moments, using a digital pen to draw over the scan and explain what was happening. While I wanted to be invested in what he was saying, considering it had to do with me specifically, I found myself drifting from the presentation and the room entirely. My ears were ringing, drowning out the sounds of Michael's voice, which was jarring to begin with.

All I could think about was the idea that Daphne had seen these results, which by Michael's explanation were significant and probably life-altering, and yet had neglected to say anything to me about it. She'd been with me for weeks, took MRI scans several times during her visit, and yet she hadn't once shown any ounce of outward concern. I had no idea what to think about it. Couldn't put a finger on the emotions I was feeling.

I didn't have an idea how long I'd been hovering in front of the computer, lost in my own head, when Michael brought me back to the room and reality. "However, despite these somewhat discerning findings of Daphne's, I do have some rather exciting news that I'm quite sure even she isn't aware of yet."

The MRI scans disappeared from the screen, and once again Michael and Daphne were there. Daphne's intense hazel eyes were laser focused on her ex-husband. "While Dr. Carter's findings were rather concerning initially, with the outstanding results of the drug trial we'd been conducting on the ISS, we decided to approach the drug company and the FDA about pushing through an emergency waiver to utilize the drug with Ruby, if she would be willing. I'm pleased to say the waiver was approved just a few minutes prior to this video conference. Which is tremendously exciting, and I hope welcome news to you, Commander Peters. We all know how passionate you are about your time in space and at the station, and your aspirations to beat records. Our hope is that we can still make that possible for you."

It was in those last moments, when Dr. Riddler had spoken about my career aspirations, my passion for my work, and my dreams about breaking records, that I'd seen through his ruse. Understood, without any doubts, what had happened with Daphne. While I'd been a mix of emotions learning that she'd withheld information from me, it was abundantly clear why she had.

The information would have been catastrophic to my career. If Daphne had reported her findings to her superiors, to my own, I would have been on *Galileo* and back on Earth right now. My career would likely have been over.

Daphne had gone to great lengths to protect one of the things I valued most in my life. And she'd put her lengthy and prestigious career on the line to do it. If she'd said anything to me at all, as devastating as it would have been, I would have likely said something, and I would have dug my own grave. Daphne had not only done her best to protect me and my career, but she'd also gone out of her way to ensure that I hadn't been the one to tear it all apart. She'd taken an extraordinary risk.

My eyes landed on her on the computer screen. She was looking back, and I knew she'd been looking at me. The expression on her face, the way those hazel eyes read in those moments, further confirmed my suspicions. She looked a mix of so many things, from surprised, to shameful, to anxious, to relieved. And I knew that she was trying to read me. Somehow, she was desperately trying to get me to understand her.

So, I did my best to let her know I had. "Dr. Carter has worked incredibly hard on the drug trial. I've seen firsthand the dedication she has for her work, and it has shown through the results that she's had so far." I was careful not to credit Michael in any way for Daphne's doings. "While I'm surprised to learn about the findings of her studies while on board, I trust that she had a plan in motion from the start. Dr. Carter is very good on her feet, as evident by her continued victories over her extraordinary career. And I would be honored to utilize the troponin activator drug to further her very successful trial, in hopes that it will not only benefit me, but future astronauts as well."

Daphne cleared her throat, sitting straighter in her chair. She looked at the camera, offering the smallest of gracious smiles. Before Michael had a chance to speak again, she took the opportunity to. "I appreciate the vote of confidence, Commander Peters. I truly hope that the decision to push the drug through for you proves beneficial for you."

"For all of us," Michael pipped in, and I felt an angry lurch in my stomach.

A FEW MINUTES LATER, the video presentation ended. Daniel was putting away the camera he'd used to record on, while James was busy uploading the video to the NASA database in Houston, who would publish it to the website in a few hours. Andrea and Tony had resumed their work at computer stations in the node we were in.

"That Dr. Riddler sure likes to talk," James said, clicking away at the keys at the computer station. I was working beside him at an adjacent station, my mind thousands of miles away back on Earth, thinking of Daphne. "Dr. Carter came up here and did all that work, and he somehow managed to do all the speaking..."

I was surprised that he'd noticed this, thinking I'd been the only one. Then Daniel surprised me too. "Figures Dr. Hale would pass off the project to someone else. Rumor has it that he's been trying to get Dr. Carter to step down and retire to a different project for years now. I'm surprised he even let her come up here in the first place."

That was something I hadn't known. Who had been keeping tabs on Daphne? "Why does he want her to retire? She's been on this project for nearly two decades. You'd think he'd want an expert." I stared at Daniel, baffled. "And it's not like Dr. Riddler is that much younger than Dap— Dr. Carter." I caught myself, swallowing deeply.

"Dr. Hale's always been a little—-er..." Daniel scratched his chin and looked toward Andrea and Tony then, who had stayed with us, the three exchanging looks.

"Sexist?" Andrea and I said at nearly the same time.

Daniel shrugged. "You said it, not me."

"You know the story about Dr. Riddler and Dr. Carter, right?" I asked them, and they all turned their focus on me, shaking their heads. "They used to be married, and research partners in college at UC San Diego." I could tell by their vacant expressions that they hadn't heard this information before. So, I spent a few minutes enlightening them on the story. When I finished, they both stared at me looking equally surprised.

"And Dr. Hale let him on the project anyway?" Tony looked at me, and then to Andrea and Daniel. "I guess it shouldn't surprise me *that* much, but if he has a history like that..."

"The whole story has been buried," I argued, feeling rather frustrated about the situation. "The university didn't do anything about it. I mean, Dr. Riddler's the head of the department now, for Pete's sake. They couldn't have cared less..."

"You're sure Dr. Carter isn't mistaken about some of the situation?" Tony asked, raising a brow. It was a simple question and an innocent one, but I'd taken it worse than I intended.

"She's not lying," I snapped, not really at Tony specifically but just into the room. "I would know if Daphne was lying about something, and she's certainly not lying about this. She's not a liar." Tony raised his hands up in apology, and I glanced at Daniel and then Andrea and Tony, then stared off behind them toward Node 2. In that moment, I'd also realized that I had let it slip, yet again, with Daphne's given name. "I'm going to go up to the cupola for a bit." And then I started propelling myself down the metallic blue railing without another word.

ABOVE ME, it was still daytime in North America, which we were in the process of passing over. I had watched it for a while, staring at Texas, thinking about Daphne, and trying desperately to shove Michael as far from my mind as possible. I hoped that she had relaxed about the situation once I'd agreed to utilizing the drug. While I still hadn't completely recovered from the news about my spine, I certainly felt better than I did. And I hoped with every fiber of my being, that the drug would help reverse the damage to my spine.

Eventually, I turned my attention to my computer that I'd been sitting in front of. I hadn't even logged in yet, my mind too busy and filled with all sorts of thoughts. I clicked through screens to get to my emails and shuffled through the dozen or so I'd gotten since I'd last checked.

Once I'd finished, I was planning to work on some projects related to the ISS for a bit to distract myself. Before I'd gone to open other programs on the computer, I went to the web browser and then to the crossword puzzle site that Daphne and I had been using to play our games. When our latest crossword pulled up on the screen, I noticed Daphne had taken a turn. I scanned the remaining clues and open spaces, figuring out an answer rather quickly.

As I was filling in the word *f-o-r-t-i-f-i-c-a-t-i-o-n*, there was a ding from the computer. I realized then, that there was a new message in the crossword puzzle chat. I submitted my answer, pleased that I had guessed right, and then pulled up the chat.

Please forgive me.

I stared at her words for a long time, unsure of what to say. While the presentation had been happening, and when I had realized what she'd done, I felt a sense of relief. Even still, I was terrified about the news of my MRIs regardless. If the drug didn't work, it was the end of my career. Not to mention the fact that I was certain everyone on Daphne's research team, at the Biomedical Research Institute, and at NASA, knew about Daphne breaking protocol.

I do, Daphne. I know why you did it. I finally replied, sending the message as soon as I'd finished typing. Then I stared at the computer screen again, watching as another answer was completed on the crossword by Daphne. While I waited for her to reply, I filled in another answer myself. We went back and forth with the puzzle for a few minutes, practically finishing it. I thought, briefly that she might not reply to me again at all.

Finally, I couldn't handle the silence. We were on our last two unanswered clues of a very large puzzle we'd chosen to do. Instead of taking my turn, I typed another message.

What if it doesn't work?

There was a long pause again, in which several more minutes passed. When I looked up at the Earth in the meantime, we were now passing over the Atlantic Ocean, South America, and Greenland, headed straight for Africa and Europe, which I could barely make out at the curve. I got lost in the view, thinking about the fact that I'd hardly traveled at all on Earth. There was so much I hadn't seen or done. What if the damage to my spine was irreversible? What if it not only took away my career, but left me unable to do other things I'd wanted to do with my life?

My mind was filling with all sorts of dread, when another noise from my computer brought me back to the cupola. It was ringing, the signal that I had an incoming video call. I thought it had been Daphne, but I was surprised that it was from Kennedy instead. Likely someone who might have been trying to reach any one of us on the ISS.

I answered, and Mason Evans' bearded face filled my screen. He looked relieved to see me and offered a gentle smile through all his facial hair. "Commander Peters, I was hoping you'd be the one I'd get a hold of."

"Everything alright, Mason?" I asked, feeling rather curious as to why he was calling, and why he had specifically been looking for me. "What can I help you with?"

"I worked some magic down here again and wanted to let you know that I intercepted this video call," he said, matter-of-factly. I still had no earthly idea what he was talking about, but I nodded regardless. Then he decided to clarify. "I'm going to connect you to Daph here in a second. She wanted to talk to you, but in private. I've got live feed from Destiny playing over the video feed right now, and I'll trash the conversation as soon as you are through."

What Daphne and I would have done without Mason's help these past weeks, I had absolutely no idea. I offered him a small, gracious smile, and a nod. "Thanks, Mason."

A few seconds later, Mason disappeared from my screen, and was replaced by a very distraught looking Daphne, who was sitting in her office. She had been focused on something else when we were connected, but quickly realized that we had and returned to the video call.

"Ruby—" Daphne said, as soon as she realized I was there.

"I'm okay, Daphne," I replied, trying my best to smile, even though I was truly feeling a whirlwind of emotions in that moment. "Like I said, I know why you did what you did."

"It was never my intention to blatantly keep this from you," she replied, her face softening a little. "I had this plan from the start and was only further convinced that it would work when I saw what success we were getting from the trial."

"I know," I replied, nodding. I wanted to say more, but Daphne didn't let me speak.

"I'm so sorry you found out this way," Daphne said, and I heard a slight crack in her voice. "We were waiting for the FDA to approve the waiver, and then I was going to tell you everything. I swear to you. I just needed everything to be set in place, for your sake."

"I don't understand why you would take such a clearly dangerous risk," I said, when she had taken a short break from apologizing to me. "Keeping that sort of information from your colleagues...I know you did it to protect me. I realized the minute Michael started talking about my career. Those were your words, not his." Daphne's face broke into a very soft smile. "But Daphne, I still don't get it. Why would you risk your career for me? These projects have been your entire life, for decades. I'm certainly not worth jeopardizing everything you've done."

Daphne shook her head when I'd finished my little speech. There was still a small smile on her face when she looked back at the camera, back at me on the screen. "I thought it would be obvious to you." I stared at her blankly. That had clearly not been the case. All I felt was a mixture of concern and frustration towards her, for making what felt like reckless choices. "Ruby, I care about you."

Her words sent a little flutter of warmth through my body. Even still, it hadn't felt like enough to justify her actions. "If you lose everything from this, I'd never forgive myself. I would never forgive you. You can't just make decisions like this and not tell me."

"I know," Daphne said, nodding at me. "I realize it was a very calculated risk. But I had the best intentions in doing it, Ruby. I swear to you. And now that the waiver has gotten approval, we can start the treatment regimen. Today, even."

"What if it doesn't work?" I asked her, feeling very bleak about the situation.

"It will work, Ruby," Daphne replied. "Please trust me."

I believed her, but the idea of losing everything, of her losing everything, was terrifying.

SIXTEEN
DAPHNE

Outside, I could hear the pattering of rain against my office window. It was a soothing sound, helping to mask the racing thoughts in my mind in those moments. I'd arrived early to Johnson Space Center the following morning, wanting to get a head start on preparations for Ruby to begin the troponin activator drug that day. Which meant organizing a slew of different things in rapid succession, including meeting with the NASA therapists who worked in conjunction with the astronauts, to restructure the exercise regimen aboard the ISS.

Dr. Timothy Harris, Director of Physical Therapy, and Dr. Mariah Stone, Director of Occupational Therapy, at NASA, were on video conference with myself and, much to my displeasure, Dr. Riddler. Harris and Stone were both at Kennedy, in Florida, where it was slightly later in the morning. Even still, I spotted coffee mugs on the desks in front of them. Unlike Texas, there were bright and sunny skies outside their windows.

Michael had brought me another Earl Grey tea, which I hadn't touched. Meanwhile, the atrocious stench of his black coffee was wafting through my office. I didn't have time to focus on it however, too engrossed in the conversation with my colleagues, and the fact that Michael had taken over the conversation, as usual.

"Thank you both for being so accommodating with these last-minute adjustments," Dr. Riddler said graciously, looking at Timothy and Mariah. "We're doing our best to get all our ducks in a row over here, and your help and patience is greatly appreciated." The other two nodded, and my ex-husband flashed them his signature smile, which made my insides twist.

"Dr. Carter," Dr. Stone was looking at me with her blue eyes, through her very purple framed glasses, her ash brown curly hair falling around her face. The curls reminded me of Ruby's and made me wonder what she must have looked like when her hair had grown out longer. I'd never imagined being so attracted to women with curly hair before, nevertheless a woman at all, but surprisingly I'd found Mariah very beautiful. Perhaps it had a lot to do with my affections for Ruby. "I was reading through your notes while you were aboard the ISS. Right now, the exercise program emphasizes maintenance of bone mineral density, aerobic/anaerobic capacity, and muscle strength/power, specifically those of the large muscles of the proximal hips and shoulders, and endurance."

"Yes," I replied, noticing that Michael had opened his mouth to speak beside me, but I'd beaten him to the punch. "Even preflight and postflight regimens don't focus enough on lower back strength, in my personal opinion..."

"I thought it was interesting you brought up the idea of incorporating yoga," Dr. Harris was the one to speak this time, clearly over whatever thought that Mariah had been formulating. Unlike Mariah, he had a very hard face, with sharp edges. His slicked back brown hair looked far less inviting to look at over his colleague's beautiful curls. "Specifically in addressing spaceflight associated lumbar stiffness and hypomobility."

It was Michael's turn to interrupt me, leaving Mariah and I staring at one other somewhat stunned. "Of course, yoga would be a more suitable option for preflight and postflight regimens. Which is why we have left it in your and Dr. Stone's capable hands to come up with some low load, lumbar core stabilization exercises, which we know are efficacious for back pain patients."

"Dr. Stone and I have been preparing a few additional exercises for their current program, and some specifically for Commander Peters to utilize during the course of her troponin activator drug treatment," Dr. Harris said.

"Dr. Carter's research seemed to indicate that adding certain types of yoga while on the ISS might actually be beneficial," Dr. Stone argued, still looking at me. "I thought her findings that she presented were rather promising. I don't see why we couldn't add a few poses to start with, to see if it had any effect."

"I'm unsure if you're aware, Dr. Stone, but Dr. Carter also neglected to inform her colleagues of the severity of Commander Peters' condition," my ex-husband said, his attention on Mariah then. "And while she may have gathered a substantial amount of very critical research onboard the ISS, we have a certain protocol here. Yoga is a bit of an—eccentric choice." Michael paused and glanced at me. I was staring at him head on then, so we made brief eye contact, and I gave a very solid effort to not glare. "For now, we'll stick with a more traditional method. Just to see how things go."

My attention turned back to the computer, just as Timothy spoke. "I think that's the better approach, Dr. Riddler, I wholeheartedly agree." Meanwhile, I could tell that Dr. Stone was trying her best to not look annoyed, just as I was. "So, we're decided then? I'll send up the finalized and updated exercise regimen to Commander Peters after this call."

"Excellent," Michael replied, nodding. "Thank you so much for your time, both of you. We look forward to speaking with you further in the upcoming days. I'm sure we'll be seeing a lot of each other."

The four of us exchanged pleasant farewells, and then I watched Michael take control of my computer to disconnect us from the call. He turned to look at me, that deceptively charming smile still plastered on his face. "I think that went rather well, don't you Daph?"

"If by well you mean that you and Dr. Harris blatantly ignoring your female colleagues' attempts at participating in the conversation, then yes, Dr. Riddler, it went well." I stared at him, dumbfounded and annoyed. "I don't see the harm in adding yoga to Ruby's routine." The slip of her name came without me even realizing it. "It's almost as if you're afraid something I suggest to you might actually be right. Or perhaps you're just waiting for the right opportunity to take credit for that too, I suppose."

Michael's eyes narrowed slightly at me. He hesitated for a few long moments, looking as though he was trying to formulate exactly what to say. "Drink your tea, Daphne. You don't want it to get cold, and we have a meeting to get to in a few minutes."

I'd almost forgotten about the meeting with Dr. Hale. Perhaps I'd been trying to push it as far away from my mind as possible. It was the first time I'd be speaking with him since word had come out yesterday about Ruby's MRI scans and my blatant attempts to minimalize the severity of the situation to my colleagues. The meeting was not going to be in my favor, I was certain of it, and I wanted desperately to have any reason to avoid it.

Instead of replying, I turned my attention to the tea on my desk. I snatched it up, removing the lid with my other hand and tossing it into the bin. When I looked at Michael again, making sure he was watching me, I nudged my garbage can out, so it was directly beneath me. Then I poured the tea out in one long drawn-out motion, watching my ex-husband stare stunned. Once I'd finished, I tossed the empty cup into the garbage behind it.

"I don't drink tea anymore," I replied, standing up from my desk. *At least not from crooked snakes of men*, I thought to myself but didn't speak, as much as I'd wanted to. I moved around him to the door, opening it and then glancing behind me. "We've got a meeting to get to," I replied, and then stepped outside without another word.

. . .

A SHORT WHILE LATER, Michael and I had arrived outside of Dr. Hale's office. We'd walked across the research building alone. I'd feared if I had to continue conversations with him for even a few seconds longer, I might have done something I'd regret. He hadn't been far behind me, however, and as soon as he arrived, he knocked. Dr. Hale's voice called out muffled, telling us to come inside.

My ex-husband opened the door and held it open for me. Of course, he'd done this on purpose. He must have known how uncomfortable and worried I was about what was about to happen and forcing me to enter first was just a way to get under my skin more. I didn't give him the satisfaction of knowing it had any effect on me, stepping inside and holding my head as high and confidently as I possibly could.

Across the room at his very luxurious looking wood desk, Dr. Hale had been working at his computer. He looked up the moment I'd entered, and his eyes had narrowed. The expression on his face, neutral, if not a little serious, was nothing unusual from him, so I couldn't get a read of what he was thinking. He motioned me to move into the room, and I heard Michael step in behind me, shutting the door.

"Dr. Carter, Dr. Riddler," Dr. Hale nodded at both of us and then nodded at the empty chairs on the opposite side of his desk. "Have a seat." As swiftly as I had thought I was moving, Michael seemed to move faster. He'd arrived just a second before me, pulling out a chair and looking to me. He'd meant it like some chivalrous gesture toward me, offering me a seat before him. As much as I didn't want to dignify it, I found myself sulking into the chair anyway.

"Good morning, Dr. Hale," Michael said, as he pulled out the other seat beside me and sat down. He was smiling again, and words could not explain how sick and tired I was getting of seeing it on his face. "I trust everything is going well."

"As well as we could expect it to be," Dr. Hale replied, clicking out of whatever he'd been working on at his computer, and then turning his full focus on Michael and me. His eyes had landed on mine, however. Even though it was still nearly impossible to tell what he was thinking, the intensity of his gaze on me sent a chill down his spine. "There's been a lot of cleaning up to do after that show yesterday, trying to explain to our funders what a ridiculous error in judgement Dr. Carter made in not fully disclosing the details of her research. Multi-billion-dollar research that was very *graciously* given to us."

"—I realize the error of my ways, Dr. Hale," I started, but my mouth quickly snapped shut when Dr. Hale's hand came up to silence me.

"Dr. Carter, if I want to hear your excuses, I'll ask you for them," Dr. Hale said, sternly. He was still staring straight at me, not even remotely giving Michael a second of attention. It was terrifying. "Your severe lack of judgement nearly cost us all. I was scrambling on phone calls all day yesterday, using every trick I had to clean up this giant mess you made. Thank God for Dr. Riddler's quick thinking about the drug trial. If it weren't for that, you'd be out on your ass right now, I don't give a damn about your tenure. What the hell you were thinking, I have absolutely no idea, but you should be thanking Dr. Riddler that you still have your job."

My ears were ringing, growing gradually louder and louder as Dr. Hale finished his little speech. I felt very much like a deer that had been stunned by headlights in those moments.

Thank God for Dr. Riddler's quick thinking.

Dr. Riddler is the reason you still have your job.

Finally, I managed to get my wits about me again. "Excuse me?" I stared at Dr. Hale, knowing full well that the amount of shock I was feeling was clear on my face. "Dr. Riddler had absolutely *nothing* to do with the plans to utilize the troponin activator drug. I had been working on the idea since I got the first MRI results from Commander Peters. I realize the position I put my colleagues in, that I put you in, sir, but let me make it very clear. This entire plan was orchestrated by *me*. Michael had absolutely *nothing* to do with this."

"I don't give a damn whose plan it was," Dr. Hale spoke, the second I'd finished my sentence. "That is the last thing on my mind. The last thing I'd be worried about right now, Dr. Carter, is who should be taking credit for the one thing that's saving your ass. You should be grateful you're still here, as far as I'm concerned."

"Dr. Hale, I think the point we should be considering right now is that we have a plan in place." It was Michael's turn to speak, and I felt myself turning to look at him. My ears were still slightly ringing, and I was certain that my blood pressure was skyrocketing through the roof. "A good plan. One that everyone seems to be on board with, including our investors. Let's give it a chance. I'm very hopeful it will work out in all our favors."

I absolutely loathed how Michael made me feel. As much as I hated him in those moments, as awful of a human being as I knew he was, those words had just the slightest touches of human decency to them. He was trying to remind Bill of the real heart of the matter. That we had a plan, and it had a very real chance of working. Regardless of whose plan it was. Regardless of what a mess I had initially made, and no matter how I tried to spin it, no matter if I had a plan at all, it had been me that had made the mess. My feelings for Ruby, that I hoped desperately no one would question me further about, if it hadn't been obvious already.

I watched Dr. Hale settle back into his office chair and take a long breath. He was focused on Michael, but he glanced briefly at me before he spoke again. "I suppose you make a valid point, Dr. Riddler," he agreed, with a small nod of his head. Then he turned his full attention back to me. "However, I want to make myself *very* clear, Dr. Carter. You're on extremely thin ice right now. So much as a wrong move of a finger, and I'll have you removed from this program faster than you could blink. I might not be able to fire you completely, given your history with the Biomedical Research Institute, but I will make certain that you never have anything to do with our occupational health and ergonomics programs ever again."

"Understood," I replied, swallowing deeply, and deciding that no matter how desperately I wanted to argue in my defense, there was literally almost nothing I could say.

"Commander Peters will be starting the first treatment of the drug this morning?" Dr. Hale's attention turned to Michael, much to my annoyance. My ex-husband nodded. "Good. I expect to be informed of everything from now on." Again, his attention turned to me. "If Commander Peters so much as blinks the wrong way, it will be documented." Both Dr. Riddler and I nodded in agreement. "Very well then. I expect updates as soon as she's started the drug. You both are excused."

Dr. Hale turned his attention back to his computer then, leaving Michael and I sitting awkwardly for a few seconds before we both got up from the desk. We both said polite goodbyes, before we weaved our way out of the office. Michael shut the door behind us and we both stared at one another for a few seconds in silence.

And then I found myself saying something I thought I never would to him. "Thank you for speaking in my defense." When I spoke, I watched Michael's face break into a soft smile. For a few short moments, he reminded me of the man I'd fallen in love with so many years ago, the man that I had thought was compassionate and kind, who understood the rigors of research, who I had believed for so long understood me and cared for me. I genuinely believed, at least for a short while, that he'd been sincere. That he had cared about me. "Of course, Daph." And then he'd ruined it when he'd continued. "I'm confident our plan is going to work out. And the impact on all our careers could be substantial, if it does."

I shuddered, turning away from him and walking down the hall without another word.

MICHAEL LEFT me for a brief while in peace before our conference with Ruby to begin her drug regimen. I couldn't focus on anything in the meantime, which was odd for me. Instead, I found myself finishing up a crossword puzzle that Ruby and I had been working on. I thought to send her a message after I'd completed the last clue, to tell her that I'd been thinking about her, but the anxiety of the conversation that I'd had with Dr. Hale prevented me from doing it.

I'd returned my focus back on busy work for a few minutes, when I noticed an email had come through on my phone, to my personal account. It was sent from Ruby's personal account and contained one line and a hyperlink.

FOR YOU. -R

I STUDIED the link in the email for a few seconds, convinced somehow that it might be a spam message or something unwanted. That perhaps it was some attempt by a colleague to pry into my relationship with Ruby. I was starting to fear that every tiny gesture between us both could be used against us at any moment, and it was terrifying.

Eventually, my curiosity got the best of me. When I double checked the email, I convinced myself that it had to be real and clicked on the link. It led to a site with a long list of what I eventually realized were songs. At the top, the title read 300 *Miles Above You*. When I looked over the list, I realized that there must have been at least a few dozen. A handful I recognized, a lot of them I didn't.

The warmth I felt from the gesture was unlike anything I'd felt in a very long time. It brought back memories aboard the space station, watching Ruby complete her spacewalk, and the adventure we'd had going out together afterward. Holding hands as we floated above the majestic Earth, in all its glory.

I'd never experienced anything like that with another human in my life. I doubted I ever would again. And I was grateful, out of anyone, that it had been Ruby I'd shared that moment with. I wouldn't have wanted it to be any other person.

I realized in that moment, too, why I'd gone to such lengths to protect her. Why I'd risked my entire career for her, as entirely out of character as it had been. Somehow, I had known that Ruby was worth the trouble. That my foolish attempts to let her keep her job, were with the knowledge of now knowing what a miraculous job it truly was.

As much as I wasn't a very big music listener, occasional classical music, like the New York Philharmonic from time to time but that was it, I was curious nonetheless. And flattered that she'd spent the time to do something like this, for me. I clicked on the first song on the list titled "Many the Miles" by Sara Bareilles. I recognized the artist, vaguely. The piano melody was light and a little peppy and reminded me a lot of the way Ruby was.

While I worked at my computer, I listened to the lyrics, which I never did.

How far do I have to get to you? Many the miles, many the miles.

It was surprising how well the words resonated with me. Something that never really happened, mostly because I never was that interested in music. But this? Knowing Ruby had made this just for me, picked these songs out with purpose… It meant everything.

Just as the Sara Bareilles song was ending, my computer rang, jerking me from my daydreaming haze I'd been in. When I focused, I realized that Ruby had been calling me for a video chat. I straightened in my chair, turning off the music. Once I had, I answered the call. "Commander Peters," I kept my voice as neutral and professional as I could, even though I'd been feeling a whirlwind of emotions from her gesture.

"Dr. Carter," Ruby was smiling at me, and her voice came out in a soft, melodic way that had me transfixed. "I'm assuming you got my email."

I grew even more rigid than I already had, worried that she'd said things she shouldn't. Even still, I tried to casually reply to her, regardless. "Safe and sound," I replied. "And thank you," I added, quickly. "Are you busy?"

"Not for you," Ruby replied, in a playful way, and again it sent a wave of uncomfortable panic through me that wouldn't settle. She was being a little too transparent for my liking. "What do you need? Want to go over the data from this past week, before our meeting?"

I nodded. "Are you in the lab?" I couldn't tell by the way the camera was positioned. It was mostly up close on her face, which I didn't mind seeing, but I was trying very hard to be professional in those moments, regardless.

"I will be in a minute, just bear with me," Ruby replied. I watched as she moved from wherever she'd been, rounding a corner and into the familiar Destiny module. "Have you been listening to the playlist?" Again, I hadn't expected her to say anything about it, but she'd done it anyway.

As carefully and casually as I could, I replied. "I have." I could sense the smile on the other end of the line, even though Ruby had disappeared from the camera briefly, to get settled at the workstation over by the rat enclosures. "Thank you for sending it."

"Of course," Ruby replied. "I'm glad you like it." Liked it was an understatement, for certain, but I wouldn't elaborate further. I heard some noise on the other end of the line, as Ruby situated what I could have only assumed was a tablet, on the workstation, and she came into view again. "Alright, I'm at my computer. What do you need from me today?"

"Can you send me the data from this week again? You took MRI scans this week too, I presume?" Ruby nodded at my questions. "Great. For whatever reason there was an error with the database when you sent over the information before, so I want to try again. And we can go over things this time around."

"Just a sec," Ruby replied, and I heard her clicking at the keys of the computer. She was a noisy typist, much like how she ate. It was something that had annoyed me to no end when I'd first met her, but now was just another thing that I missed. "Okay. It should be sent." Sure enough, the files were in my inbox. I pulled up the data on my computer, scanning through it for a few minutes in silence.

"Let's go over this together, if you don't mind." Truthfully, I could have done this on my own every time I'd had these meetings, but it was an excuse to spend time with her, alone, without the prying eyes of my ex-husband. To see her face-to-face. Any excuse for her company was good enough for me.

Just as we were about to start, there was a knock at the door. I glanced upward, feeling an annoyed glare stretch across my face at the disturbance. I took a breath through my nose and then looked at Ruby, briefly. "One second, Commander." Then I called for the person on the other side of my office door to enter. The minute it opened, I'd wished I had pretended I wasn't there.

Michael smiled at me in the doorway. He had a sandwich and chips in his hand and was staring me down behind those iconic glasses of his. "Daph. I saw you were on a call with Commander Peters. Thought we could get our drug trial stuff out of the way, what do you think?" The idea that he'd somehow known that we'd been speaking didn't sit well, but I nodded and watched as he entered the room and shut the door behind him. So much for a moment alone with Ruby.

"R—Commander Peters," I nearly stumbled over her name, quickly correcting myself. "Dr. Riddler is here. He'd like to go ahead and get started, if that's alright. We can put our research conversation on hold for a short while."

"Of course," Ruby replied, just as Michael had landed beside me. I could tell by the way she was looking at me, and the tone of her voice, she had some reservations. But there was nothing either of us could do but let him, as much as I hated it. "Nice to see you again, Dr. Riddler."

"Oh Ruby, call me Michael, please. We're all partners here. I'm not into formalities much, isn't that right, Daph?" I felt Michael nudge me gently, and it was all I could do to remain still and calm. I nodded.

"Michael it is," Ruby said, still in that slightly off tone of voice.

"Now then. Let's get started, shall we?" Michael asked, clapping his hands together.

EVEN THOUGH THE brief physical and administering of the troponin activator drug only took thirty minutes or so, Ruby and I spent nearly two hours with Michael, who was insistent upon going over every shred of information regarding new protocols for this project. By the end of it, I felt more mentally exhausted than I had in a very long time and could tell by the expression on Ruby's face that she was equally as done.

When Michael finally excused himself from my office, I'd already disconnected from the video chat with Ruby. It was just me, alone in my office. Once I'd settled back in my chair and focused on my computer again, I pulled open the playlist Ruby had sent and started up the songs. They played softly in the background as I worked. I managed to focus on what I was doing for a few hours, before I went to check my phone. Ruby had played her turn on our new crossword. I studied one of the unsolved clues, and quickly entered the answer.

After, I saw Ruby's message she'd left me in the chat. *I really hate your ex-husband.*

Me too. I replied, smiling softly. *Have you done your sweep yet?* It was a mention of her spacewalk excursion for the week, which generally took place today.

Just finished up, Ruby replied, a few seconds later. The chat box cursor blinked rapidly as I sat, wondering what else I should even say. Before I could manage a reply, Ruby sent another. *Can I call you in a few hours? Are you almost done with work?*

I'll be home in a few hours, I replied, after glancing at the clock. *Call me anytime.* Once I sent the message, I closed out of the crossword, determined to focus for the remainder of my time in the office, even if it killed me. There was too much work to be done, and every moment of my time lately had been spent trying to prove my worth over Michael, which often felt futile. Especially now, with my job hanging precariously on the line.

BY THE TIME I'd arrived back at my condo with takeout from a Thai place down the street, I'd barely sat down at my kitchen table when my phone rang. A video call from Ruby's personal cell. I answered quickly, and the short raven-haired woman's face filled my screen.

"Ruby," I said, my voice laced with a hint of concern. "Is everything alright?" I wasn't quite sure why she'd needed to call me and hoped nothing was the matter, even though it made me happy to get to speak with her. To hear that lispy voice of hers again. To see her soft face.

"I just wanted to talk to you. Hear your voice. See you." Ruby admitted. My heart raced in my chest at her admissions, panicked that she'd admitted so many things out loud, where anyone could hear her.

"—Ruby," I began to interject, and she smiled at me and held up a finger.

"Mason's intercepting this call," she said, simply. "And I'm tucked away in my sleeping quarters." She panned the camera around, showing me the empty room, and the small space she slept in. I missed that space across from her, where I used to see her sleeping sometimes. Missed that peaceful look on her face when she'd been far away and dreaming. "It's just me and you."

It had been one of the few times we'd had privacy in our entire relationship. Even onboard the space station I hadn't felt that way much, considering everything and everywhere was recorded most of the time.

"It's nice to see you," I said, a small smile breaching my lips. I spoke quietly, even though there was no one to hear me and Ruby wore headphones. Somehow, I still feared that someone might be listening to us. Which felt exponentially worse after the conversation

I'd had with Dr. Hale today, regarding my job. For a few moments, I thought to mention it to Ruby, but changed my mind.

"You too," Ruby said, staring back at me. The way her eyes pierced into me felt like they were daggers, digging into my body, carving out pieces of my heart with every second. For what felt like forever there was silence between us, before both of us spoke nearly simultaneously.

"Ruby—"

"Daphne—"

There was silence again, and then both of us laughed. "You go first," Ruby said, quickly, nodding at me. Did I have the courage to speak? To say what I wanted to say? Part of me still feared that at any moment someone would see this, would hear my words and it would be the end of me.

But I couldn't not tell her. Not when it was all I could think about. "I can't stop thinking about you." I admitted, taking a breath before I spoke again. "Every time I see you, I wish I could touch you again. I think about those last moments together on the station, and I wish so much that we had kissed for longer." I hesitated, unable to read what Ruby was thinking by her facial expression. She just seemed to be listening intently, and now that I had started, I couldn't stop myself. "I'm constantly thinking about you, and I've never felt that way about another woman before. I keep wondering before I fall asleep at night, what you smelled like. I wish I'd paid more attention to it."

"Lavender," Ruby replied, finally, and there was a small smile on her lips. "The stuff they send up for me to shower with smells like lavender. You used it too when you were up here, remember." Somehow, I'd still forgotten, and the smell felt so distant.

"I wish I could remember it," I said, staring back at her and leaning back in my chair. My fingers brushed against the screen of my phone, trying to recall what her cheeks felt like beneath my fingers. Losing myself in that idea, until Ruby's voice interrupted my thoughts.

"If it's any consolation, I can't stop thinking about you either," Ruby admitted, and her words sent my entire body aflame. A broad smile stretched across my face. "I wish I could have kissed you longer too. I think about it all the time. The way you tasted…"

"I miss the feeling of my fingers in your hair," I said, my eyes focused on those short black curls that floated on top of her head. "You have the most beautiful hair."

"I loved that," Ruby sighed, her eyes having closed momentarily, but they opened again. The two of us stared at one another for a long moment.

"Perhaps I can take you on a proper date when you get back home," I said, thoughtfully. Despite everything that had happened today, the idea was still inviting. There was still a smile on my face that had been there since she'd admitted her feelings to me. That we'd felt the same. "Kiss you again before we leave. If I can leave you ever again after this." It was a small joke, but it made Ruby laugh lightly. "I had never kissed a woman before."

"It's the best thing you'll ever do," Ruby replied, swiftly. "Well, that and— you know." There was silence on the line after, and Ruby was grinning broadly. It took a few moments to realize what she'd been implying, and my face went red with embarrassment.

"—I'd like a few dates before any of that happens," I said simply, once I'd managed to recover. Ruby was still smiling at me. "I'm an old-fashioned woman, Ruby."

"We'll see about that," Ruby shrugged. She was about to speak again when there was a rustling and commotion on her end. She glanced around briefly, and then turned her attention back to me. "I have to run. Talk to you later." And then, just like that, she'd disappeared.

I'D FINISHED up my dinner and was disposing of the leftovers when my phone chirped on the table, signaling a message, though I wasn't sure what exactly. When I looked at the clock it was after eight, although it wouldn't have surprised me if someone at work had contacted me for something, even at this hour.

When I reached my phone, I was surprised to see it was a text message from Ruby's personal phone. I assumed she hadn't called me back because of the company arriving. With how our discussion had gone, neither of us could risk being overheard.

The message inside was encrypted. A photograph or file of some sort. I clicked to open it and waited for a few seconds while it loaded. When the image started to pop up on the screen, I nearly dropped my phone in surprise.

It was dimly lit, and by what little I could make of the background, I assumed that Ruby was still in her sleeping quarters. My attention didn't remain on the surroundings for more than a half second, my eyes staring at the focus of the image, Ruby herself.

There had been many times I'd seen photos or television shows or movies with naked women. Art I'd viewed at galleries. Once on a beach in California, even. But it had never been like this. Never had a woman shown herself for me. It was only her from the waist up, but I couldn't take my eyes off her. She was the most beautiful thing I'd ever seen.

And her breasts, small soft mounds of flesh, with dark brown areolas and hardened nipples. I'd never looked at another woman's breasts like I was looking now, in my entire life. Imagining what it would be like to brush them with my fingertips, how her nipple must have felt as it hardened. How soft her skin was. I wondered what she tasted like, how the texture of her skin would feel against my lips. The kinds of sounds she might have made when I touched her.

All the thoughts that overcame me were overwhelming. I felt a heat between my legs, a deep, strong stirring that I couldn't recall ever feeling as intensely as I did in those moments. The panic I should have felt wondering if someone had seen the picture she'd sent, the worries I had about people watching... They were so far gone. I couldn't have imagined them even existing.

My mind was lost on her. Another chirp from my phone. I closed out of the image, returning to the text messages. *Still feeling old fashioned?*

I laughed and then licked my lips, typing back a response. *You're very convincing.*

And you haven't even seen all of me yet. God, the idea that as entranced as I had been about what I'd seen, and there was still more... I could barely stand on my wobbly legs, making my way into the living room and onto my couch. Just as I'd sat down and let out a deep breath of air, there was another text message from Ruby. *You aren't going to reciprocate?*

When I read the message, I hesitated, blinking at the text on the screen. Reciprocate? For a few moments I wondered what she'd meant, dumbly. Then it occurred to me, and the heat between my legs shot up to my cheeks. I typed back a reply. *Someone might see this, Ruby.*

No one will see. Just me.

I stared at Ruby's reply for a little while, contemplating what to do. The idea of exposing myself to her in that way, to another woman... I'd never done anything like this with anyone. But the idea of sharing that part of me with Ruby. It was bringing back that rush of feelings and that heat inside of me, all over again.

There were no text messages exchanged for a few minutes while I removed the upper half of my clothing. The cool air of the fan above me made goosebumps on my exposed flesh, and I felt my nipples hardening. While Ruby's breasts had been small and supple, mine were quite a bit larger and showed their age a bit. Looking down at them I felt somewhat self-conscious, wondering what someone as youthful as Ruby would think about an older woman's body.

But she'd asked, and the desire to give to her what she'd wanted was strong. I pulled open my camera, turning it to take a selfie of myself. The only other time I'd used this was when I'd taken the photo of me with the ISS to send to Ruby. It felt awkward and strange seeing myself on camera, especially naked.

I took at least a dozen pictures, until I finally felt satisfied with one. A small little smile was on my lips, my free hand resting above my head as I laid across the cushions of the couch, staring up into the camera. Instead of taking too long to study the picture, in fear my self-consciousness would prevent me from sending it, I quickly attached it to the text message, encrypted it, and sent it back to Ruby.

Every second of those next few minutes felt like they lasted an eternity. Briefly, I wondered if Ruby had even gotten my text at all. Just when I'd gone to text her to see if she was still there, a message appeared.

You're so beautiful.

My eyes studied over the words, in somewhat disbelief. Hardly able to imagine that anyone would ever call me beautiful, and certainly not now as I'd gotten older. Those words felt foreign and strange. Yet, even still, I trusted them when they came from Ruby. I knew she was being honest. It wasn't in her nature to lie.

Not nearly as beautiful as you. I replied to her, scrolling back up to the picture she'd sent. I opened it bigger again, staring at her marvelous glowing skin, and those perfect breasts of hers. Before I knew what I was doing, I surprised myself, my free hand snaking its way down my body, and I found my fingers rubbing against the burning heat between my legs.

The way it felt, touching myself while looking at her... I didn't often do this sort of thing, and never in my life had I done it because of another woman. All I could do was moan softly into the room with delight, overwhelmed by the sensation. Once again, my mind was drifting to thoughts of rolling my tongue over that hardened nipple and feeling that tiny body buck against me when I did. Kissing down her stomach to her belly button. Tasting her skin.

My phone chirped again, and I closed out of the image so I could see what she'd written, removing my hand from between my legs. I very nearly dropped my phone.

I'm wet for you, Daphne.

I surprised myself knowing exactly what she'd meant by those words, and I found I was wondering if I was too. My hand dipped under my khaki work pants, and under the elastic of my underwear, through the small patch of pubic hair and between my folds. It had felt like ages since I'd last touched myself.

My fingers danced over my clit, which had me moaning into the room in delight. I let them stay there for a few seconds, before pulling my hand out to reply to Ruby, surprising myself for being as salacious as she had been. *I'm wet for you too, Ruby.* Wet had certainly been an understatement, I was very much dripping with desire for her, something I never thought I'd experience with a woman.

Once again, I'd brought up that photo of Ruby, my mind wandering in a million directions. All of them involved us both naked in a bed, kissing and touching one another in every place we could. My hand had made its way into my underwear again, fingers circling around my aroused clit, feeling the warm heat from my body. Every touch I gave myself was followed by a gentle moan or sigh, unable to contain my arousal.

Suddenly, my phone began to ring. A phone call from Ruby's personal cell. I managed to answer with my free hand, putting the phone on speaker. "Are you touching yourself, Daphne?" Ruby's voice was in a sexy whisper that caused me to pant into the phone. "I told you that you weren't old fashioned."

"How can I resist when you send me things like that?" I panted in reply to her, fingers still rolling around the wetness between my legs. "All I can think about is your beautiful breasts. What I wouldn't give to feel your nipples against my tongue. Hearing you moan..."

"*Oh, Daphne,*" Ruby's hushed voice purred into my ear, and it raised every hair on my neck and gave me every goosebump imaginable. My clit throbbed and my fingers ran against it in a fury. "You think hearing me say your name is sexy... Wait until you have your fingers inside me while I'm coming, and you feel me clenching around you while I'm moaning and writhing and gasping..."

"Oh, dear God," I gasped, my body bucking against the couch. I could feel the wave about to wash over my entire body, and I let myself fall into it. My entire body trembled, and I moaned loudly into the phone, sucking in breaths of air in between.

"Say my name, Daphne," Ruby whispered in that seductive tone of hers, with that little lisp mixed in. "Say my name while you're coming."

"Ruby— *Oh God, Ruby. Oh God...*"

My entire being let go. I couldn't recall ever being as vocal and careless as I had in those moments, but it was the only thing I could manage to do as those waves of pleasure crashed into me. I continued moaning and whimpering her name, still rubbing my clit until it was too sensitive to touch any longer. And then I laid for a minute trying to catch my breath.

Ruby gave me a good while to recover before she spoke. "And here I thought you'd be quiet when you were coming." She let out a little laugh. "Way to prove me wrong." Truthfully, I'd surprised myself how vocal I'd been. I couldn't recall ever being like that in my life, but she'd done something to me. Unraveled me somehow.

"I'm sorry," I replied, feeling somewhat self-conscious about it then.

"Don't be," Ruby replied. "It's going to be all I think about when I'm touching myself in a few minutes." I swallowed deeply. "And twenty bucks says you're going to be again too, now that I said that."

A laugh escaped me. "I guess you'll never know."

"Sleep well, Dr. Carter." Ruby said, and then she disconnected without another word.

SEVENTEEN
RUBY

Above me, we were passing over a darkened Asia, specifically Russia. Even with the computer systems to triangulate our exact location, I'd seen the patterns of lights so many times now, I knew exactly where we were. Russia was always fascinating to pass over, so much of its giant landscape shrouded in darkness at night, with bunches of lights around major cities like St. Petersburg.

I was admiring the view for a few minutes, as I often did, when a ringing interrupted my thoughts. Truthfully, with how much I'd collaborated with Daphne and Michael over the last few months, since I'd begun the troponin activator drug trial, I half expected it had been them. Instead, I found it was my mother, Mary. I hadn't spoken to her in a while, so it was a welcomed surprise, to say the least.

When I answered, her face stretched across the computer screen, blonde hair up in a bun on her head, blue eyes staring at me from behind those infamous coke bottle glasses. She was smiling brightly the minute we'd connected, and the sight caused me to smile back in return.

"Well goodness, is it wonderful to see you," Mary said, beaming at me. By the looks of it, she was taking her lunch break in her classroom. There was her usual turkey sandwich and chips on her desk in front of her, a mess of writing on the whiteboard behind her. I couldn't make out what it said, but that was mostly because I was so fixated on my mother.

"It's good to see you too," I replied, brushing hair away from my eyes and turning myself more toward the computer. Luckily the light had been on in the cupola, otherwise she might not have seen me. "How's everything in Florida?"

"Oh, you know, mostly the same as always," Mary replied, shrugging. "Got a classroom full of rambunctious kids, so I'm sure you know how that goes." I couldn't help but laugh and nod. Even with my exceptional career, there had been times in my high school years I'd been that same sort of student, wild and untamed. My mother had always been a very patient human, however. "Dad wanted me to check on you, make sure you were doing okay. I hope I'm not interrupting you."

"Not at all," I replied, taking the computer and turning it to offer Mary a view outside the windows, overlooking the dark Earth above me. "Just hanging out in my usual spot. You probably wouldn't know it, but we're passing over Russia right now."

I watched Mary, who was looking at the view in awe. It never ceased to captivate me, no matter how many times I saw it, so I couldn't imagine what it was like for people who very rarely got the chance to. "I don't know how you focus up there," my mother laughed.

"I don't sometimes," I admitted, laughing along with her. "But I wouldn't trade the view, regardless." Mary nodded in agreement, and I turned my focus back on her, and moved the computer back to where it had been situated.

"How are you feeling?" Mary asked once I'd situated the computer. Even though she hadn't elaborated on what she meant, I knew. I assumed everyone on Earth, both NASA and any interested civilians who followed the ISS, knew about the drug I'd been taking. I hadn't spoken much to Mary about the issues they'd found with my spine, preferring not to dwell on it too much until I absolutely had to.

Luckily, I had good news to share. "It's actually going pretty well," I admitted to her, shrugging. "I was a little bit nervous at first, but our most recent MRIs have been showing some reversal in the atrophy. Dr. Carter doesn't think I'll be completely back to normal, but I'll have decent improvement by the time I come home." Thinking about it made me realize it was only a few more months from now. The time was passing by rapidly. "I'm feeling optimistic."

Mary was smiling at the news. "Everything I was reading says you haven't had any side effects either?" I nodded in reply, and she seemed relieved. "That's wonderful, Ruby. Just think how many people you're probably helping by doing this. They're going to owe a lot of it to you."

"And to Daphne," I replied, not even caring that I'd spoken her first name. I'd also made sure I hadn't credited Michael, who was still weaving his way into every milestone of this venture, whether Daphne or I liked it or not. "She's the real reason this is all happening. I don't know what I would have done had she not stuck up for me the way she had—" I realized I'd started to go off on a tangent. A tangent that I had very much wanted to talk to someone about for a while. Someone besides Daphne herself.

I hesitated briefly, looking at Mary. "Can you give me just a minute?"

My mother nodded, and I clicked out of the video chat, still leaving it running but opening a chat window. It was to Mason Evans, down at Mission Control at Kennedy. He'd been a saving grace for me these last few months, and once again I was going to ask him for help. *Do you think you can give my mom and I a minute? I'd rather not have everyone listening in.* It was an innocent enough of a request. A kid could want a few moments with her mother, regardless of the reason. I waited impatiently for a minute or two, until Mason finally replied.

Gotcha covered. Let me know when you're through.

After he'd responded, I returned to the video chat. Mary was busy munching away at the sandwich she'd been having for lunch, nearly finished with it. "Okay, I'm back," I replied, smiling at her when she glanced back at the computer. "I just wanted to have a minute to talk to you without feeling like everyone was watching us."

Mary nodded in understanding, but I watched her eyes narrow a little with concern. "Is everything alright, Ruby?"

I glanced down, making certain that I was alone, though I doubted any of my colleagues aboard the station now would have made any sort of fuss over what I was about to say. Hell, Daniel already knew most of it anyway. "Everything's alright, Mom," I replied, nodding and trying to do my best to be reassuring. "At least, it's nothing emergent or anything. I just wanted to talk to you about something."

"About Dr. Carter?" Mary guessed, and the surprise I felt must have shown on my face, because she looked pleased. "I sort of had a feeling." I worried then, if she had guessed so easily, had our feelings for one another been obvious? Was it as apparent to everyone else that knew us and worked with us? I certainly hoped not. Mary quickly reassured me. "Call it a mother's intuition," she explained, shrugging. "I can just tell when you talk about her. You haven't talked about a person like that in a very long time. I'm happy for you, Ruby."

"She's wonderful," I said, sighing softly. "I've never met anyone like her in my life. I never thought I could feel like this for anyone in my life. I can't explain it."

"Clearly she thinks the same about you," Mary replied, and I raised a curious brow. "If she was willing to do what she did about the research project..." She'd been referring to Daphne covering up the MRI information. Initially, Mary had called me livid that she'd done such a thing, but after I'd explained the circumstances, she'd been relieved. "A woman like that wouldn't put her neck on the line for just anyone. But I understand what she sees."

"You're not biased at all," I laughed, shaking my head. Mary smiled back at me, shrugging. "I still can't believe that she did that for me."

"People do crazy things for the ones they love," Mary said, matter-of-factly. I felt my heart skip a few beats in my chest at her words. Baffled that she'd even suggest them. Daphne and I had known each other a handful of months now, most of which had been at a distance. Yet even when she'd said it, even when I'd briefly thought to argue, at the same time it made me wonder. Could Daphne have loved me? Did I think I was falling in love with her?

Mary interrupted my thoughts, bringing me back to the conversation. "Did I ever tell you the story your dad used to talk about, when he first met your mother?" The mention of my biological parents pained me a little bit, but my curiosity still got the best of me. It was a story I hadn't heard before. I shook my head. "Well, I know we all tell you that you get your courage and ambition from your father, which you certainly do. But you get your stubbornness from your mother, that is for certain."

"I am not stubborn—" I argued with her briefly, and Mary held up a finger to pause me.

"Elizabeth worked for the New York Times when she first met your father, as you know," Mary explained. My mother had been a journalist nearly her entire life, and while I hadn't ever really known her, I'd read a lot of her work over the years. "She was doing some press for NASA, trying to get them some publicity, get their work more in the public eye. I remember when she took that first trip down to Cape Canaveral. We were all still living in New York at the time."

I leaned back against the blue metal support beam in the cupola, glancing briefly up at the Earth while Mary talked. Russia was nearly past us now, the Earth starting to glow again in sunlight as we moved toward North America. "Well, Ruby, let me tell you... I had never seen your mother so livid as she was when she came back from that trip. She'd met Jeffery, of course." Jeffery Peters, my father. "He was fresh out of the training program, gearing up for his first mission into space. A hotshot rookie, your mother had called him. Apparently, they'd butted heads a lot when they met. Your mother was convinced he'd never make it as an astronaut. He was too arrogant, too full of himself. She wrote that first article about him and I was certain she'd never hear the end of it." Mary paused, looking thoughtfully away from the screen for a minute. Eventually, she turned her attention back to me. "But you know what happened?"

"What?" I asked, shaking my head. Obviously, they had to have gotten over their differences, or else I would have never existed. But I was curious, regardless.

"I bet Jeffery called Elizabeth a thousand times asking to take her out to dinner to prove her wrong about him, and I thought she'd turn him down every time. She was relentless." Mary smiled then, shaking her head. "But then he took his first mission to space, and your mother was covering it again..." I remembered the mission she'd been referring to. It had been one of the many things I'd followed about my father over the years. "And he called her up when they'd gotten to orbit, and they had their little interview for the Times like she wanted, and at the end he showed her that view—"

I could remember, in vivid detail, the first time I'd seen the view of the Earth from outside the shuttle windows, when we'd cleared the atmosphere. Nothing in my entire life could have prepared me for that moment. Nothing could or would ever compare.

"Your dad told your mom that there was no one in the entire world he wanted to share that view with more than your mother," Mary said, finishing the last bit of her story. "And that was that. Your mother never had another bad thing to say about the man."

For whatever reason, the story made me think of Daphne then, and those moments we'd shared when I'd taken her outside of the station. When we'd floated three hundred miles above the Earth, holding hands. The entire universe had stilled in those moments. It had just been her and I. And there had been no one else I'd wanted to share that with, more than her.

I turned my attention to Mary again. "I can't have feelings for Daphne, Mary. Not after everything. Her career is hanging by a thread as is, if they found out we had feelings for one another...that Daphne jeopardized the research because of me, and her feelings about me... She's been working for decades on those projects. I couldn't possibly take them away from her. She's risked enough for me as it is."

"So, you want to end things between you then?" Mary asked me, and her question caught me off guard. It certainly had sounded like that's what I wanted, but in truth, it was the last thing on my mind.

"—I," I tried to formulate words to say, but found I couldn't figure out exactly what I wanted. "No, I don't. I just wish things were easier. Wish we could have what we wanted, without it being such a risk to our careers." And then my mind wandered back to my dad, and the story that Mary had just told, and I couldn't help but recall him in an interview before the *Eclipse* launch.

Mary seemed to have the same train of thought as me. "Didn't your dad say once that life is inherently risky—"

"There is only one big risk you should avoid, at all costs, and that is the risk of doing nothing," I replied, finishing the quote. I could hear his voice in my head, the tone, the inflections. The facial expressions he'd made when he said it. In those moments, I could see myself in him, in certain ways. I'd been so grateful to have inherited so much from him at all.

"You're so much like him, Ruby," Mary said, smiling softly at me. "I see it in you with everything you do. And I'm pretty sure, even with how much your dad loved his work, as much as you love yours, he would have told you that sometimes it is worth the risk."

"Sometimes it is worth the risk," I repeated, feeling a warmth flow through me in that moment, spreading from head to toe.

A FEW MINUTES LATER, I disconnected from the private video call with my mother. Before I had an opportunity to let Mason know we'd finished, another call came through. This time, it was from Daphne. I answered, expecting that it would be her and Michael together waiting for me. Instead, I was surprised to find that it wasn't the case at all. Daphne had another woman on a separate video chat with us.

The woman looked familiar, curly ash brown hair, blue eyes, but it was those very unusual purple framed glasses that sparked my memory. Dr. Mariah Stone, the head of the Occupational Therapy department at NASA. I had spoken with her maybe once or twice before, but it had been several years ago. It was therapists who worked under her authority who oversaw my care pre and post flights, and even during my time on the station. She and I had very little reason to speak, so I was surprised to see her on the call.

"Good afternoon, Commander Peters," Daphne said, offering me a small smile. Like Mariah, she was wearing her own black framed glasses, that accentuated her beautiful hazel eyes. "We aren't interrupting anything?"

I shook my head, returning her smile. "Not at all."

Daphne nodded. "I have Dr. Mariah Stone on the call with us," she explained. "I believe you two have met before?" We both nodded, and Daphne looked satisfied. "Good. We'd like to talk to you about your latest MRI scans and your treatment plan."

Her words admittedly scared me a little bit. I wasn't quite sure what she was going to say, and if it would be good or bad news, but I nodded again anyway. "What's up?"

"As you're aware," Daphne said, looking as though she was doing a little clicking around on her computer. A few seconds later, an MRI came up on the screen, presumably my own. "The troponin activator seems to be working for you. There's been quite a substantial improvement in your disc height changes over the last few months. Which is excellent news." I nodded in agreement. "Dr. Stone and I have been discussing how to further improve your condition, to best prepare you for your return to Earth in a few months. We both believe that if you added some yoga routines to your current exercise regimen, it may increase the benefits you're receiving presently. There's been some pretty substantial research suggesting that it could help."

I raised a brow, deciding to speak what I was thinking. "Why hasn't this been brought up before? We could have done this months ago when I first started the drug."

Daphne and Mariah both looked questionable, and I couldn't quite figure out what was going through either of their minds. Dr. Stone was the one to reply to me. "Dr. Carter and I discussed this with Dr. Hale, Dr. Harris, and Dr. Riddler before we began utilizing the troponin activator, but unfortunately we were shot down. They believed the adjustment to your exercise routine was a bit too radical for the time being."

"Yoga is radical?" I was surprised to say the least. "If there's been proven evidence of its success, then what would be the hurt? I don't understand."

"We weren't sure either," Daphne admitted, although I was quite sure that all three of us knew a probable reason as to why. If Daphne or Mariah had suggested it to the others and it hadn't been taken seriously, it could have very likely been because it was two women suggesting it. One of them being Daphne, who Michael was determined to undermine in every way. The idea that they hadn't taken either of them seriously made me angrier than I cared to admit. Especially since it was impacting my well-being.

"The proper procedure for this type of thing usually is a process of elimination type of thing," Dr. Stone clarified for Daphne and me. "Generally, we will utilize one method at a time, to see if it is useful in conjunction with the drug. Unfortunately, Dr. Hale favored a more traditional approach to begin with. Dr. Carter and I just recently pitched the yoga routine to him again, but he was still very against it."

"So, why are you calling? You want to do it anyway?" I wondered aloud. When neither of them replied and just looked back at me, I knew I had gotten my answer. "Isn't that going to get you both in trouble? Going over all of their heads, when you were explicitly told no?"

Daphne had been more and more daring as the months went by, so I wasn't entirely surprised that she was putting it all on the line again. But her reply to me had surprised me a little. "My primary concern is finding the most effective way to reverse the atrophy of your spine and give you the best possible chance of having a successful and healthy return to Earth. I'm not in this to win approval from Dr. Hale or Dr. Riddler, or even Dr. Harris. Dr. Stone and I agree that we can ask for forgiveness later. Right now, you and your health are priority."

I couldn't help but smile at her words, gracious that she cared so much. Surprised that someone like Dr. Stone was so confident in their plans that she too was putting herself at risk. "So, what do I need to do?"

THE THREE OF us worked for over an hour, discussing how my exercise regimen would change. Dr. Stone would send me a list of yoga stretches to attempt, and I'd take excessive notes for their research. For now, we'd keep everything on the downlow, but if there was record of success with the addition of these exercises, Daphne and Dr. Stone would then take it up the chain of command and deal with it. When we finished our discussion, Mariah disconnected from our video call, leaving Daphne and I alone. It was welcomed, and very much appreciated, since neither of us had really had an opportunity to work alone together in months.

I had Daphne wait for a few minutes so I could relocate to the Destiny laboratory, and let Mason know that my private conversations had ended. When I arrived at the computer station next to the housing for the research specimen, I connected back with Daphne to the video call. She seemed as if she had been right in the middle of something, but quickly turned her focus to me.

"Harold was being a bit grumpy and temperamental earlier," I said, fetching him from his compartment. I showed him to the laptop camera, smiling at Daphne, who was watching me. Then, I proceeded to do the normal series of visual checks and vital checks on the rat, that I hadn't gotten to do earlier because of his mood. "Seems a bit better now though. As soon as I get his info for the day, I'll send everything over."

"Take your time," Daphne replied, doing her own set of things on the other end of the call. The two of us worked in silence for a few minutes, until I heard some noise. When I glanced back at the computer, Daphne was ushering someone into her office. A few seconds later, I heard the familiar and rather annoying voice of Dr. Riddler, who had apparently come to visit. There was a third voice that followed, one that I didn't quite recognize.

Daphne eventually turned her attention back to the computer and to me. "Commander Peters, Dr. Riddler has arrived and seems to have a guest he'd like to introduce to us." There was a weird expression on her face. She looked distraught, if I had to put a label on it. I waited for a minute as Dr. Riddler got settled beside Daphne, and then a third person joined. He was a younger man, not quite my age, but not as old as Daphne and Michael either. He had dusty brownish blonde hair and green eyes, and sported a beard like Mason's, but it was cleanly cut and short.

"Hello Ruby," Michael said, giving the camera a wave. I nodded but didn't reply to him. "I hope I'm not interrupting you two." He was, but again I didn't dignify him with a response. "I just wanted to drop by to introduce a new face to the research team."

Beside him, Daphne's mouth had dropped slightly open, and she was staring intensely. "Daphne, Ruby, this is Dr. Walter Mills. He was a student of mine at UC San Diego a few years ago, and just graduated from the astronaut program a few months ago. Dr. Hale and I, after much consideration, have decided to make him Ruby's replacement to continue our research at the ISS."

"Pleasure," Dr. Mills said, nodding at the computer screen. "I've heard good things about both of you, and I'm looking forward to being a part of the team." It was clear by Daphne's facial expression that she had not known any details about this decision, and it had been made entirely without her. "Dr. Riddler has been getting me up to speed with everything."

Michael and Daphne exchanged a look, in which Daphne's facial expression grew slightly darker, while Michael flashed her that smile that I had grown to dislike with a passion. "I'm sure you'll approve of my decision to bring Dr. Mills aboard. He was best in his class at UC San Diego and did exceptionally well in the training program. It will be nice to have a trained biologist aboard to manage everything."

It was a slight jab at me and my lack of background, I was certain. "Perhaps you should have let Dr. Carter be a part of that decision," I argued, feeling just about as annoyed as I'm sure Daphne was feeling in those moments.

"Dr. Carter will be more than able to be involved in any capacity she chooses," Michael tried to assure me, but it did anything but. It was just empty words, masked by the façade of kindness. Michael had little intention of keeping Daphne involved. If anything, he was trying to push her out of her own research. But, in as short of a time as I'd known Daphne, I knew for certain that she wouldn't go down without a fight.

"I certainly hope so," I replied, staring Michael down on the opposite end of the computer. Then, I focused on Walter, offering a kind smile that was certainly more genuine than Michael's had been. While I wasn't happy with the decision that he'd made without Daphne, it didn't mean that I wouldn't be kind to my replacement and do my best to ensure that the research was well taken care of.

I spoke again. "It's nice to meet you too, Dr. Mills. I look forward to getting to know you better and helping you acclimate once you arrive. There's nothing like it up here, I assure you."

"Indeed, there isn't," Dr. Carter agreed. There was a subtle change of her facial expression. When I turned my attention to her, she was looking straight at the camera, at me I presumed. Daphne's journey to the space station had changed her life forever, I was certain.

And it had changed mine, too.

EIGHTEEN
RUBY

While the Earth passed above me through the windows of the cupola, my eyes were transfixed to the computer screen on the console in front of me. My first childhood crush, Han Solo, and his faithful companion Chewbacca were just being sentenced to death by Jabba. On my phone, next to the computer, I could see Daphne on video chat, her intense gaze locked on the screen as Leia strangles Jabba to death.

Had it been a few months prior, Daphne would have complained about the idea of watching a movie, or how unrealistic it was, but surprisingly she'd learned to relax a little and enjoy herself. And she had seemed rather surprised about Star Wars, a fact I hadn't expected. She'd never seen the series before, and I'd been flabbergasted when she'd explained this midway through this long-distance thing we had going on. Whatever it was.

"You haven't seen *Star Wars*?" I'd said in disbelief. "How can someone not have seen *Star Wars*? I think that's statistically improbable."

"Plenty of people haven't seen *Star Wars*," Daphne had argued.

So, for the last few Fridays, we'd watched through the first five movies, finally concluding with the sixth, *Return of the Jedi*.

"Now Luke is going back to see Yoda—" I started, but Daphne waved at me to silence myself. I laughed, settling back against the wall of the cupola, and admired her as she watched the movie, completely entranced.

It was a long time before I finally heard her clear her throat. I was surprised she'd diverted her attention from the movie at all. My attention turned quickly from the movie, across to my phone screen, where she was studying me.

"Are you excited to be coming home soon?" Daphne asked me. It was only a matter of days now until I'd leave the space station and return to Earth. She knew it must have been a heavy question to ask, and I wondered how long she'd been waiting to say it. It meant a lot of things. And honestly, it was hard to articulate what I really felt. The other times I'd been up here, it had been a bleak affair, leaving, returning to my reality on Earth.

Now, Daphne was a part of that reality, and truthfully, I was desperate to see her. To ensure that these past few months hadn't been a dream. To know that she was real, that I could do something as simple as touch her. But even still, I knew the look on my face had to reveal the fact that I had mixed feelings about everything, even if I wanted to just be happy about it.

Every time I left, I wondered if I'd ever come back. This time was no exception. I'd spent eighteen months up here now, far more than any of my colleagues. Adrik hadn't been wrong that I wanted to break the record. If I had it my way, I wouldn't have ever left.

Except now there was Daphne. I had a reason to leave. A reason to be home.

"I am," I finally answered. *Mostly to be with you.* I didn't say it, since this time around there were likely people watching us. As much as I wanted Mason to run interception on all of Daphne and my interactions, it wasn't always possible. So, I kept it professional. "I'm excited to see my parents. To be able to drink a hot cup of coffee again."

Daphne made a face, and I couldn't help but laugh. Then she turned her attention toward me, and I could see a softness in her eyes. She seemed to read right through my façade. She didn't try to make me feel better, only empathized. "I can't imagine what it must be like. I know that I still miss being there from time to time, and I was barely even there."

A bleak smile broke on my face, and I nodded in reply. "It's a gift to be here." I couldn't help but sigh and decided to turn my attention briefly back to the movie, just in time to see Luke explaining to Leia a big secret. "Don't miss this—"

"He explained already," Daphne assured me. "I was listening."

"I don't know how you do things at the same time," I replied, baffled.

There was a strange smile on Daphne's face then, that I caught when I glanced at my phone. "I am quite a multitasker, I admit," she replied, matter-of-factly. Then I watched her hold up her phone to the screen of her computer, which she was using to video chat with me from her condo in Houston. I squinted as the image on her phone came into view.

It was a boarding pass. Marked just a handful of days from now. A flight from Houston to Orlando. I stared at it, blinking. While I knew in the back of my mind what she'd done, I still found myself at a loss of whether it was true or not. "You're coming to Florida?"

Daphne smiled at me, softly, and nodded. Anyone with half a mind would have read through our innocent friendship and saw something more, especially with the way she was looking at me then. "I didn't want to miss it," she said simply, and I knew there was more she wanted to say but couldn't.

Then she continued, likely to hide any shred of evidence of her feelings. "Michael appears to also be coming along." There was a slight annoyance in her tone, but she kept it to a minimum. "He'd like to fit some meetings in about the research, and we wanted to oversee your recovery, for our data. Dr. Miller is coming with *Galileo*, and Michael and I have gotten him up to speed as best we can. You'll need to get him acclimated like we talked about."

We hadn't talked much about Walter Mills. The man who would be handling Daphne's research, who had been hand selected by Michael to take over. Daphne had struggled so much to trust me with everything, I couldn't imagine what it was like for her to have someone completely new working with them now. But I hadn't really asked her much about it.

"Pay attention to the movie, Commander," Daphne finally interrupted my thoughts, and I drifted back to the movie then. It was near the end now. Our last movie together. My last movie aboard the space station. I glanced upward, looking at the Earth above me. It was night now, lights twinkling in every direction. For a few moments I was transfixed by it, taking it all in.

Then I turned back to *Star Wars*, back to Daphne. Tried to think about the fact that while I was leaving the space station in a few days, it meant, too, that I was going home to her.

THE DAY of *Galileo*'s arrival was a whirlwind. It always was when new shuttles came to the space station, but even more so when it was your turn to leave. The craft would stay for a day while we briefed the new crew members and got them up to speed, and then Daniel and I would head back to Earth together with James Mertz, while Tony and Andrea stayed behind.

I remembered one time visiting Oregon, driving along a mountain road to get to Portland. It was slippery, and I was doing a bunch of curves, focused on trying not to run into anyone as I did. I couldn't really see anything, because there was one cliff falling on one side of me, and one cliff going up on the other side. But I remembered suddenly coming around a corner, and saying, "Oh, wow!" because there was a whole valley in front of me. I pulled over just to be able to bask in it, to stop and look out. To see where all those little myopic turns had taken me.

A spacewalk felt very much like that. There were a million little steps once I left the hatch and was trying to get where I were going. Most of which were all boring and minuscule, and all on a checklist that I had to get right, so it was painstaking at times. But then suddenly, I was in a place I hadn't expected, where I realized how beautiful it all could be. How stupefying, where all my thoughts just stopped—and all I could do was take it in.

The last spacewalk I took before *Galileo*'s arrival at the International Space Station was like coming around a corner and seeing the most magnificent sunset of my life, from one horizon to the other. The entire sky was on fire, with a million colors. The sun's rays looked like a beautiful painting up over my head. I wanted to open my eyes as wide as they would go, just to soak up the image. To try and remember every detail. It was like that every time, but this time especially. This time I was hyper aware of what was happening.

The Earth was like the most beautiful music filling up my soul. No song on my playlist could ever compare. It was like seeing a gorgeous person, where you just couldn't help but stare. Like when I looked at Daphne Carter.

"Ready, Ruby?" My thoughts were interrupted by the sound of Tony's voice in my ear. I was floating in my favorite spot on the entire outside of the station. Looking down at my beautiful planet. We were flying right over the United States, practically over Florida. I could just let go of all the tethers attaching me to the station, and maybe I'd fall straight down and find myself landing on Cocoa Beach, my home.

"Ready," I replied, managing to break my attention from the view to focus on what I'd come out to do. It was mostly just a typical outside sweep, a normal weekly routine for us. They'd let me do the honors, since I'd be leaving and unable to have another opportunity. I wasn't even sure if I'd have another opportunity again in my lifetime, but I certainly hoped I did. Because it was the most magnificent thing I would ever do.

"WELCOME ABOARD, COMMANDER," Daniel greeted the astronauts that would be replacing us. The first, I'd never met before. He was a smaller man, shorter than me and who had supposedly needed a specialized suit tailor made for him. Commander Adam Lynch had graduated from the astronaut program a few years after me. He'd been up to the ISS once before, but it had been several years. His dark brown hair was frazzled when he took off his helmet, and his sharp blue eyes were scanning the room as he floated inside.

"Thank you," he replied, shaking Daniel's hand. Then Andrea, Tony, James, and I took turns greeting him as well. He moved from the hatch shortly after, to let the other astronaut through.

This time, I knew who he was. We'd been working together for a while now, in preparation for his arrival at the space station. Dr. Walter Mills had been pleasant enough to be around, but even still, he felt about as stifling as Michael did at times. He'd never been to space before, so he looked very overwhelmed when he exited the shuttle.

While I helped Walter inside, James and Daniel escorted Commander Lynch. We all went for a brief tour around the station, which wasn't new for Adam, but had been quite an experience for Walter. He'd asked a lot of questions, which all of us were happy to answer, and Daniel seemed rather enthusiastic about his curiosity.

Eventually, we all ended up in the Destiny Laboratory. While the rest of the crew went elsewhere, Walter and I remained so I could get him acquainted. The minute everyone had left, he turned his attention to the rack of research specimen on the wall. The ten rats that I'd grown very attached to in the past six months. "These must be for our project."

Our project. While I knew that eventually Daphne's research would have to be handed over to another astronaut, since I would be leaving, it still felt weird hearing Walter say the words. Like somehow, he'd meant it was Michael's project too, which even after all this time, I didn't admit. Walter had been hand selected by Michael after all, a prodigy student of his at UC San Diego. "All are in perfect health as of their last checkups yesterday," I said matter-of-factly. Then I introduced him to each of the rats, one by one, calling them by my pet names, as well as their alphabetical designations.

"I heard that you'd named them," Walter said, scratching his chin when I'd finished. "I thought it was a little childish, truth be told." His words took me aback, and I found my mouth dropping open. "But you aren't a scientist, after all. We can't expect all of you to understand the professional standards of research."

For whatever reason, this conversation reminded me of one of the very first I'd had with Daphne when she'd come aboard the space station. She too had disagreed with me about my nicknames for the rats, but I'd argued with her anyway. Now, it felt a little different. Daphne had never been outright condescending to me, but the words that had come out of Walter's mouth had very much felt like an attack.

Even still, I did my best to remain civil. I took a deep breath, letting the air roll out through my nose, and then I replied. "There's actually been several studies done over the years that indicate the validity of assigning 'real' names to research specimen. I know I'm not a 'real' scientist, Dr. Mills, but I can assure you that I am exceptional at reading research papers. You can ask Dr. Carter herself."

Walter raised a brow at me, briefly giving me attention, before he turned back toward the rats. "Ah yes, those 'studies' you referenced to Dr. Carter, I remember this. And if I remember right, Dr. Carter explained to you that those studies weren't exactly the most valid of data. Coming from some subpar universities. None of which had multiple trials..."

Déjà vu, I thought to myself. Still, as arrogant as Daphne had sounded when she'd argued with me, she'd never once made me feel small and insignificant about it. She'd just been arguing her own points, the things she believed. Walter sounded as if he was speaking to an ignorant child, which was horribly infuriating.

"Either way," I replied, still trying to keep my tone neutral. "Dr. Carter actually ended up agreeing with me, because, Dr. Mills, there's no harm in utilizing nicknames. I'm not putting the research in jeopardy. It's a name. And if you'd put your arrogance aside for a moment, perhaps you'd realize that fact." I hadn't meant to speak the last sentence, and it had come out so harshly that I'd surprised myself. I snapped my mouth shut as soon as I'd finished.

Walter, who had been engrossed in evaluating the rat enclosure, had turned his full attention back to me again. I couldn't read the expression on his face, whether he was stunned by my words, annoyed, or what he'd been feeling. He didn't bother in enlightening me, instead changing the subject entirely. "Let's go over the recent data you gathered yesterday, and then I need to conduct all the astronauts' physicals."

It was an abrupt segue, and a blatant attempt at ignoring my comment, which I wasn't sure if I was grateful for or annoyed by. Either way, I nodded, and the two of us worked together at the computer station, analyzing the data I'd gotten. Then Walter conducted my physical, which hadn't been done by another medical doctor since Daphne had left the station. As much as I hated to admit it, he was thorough.

The last few weeks of MRIs had been fantastic news on the troponin activator drug trial, especially regarding the emergency waiver that had been made for usage for me aboard the ISS. When Dr. Carter and Dr. Stone had implemented a series of yoga routines into my regular exercise regimen, it had made a substantial difference in my recovery. Daphne hadn't made it aware to her supervisors or other colleagues yet, outside of Mariah, what we'd done. But the results were very promising.

While Dr. Mills was examining my MRI scans for the day, I was busy cleaning the rat enclosures, to spend what little time I had left with them. I'd said my goodbyes to Delilah, having put her away, and had retrieved Jeffery, the last rat. He was surprisingly active for this time of day, fidgeting in my grasp. I pet him gently down his spine, holding him close to my face.

"Don't get into any more funny business with Walter, okay?" I whispered, softly brushing a finger over his head. Jeffery was one of the few of the research specimens who enjoyed being pet. I had a feeling it was because of when he'd gotten sick early on after his arrival, and I'd done everything I could to nurse him back to health. The two of us had bonded quite a bit, and as much as I never thought I'd get attached to a *rat* of all things, here I was.

"Got word you wanted to do my physical?" I heard a voice from behind me, and when I looked over my shoulder, Daniel was floating in the doorway, at a weird angle, having come from around the corner. My moment with Jeffery had ended, and I put the rat back up carefully, and wiped the condensation that had built up on the edges of my eyes away.

"Yes, Mr. Richards, please come in." Walter looked up from what he'd been doing at the computer, presumably entering notes about my latest scans. "I was just finishing up with Commander Peters, so you made perfect timing."

"How did my scans look?" I asked, curiously. Not that I'd be surprised by his answer. We'd just taken MRIs last week, and there'd been a tremendous improvement over the last month or so. Dr. Carter and the rest of the orthopedic staff at NASA had all agreed that they'd be surprised if I had any back issues at all upon my return.

"About the same as last week," Walter replied, glancing at me briefly. "You've shown remarkable improvement over the last month. It's been quite surprising, really."

"Must be all that yoga she's been doing," Daniel piped in, making his way across the room toward us. The minute he'd spoken the words, the second they'd left his mouth, my entire world froze. I was no longer paying attention to anything else in the room, except for what he'd said. A million thoughts were racing through my mind. I'd been extraordinarily careful in keeping my new routine on the downlow from my colleagues, so I had no earthly idea how Daniel had known what I was doing. Then there was the even worse thought, that Walter had found out, which meant for certain that Michael would know soon enough.

I tried my best to come up with something to say, quickly. "I was doing some research online and thought I might include some yoga into my exercise routine." Somehow, I mustered up enough courage to look Walter in the eyes, who was staring me down, expressionless. "Just thought it couldn't hurt, you know. Mix it up a little."

Walter scratched at his chin, looking deep in thought. It was the longest minute of my life waiting for him to reply. "You didn't think to make record of this in your logs? There's a reason we ask all of you to take meticulous notes of everything."

"Well," I shrugged, forcing a small laugh and a shrug. "I'm not a scientist, after all. It honestly slipped my mind to even mention it. Just a little recreational activity, I didn't think anything of it. I apologize."

Again, there was a long moment of silence. Daniel had come to Walter's other side, and I could see him looking questionably at me, but I ignored him in those moments. My entire focus was on Walter, who I still couldn't get a read on. "I'll need more information about what you've been doing, Commander Peters. It might not be as efficient as if you'd documented this during the fact, but I suppose it will have to do."

"Of course," I replied, nodding. "I'd be happy to make some notes for you." Walter had turned his focus back to his computer then, and I still stared at him, trying to make sense of what could possibly be going through his head. Worried about what he'd tell Michael, the minute he'd have opportunity. Hoping that the things I'd said had been enough to keep the blame off Daphne. I'd been ignorant, that was all.

Walter turned his focus on Daniel then. "Let's get started, Mr. Richards." And then Daniel joined him, and I decided in those moments that I needed to be as far away from him as humanly possible.

. . .

ALL AFTERNOON I spent trying to get into contact with Daphne, to warn her of what had happened with Walter. My efforts were in vain, which was unusual for her, since she nearly was always working. Finally, I sent her a short email, with no subject.

Contact me ASAP.

I left the rest vague, fearing that if I even made any sort of indication of what I needed, it would just point fingers at Daphne. Once I'd sent the email, I brought up the web browser and navigated to Daphne and my crossword puzzle. We had just a few more answers to fill in before it was completed. Our last one that we'd do long distance, at least for now. The next one would be in person, and I was so excited about the fact, I could barely contain myself.

I pondered on one of the clues for a few minutes, before deciding on an answer and filling it in. Once I had, I turned my attention to the chat box. Daphne hadn't said anything since our last interaction a few days ago. I watched the cursor blink in the text area and tried to decide if I should say anything at all or let her be.

Are you there? I felt silly asking, but I desperately hoped that she was.

Surprisingly, she answered after a few moments. *Yes. I'm home sick with a cold.* That had explained her lack of response to my contacts. I worried about her, about to ask her how she was doing when she replied. *I'm on the mend, I just wanted an extra day to recover.*

I'm glad you're okay, I replied swiftly. For a long while she didn't reply, and I wondered if she had fallen asleep or forgotten about me. I flipped through my social media sites for a bit, admiring pictures of Earthly things, the things I'd be returning to in a few short hours now. Admittedly, I was a little excited about seeing palm trees again. Going running on the beach and watching the sunrise over the ocean.

There was a tiny bleep from the computer, and I realized it was a notification from the chat box on the crossword puzzle site. I clicked back over.

Are you okay? She'd typed just a short sentence. I didn't even need to ask her to clarify, to know what she'd meant by it.

For a few minutes, I just stared at the computer, unsure of what to say in reply. I didn't want to admit it. Didn't want to talk about it, really. I felt such a mix of emotions, it was hard to sort through. Finally, I managed to type something. *A little sad,* I admitted. And then I decided to change the topic, fearing that if I thought about my leaving the ISS for too long, I'd never recover from it. And surprisingly, it had nothing to do with what had just gone down with Walter a short while earlier. I didn't want to worry her. Not yet. *Are you going to kiss me?* I asked her.

There was another long pause in the conversation, to the point that it bothered me a little. But eventually Daphne replied. *I haven't stopped thinking about it.*

The response had plastered a stupid grin on my face. *I'm so happy you'll be there.*

I'm so happy you're coming home. She replied. And I stared at the message, once again filled with a whirlwind of emotions. Some happy, some sad. Some a mix in between. I didn't respond, and eventually Daphne filled in another answer on the crossword. We went back and forth a few more times, until it was finally completed.

When it was over, and the site congratulated us on finishing, I stared blankly at the computer for a long while. Neither Daphne nor I had said anything else to one another. And then, out of nowhere, I found myself crying. Staring at that crossword puzzle embodied the entire idea that I was leaving. That this adventure of mine was finished, another chapter of my life complete. And whether I would ever get another chance to be here, was entirely up to fate at this point. The only thing I knew for certain was that I was going home.

To my family. To my colleagues. To the world I knew in Florida. And to Daphne Carter.

PART THREE
DESCENT

NINETEEN

DAPHNE

In a research lab adjacent to the Vehicle Assembly Building at the Kennedy Space Center, I was working through the latest data that had come through regarding the drug trial and the astronauts aboard the ISS. The data that Walter had gathered since his arrival. The information would be used for the research paper that documented the changes in the astronauts since my visit six months prior.

When word had gotten out that I'd be attending *Galileo*'s return to Earth at Kennedy, somehow my ex-husband had decided that he and Dr. Hale would also be coming along. "For work," he'd argued, though I knew it was far more than that. He was keeping tabs on me for literally everything nowadays. I'd just decided to accept that fact, even though it was frustrating beyond belief.

The fact was it didn't matter what Michael did. Not now, not in these next few days, these next few hours. When Ruby Peters arrived back on Earth, when she was in my arms... Nothing he did could take that away from me. It wouldn't, no matter how hard he tried. Even if we had to keep it a secret between us.

The sun was shining outside, white puffy clouds danced across the sky. The palm trees were blowing in the balmy wind, and I stared at them for a little while, transfixed. Then my eyes went to the Vehicle Assembly Building, thinking about Ruby's arrival shortly. It was only a matter of hours now. And even better, Michael had left me alone in the laboratory that morning, so I wasn't bothered by his incessant chatter and mindless conversations.

Instead, Mason had joined me, having brought me an Earl Grey tea, while he sipped on a coffee. And for once in my life, I hadn't minded the smell. It just made me think of Ruby all over again. "They should be here soon." Mason interrupted my thoughts. He was staring at me, looking up from a computer he'd been working on, drinking from the white paper coffee cup. He smiled at me through his facial hair. "Are you getting excited?"

Excited was the understatement of the year, for certain. A little part of me still felt anxious admitting it, like if I spoke the words aloud, they might condemn me. But I nodded anyway, and felt a small smile breech my face. "I am," I replied, simply.

"We should probably get on over there," Mason replied, closing out of whatever he was working on at his computer and getting to his feet. "Don't want to miss all the excitement." My stomach churned with his words, but I tried my best to ignore it. I nodded, and once I'd finished up with what I had been doing, I followed him out of the room.

AN HOUR LATER, I stood at the viewing room of the runway, a nervous wreck. I'd never felt more anxious in my entire life. Adrenaline was coursing through me at a thousand miles an hour. I paced back and forth, ignoring the fact that my colleagues were there. At least some of them were. Strangely enough, Michael and Dr. Hale were absent, but I didn't think about it much. Too wrapped up in the idea that *Galileo* was moments from arriving.

At least Mason was there. Along with about three dozen other NASA employees, and a collection of tourists that were visiting the space center and who had received special passes to watch from this viewing area.

"James and Ruby have landed shuttles so many times, they can do it in their sleep," I heard Mason say beside me, nudging me gently. "You can quit your worrying." Had I been that obvious? Hopefully not. But Mason had known about my feelings for Ruby, regardless, so I supposed it didn't matter in those moments. I sighed, still nervous regardless.

All at once it came into view, in a fiery streak and an explosive sonic boom. A long distance away from us still, but visible. The entire room grew quiet as we watched *Galileo*'s descent into the atmosphere, drawing closer and closer to the runway it would land on. My breath hitched in my throat in anticipation.

Ruby Peters was on that shuttle. Closer than she'd been to me in six months. And soon to be in my arms. Not soon enough, I supposed, but still soon.

The shuttle slowed, and the entire room watched as it angled its way perfectly toward the runway, until it finally bounced down onto land and started decelerating at a rapid pace. I watched as it came to a near halt, and then slowly began rolling down the runway. The entire room clapped in applause, both Mason and I joining in.

"Ready to go see your girl?" Mason asked me, in a whisper. He'd said it quietly enough that I was certain no one had overheard. Ready was by far an understatement, and I doubted we'd have time completely alone for a while still, but to see her in person... To know she was close enough to touch now, and safe back on Earth. That was all I needed.

A SMALL GROUP of us headed out of the building on golf carts to meet up with the shuttle. It was a standard procedure to wait for the vehicle to cool down first before we were allowed to approach, but it took us nearly that long to arrive. We waited, while some of the Kennedy shuttle crew went to get the astronauts and help them outside. Medical personnel had to greet and assess them first, as their journey and stay on the ISS was taxing. Their time in microgravity would leave them unable to walk on their own for a while, until their muscles readjusted to Earth.

The crew was inside for a long while, and it felt like an eternity waiting. Finally, I saw some of them exiting, assisting the astronauts in wheelchairs. Even after a short visit to the ISS, it had taken me a few days to acclimate back to Earth's gravity. It would take these astronauts significantly longer, especially Ruby and Daniel, who had been in space for a year.

I waited patiently as they unloaded, until last, but certainly not least, I saw Ruby. Her helmet had been removed, her short, curly raven hair in disarray on her head. It felt as if I was seeing her for the first time again, on the space station. I was too far away to make out the small details about her, but even from the distance I was at, she took my breath away.

They were wheeling the astronauts down the ramp alongside the shuttle, toward a special tent that house doctors and medical staff that would check them before they traveled to the facility they'd stay in for a while to recover. I'd left the golf cart, just as they'd reached the ground, with full intentions of meeting them before they'd tucked Ruby away in the tent. I hadn't cared who was watching.

I'd barely started my way there, when another golf cart arrived next to the small fleet that had been waiting. My attention turned toward it, and I was surprised to see Dr. Hale and Michael sitting in the back seat. They'd distracted me from my initial plan of going to meet Ruby, surprised that they'd arrived late, much after the shuttle's arrival.

Dr. Hale was scanning through the crowd, until he'd spotted me. Our eyes met, and he nodded, and then I watched him motion at me to approach. There was a strange feeling that overcame me then. It felt a mixture of curiosity, mixed with a tinge of worry. What could he have possibly wanted? I had things to do. A woman to see, before she was whisked away, and impossible to find for hours, possibly days more.

When I reached the golf cart, Dr. Hale motioned toward the empty seat in front, next to the driver. "Please sit, Daphne."

I stared at him confused. "Is there a reason I need to sit?" I replied, glancing at Michael, who was also looking at me with a strange look on his face. It was not his usual deceptive smile, but a look that sent a chill down my spine. He looked deathly serious, just like Dr. Hale.

"Sit down, Daphne." Dr. Hale's voice came out as stern as I'd ever heard it. I didn't question him for another second, sitting down obediently in the passenger seat. As soon as I had, Dr. Hale patted the driver on the shoulder, and the cart took off. I glanced over toward Mason, who was sitting in the golf cart I'd traveled out with him in, and he was watching me as we drove off, looking as completely confused as I'd felt in those moments.

Instead of inquiring as to where we were headed, I sat quietly, watching *Galileo* disappear in the rearview mirror, feeling horrible that I hadn't been there with Ruby upon her arrival. We drove across the KSC campus, until we'd reached the familiar building where I'd been working in the science laboratory. The golf cart was parked, and I followed Dr. Hale and Michael, as we made our way down white, florescent lit hallways, and into the conference room that had become quite familiar to me now.

The room housed a few people, who were chatting amongst themselves when we entered. Everyone went quiet when the door had opened, all the attention turned on the three of us as we wandered inside. There was a sinking feeling in my chest again, recognizing some of the faces. Dr. Timothy Harris and Dr. Mariah Stone. A few faces I didn't recognize. And then Dr. Stephens, the head of the entire research division at NASA, at the far end of the room.

Dr. Hale and Michael sat at empty seats near the door, leaving an open seat toward the middle of the conference table. Dr. Stephens cleared his throat, and my attention turned toward him. He nodded at me. "Have a seat, Dr. Carter."

I took a long breath, trying to steady myself, before I made my way to the empty chair that was left, and sat myself down. My attention turned toward Dr. Stephens, who looked as though he was going to be the one starting this conversation, whatever it happened to be about. He was sitting almost directly across from me now, and I watched as he slid across the table a small pile of papers.

"Take a look at these," Dr. Stephen's said, as I outstretched my hand to take what he'd pushed in my direction. It took me a couple of seconds to figure out what I'd been looking at on the top of the pile, but the moment I realized, I felt all the blood drain from my face. My pulse skyrocketed; my palms began to sweat. There was a thudding in my head, likely a rise in my blood pressure. All the air from my lungs had ceased to exist.

It was correspondence from Dr. Walter Mills. By the wording at the beginning of the email, it was just a few days prior, after he'd arrived at the International Space Station. The first few sentences detailed that he'd begun the transition with Ruby, and about the research specimens, and various other things regarding the drug trial.

Then I'd reached the paragraph that had brought me to a halt. Walter spoke about Ruby and the new yoga routines she'd been conducting over the last few months, which seemed to have substantially improved her spinal health. He spoke about how the information hadn't been recorded, and that Ruby had mentioned it had been her entire idea, just as a "hobby." Once I'd read that part, my eyes glanced up to find Dr. Stone. She looked about as panicked as I felt in those moments. I finished the email, to which Walter wrote his suspicions that both I and Dr. Stone had something to do with this, and that it had been undocumented on purpose.

I looked upward, toward Dr. Stephens, opening my mouth to speak. He beat me to the punch. "I need you to look at everything, Dr. Carter." He nodded back to the stack of papers.

Never in my life had I not wanted to do something more,

dreading what else was in this stack of papers. I flipped through them. Pages of correspondence between Ruby and me. Notes and transcripts of mine from when I'd failed to disclose about the severity of Ruby's MRIs. Transcripts of many of Ruby and my movie nights over the last few months. Even screenshots of the crossword puzzle site we'd completed together. Luckily, I found no trace of the chat logs.

My heart was ripping through my chest by the time I'd looked through everything. Clearly, the evidence they had on me was damning. They had enough of it to make accusations at this point, and I knew for a fact what was coming, as much as I prayed it wasn't. We'd tried so hard to stay quiet about things. Done our best to make light of the situation, as to not draw suspicion. Yet somehow, they'd figured it out anyway. And I had every feeling that most of it, if not all of it entirely, had been my ex-husband's doing.

Even though this conversation had been with Dr. Stephens and myself, I couldn't help but look up and over toward Michael, on the opposite side of the table, next to Dr. Hale. He was watching me curiously, with those dead brown eyes of his. He wasn't even trying to hide the very smug look on his face in that moment. And if it hadn't brought the possibility of me being arrested, I would have flung myself across the conference table and strangled the ridiculous excuse of a man with my bare hands.

Dr. Stephens brought my focus back to him. "Would you care to explain?"

I had no earthly idea what to say. "Dr. Stephens—"

"You've been with us for what, nearly two decades now? Is that correct?" Dr. Stephens interrupted me, staring me down. I nodded, and he continued, his expression neutral. "Two decades you've been working on this project, in this department. Two decades that you built your entire career around."

"I'm completely committed to my research," I argued with him. *What else could I say?*

"Clearly you're more reckless than I thought you'd ever be," Dr.

Hale spoke this time, instead of Dr. Stephens. My attention turned to him, and unlike Dr. Stephens neutral expression, he was downright glaring at me. He was pissed. "This is a multi-billion-dollar project, Dr. Carter. Billions of dollars that were graciously awarded to us to conduct this *groundbreaking* research."

"I realize this fact—" I tried to speak again, but instead was interrupted by a slamming of a hand down on the table. Dr. Hale clearly hadn't wanted me to detract from what he'd been saying. He wasn't hearing any excuse I made at this point. He knew better.

"What the hell were you thinking, Daphne?" Dr. Hale said, his body leaning forward so he was looming over the table. "First you withhold critical data from us regarding Commander Peters. Luckily, you had Dr. Riddler to thank for rescuing you from that situation, otherwise I would have acted sooner about all of this." I couldn't believe what I was hearing. Michael was getting credit for my idea to use the troponin activator drug on Ruby. This wasn't the time to argue with him about it, however. "And then for you to go behind your colleagues' backs, your supervisors' backs, and authorize a new protocol for Commander Peters, when you were explicitly told no..."

My eyes flicked over toward Mariah, who was looking mortified in her seat. She mouthed an apology to me, but I didn't dignify it with a response. She wasn't to blame for this, not in the least. I'd been the one to approach her, and the one to approach Ruby. This was ultimately my own doing. Even still, it seemed as though, perhaps, they hadn't figured out why. I hoped desperately that Dr. Hale was only upset because of my disregard to authority.

Then I realized I was mistaken, when Dr. Stephens spoke again. "Dr. Carter, would you care to enlighten us as to the nature of your and Commander Peters' relationship?"

There was an intense ringing in my ears, so horrendously loud that I was having trouble making out any sounds in the room. I forced air into my lungs, taking a few terrified breaths of air before I managed to say anything at all. "I don't understand what you mean..."

Dr. Hale spoke before Dr. Stephens could get in another word. I barely heard him over the sounds my body was making, completely shutting down on me. "At first I couldn't believe this," he said, his blue eyes laser focused on me. I wanted desperately to look at Michael, to know what he was thinking in those moments, but I couldn't break away from Dr. Hale. "I couldn't imagine a universe in which Dr. Daphne Carter, the woman who worked her way up from nothing to get where she is now, would do something so obscenely reckless. She is a scientist, I thought. One of the foremost researchers in her field. Dr. Carter wouldn't dare do anything to jeopardize decades worth of work. Not for some fleeting, meaningless crush on a rookie astronaut—"

"Ruby is *not* some rookie astronaut—" I found myself nearly yelling in response, interrupting Dr. Hale's speech to me. Words that spilled out from me before I had a chance to think about what I was doing. One sentence that would condemn me, but in those few moments I hadn't even cared. Dr. Hale, Dr. Stephens, the entire room could viciously attack me as much as they wanted, but there wouldn't be a moment that I'd find it acceptable for them to tear at Ruby.

The room was dead silent. Dr. Hale sat paused, mouth still hanging slightly open from when he was speaking before. Dr. Stephens looked somewhat surprised. And when I looked at Michael, he was still sitting there, looking both stunned, but also still with that arrogant, horrifyingly smug look still on his face.

I cleared my throat, realizing in that moment that I was defeated. There was no way I would recover from this. No words I could say at this point to try and stop this from happening. So, instead, I told the truth. "Dr. Hale. Dr. Stephens." I made eye contact with each of them before continuing. "I am very aware of my status in this community, and of the tremendous amount of work I put into my career. The tremendous amount of responsibility on my shoulders." I took a breath, focusing back on Dr. Hale then. "Never in my wildest dreams would I have imagined that my life would take the turn it did. I'm a woman of science. A woman who worked tirelessly for decades to get where I am today. And I wholeheartedly understand both the importance of the research I was conducting, and the importance of my role in conducting it."

"Clearly not." A voice interrupted my speech. This time, it was not Dr. Hale, nor Dr. Stephens. Instead, my ex-husband spoke beside them, leaning forward in his seat and casting a very menacing gaze at me. "Clearly you had absolutely no regard for any—"

My eyes were on Dr. Hale, knowing that I was at his mercy. Not Michael's. I didn't let him finish what he'd been saying. "—I fell in love with her," I admitted, and as terrifying as it had been to do, I didn't regret it. Not in those moments. It was as if I needed to confess it to myself, just as much as I had to explain it to my colleagues. I needed to understand why I'd done the things I did. Why I had put my entire career in jeopardy, for one singular person. A thing I would have never in my wildest dreams imagined myself doing. "I fell in love with Ruby Peters. Something I didn't expect was possible, something I could have never predicted. I fell in love with a woman, another person, who understood me completely. Another person who understood what it was like to live this life we live, these careers we've chosen. A person who believed in me and the work I did, as much as I believed in her and her work."

I turned to Michael then, who was staring at me. His smug look had shifted slightly to an expression more neutral. He'd been listening to what I was saying. "There was a time in your life that you felt that way too, Michael." I stared at him; my expression as soft as I could make it in those moments. Surprised that I had thought, even for a second, that he might understand me. Then my attention turned back to Dr. Hale, and to Dr. Stephens. "I was wrong in my actions regarding the trial, regarding this research. I made questionable decisions that could have very well jeopardized everything we'd been working for. I admit this, I do."

Dr. Hale looked as though he was going to speak, but I raised my hand to stop him. "But I will never, not for a second, tell you that I regret anything that happened. I will never, not for a second, tell you that I wouldn't do the same things again. And I realize this might be the biggest mistake that I make in my life, admitting this to you. Admitting that I was wrong..." I trailed off for a minute, taking another breath. "But I had the best intentions, Dr. Hale. I swear to you, this. They may have been clouded by my feelings for Ruby, which I never expected to happen, but I have always cared for these projects. I will always care. And so did Ruby."

The room went quiet again for what felt like the longest few minutes of my life. Dr. Hale and Dr. Stephens spoke alone, while Michael was busy looking at papers in front of him. Meanwhile, Dr. Harris and Dr. Stone were conversing at one end of the table, and when I looked at Mariah, she glanced back at me and nodded softly.

"Dr. Carter," Dr. Stephens eventually broke the silence. I waited, terrified of the words that were about to come out of his mouth. I knew what they were going to be, but I was in denial until it happened. Couldn't believe that it could, until it did. "I'm afraid you've left us no choice but to remove you from the spinal research program indefinitely. You, of course, will remain on our staff and employed with the Biomedical Research Institute. However, your two-decade tenure with this research is officially over. Dr. Riddler will be taking your place as head of the department."

I was reliving the nightmare of my medical school days, all over again. All I could do was stare at Dr. Stephens, feeling myself lose all control of my body. There were tears beginning to well in the corners of my eyes, but I wouldn't cry. Not in front of them. Not in front of Michael. I cleared my throat, getting unsteadily to my feet. I didn't once look at Michael, only straight ahead, toward Dr. Stephens and Dr. Hale. For a moment, I thought I might say something eloquent to them. Thank them for the time that I had on staff with this research. That I accepted the result of my actions and would take it in stride.

But my emotions got the best of me. I nodded a few times, and then turned away, heading out of the conference room doors without another word. Waiting outside, I was surprised to find my oldest friend, Mason Evans, leaning against the wall. When he saw me, there was a look of shock on his face, as I'm sure was on mine as well. How he'd known where to find me, I had no idea.

"—Mason," I could barely speak his name.

"Not here," he said quickly, grasping a hold of my arm lightly and moving me down the hallway. We reached a door, leading into the stairwell. Once he'd closed it, I flung myself into his arms, and let myself go, sobbing. I couldn't remember the last time I'd cried, and it hadn't mattered. Mason wrapped his arms around me, and for the first time I was truly grateful to be hugged by that big burly man. Grateful I had a friend at all, to comfort me in that moment.

TWENTY

RUBY

When the door to *Galileo* finally opened, after a brief stay inside for the vehicle to cool down from having reentered the atmosphere, the first thing I noticed was the brilliant cerulean color of the sky. The gorgeous fluffy clouds that were sprinkled on it, mixed with the golden hues of the rays of sunlight. The balmy Florida air trickled in, and it warmed my entire body.

"Welcome back to life on *terra firma*," one of the NASA medical team had entered the cockpit of the shuttle. James and I had been strapped next to one another, and we were assisted in removing the harnesses. Every part of my body felt heavier than I'd ever expected it too. When we'd landed, I remembered feeling the weight of my lips and tongue. The moment I'd spoken to James and Daniel, a few seconds after, I had to change how I was talking. Something that came so natural to me, felt so strange now back on Earth.

While I was relieved to be on the ground and enjoying the sight of Florida sunshine and blue skies outside, it too felt like I was suffering from the world's worst hangover. I felt dizzy, which was to be expected since vertigo was a common occurrence for astronauts that had spent a significant amount of time in space.

Once we were unhooked from our seats and briefly checked over, the medical team assisted James, Daniel, and I from the shuttle in wheelchairs. It would be a few weeks before we were able to function entirely on our own again, as our muscles acclimated back to Earth's gravity and our bodies recovered from the extreme shift in our environment. We spent an hour in a medical tent just off the runway, where we were assessed about our general condition upon arrival.

The entire time, I looked for Daphne. Every person that wandered in and out of the tent, I expected to be her. I could barely lift my head, but I would try, every time I heard a noise. Expecting that at some point, she'd come for me. That I'd get to see her in the flesh again. But she never showed, nor did Dr. Riddler or any of her other supervisors, which I found particularly odd.

Daniel, James, and I were escorted to a medical facility on site, where we'd spend a length of time in close watch by doctors on staff and other therapists, as we recovered from our trip. The trip there I barely remembered, fading in and out of consciousness both from exhaustion and overstimulation.

In my fading dreams, I saw her. Beautiful blonde hair, blowing in the Florida breeze. Hazel eyes watching me. There was a small smile on her face. "Ruby," she would call to me. "I'm here Ruby. Ruby, I'm here..."

When I finally managed to stay awake for longer than a few minutes at a time, several days had passed. I'd spent nearly all of it in a hospital bed, Daniel on one side of me, and James on the other. It was early in the morning when I'd come to, and my first sight upon opening my eyes had been Daniel, watching an episode of *The Office* on a television in our room, and being assisted in eating breakfast.

The smell of fresh bacon mixed with the aroma of a hot pancake filled my nostrils. It felt like decades since I'd last tasted a piece of bacon, and it made my stomach rumble. All the nausea I had for the first few days was mostly gone. Surprisingly, I felt like I had quite a substantial appetite in those moments. I blinked a few times and stretched as best I could, which wasn't much.

It had been enough to catch the therapist who had been assisting Daniel, and Daniel himself, to look over at me. My friend still looked very weak, but he gave me his best smile through that bushy mustache of his, when our eyes met.

"Well good morning, sleeping beauty," he said, chewing down a piece of bacon he'd eaten. "James and I were taking bets how many more days you'd be out of it. How ya feeling?"

I blinked a few times, trying to adjust to the florescent lighting of the hospital room. Then I moved my mouth again, still feeling awkward when I tried to talk. "Better than I did," I replied, turning my head to look in the opposite direction and finding that James was also awake, and watching me intently.

"Glad to hear it," James replied, smiling at me like Daniel had. "Daniel and I both just had breakfast. I'm sure they'll bring you some if you want it."

"Yes, please. I'm starved," I replied, and I heard everyone in the room laughing.

The therapist, who had been helping Daniel eat his breakfast, promised me some food as soon as possible, and disappeared from the room. Just as he'd turned the corner, another set of bodies came from the opposite direction, and walked inside to meet us. A long, wavy and dusty brown-haired woman, with green eyes. And twin boys, who looked so strikingly like Daniel Richards himself, that there wouldn't be any doubt that they were his.

"Elle," Daniel's voice cracked into the room. I turned, watching him as his wife and children came to his bedside. We'd already known that Elle was going to be a few days late getting to Kennedy. She'd been caring for her elderly mother across the country in Portland and had taken her children with her. Clearly this had been the first time they'd seen one another.

I watched them embrace, admiring the softness in Daniel's eyes looking at her. They kissed, and hugged one another, and then Daniel took his two sons into his arms, who looked just as overjoyed to see him as his wife. It was magical watching them. I could only imagine how Daniel must have felt seeing his family after an entire year away from them. I'd only known Daphne a short while, only had been away from her for six months, and it had felt like an eternity. I wasn't sure how I had lasted.

The thought of Daphne made me turn away from Daniel and his family reunion. Instead, I looked in the opposite direction at James, who had also been admiring the happy scene. We met eyes, and I paused for a minute, unsure of what I even wanted to ask him.

"Dr. Carter hasn't come by, has she?" I felt silly asking, like saying something like that would give me away, give us away, entirely. But I couldn't *not* ask. I was desperately wanting any information about Daphne's whereabouts. James shook his head, and I felt my heart sink deeper into my chest.

"Dr. Riddler came by yesterday," James noted. "Just for a few minutes. You were out of it still, but he talked to Daniel and said hello to me. I think he was pretty busy." So, Dr. Riddler was here, and had been to visit. The idea that he'd come, but there'd been no sign of Daphne, worried me greatly.

Just as my mind began to wander, the therapist returned with a tray of breakfast food for me to eat. When he'd joined me beside the bed, I lost track of my thoughts about Daphne, too hungry to eat. But before I took my first bite, I thought to ask one question.

"Can someone get me Mason Evans?"

A FEW HOURS LATER, after some physical and occupational therapy, an appointment with a pulmonologist, a blood draw, and my vitals measured, I was finally left alone for a few minutes. James had been taken for scans, which I'd also get later, and Daniel had gone somewhere to visit with his family for a while.

I'd just settled in the bed, watching another rerun of *The Office* that I vaguely remembered seeing memes of online at some point, when there was movement outside the door. Mason had yet to come visit, so I'd hoped it was him. Instead, I was disappointed to find that it had been Michael Riddler.

"Ah, the woman of the hour," Michael said, as he rounded the corner into the room. He shoved his glasses up his nose and offered me a pleasant smile, that I'd grown to hate as much as Daphne did. He moved across the room, picking up a blood pressure cuff hanging from the wall and coming to my bedside. "Mind if I take some quick vitals?"

Honestly, I did mind. They'd just got through poking and prodding me for hours, and I wanted nothing more than to have a short while with peace and quiet. This little visit from Michael wasn't really for vitals. He was just being his nosy, overbearing self. But at the same time, I was dying of curiosity, wondering where Daphne was. Which, if anyone knew where she was, after how close of tabs he'd been keeping on her lately, it was Michael.

I nodded, and Michael wrapped the blood pressure cuff around my exposed upper arm. He pulled the stethoscope from around his neck, placing the tips into his ears. "Take a few deep breaths for me Ruby." I did what I was instructed to do, while Michael pumped the cuff and listened.

When he'd finished, he logged onto a nearby computer, presumably taking notes of his findings. I let him work, enjoying the idea that I didn't have to make small talk. Before he'd completed whatever it was that he'd been working on, I found myself needing to ask.

"Is there a reason Dr. Carter hasn't come by yet?" I asked, wondering if I even wanted to know the answer to the question. There was a very sick feeling in my stomach. Hoping desperately that something hadn't happened to her, and there was a logical explanation.

Michael looked up, having finished typing. He gave me a strange look and a facial expression that I couldn't get a read on. There was a long drawn out pause before he replied. "Ah, well—I'm afraid Dr. Carter had some last-minute work to do in Houston."

I didn't believe him for a second. "Really? I would have expected she'd come with you. Our post-flight medical exams are pretty important to her research." I watched Michael's face twitch at the sound of me saying *her* research. It was slightly satisfying knowing that fact. "Is she coming soon, then? After she gets done with her work?"

Another long hesitation from Michael. I didn't like it. Not one bit. "I'm not certain, Commander. I'll look into it for you." His face was still expressionless. "And if you're done inquiring about Dr. Carter, I'd like to finish my exam."

"Have you seen Mason Evans?" I asked, annoyed that I still hadn't gotten in touch with him either. Michael gave me a look then, one that I understood. His eyes had narrowed, and his lips drew in a straight line. I sat back on the bed, deciding to stop asking questions and let him do his job. One way or another I'd find out, and the more I was without answers, the more I was starting to feel like the situation wasn't good. Not at all.

BY THE TIME Michael had left me, both James and Daniel had returned to the room. I'd changed the channel on the TV and was surprised to find that the original *Back to the Future* movie had been playing. While I'd seen it a thousand times already, and only a few short months ago with Daphne, I couldn't help but stop to watch it. Thinking about that first "date" we'd had. Even with an audience watching, it had been a wonderful time. Enjoying Daphne's expressions having never seen it before.

"Ah, I love this movie," James said, as a nurse assisted him back into bed. "Didn't you just watch this not too long ago?" I exchanged a look with him.

"This girl can quote the whole damn thing practically," Daniel said, leaning back into his bed, that had been adjusted so he was mostly sitting up. "I remember the first time we chatted for longer than a few minutes, she said something about being 1% bisexual for Michael J Fox."

The memory brought a laugh from deep inside of me. It felt

strange, laughing. Just like everything else had once we'd gotten to Earth. Like it was foreign, and I wasn't quite sure how to do it. Either way, I was smiling too, amused that he'd remembered such a small, trivial thing. "I can't believe I said something like that."

"I looked a lot like Michael as a teenager," James said, thoughtfully, and I turned to glance at him. "Just saying, Ruby."

"Never in your wildest dreams," I replied, smiling at him and shaking my head.

"She's all about the ladies," Daniel piped in, and when I looked at him, he gave me a small wink. While none of my other colleagues from the ISS had any idea about my feelings toward Daphne, at least I had desperately hoped not, Daniel and I had spoken a few times about her. He'd known, and I had trusted him dearly, being one of my oldest friends from the astronaut program, and probably my closet colleague.

The comment, however, made me think about Daphne yet again. Everything did, truthfully. Until I got to see her, to know she was okay, I didn't think it was possible I would stop. I couldn't stop. My worrying was too strong.

Before I could reply to Daniel, someone entered the room. When I looked up, I couldn't believe it. Relief filled my entire body. Mason's stocky frame loomed in the doorway. He was wearing one of his classic plaid shirts, sleeves rolled up his arms, and a pair of jeans. I didn't focus on his clothes very long, however, worried about the very serious expression on his face.

The other two guys in the room with me had also taken notice to Mason's appearance. "Well, hey there, buddy. Long time, no see." Daniel was the one to speak first, when Mason stepped inside the room.

"Daniel, James," Mason looked to each of them and nodded. "Glad to see you all got back here in one piece." It was a polite thing to say, a very usual thing to say, but for an astronaut, it really was a relief, without a doubt. Space flight was dangerous. One of the more dangerous things a human could do with their life. But as someone who had been dreaming of it since she was a kid, it was all I could ever think of doing, regardless of the stakes involved.

"Ruby, can I speak with you a moment?" Mason's voice interrupted my thoughts. I looked up at him, that strange, very serious look still on his face. The sinking feeling I'd had earlier returned, in full force. I nodded toward the wheelchair off to one side of the room. He went to fetch it, and then, without the assistance of the hospital staff, helped me into it, like he'd been lifting a feather.

"Maybe I can hire you to carry me around everywhere," I tried to make a small joke, as he sat me down in the wheelchair. Once I'd settled, he connected my IV line to it. When Mason didn't react very much to my joke, I found myself struggling to breathe. There was something wrong. When Mason Evans was serious, there was something wrong, without a doubt.

He didn't speak again until he'd wheeled me out of the room, down the hall, and into an empty and dead-end hallway. Once he'd parked the chair, he came around to face me, and I watched him, the burly man that he was, take a knee.

"It's Daphne," I said, knowing full well what was coming. There was no way that it wasn't. I forced myself to breathe for a second, before I asked. "What happened, Mason?"

Mason's eyes met mine, and a chill shot down my spine. It was like I'd known exactly what he was going to say, before the words even came from his mouth. The look he gave me spoke everything he didn't even need to. But then he made it real, the sounds of the words filling the deathly quiet space around us. "They let her go."

TWENTY-ONE
DAPHNE

In Houston, the milder spring temperatures and weather had been replaced with hotter days as it transitioned into summertime. Outside didn't matter much to me usually, since most of my time was spent indoors. I barely was ever out in the sunshine either, unless it was an exceptionally long day out.

Today, there wasn't a cloud in the sky. I'd paused for a minute working to admire how beautiful of a day it was. It was something I didn't do often, but for whatever reason it felt like a little bit of comfort. Across the Johnson Space Center campus, there was a giant tour happening. I watched the crowd as they made their way through the courtyard.

I remembered the first time I'd arrived here, and the tour I'd been given for orientation. It had been a group of twelve of us, and I had been the only woman there, and the only doctor. Things had changed drastically in the two decades since I'd arrived, but that memory of feeling like I'd accomplished something incredible by being there... That would never fade.

"Dr. Carter," a voice from behind me interrupted my thoughts. I turned from the window, face-to-face with a young blonde-haired, blue-eyed man, dressed in a navy-blue NASA polo, and a pair of khaki pants. He was so close to me, that I could smell his minty breath. "I do hope I'm not interrupting your daydreaming. I wouldn't want to have to remind you of the deadline for this research paper is coming up fast."

Dr. Drew Porter was a brand new, freshly graduated, hot shot doctor from Cornell, with an ego that suffocated every living thing around him. Put into a leadership role the moment he'd been hired. He knew no bounds with his condescending remarks, took pleasure in demeaning everything around him that felt the least bit underqualified.

And he absolutely hated me.

"I'm nearly finished," I replied, keeping my voice steady. "Just waiting on an email with some last-minute data from our control subject. I was told it would be any time now."

Drew looked no less annoyed with me, even with my reassurances. "There's a million other things you could be doing, Dr. Carter." He clicked his tongue, sitting down beside me in an adjacent chair. "Listen, I've told you this before. I'm not a micromanager."

You most certainly are, I thought, bitterly.

"I don't like having to constantly be on you about getting things done," he continued. I kept my gaze straight ahead, looking at my computer and clicking through screens while he talked. The urge to say something stupid if I looked him in the eyes was strong. "You're an intelligent woman. Hell, you ran a whole department for years. We all know how capable you are. So, please explain to me why you can't do something as simple as get your work for this paper done. Is this too mundane for you? Are you bored?"

Yes, I thought miserably in my head. *More than you could possibly understand*. I didn't say it though and forced myself to shake my head. "I'll stay focused, Dr. Porter. Thank you for the reminder." The idea that I was bending to his will, that I had no backbone to stand up to him, was crushing me. Part of me felt that leaving NASA and this career all together was far better of a fate than staying here and being treated this way.

But I didn't have the heart to leave. I wasn't going to give Michael Riddler the satisfaction of knowing that he'd completely defeated me. If I had any way to remind him that I was still there, that I was still trying everything in my power to not let him win… I was going to do it. Even if it meant that this twerp of a man had authority over me.

Drew got up from his seat then, and much to my displeasure, patted me on the shoulder. "Very good, Dr. Carter. I'm glad all that work ethic from your years managing that department didn't go to waste when they let you go."

My entire face twitched. It took every single bit of willpower I had not to react to his words. He'd said them on purpose, trying to dig into me just a little bit more. Deflate me more than he already had. I wouldn't let him. A line had to be drawn. "There's plenty of things I'm still quite capable of, Dr. Porter. My lack of tolerance for arrogant, self-centered men hasn't gone to waste either."

I watched Drew's mouth snap shut. He stared at me, looking a mixture of shocked and annoyed at my words. There was silence for a few moments, where I waited for him to scold me for my very purposeful jab at him. Instead, I was surprised when he backed up a step, took a deep breath, and replied very calmly to me. "Let's try not to get sacked from two positions in less than a year, Daphne. Shall we?" And then I watched him turn and leave me without speaking another word.

"Touché," I muttered under my breath, returning my focus to my computer.

When I checked my email again, hoping for data about our control subject, I was disappointed to find it still hadn't arrived. Dr. Porter oversaw the genetics division of the biology department at NASA. He'd been involved in an intimate project, far smaller of a scale than the work I'd been doing, observing the shifts in gene expression in twins, one of which had gone to the ISS, while the other remained on Earth. If I'd cared more about genetics, I might have been rather fascinated with the results, which showed significant changes. Genetics didn't interest me, however intriguing it might have been to most biologists. My entire life's work had been focused on the spine, and I didn't see that changing any time soon.

Even if I would likely be stuck in this position until I retired. The thought was absolutely mortifying, so I tried not to dwell on it often.

Just as I was about to close out of my emails to move on to other things, in fear I might be in for more lashings from Dr. Porter, a new message came in. I'd hoped it was the data I needed but was not surprised to see that it was yet another email from Ruby Peters.

It had been just over a month since she'd returned to Earth. A month of not being able to see her, like I had wanted so desperately to. A month that I hadn't explained what had happened to her and left her completely in the dark. I was certain that Mason had enlightened her, at least enough. But it was for the best. As painful as it had been to distance myself from her, I couldn't bear the thought of jeopardizing her career, after mine had been stripped from me. All I could think of every moment that I wished I'd just answered her, was one of our first conversations.

It was a disservice to Marie Curie herself not to help another woman succeed.

Not surprisingly, she was still persistent and stubborn as ever. I received several emails a day, both on my work email account, and my personal one. An excessive amount of phone calls. Even messages from our crossword site that indicated she'd started another puzzle without me. She was clever, and smart, and she deserved the career that she had worked so hard for. If that meant I couldn't be with her, that we couldn't speak to one another, then it would have to be.

The email that had arrived in my inbox had no subject. Normally, it would have shown a small snippet of what had been written inside, but there was nothing this time. My logic had been, if I didn't open her correspondence, if I showed that I wasn't interested anymore, no matter how much she pursued me, that they had nothing to condemn her with. This was my cross to bear, not hers.

My curiosity was getting the best of me that day, however. I found, after the demeaning conversation with Drew, that I wanted nothing more than the comfort of one of the very few humans that had ever understood me. There was nothing tethering me to reality in those moments, just the overwhelming desire to have her in my life again.

I'd just about clicked on the message, when another email arrived. The data that I had been waiting on for hours. The painstaking curiosity dwindled a bit, and my mind returned to what needed to be done. There would be no more belligerent comments from Dr. Porter today, if I could help it. I'd do what he'd asked of me, even if it was the hardest thing I'd ever do. And I'd made the trip to the International Space Station. I'd been a civilian in space.

Ruby would have to understand. I wasn't going to give her a choice.

WHILE I USUALLY WORKED WELL INTO the evenings when I'd been head of the occupational health and ergonomics department, I found I wanted any reason to escape this last month. My condo had become a welcome comfort, a safe haven from the chaos that had become my life. And my time in the evenings had become dedicated to the pursuit of baking.

Tonight, I'd decided on pumpkin muffins, despite the summer season. After the day that I'd had, it was all I could think about making. They were my absolute favorite treat, one that I believed that I could eat every day for the rest of my life and never get sick of.

Once I'd mixed the batter and poured it into muffin tins, I popped the dozen into the oven and set the timer accordingly. After, I retrieved a bottle of a local red wine from the fridge. I very rarely drank, but it had been a gift from my intern Jenny, when I'd left the department. A fruity wine, that even a non-drinker like myself would be able to enjoy. I hadn't touched it since I'd received it, but tonight felt like a night for it.

With a full regular sized glass in hand, since I had no wine glasses available, I made my way from the kitchen to my couch. For years, I'd barely used it. Then Ruby had come into my life, and it had become one of my favorite places in my house. Even after having not spoken to her in over a month, I still took comfort in it when I came home in the evenings.

I flipped through the television stations, mostly everything uninteresting. Honestly, I just needed something homey and light. Something to distract me from the terrible day I'd had. The terrible week. The terrible month. Something to stop the barrage of thoughts, begging me to contact the one person I wanted in those moments. The one person I could never have.

Then I saw it. Just a tiny blip of a scene as I clicked through channels. I remembered it vividly in my mind, so it was hard not to recognize. The last movie Ruby and I had watched together. It was the scene in *Return of the Jedi*, when Princess Leia had freed Han Solo from the carbonite prison he'd been encased in. One of my favorite scenes from the film, when they had reunited. Even though Harrison Ford had reminded me in many ways of a young version of my ex-husband, and Han Solo's cocky arrogance had been eerily similar.

Just as I'd taken my first sip of wine, settling in to watch the remainder of the film, my doorbell rang through the condo. I couldn't recall there ever being a time that I'd heard it. The sound startled me at first, causing me to jump in my seat. Then I spent a few moments trying to understand what it had been, finally realizing that it was the doorbell.

The only person I could possibly imagine it being was Mason. He was the only friend of mine that had ever been in my apartment, years and years ago. The idea that he'd come all the way here from Florida filled me with a rush of anxiety, wondering what he could have possibly wanted. Perhaps it hadn't been him at all. Someone who had rang the doorbell by accident.

"I'm coming," I called across the condo. After I set my glass on the island in the kitchen, I weaved my way around to the other side of the room, where the front door was. Before I opened it, I took a deep breath, preparing myself for whatever might be on the other side of the door. I wasn't particularly in the mood for visitors.

Nothing could have readied me to see Ruby Peters on the other side. I'd been gracious in that moment, when it had flown open, that I had not been holding the glass of wine. It would have most certainly crashed to the floor in my surprise.

"Ruby," I said, barely managing to speak her name. My voice came out breathy and hardly audible. I stared at her, stunned, trying to process that she was there. Somehow, she'd figured out where I'd lived, likely due to Mason. And where I expected to feel panicked, to immediately tell her that she needed to leave and I couldn't see her anymore, I didn't. Instead, I stood motionless, just staring at her. Disbelieving that she was even real. She must have just been released from the medical facility at Kennedy, having come the minute they'd let her leave.

No longer was that short curly black hair of hers floating in the microgravity of space. No longer was her very essence dampened by a computer screen, by three hundred miles of space between us. She was there, standing perfectly still in the doorway. Brown eyes wide and beautiful as ever. I could hear her breathing in the silence that had existed between us in those moments. She was inches away from me now. A foot, at most. If I reached out, I could touch her again. Know that she existed.

It was everything I had ever wanted, for her to be there. Real, in the flesh, no longer a figment of my imagination. No longer a voice in my head, an image in my mind. I saw her, as real as everything else around me in those moments. Yet nothing else around me existed. Only Ruby. My beautiful, perfect Ruby.

"What the hell were you thinking?" Ruby's tone was a jarring contrast to the warm, pleasant thoughts I was having. It yanked me firmly back to reality. I blinked, and stared at her, trying to realize what she'd just said. "It's been an entire *month,* Daphne. You didn't say a word to me. Vanished, with no explanation. You could have been dead for all I knew—"

"Mason had to have told you..." I started, unable to think clearly with her standing there, even if she seemed to be furious with me in those moments. I was too enamored by her presence.

"Mason told me," Ruby confirmed, but her tone was still firm, even slightly pissed. Even with her eyes having narrowed, they were gorgeous. A beautiful, warm walnut color. Never in my life did I think I could be more attracted to someone with brown eyes, but hers consumed me, every time she looked at me. "I needed *you* to tell me, Daphne. I needed *you* to be there. I needed *you* to let me know that you were safe, that you were okay. Not your friend. You."

"I was trying to protect you, Ruby," I argued, finally managing to find words to say to her, despite how angry she seemed. There were things I wanted to say in my defense, things that I hoped would make her understand my actions. "I was trying not to tear you down with me. You know Michael, you know what he's capable of. He may have figured out how to destroy my career, but I would be damned if he took away yours."

"I'm a grown woman, Daphne," Ruby said back, firmly. Her tone had softened just slightly, eyes not quite so narrow as they had been. But she was still deathly serious. "I know what I'm doing when it comes to my career. I know what I'm capable of. I know what Dr. Riddler is capable of. I could have handled it, whatever happened..."

"Ruby—"

"But I can't handle losing you, Daphne," she said, and I watched her take a small step forward, closer to me. Diminishing what little space there was between us. So close now, that I could feel her steady breaths beating against the lower half of my face, as she looked up into my eyes. "Don't you get that? Don't you see after all this time? After everything?"

"It was the only thing I could think of to do," I explained, finding it increasingly difficult to breathe, with her standing so close to me. "The only thing that made any sense. I wanted to protect you, to keep you safe from Michael. I never meant to hurt you."

"But why did you—"

"Because I love you." The four words spilled from my mouth, as effortlessly as they had been the air I'd been breathing. It felt natural. Completely normal. Completely right.

Ruby stared at me, this time the one without words to say. Her mouth hung slightly open, and once again I could hear her steady breathing.

It was like beautiful music to my ears, knowing she was alive, right there in front of me. That subtle sound that said that you were a living entity, that you existed in the universe. I remembered it so vividly when she was breathing over the hot microphone inside the space suit, when we'd floated together above the Earth. In those moments, looking at the serene way she smiled, the softness of her face, the glow of the planet in her eyes...that was when I had known. The very moment I had understood her and realized that she had been a fundamental part of me that I'd been missing my entire life. A singular thing that I didn't realize I'd needed.

I had those same feelings now, staring at her in my doorway. Completely enamored by everything about her. There was nothing I needed more in those moments, than for her to exist. And I hadn't realized how desperately I did, until she'd been there, right in front of me.

Suddenly, the small distance between us, those tiny, final few inches that separated me from her, dissipated. It wasn't clear who had moved first, or if we had both just moved together, like one singular entity that knew exactly what to do. But my hands found her face again, the soft warmth from her cheeks, as wonderful as sunlight on my skin. My fingers wove into those marvelous curls of hers, feeling their soft texture.

Our faces came together, closer than they'd been in seven

months. The two of us paused, lips hovering over one another's. My eyes had closed, completely lost in all my other senses, trying to take every part of her in. I listened to our steady breathing that had fallen together in a synchronous rhythm. A soft tickle against my lips let me know that Ruby had ran her tongue across hers. The image in my mind made me lose all control.

My body moved forward, pushing us together. Ruby took steps back, and I onward, neither of us separating, until she'd been pushed up against the wall opposite to the door. Then our mouths came together, in such a fiery blaze of heat and longing, that the only thing I could focus on in those moments was kissing her. The feeling of her soft lips falling over mine, damp from when she'd licked them moments earlier. The kiss sent my stomach into a wild swirl.

I listened to the soft, irresistible sounds that our mouths made, each time we broke and came back again. Smelled what seemed to be remnants of something spicy on her breath, mixed with the sweet scent of lavender from her hair. Felt the delicate way she caressed me with her lips, mixed with our exhilarating desires to really feel each other, completely. To know that we both existed, that this moment was real.

Ruby Peters had come back to me.

When we finally broke, it felt painful. I wanted nothing more in those moments than to kiss her forever. There was nothing stopping us, not right then. It was just her and I in that hallway. Just her and I, together at last. But when I'd taken a step back from her, to look at her face again, reality had come back with brutal force. And it was horribly painful.

Then Ruby said a few words that made it all fade away. "I love you too, Daphne."

I sighed, drawing my hand up to cup the soft skin of her cheek again, wanting to feel her against me every second. To never let her fade away again. As beautiful as her words had been, as much as I had needed to hear them in those moments, they too, were devastating.

"We can't," I said, my voice having grown incredibly soft and fragile. It was difficult for me to hang on in those moments, knowing the gravity of the situation. The reality we faced.

"Yes, we can," Ruby's hand came up to wrap around my own, that was still holding her. I watched that warm smile as it stretched across her face, brown eyes looking so deeply at me, that it felt as if she was diving into my soul, if it existed. "You've spent two decades trying to fight these battles alone, trying to be a strong, independent woman, in the face of so much adversity. You did it, Daphne. You lived that life, more bravely than I could have ever imagined another human to be. I'm so proud of you, so honored to know you, to be in your presence..."

Never in my entire life had I heard someone speak to me the way she was. The validating words that came so naturally from her. I knew every part of it to be true, didn't question it for a second. She would never lie to me, that wasn't in her character.

"Only a person who has been through the same sort of journey would ever be able to understand that, you know," I replied, feeling a small smile breaching my face, as my thumb stroked against her cheek. Ruby squeezed my hand in return. "There's not a person in this universe I know braver than you, Ruby Peters."

Ruby's smile widened, if that were even possible. We paused for a moment, both of us just staring at one another. Basking in each other's presence, in the idea that we were together. Then she spoke again. "What I'm trying to say, Daphne," she stated softly, drawing my hand down from her face, and weaving ours together, in one graceful motion. "Is that you don't have to be alone anymore. Neither of us do. We're a team, now."

I wasn't sure what to say, and I admitted it. "I don't know what to do."

Inside, I heard the buzz of the oven timer, distant in the background.

The smile that had been on Ruby's face, turned more into a grin then. That kind of quirky grin I'd known her for when we'd first been together on the ISS. The kind of grin that indicated that she knew exactly what she wanted, what she was doing. It was the kind of act that instilled confidence within me, even without knowing a single thing.

"Well lucky for you, I have a plan."

TWENTY-TWO

RUBY

Through the speakers of the car, a violin and piano played an upbeat duet. The cheery music blended in with the sounds of the wind rushing by the open windows outside, and the waves crashing into the beach to the right of us, and the seagulls above. I could smell the scent of saltwater in the air and enjoyed the warm sunlight on the cloudless summer afternoon in Florida.

It was the perfect day out, and what made it all the better was the blonde sitting beside me, her hand outside the window dancing in the wind, as I drove down the beachside road up north. I didn't think I'd seen Daphne more relaxed than she was in those moments, getting lost in the scenery and the ambiance.

"What's this song?" I asked, curiously, glancing over in her direction.

Daphne met my gaze for a half second before I looked away toward the road again. She looked thoughtful, a small smile on her face. "*Sonata No. 17 in C*," she explained, matter-of-factly. "Composed by Mozart. This rendition is by Juliet Hamilton and Emma Harvey. Have you heard of them?" I shook my head, not having been a big classical music listener. But I'd decided to let Daphne pick the music today, as we made our short road trip from my apartment in Cocoa Beach. "They played for the New York Philharmonic, but I believe they're in London now."

"It's a beautiful song," I admitted, turning along the road a bit. "Very peppy."

I heard Daphne laugh beside me, and it was the sweetest sound, blending in with everything else around me. "I'd hoped you'd like it. I made this playlist just for you."

A warmth spread through me at her words. Months ago, I'd sent Daphne a playlist of songs while I'd still been aboard the ISS. Never in my wildest dreams had I imagined she'd take the time to make me one in return. But here it was, and it nearly took my breath away.

"You made a playlist for me?" I said, feeling slightly overwhelmed at the gesture. When I glanced at Daphne again, she was still smiling and nodded. "—I don't even know what to say."

"You don't have to say a word," Daphne replied, as the Mozart song ended. "Just listen." Just as I was about to ask if there was anything other than classical music on this list, the next song started. I instantly recognized it. A Van Morrison song that I hadn't heard in ages, but the minute the music began to play, I knew exactly what it was.

Daphne must have realized that I had and grew gently stern with me. "I'd prefer it if you focused on driving instead of dancing." When she said it, I laughed, swaying a little in my seat. I peeked over at her again, and Daphne was shaking her head, but still smiling.

"Am I your brown eyed girl?" I said, before Van Morrison had even sung the lyrics. When I looked at Daphne again, she'd covered her face with a hand, and it caused me to laugh. She shook her head, refusing to look back at me. "This was charmingly cheesy of you, Daphne. I didn't think you had it in you."

Daphne sat back in her seat, and when I glanced at her again, she'd resumed looking at me. Though there was a hint of redness to her cheeks, she was still smiling. "I'll have you know that while I'm mostly a very predictable human being, I still am surprising on occasion, Ruby."

"Indeed, you are," I replied, grinning as the lyrics of the chorus kicked in. While I sang along, swaying in my seat while I drove, I could make out Daphne beside me, shaking her head. Her hand had resumed catching the air outside the car, and she'd relaxed in her seat.

When I looked at Daphne a minute or so later, her attention had turned completely focused outside, admiring the beachfront we were passing. While most of Florida's coast was filled with high rise hotels and condominiums, this patch was wide open, allowing for an unobstructed view of the ocean. The sun was getting lower in the sky now and if I had to guess there were thirty minutes or so until it would disappear completely.

"I know it's not the same as watching sunsets on the Gulf," Daphne's voice interrupted my thoughts, and I focused on her. "But I don't suppose you'd mind if we pull over and enjoy it on the beach anyway?" A smile stretched across my face and I slowed the car, making the turn into a parking lot that was surprisingly mostly empty.

Once I'd parked, I spoke again. "Now we didn't bring swimsuits," I noted. "And as delightful as skinny dipping with you in the ocean sounds, I don't have towels either. So, we'll just have to refrain, no matter how enticing it is."

Daphne's cheeks flushed slightly pink again, and she'd opened her mouth to speak, but nothing came. Instead, she hopped out. I followed behind her. She'd paused in front of the car, and I'd admired her for a moment. While I had nearly always saw her in professional clothes and NASA polos, today she'd dressed very relaxed. A loosely fitting, white cotton three-quarter-length blouse, that was blowing lightly in the wind, and a pair of khaki capris, and sandals. Meanwhile, I'd dressed down more than her, in a pair of jean shorts and a NASA tank top.

When I reached Daphne, I noticed she'd been holding out her

hand toward me. It took me a moment to realize what she'd wanted, but when I did, I couldn't help but smile. I wrapped my hand in her own, intertwining our fingers, and then the two of us set off onto the beach.

The sky was a mix of beautiful shades of honey and apricot oranges, mixed with coral and bubblegum pinks. I didn't think I'd really stopped to admire a sunset since I'd returned home from the ISS, but tonight was certainly a glorious one. Perhaps the best one I'd ever experienced in my life, when Daphne had been by my side to share it.

"It's a wonderful evening," Daphne noted, as we walked through the sand toward the shoreline. Out of the corner of my eye, I saw her blonde hair catching the wind, and the serene look on her face. I took a deep breath in, enjoying the smell of salt in the fresh air. She squeezed my hand. "Thank you for the trip."

"It hasn't even started yet," I reminded her. We hadn't gotten to our destination yet and had only left a little over an hour earlier, after Daphne had dropped off her small bag of luggage for her weekend trip here. "It's our first *real* date, after all. I had to make a good impression..."

"I would be perfectly content doing nearly anything, as long as you were here with me," Daphne replied, and I watched her tuck a few strands of hair behind her ear. Those hazel eyes were looking at me, a small smile on her lips. She was being delightfully cheesy today, and I was very much enjoying it.

"Even taking another shuttle ride?" I asked, raising a brow and grinning.

"I did say *nearly*," Daphne reminded me, and I laughed. "I'm certain whatever you have planned will be perfect." I nodded in reply and the two of us went quiet for a few minutes, coming up near the edge of the water. Daphne took her sandals off once we'd gotten onto the wet sand. She let go of my hand, and I watched her walk until her feet had hit the gentle waves that were rolling onto the shore.

Daphne stood, looking out into the vast expanse of water, her blonde hair dancing around her head, and the edges of her blouse and capris catching the wind. I stood and watched her from a short distance away, taking in her innocence in those moments. The peace she seemed to have been feeling.

It had been a long week, all things considered. She needed this brief bit of time, and I was happy to have been sharing it with her. Eventually, I came up beside her, once I'd removed my own sandals, and interlaced our hands together again. The cool water rolled up over my feet and I enjoyed the way it felt, rhythmic and calming.

"How are you feeling?" Daphne asked me. It had been a question she'd asked frequently over the last week since I'd arrived at her doorstep in Houston. The minute I'd been released from medical care at Kennedy, I'd taken a plane right straight to her. She still seemed to be rather concerned about my health, regardless that I'd been cleared by the staff. While I knew it was mostly because she genuinely cared about me, it was in her nature to constantly be on top of an astronaut's health, especially related to their spines. It had been her job for decades, after all.

"I'm doing okay," I admitted, watching as a seagull flew by us overhead. "I still have my physical therapy and occupational therapy for the next few months, but all things considered I think I'm doing really well." Daphne looked satisfied, seeming to relax a little. But her question had prompted me with one of my own. "What about you?"

Daphne had known what I meant. I was certain. She turned her full attention toward me then, and we focused on one another, instead of the world around us. It was just me and her. "I'm worried about it," she admitted. "I'm trying not to get my hopes up. There's a high probability it won't work out the way we intend it to."

"So, we'll try anyway," I argued, squeezing her hand, and offering a small smile. "They scheduled the ethics hearing next week. We'll go, say our piece, and whatever happens, happens, right? There's nothing to lose, Daphne."

"There's plenty for you to lose," Daphne replied, looking a mix of stern and worried. "This entire plan could backfire and cost you as much as it's cost me." She didn't look convinced, and suddenly I felt bad I'd even mentioned the situation at all, having enjoyed her peaceful and happy aura the last few hours.

"Marie Curie," I reminded her, a small smile forming on my face. The name, I hoped, would be all she would need to hear.

It seemed to have been the case. Daphne sighed softly and nodded. She returned my small smile, and I watched her take the hand that had been holding my own, and gently place it against my cheek. I leaned into it, enjoying its warmth and softness. She leaned forward, planting her lips on mine, just for a few moments.

When she broke away, she brushed her thumb against my cheek. Her face had relaxed again, those hazel eyes softening, and that smile still there. We just stood there, neither of us saying anything at all. It was only the sounds of the ocean and the breeze and the seagulls then. A stark contrast to the soundless void of being out in space. Earth was miraculous in that way.

And so was Daphne.

The sun was nearly set, the sky growing dark then. Daphne seemed to realize this too, and let her hand fall from my face, wrapping it in my own again. "Should we go?" she asked me.

"Let's," I replied, starting to lead us off the beach, hand in hand.

THIRTY MINUTES LATER, we arrived in another empty parking lot on the campus of Seminole State College. The Emil Buehler Planetarium was the closest one to the space coast and was tucked away between beautifully lit buildings on the college grounds. It was a small place. I'd only visited twice before, many years ago. When I glanced at Daphne after I'd removed the keys from the ignition, she was staring, very confused.

"All your questions will be answered momentarily," I replied, nodding for her to exit. In the back of the car, I fetched a large bag that I'd brought along with us, while Daphne closed the door for me. Then the two of us walked up the concrete pathway to the front of the building. The sign outside gave my plan away. When I glanced at Daphne, she was smiling. Before I could manage to knock a familiar face met me at the door.

Elle Richards, Daniel's wife, was the assistant to the General Director of the planetarium and astronomy department at the college. She'd been working at Seminole State for as long as I'd known her. The last time I'd been up to visit, myself and several other NASA colleagues, including Mason, had been given a private tour and show.

"Right on time," Elle said, holding open the door for us. She was a pretty woman, who I'd always joked with Daniel had been "way out of his league," but she also was one of the kindest people I'd ever met. "Nice to see you again, Ruby."

"You too, Elle," I replied, offering a smile as I came through the doorway. Once we'd both made it through, Elle locked it behind us. It was just us tonight, exactly the way I had wanted it to be. I glanced at Daphne, who had paused once we'd all made it inside. "Elle, this is Daphne—"

"Dr. Carter," Elle said, and without hesitation walked up and hugged her gently. Daphne had gone slightly rigid at the gesture, and I watched her lightly pat Elle on the back. When they broke, she spoke again. "I've heard a lot of nice things about you, between my husband and Ruby..."

"Your husband?" Daphne asked, curiously. "Daniel Richards, I presume?" Elle nodded, and Daphne looked pleased that she'd guessed right. "And please, call me Daphne." It was strange hearing her ask someone to call her informally. Ever since I'd known her, she'd been an all-work, no-play kind of person, so the idea that she was trying to be casual with anyone was surprising. She seemed to have relaxed quite a bit. "Daniel is a very kind man, which I'm certain if you married him, you must certainly be the same."

Elle beamed at her and shrugged. "My husband is quite the charmer." She waved us inside. "Come on in." She looked at me as Daphne and I followed her through the lobby, toward the opposite end of the building. "I've got everything all set up, and I've got the NexStar upstairs and ready to go..." She paused a second.

"I'll let you two be," Elle said, holding out a set of keys in her hand toward me. I took them carefully, tucking them away in my jean shorts pocket. "Just lock everything up before you leave, and you can swing by our place on your way home and leave those in the mailbox." I nodded, and then Elle leaned in to hug me goodbye.

Once she'd left the two of us alone, I turned my attention to Daphne. There was a perplexed look on her face, that was a mixture of curiosity and confusion. "What is a NexStar?" she asked, as I wrapped my hand in her own.

"How about I just show you?" I replied, smiling at her.

Outside, it had grown very dark. It was a perfect evening, cloudless, so you could see stars in every direction. I enjoyed this area of Florida quite a bit, due to its low light pollution. It wasn't the very best place to stargaze in the state, but it was close. I'd taken Daphne up to the rooftop of the building adjacent to the planetarium, where Elle had left the Celestron Nextar Evolution 8 telescope set up on one side, with a pair of lawn chairs. It was Daniel's several thousand dollar present he'd bought himself when he'd first graduated the astronaut program.

"Very original of you," Daphne said, once she'd realized what I'd done. She was smiling however, a bright smile that stretched across her face. While she'd been teasing me, she looked genuinely happy at the idea.

"Just wait," I replied, glancing at her briefly as we made our way over to the opposite side of the roof. "You can see Jupiter with this thing." We stepped up to the telescope together, and Daphne sat down while I spent a few minutes fiddling with setting it up. It had been a year or so since I'd last had an opportunity to use it. Once I'd found what I was searching for, I focused on it and then stepped away, motioning for Daphne to look.

Daphne approached the telescope timidly, like I'd asked her to jump off a waterfall and she'd been testing the waters and looking over the edge to make sure it was safe. We met eyes, and she looked as though she was wanting permission. I nodded and watched as she leaned forward to press her eye against the lens.

I wasn't quite sure what was going through her head for a while. The two of us were completely silent, and I didn't mind much, enjoying the view of Daphne with the telescope. Eventually, I heard her let out a soft sigh, and then stand back upright, looking up at the night sky for a while, like she was contemplating her very existence.

She turned to me. "You know, I never would have thought myself a person to take much interest in astronomy." I watched her glance up at the skies again, before her hazel eyes returned to me. "I've always been so focused on biology, on medicine, my entire life. It was there, of course, working with astronauts how could it not be, but—I just never thought I'd care."

"It changes, doesn't it?" I said, thoughtfully, quite sure I knew where she'd been going. "When you see the Earth from space for the first time. It really puts things into perspective. Have you ever heard that Carl Sagan quote about the pale blue dot?"

"That astronomy is a humble and character-building experience," Daphne said, without a second of hesitation. I smiled, nodding in agreement. "How small we really are."

"I take it you liked seeing Jupiter," I said, nodding at the telescope. Daphne's face broke into a smile, and she nodded. After I set up the telescope for her again, I let her view a few more planets, the moon, and stars. It was highly likely that she'd be content just spending the entire night out here, stargazing. The thought made me happy, but I'd had other plans in mind.

While Daphne was looking at the moon again through the telescope, I spoke. "I'm going to let you stay up here for a few more minutes, while I go back downstairs. Come meet me in the planetarium in say—" I looked at my watch on my hand, trying to make a good guess. "Ten minutes?"

I expected for Daphne to ask where I was going, or what I was planning to do, but she instead seemed rather distracted with what she'd been looking at. "I'll be down shortly," she agreed, and I couldn't help but smile and watch her for a few moments before I disappeared.

DAPHNE HAD ARRIVED DOWNSTAIRS, twenty minutes later. I'd almost left to go fetch her, thinking she'd gotten so caught up in stargazing that she'd forgotten. I'd finished setting up the giant projector in the middle of the room, per instructions that Elle had left. On the far side, away from the doors, was an open spot, free of chairs.

I'd spread a blanket out, along with a collection of picnic-worthy food and drinks. Above, footage of the Earth beneath the International Space Station was playing. Daphne was looking up in awe as she entered, transfixed by the video that was spread across the dome above us.

"This was the first show I ever saw when I came to this planetarium," I explained to her. "I'd just moved to Cocoa Beach to start the astronaut training program at Kennedy, and I took a trip up here. I just remember how surreal it felt to see it, realizing I'd get to in person one day."

Daphne had been making her way around the outer part of the room, avoiding the lines of chairs in the middle. She found me on the opposite side, and sat herself down on the blanket. It seemed as if she couldn't make up her mind whether to focus on the video playing above us, or on me. She smiled, wordlessly, and then I watched her lay down on her back, staring upward. I joined her, looking skyward as the International Space Station was passing over an upside-down India. I got lost in the view for a while, hearing Daphne beside me, breathing steadily.

"I could look at you, lost in that view, for the rest of my life," Daphne spoke softly.

I glanced over at her, realizing she'd turned on her side and was focused entirely on me. A smile dance across my lips, looking into those eyes flecked with blues and greens and browns. In some ways, they reminded me of looking at the Earth, and perhaps that was one of the many reasons they always demanded my attention.

"It's an amazing thing to watch," I argued, still unable to stop myself from smiling. My hand reached up to tuck some of her blonde hair behind her ear, away from her face, so I could see her clearly. Her delicate skin glowed in the light surrounding us in that dome.

"Not nearly as amazing as watching you," Daphne replied, leaning into the delicate touch of my fingertips against her cheek. Her abundance of cheesy lines throughout the day finally got the best of me, and I found my hand wrapping around the back of her head, drawing her close.

Daphne dropped, in one delicate motion, her hand moving to rest on the opposite side of my body, as our faces drew together. Our mouths lingered, almost touching. I could hear her breaths, having quickened slightly, and felt the heat against my face. I waited until the ache to feel us touch was nearly unbearable before I planted my lips to hers. Daphne let out the gentlest of sighs when we kissed, and it lit me aflame.

I drew up, pressing against her and turning her until she'd come to fall on her back against the blanket I'd laid out. When I laid on top of her, I let the contours of our bodies come together, and for the first time felt what it was like to be completely wrapped up in her. We kissed again, this time more deeply before. My tongue danced against Daphne's lips, until it was met with hers. She let out the smallest of moans again, and it was the most mesmerizing sound that I could have ever imagined hearing.

My mouth left hers, drawing against her soft cheek, and then down into the divot of her neck. Daphne had wrapped her long fingers into my curly hair, and I felt her body buck against me as I planted kiss after kiss into her skin. Smelling the faint scent of her, surprisingly reminding me of what the beach had smelled like earlier that day, fresh and crisp and delightful.

All at once, Daphne cleared her throat, and I drew upward so I could look down at her. Her hazel eyes had softened, and I felt her fingers stroke against my face while she studied me. There was a drawn-out silence between us, just watching one another.

"I've never been with a woman before," Daphne admitted, though not so much in a bashful way, as much as a statement of fact. "I'm not certain I'll be any good at it." It was strange, hearing a woman so undeniably intelligent and distinguished in so many ways, be so vulnerable in admitting her shortcomings. Except they weren't shortcomings, not to me anyway.

"I've never been with you either," I reminded her, dipping down to draw a small kiss against her mouth, before coming back up again. "We're in this together, Daphne."

Daphne's look of concern faded back into a smile, fingers still dancing against my face. They drew around the back of my head, and she pulled me downward again, without another word. This time it was me who gasped softly when our mouths met. The two of our bodies moved in a synchronous rhythm, rocking against each other. I kissed along her cheek again, down into her neck, while my fingers made quick work of the buttons on her blouse.

Before I knew it, Daphne had sat up, letting me draw the white fabric over her shoulders, and off her. My hands reached behind her body, undoing the white lacy bra she'd been wearing. I'd barely been able to look at her, when Daphne decided to follow suit, pulling my tank top over my head, revealing my naked flesh underneath.

The two of us sat together, half naked, underneath the dome of the planetarium, the beautiful glow of the Earth above us. The lights illuminated Daphne's delicate features, from the curves of her face and neck, the prominence of her collarbone, and her shapely breasts. I was so focused on taking every bit of her in, that I hadn't noticed she'd been doing the same thing.

My fingers danced across her naked shoulder, drawing down her arm. I watched goosebumps form as they did, and the touch drew Daphne's eyes to look at me. Carefully, I fell back into her, bringing her back to the blanket on the floor. My fingers drew underneath the hem of her capri pants, tugging them down the length of her, until she was lying completely naked. Then I followed suit, removing my own pants, before my focus returned to Daphne.

I got lost in her for a long time, tracing over her repeatedly in my mind. Memorizing all the features of her I'd fantasized and dreamed about for months, now completely real in front of me. Eventually, I drew forward, leaning down to plant soft kisses at her belly button, and making my way up the length of her. Each time my mouth touched her flesh, Daphne moaned lightly into the room, hips bucking against me.

When I'd reached her face again, pulling us together so I could feel the warmth of her flesh against me, I rested my hands on either side of her. We met eyes, hazel on brown, and became completely frozen in time. I listened to her steady breathing, almost in time with my own, our bodies like the waves of the ocean, as our chests moved up and down.

Daphne drew her fingers up to my cheek again, sliding them back around my neck and into my hair. Her face was still gentle, but had grown a little more serious, too. I watched her mouth open just a fraction, felt her body writhe gently into my own, and listened to the soft pants she made when we came together.

Then she whispered, just audibly enough for me to hear her, in a tone so sensual, it was like silk wrapping around me. The sounds sent a violent shiver down my spine. "Ruby," Daphne was looking straight at me, those eyes wide and full of longing and desires beyond my possible comprehension. I could see the light of the Earth above us, reflecting in her eyes. And then she spoke three words that sent me crashing over the edge.

"I want you."

TWENTY-THREE

DAPHNE

Marveling at Ruby Peters, with the sight of the magnificent glowing picture of the Earth behind her, I found I was without any words that could comprehend the emotions I felt. It brought back memories from the first time I'd seen the Earth from the cockpit of *Galileo*, months ago. The serenity that had washed over me, when Ruby I had been floating, hand in hand, on our spacewalk. Every evening that I'd spent watching videos of her, hiding away in the cupola.

Nothing could compare to this moment, now. I'd watched Ruby look over every piece of me, naked and vulnerable beneath her, and where I was certain I would feel self-conscious and worried, all I felt was calm. My breath came out in steady rolls, as Ruby lingered above me, having pressed our bodies together.

The first thought I had when I had felt the warmth of her skin against mine, was how soft it felt. Such an undeniable contrast to anything I'd ever experienced before, like the difference between cotton and silk bedsheets. I felt her breathing against me, how we'd both fallen in rhythm with one another, along with the gentle bucking of our hips.

Ruby fell, encompassing me as much as her small frame could, and kissed me deeply. She took the air from my lungs, and I found myself gasping when we parted. Then her lips trailed again, from my mouth, against my cheek, and down into my neck. Every tender touch she made was a constant reminder that I was with a woman, and not just any woman, but with Ruby.

The trail of kisses drew to my breasts. Every concern I had about what she might have thought about them, a little more telling of their age than her own, vanished when I felt her lips fall around my hardened nipple. I gasped, my hips bucking again. The noise seemed to encourage Ruby, whose tongue had flicked against me. Sound after sound came from deep within me, with every touch she gave.

I'd never had someone pay such delicate attention to this part of me. Ruby knew what she was doing, that was evident. Even as a doctor, I'd never expected to marvel so much at what a tongue could do. The way it would feel as it danced across my flesh and teased at my nipple. And just when I'd thought I couldn't possibly reach a higher level of ecstasy than I was feeling in those moments, Ruby planted her mouth over my other breast, and I found it was even more sensitive than the first.

"Oh, Ruby," I found myself gasping, my body writhing underneath her. My fingers wrapped into her hair, holding on to her head as her tongue worked effortlessly against me. When I looked down to watch her, she'd glanced upward, and we met eyes. The sight of her, staring at me, tongue outstretched from her mouth, flicking against my hardened nipple, sent a raging wave of heat between my legs, the likes of which I'd never felt before. I couldn't watch for long, falling back against the blanket, hands still around her head.

Ruby finished with my breasts, and I felt her mouth drawing softly down the center of my body, over my belly button, and down to the crest of my pubic bone. She paused, and I found myself propping the upper part of my body up to look at her. When our eyes were locked together, it felt as if the entire world had paused in those moments. Both of us were breathing steady and calm, and I realized Ruby was subtly making sure I was okay.

I offered a small smile, reaching out with one hand to touch her cheek. Ruby turned her head, to catch my fingertips with her lips. She kissed them, and then I dropped my hand back down, and laid back down. My eyes looked upward, feeling encapsulated by the beauty of the Earth glowing above me.

The feeling of Ruby's mouth against my flesh resumed, drawing against my belly button, and then in slow, purposeful motions back to my pubic bone. She lingered there a while, letting me feel the steady breaths she took against my flesh. My hips bucked occasionally with anticipation, wanting desperately for her to touch me.

Just when I thought I couldn't handle waiting any longer, when I was about to sit up again, Ruby's mouth returned to me. She kissed down the inside of each of my thighs. Then I felt her delicate fingers brush against the skin of my pubic bone and my thighs, following the same path her lips had taken. The touches made sounds I never expected come from me.

I'd been looking up again, just as the glow of the Earth began to fade into night, and that unbelievable sight of a world of lights enveloped Ruby and I below. As the room faded into darkness around me, I felt Ruby's mouth kiss up between my legs, a little path down the folds of my lips. The touches were firm and slow. Deliberate. She wanted me to feel each one, each tantalizing move she made against me. Ruby intended to unravel me completely, and I wasn't sure if I would ever come back from it. I didn't care.

Golden lights flickered above me and the illuminated space station. As I watched them twinkle over us in slow motion, I felt too, as Ruby's fingers danced against me. She splayed me open, the cold air hitting me in places that brought entirely new sensations I'd never felt. The touch of Ruby's fingers was enough to send me catapulting into oblivion, but it was nothing compared to the moment her tongue drew over me.

There was nothing to compare the sensation to, no words that could adequately describe the way it made me feel. Experiencing Ruby touch and taste me was otherworldly, like my entire being was floating high above the Earth in those moments. Once again, it felt as if Ruby was like the most seasoned ballet dancer, elegantly performing against my body, as if she'd practiced thousands of times before.

Before I could even comprehend what was happening, Ruby, whose tongue had been causing my whole body to ripple with waves of ecstasy, slid fingers deep inside of me. I writhed and bucked, a moan erupting so loudly from within me that it echoed off the walls. Every part of Ruby that had been touching me, had taken on a very steady rhythm. A rhythm that I relaxed into, letting my whole body succumb to. Reveled in the feeling of it, of Ruby pleasuring me.

The cliff I'd been precariously hanging on to, only by threads at that point, ceased to exist any longer. I fell, my entire body washed over by the steady draws of Ruby's tongue, and fingers curling within me. My movements were not my own, the sounds I made were out of my control. The world vanished, and it was only Ruby and I, and the indescribable sensations that overcame me, for what felt like an eternity.

When my body finally relaxed, and my focus returned to looking above me at the flickering lights of Earth's night, Ruby's fingers and mouth left me. I was lightly panting, as I felt her body draw over mine, until she'd come to stare down at me.

It had grown very dark in the room, but I could still make out bits and pieces of her, and the soft glow of her eyes. She was smiling at me. I watched her lean down and kiss me, without any reserve, tongue delving into my mouth. The passion in her kiss brought that heat back between my legs, but when I tasted that unusual taste in my mouth, I realized why she'd done it. It was me that I was experiencing, the result of Ruby's efforts. I savored the taste, surprised by how much I enjoyed it, and what it had meant.

Our mouths broke, and I felt Ruby's lips brush against my ear, her breath on my neck. She whispered to me, barely audible, and it caused every hair on my body to rise. "I need you to touch me."

The next few moments felt like they'd been practiced a hundred times, with how effortlessly it happened. Ruby separated from me slightly, enough so my hand could come between us. My fingers felt the patch of hair on her pubic bone and traced her lips. When they dipped between her folds, I was surprised how wet she was, and the idea of it made me gasp. The realization that I'd done this to her, we'd done this, was hard to comprehend.

"How does it feel?" Ruby asked me, her voice still quiet. Those brown eyes were lost in my own. I couldn't have imagined how anything in the world could have been more beautiful.

Then the light began to illuminate the curve of the Earth, and it all lit up before my eyes. My fingers seemed to, somewhat effortlessly, find the place on Ruby that made her entire body come alive. I worked against her, circling and flicking, experimenting with every touch I could think of, until I'd discovered the spot and the motion that sent her writhing against me. Ruby's eyes closed, mouth hung open while she panted and moaned as I touched her.

All the while, the Earth glowed again above her, making her black curls glisten, her skin vibrant as ever. And I watched the most miraculous scene unfold, something beyond anything I could have ever imagined. Ruby cried out my name into the room in a violent gasp of air. She bucked against my fingers that were covered in her arousal. I continued my motions, what I discovered she liked most, reveling in her entire being as she came. No other place, no other moment, could have been more perfect than this. The brilliant view of the Earth behind her. Exactly like I'd pictured her a thousand times before, but never as unbelievably beautiful as now.

Ruby came for a while, and I continued my motions until she'd started to fall against me. After I'd removed my hand between us, we weaved together, in a tangled mess of two naked bodies. We laid side-by-side on the blanket, staring at one another. There was a gentle smile on Ruby's lips, that I could feel I was reciprocating. Her hand came up to stroke the side of my face, delicate fingers on my cheek.

"You can't imagine how long I've been wanting to do that," Ruby said, quietly, those brown eyes studying me.

"So have I," I replied, reaching for her hand that was touching mine and wrapping them together. We laid there for a few minutes, neither of us speaking, and then I added. "I hope I wasn't too dreadful at it."

Ruby laughed, drawing forward to plant a small kiss on my lips. When she broke from me, she nudged our noses together for a second and then replied. "You were perfect."

"DO you remember the feeling when you broke through the atmosphere? When the entire universe seemed to pause, and all you could do was stare out at the Earth and marvel at how beautiful it was?" Ruby's attention was upward, staring out of the cupola window at the glowing planet in the light of day.

"Vividly," I replied, watching from below her, admiring the way she looked when she was taking in the view. I could have watched her all day, that childlike innocence about her, filled with wonder and wide-eyed fascination. She'd seen this view a hundred times, and it never grew boring to her. I didn't see how it could.

"That's what got me through," Ruby said, her brown eyes turning their attention back to me. There was a small smile on her face when she looked at me. I loved that smile, the way it danced on her lips and brightened her entire being. "All those years of school, all those times of doubt and frustration, like I was never going to measure up to my male colleagues. That I'd never make it as an astronaut. All I could do was think about getting that moment, when it was just me, staring at my planet, my home."

There was a small bit of silence between us, both of us just staring at each other, calmly. Eventually I cleared my throat, realizing how long we'd been glued to one another. I looked at my computer instead, and then decided to speak. "I remember that interview fondly." Ruby raised a brow when I glanced at her, like she wasn't sure what I was referencing. "The one you mentioned to me the other day, when I'd first started at the Biomedical Research Institute..."

"The one where you talked about wishing you could see the Earth from an astronaut's point of view? That you'd suffer through the shuttle launch and all the training, just to have that moment?" When Ruby finished, I nodded.

"I don't believe I've ever told anyone this before," I admitted. "When I was little, my father gave me an astronomy book. It was one of the few memories I have of him that I truly cherish. We used to sit together at night in my bed, and he'd talk to me about it. And I remember even when I was so small, that I knew that's all I wanted in my life. Was to do something with that. To cherish that memory. I suppose it's my way of honoring my father a little bit, regardless of what happened to us over the years."

"It's funny how we had the same aspirations, but how it led us on different paths," Ruby said, thoughtfully. "I would have never guessed you'd want to be a doctor, if you had memories like that growing up."

"I became a doctor because of my mother," I replied. "But I still had the same dreams. They just—shifted a bit, I suppose."

"I'm glad you had the dreams you did," Ruby said, and I looked up at her, admiring the warmth of the expression on her face. I couldn't help but reciprocate. "That you never gave up on them."

"I'm glad, too."

"DAPH—" A voice interrupted my daydream, bringing me back to reality. I'd been staring at a rather large photograph framed on the wall at Kennedy Space Center. A vivid picture of the cupola at the International Space Station. While there was no Ruby, she was all I could think about every time I saw it. Those memories of us together, that I would cherish for the rest of my life. "You doing okay?"

All at once, the overwhelming rush of feelings came back to me. My stomach tumbled with nerves. I realized that my palms were sweaty, and my heart was thudding inside of my chest. It was all I could do to remind myself to take steady, calm breaths.

"The best I can be, given the circumstances," I replied, swallowing deeply. When I glanced down at my watch, I realized that the hearing was scheduled to begin any moment now. No one had come to escort me inside, so I'd waited with Mason. Ruby hadn't even arrived, and she'd promised she'd be on time. The idea that she wasn't there made me incredibly anxious.

"It's going to be fine," Mason reassured me, and I felt his familiar hand squeeze my shoulder gently. Surprisingly, I found myself taking a few steps to wrap my arms around his neck and embrace him. He hugged me back, like a giant warm comforting teddy bear that I needed in those moments. "You're going to be fine."

"I certainly hope so," I replied once I'd broke away from him. As soon as we'd separated, I saw out of the corner of my eye that someone had rounded the corner, heading in the direction of the large conference hall where the hearing was taking place. While I had hoped that it would be Ruby finally arriving, I was disappointed to see that it had been Dr. William Hale and my ex-husband, Michael.

It had been months since I'd last seen Michael. He looked the same as the last time I'd seen him, except more formally dressed today than usual. I could barely look at him as he approached, feeling too many strong emotions when I did. Never had anything infuriated me more than the image of him there in front of me, and of what he represented in those moments. That he was a large part of the reason why I was even here right now, and that he'd done what he did best, and taken away my dreams from me, once again.

"Dr. Carter, Mr. Evans," Dr. Hale spoke, and I turned my attention to him, deciding that it was best if I ignored Michael as much as I could. "I'm glad you could make it. I don't suppose you want to head inside?" Michael had gotten the door, holding it open. When I looked, I made out a massive crowd of people in the auditorium. It wasn't completely full, but there were far more people than I would have ever anticipated.

"I need just another moment," I replied, then glanced at Mason briefly. "You all are welcome to go inside. I'll be along shortly." Dr. Hale looked as though he wanted to say something else, but he refrained and nodded. Mason studied me for a few moments, but I nodded for him to join them, and the three ended up going inside without me, the door shutting behind them.

Just as they'd left me, there was more commotion in the hall. Familiar voices that I recognized. When they turned the corner, relief flooded through me. Ruby Peters appeared in front of me, dressed more professionally than I'd ever seen her before. Beside her, was Daniel Richards, who also had dressed up for the occasion. And much to my surprise, right behind the two, was Adrik Ivanov, who I would have never in a million years expected to see.

"Sorry we were running late," Ruby said, walking up to hug me gently. I hugged her back for a few seconds before we separated. "I had to run and pick Adrik up from the airport."

I glanced up at Adrik, who was smiling at me softly. I could barely speak words. "Mr. Ivanov, I never expected you to come," I started, feeling gracious because of his appearance. "Nor you Mr. Richards. It wasn't necessary."

"Of course, it was," Daniel said, smiling at me. "Ruby said you needed us, and Lord knows I'd do absolutely anything for this woman." He nudged Ruby softly.

"Everyone is inside," I said, glancing at the doors. "I suppose we should be too." The three nodded, and the men filed in first, leaving Ruby and I behind.

Ruby glanced at me, as if she was trying to read how I was feeling. I was certain that it was obvious in those moments, but I did my best to offer a gracious smile anyway. "Thank you for bringing Mr. Richards and Mr. Ivanov. I'm not sure it's going to make a difference, but I appreciate the gesture regardless."

There was a strange look on Ruby's face then. She was smiling softly, and she reached for my hand, gently squeezing it. "Everything is going to work out, Daphne. I promise." She had such a calmness about her, almost how Mason had sounded minutes earlier. I wished I felt the same, but all I did was fight off the overwhelming sense of dread that was overtaking me. Hopefully she was right, Mason was right. It was all I could do, was to be hopeful.

THERE MUST HAVE BEEN at least fifty people in the conference hall when I'd finally had the nerve to step inside. Ruby followed behind me, and we made our way to empty seats on the far side of the room. I was gracious that it was an exceptional distance away from Michael, who I wanted nothing to do with in those moments. I spotted a few familiar faces, colleagues that I worked with, some on my team. Jenny, my intern. Dr. Mariah Stone, the occupational therapist who helped Ruby with her yoga routine. But most of the room was strangers, which made me even more nervous.

Once I'd settled in my seat, Dr. Hale made his way to the front of the room. I watched him, following every move he made. Meanwhile, my hands fidgeted in my lap, until I felt Ruby reach over to wrap hers in my own. We were directly in front, nothing to block everyone from seeing us, but I didn't care. Her gesture had meant everything to me in that moment, a simple one to remind me to stay calm, and I was gracious for it.

"I believe we're all here, so we can get started," Dr. Hale said, speaking loudly into the large room. "My name is Dr. William Hale, and I am the director of biological research here at NASA. As I'm sure all of you are aware, we are here today to evaluate the ethical nature of Dr. Daphne Carter's work over the past year, and what that means for her future career here."

Dr. Hale focused on me for a short moment, and I felt dozens of other eyes. I took a slow, rolling breath, trying to steady myself. The only thing tethering me to reality in those moments was Ruby's hand wrapped around my own. Dr. Hale continued, taking a few minutes to explain about the program, and the research that had been conducted. My twenty years of research. When he finally finished, he turned his attention back to me.

"Dr. Daphne Carter has been working for our program for nearly two decades now. As most of you know, she is an exemplary employee, who has had much success in her career." I was surprised by his flattery, expecting him to do nothing but criticize me. But then it came. "However, these last few months, Dr. Carter has been nothing short of a disappointment to her lifelong career, and to our program. She's broken rule after rule, kept information from us, went behind her superiors' backs, and, not only that, but she engaged in a romantic relationship with a fellow employee who was a part of her research studies, possibly invalidating the research that was done."

I felt myself sinking into my chair then, as if I was falling into a well, unable to stop myself. Again, Ruby's hand around my own, was my only comfort in those moments. I tried my best to breathe, albeit shakily. "We had asked her here today to give the opportunity to evaluate her career here at NASA, the research she's done, and allow her and her colleagues to testify on her behalf. But rest assured, I believe you will find that there is very little that could be said to justify the excessive amount of defiant behavior the woman has shown."

Dr. Hale turned to look at Michael and nodded. My attention went to my ex-husband then and I watched him get up from his seat and walk across the floor to the center of the room. He turned to look at the crowd and offered his signature charismatic smile. A smile that sickened me to my very core.

"Good morning. For those of you who don't know me, I'm Dr. Michael Riddler. Currently the head of the Occupational Health and Ergonomics division of the National Space Biomedical Research Institute, and who replaced Daphne when she was asked to step down from her role. I've been involved with this research for a while now, and even before I came on to help with NASA's program, I was doing very similar research at my position at UC San Diego."

Michael took a moment to scan the room, until he found where I was sitting. There was still a smile on his face, and he nodded to me. The moment he had, I looked away from him, refusing to acknowledge his presence. He continued. "Dr. Carter and I have a long history together, both professionally and personally. She and I met in medical school, did research alongside one another, and were even married for a few years. I absolutely adored her when I met her. Anyone that knows her well knows what a passionate and career-driven woman she is, and how dedicated she is to the research she does. I enjoyed every minute of my time working with her all those years ago."

I wasn't quite sure where he was going with this. Part of me was flattered that he was saying anything nice at all about me. It gave me a small sense of comfort that he hadn't forgotten those years we'd been together and liked one another and had enjoyed working with one another. But it was a false sense of security, I knew better than to assume he had any good intentions with what he'd been saying.

And I'd been right. "However, Daphne has also always shown a little bit of defiance about following the rules. In our career at UC San Diego, she was found guilty of the same sort of behaviors she exhibited over the past few months, neglecting to share all the data she found, skirting around protocols and rules. Dr. Carter has very much always been of the mindset that she can play by her own rules. Which, of course, in a scientific field is frowned upon."

My hand had clenched around Ruby's then. My heart having sped up in my chest. It was all I could do to remain seated. All I could do not to shout at him from across the room, deny the accusations he was accusing me of. Except he wasn't entirely wrong. While I'd certainly been excused from UC San Diego on false grounds, I had always been the type to figure out things on my own. I didn't always stick to protocol and procedures, which of course could get me into trouble. It was most of the reason I was sitting there then.

"So, naturally, I was surprised, two decades later, that Daphne was *yet again* repeating the same behaviors. Skirting around the rules, not following protocol. And, truthfully, I was flabbergasted that she'd do such a thing, with the career that she had. I thought it was a young recent college grad sort of defiance she had. I thought after years and years, it would have changed. The whole defiant childish behaviors of hers would have worn off."

Michael was pacing back and forth across the room, casting glances at various people while he spoke. He met eyes again with me, and shook his head, like he was disappointed in me and could hardly meet me eyes. The idea infuriated me, to the point that once again I was seconds from standing up and shouting at him. Again, I refrained.

"What was *most* surprising, however, was not only did Dr. Carter decide to break rules and not follow protocol, but so did Commander Peters." I watched Michael's eyes shift to look at Ruby's, and a chill shot down my spine. "An astronaut with as extraordinary of a career as Dr. Carter herself, who worked tirelessly to get where she was. How someone that capable, that smart, could do something so reckless—jeopardize her entire career... It's a shame that it came down to this. I'm certain that I heard Ruby had wanted to set records for the astronaut with the longest record in space. And for her to want to risk that all by testifying today—"

"Ruby has nothing to do with this!" I'd lost my temper finally, unable to hold it in any longer. My hand had ripped from Ruby's, and I'd gotten to my feet. "You can accuse me all you want, Michael. Destroy my career, burn me to the ground. But I refuse to let you take her down with me." I glared at him, feeling a vein in my forehead throbbing. My fists were clenched. It was all I could do not to storm across the room to him in those moments, but somehow, I just stood my ground.

Dr. Hale was the one to speak, instead of Michael, getting to his feet. He turned toward the crowd, glancing at me momentarily with a very stern look on his face, before looking elsewhere. "I think we may need a short break before we continue. Some of us seem to need a little breath of fresh air." He'd meant me. I didn't care. I stormed from the room without another word, Ruby following closely behind.

"—I won't do this." The moment Ruby and I had left the room together, we wandered down the hallway to an empty stairwell, closing the door behind us, and then I'd spoken. "I won't let you go down with me."

"I'm not going to," Ruby replied, matter-of-factly. "Let Michael say what he wants about me. I promise you. Everything is going to be okay."

I stared at her in disbelief of what I was hearing. That she could be so confident in those moments, so collected and all-knowing. She was wrong, of course. Michael would do everything in his power to assure that both of our careers went up in flames. I knew him well enough.

"No," I replied, shaking my head, just as Ruby reached out for my hand. I turned away from her, feeling rather frustrated in those moments. "I'm done. I'm not going back in there. If he wants to destroy my career, if this is what it comes down to, so be it. But I refuse for you to sacrifice yourself, too. I won't allow it."

"Daphne will you just trust me?" Ruby said, wrapping her hand around my wrist. It caused me to turn back to face her, staring into those warm brown eyes of hers. They instantly calmed me. "Do you remember the Marie Curie quote? The one you love so much?"

"Nothing in life is to be feared, it is only to be understood. Now is the time to understand more, so that we may fear less." I recited, verbatim. It was the singular quote I would never forget, for as long as I lived. "I'm not *afraid* Ruby. I'm using what knowledge I have of my ex-husband. I know what he's capable of, what he'll do to you if he can. And if this doesn't happen if I walk away now... You'll be safe. You don't have to do this."

"But you *are* afraid Daphne," Ruby said, reaching up to place a hand against my cheek. It felt warm, and comforting, and inviting. Exactly what I had needed in those moments. "You're afraid for me. Afraid for what might happen as consequence of all this. But I'm here to tell you that it's all going to be okay. You've got to trust me. Understand me and what I'm saying."

I had no earthly idea what she meant by that and had no more confidence about the situation than I had the few moments before we'd arrived. But there was something so sincere, so reassuring in the way that she looked at me, that I couldn't help but try to believe her. Even if it was the hardest thing I ever had to do.

"—I'll do my best," I replied, shaking my head, and allowing myself to breathe a moment. We took a seat on the stairwell for a few minutes, and Ruby let me breathe and try to steady myself. Then Ruby smiled at me softly and took my hand. The two of us made our way back into the conference room without another word to one another. And I was still filled with as much dread as I had been before, but I was grateful, too, that Ruby was there with me.

As Ruby and I had made our way inside, I realized that the hearing was still going on without me. In the front of the room, Daniel Richards and Adrik Ivanov were standing, along with Dr. Mariah Stone and, on video chat, James Mertz, Andrea Bratcher, and Tony Reynolds, all still aboard the International Space Station. While Ruby and I made our way back to our seats, I realized that there was a discussion about me.

"Dr. Carter was with us aboard the ISS for three weeks conducting research," Daniel was speaking. "She was working on two projects, one of which included all of us."

"And I am to believe you were aware of the nature of Dr. Carter and Commander Peter's relationship?" Dr. Hale spoke from his seat across the room, staring at Daniel. I swallowed deeply at his question, dreading Daniel's reply.

"I was," Daniel replied, matter-of-factly and without hesitation. "Not at first, but shortly after the doctor left. But honestly, Bill, I don't know what the hell the two of them having a relationship with one another has anything to do with anything. It didn't impact her research, at least not from my perspective."

"Mr. Richards, she blatantly withheld information about Commander Peters' health in order to ensure that she didn't have to leave the station..." Dr. Hale was staring at him in disbelief. "Dr.

Stone and Dr. Carter completely undermined my authority, and the authority of Dr. Riddler, to pursue an alternative form of exercise treatment without clearance. If you don't see the ethical dilemma here—"

"Dr. Carter got us to the next phase of the trial, right? Ruby got to utilize the—er—tro—I'm not even going to try to pronounce the thing. The drug from her trial. Ruby used it, and it ended up helping her." Daniel argued, staring back at Dr. Hale. "And honestly, Bill," I was surprised that Daniel was using Dr. Hale's first name so blatantly. "I would have probably done the same thing had I been in her position. Everybody who knows Ruby knows how much she loves her job. Sure, Dr. Carter could have gone about it differently, but it all worked out. And honestly, that's all the suits want, right? Their drug trial was a success. Dr. Stone's exercise regimen was a success. All I see is wins for NASA here, and you trying to throw Daphne under the bus anyway."

Dr. Hale's mouth had dropped open slightly, while Daniel looked rather proud of his speech. When I glanced over at Ruby, she was giving Daniel a small thumbs up, to which he nodded just barely in reply. "—I think we've heard enough. Thank you for your time." Daniel nodded, and he and Adrik left the stage, while the feed from the ISS disappeared. I was certain that the crew was still watching the hearing, but we couldn't see them now.

"Commander Peters, if you'd be so kind as to come up now." Dr. Hale had turned his attention across the room to where Ruby and I had been seated. I watched Ruby nod, filled with that overwhelming sense of dread again, as she got to her feet. I watched her come to stand in the center of the room, looking out into the audience of people watching.

"—Good morning," Ruby said, offering a pleasant smile, but I could still tell she was nervous, and I was genuinely worried for her. Worried about this entire situation, wishing desperately I had stopped it before now. She glanced away from the crowd for a moment, toward the doors, not speaking. Then I watched her walk across the room, holding up a finger. When I looked to where she was heading toward, I realized the door had been cracked slightly open.

Ruby went to open the door, and I could faintly hear her conversing with whoever was outside but couldn't make out what they were saying. The entire room was dead silent, until suddenly the door opened all the way, and Ruby stepped back into the room.

What happened next, was something I could barely comprehend. I watched, completely unable to move or think, confused, and overwhelmed at the sight, as the room began to fill. Dozens upon dozens upon dozens of women, filing into the room. I didn't recognize most of them, a face or two that I'd worked with before, some I'd seen at Johnson or Kennedy in passing. By the time the door finally closed, there must have been over a hundred women standing in the open space, Ruby coming to take her place in front of them.

"What the hell is going on here?" Dr. Hale said, having gotten to his feet.

"Dr. Hale," Ruby said, stepping forward, so she was standing directly in front of him. She looked as serious as I'd ever seen her before. "Did you know that women only make up a third of NASA's workforce? Eighteen thousand employees, and only six thousand of them are women."

I watched Dr. Hale sit back down promptly in his seat, wordlessly, mouth hanging open still. He shook his head in disbelief. My ex-husband sat beside him, looking just as stunned.

Ruby continued. "And, even more surprising, only *sixteen* percent of those women have senior or leadership roles." She glanced over, looking at me, and I could only stare back at her in disbelief, wondering what on earth she could possibly be doing. Only able to slightly comprehend the words that were coming out of her mouth. "One of which, was Dr. Carter. The woman you just fired from her two-decade long position, and replaced with, well...*a man*."

Dr. Hale cleared his throat. "Commander Peters, if you're implying what I think you're implying—"

"Oh, I most certainly am, Dr. Hale," Ruby said, glancing from him, to Michael, and then back to me for a moment. "And I have six thousand female employees at NASA ready to back Dr. Carter up on that fact." She glanced at the women behind her. "Including these women of senior management positions who have all agreed to step down if anything were to happen to Dr. Carter in preventing her from continuing her research. That's a lot of jobs you'll need to replace, a lot of explaining you'll have to do to the public..."

"Commander Peters are you *threatening* me right now?" Dr. Hale stared at her in disbelief. I couldn't help but wonder the same thing, worried that everything Ruby was doing was jeopardizing her career even further.

"No, Dr. Hale," Ruby replied, matter-of-factly. "I'm *telling* you. If you let Dr. Carter, go, if you replace her with Dr. Riddler, who has a history of taking her research from her in the past...well, I think it will show everyone just who you really are. I don't think I have to threaten you. I think your actions would speak for themselves. And the actions of these women who would leave as a result."

The entire room was silent. No one breathed, no one moved. A hundred women stared at a wordless Dr. Hale and Dr. Riddler. Ruby looked as confident and calm as I'd ever seen her before, and all I could do was stare at her in disbelief of what she was doing.

Then Dr. Hale said the last thing I ever thought he would say, and I wasn't sure what to think about it. He got to his feet, Michael following behind him. "I need a moment." He turned, nodding to a few other individuals in the room, and then the group of them disappeared out of the conference hall without another word.

While they were gone, Ruby came to get me, and she introduced me to some of the women who were standing there on my behalf. It was all I could do just to thank them and shake their hands, stunned that they'd come at all. And so many of them, willing to sacrifice their careers for me. I didn't understand, couldn't possibly fathom why someone would do that.

Ruby and I stood off to the side of the room then and met each other's gaze. "What on earth are you doing, Ruby?" I was in disbelief.

The only thing that Ruby did was smile for a moment at me, which I almost felt irritated by, until she decided to speak. "It is a disservice to Marie Curie herself not to help another woman succeed. I told you this one of the first times we ever spoke to each other, remember?"

A smile broke across my face, a soft one, but one none the less. Ruby wrapped her arms around my neck and kissed me softly on the cheek. We stood together for a few moments, and then broke apart, just as the doors of the conference room opened and Dr. Hale and the small group that had left, reappeared.

Dr. Hale strolled across the room, while the remainder of the group stood by the door. All I could focus on was Bill, whose expression I couldn't read. He came to stand directly in front of Ruby and myself.

"On behalf of the Biomedical Research Institute and the Biology Department of NASA, Dr. Carter, I'd like to personally welcome you back as the department head of the Occupational Health and Ergonomics division." Bill outstretched his hand, and I stood stunned for a few seconds, unable to comprehend what was happening.

"Daphne, I think this is where you shake his hand," Ruby said, nudging me softly in the side.

I did what I was told, outstretching my hand, and shaking Bill's back, as confidently as I could manage. "—Thank you, Dr. Hale." Bill nodded, and then turned his attention the rest of the room. "This meeting is adjourned. Thank you everyone for attending."

The room began to empty, and I watched people filing out. Meanwhile, Bill and a few others were collected by the doors, including Michael, who looked completely stunned at what had just happened. All at once I couldn't help myself and wandered over to him.

"Michael," I said, once I'd gotten within earshot. He looked up at me, wordlessly, which was a rarity for him. I stopped in front of him, outstretching my hand and placing it on his shoulder. Michael's brown eyes, dull and lifeless as ever, looked back at mine, still looking completely stunned. "I just wanted to let you know that you're welcome to come work for me if you'd like." And then I let go, turning away from him without another word.

Once the room had emptied, some coming up to congratulate us, and some leaving without saying anything at all, it was only Ruby and I left together, alone. She was looking at a photo hanging on the wall, a picture of the Shuttle Eclipse, that had exploded years ago, killing her father. I watched her for a few moments, before she turned her attention back to me. She was smiling, softly, as she wandered over.

"Come to Houston with me," I said, once she'd reached me, wrapping our hands together.

"You want me to move to Houston?" Ruby said, blinking in surprise. We'd barely been dating in person, but I hadn't doubted my question, not even for a second.

"I don't want any space between us anymore."

EPILOGUE

Ruby

Daphne let out a delightful moan, as she laid half naked and sprawled out across her leather sofa in the condo. I was on my knees, my face buried between her open legs. She was dripping with arousal, and I could feel her beginning to clench against my fingers that were deep and curling inside of her. I knew she was close.

There were gasps of air coming from Daphne then, and when I looked up at her, her head was rolled back, fingers interwoven in my hair, holding my face against her. My tongue worked swiftly, knowing exactly what she liked now. The little flicks and swirls that sent her tumbling over the edge.

Suddenly she bucked, and I felt her clench tightly around my fingers. She moaned my name, writhing beneath me as she came. I loved watching, knowing that it was me that had undone her. That it was my touches that had brought her to such levels of pleasure.

Daphne came for a while, and I continued with my mouth and fingers, until she'd gone slack against the couch. When I moved away from her, I pulled myself off the ground, crawling over her body until I was straddling her.

We kissed, deeply. Daphne always seemed to enjoy tasting herself on me after I pleasured her, and even though she'd already made me come a short while earlier, I could feel the heat reappearing between my legs then, begging for more.

When we broke, Daphne was panting lightly. Her hand came up to stroke my cheek gently, and she was smiling. "As much as I would like to continue this, we're running late." I watched her check her watch on her arm. Late for what, she wouldn't tell me. But I nodded anyway, and then helped her from the sofa.

GALVESTON ISLAND WAS a place I'd visited only a handful of times in my life, when I'd made trips to Houston for work, or once with Daphne since I'd moved here. It was a beautiful place, but a little too touristy for my liking. Daphne drove us that evening, to a small restaurant that overlooked the water.

As we walked inside, she took my hand gently in her own. We turned immediately when we entered to the right, and I felt Daphne lean into me, whispering into my ear. "Act surprised."

"SURPRISE!"

A loud burst of shouting erupted when we entered the room. There were at least a dozen people, and it took me a moment to realize who all had been there. Daniel and his wife and children, Tony, and Andrea, Dr. Mariah Stone, Mason Evans, and surprisingly even my aunt and uncle, who came rushing to me the moment we'd entered. I had just seen them a week prior, but it was a surprise and pleasure to see them again.

"What on earth are you all doing here?" I asked, feeling somewhat dumbfounded.

Mary pointed behind her, to a large banner that stretched across the wall.

Congratulations Ruby!

"You didn't think we weren't going to celebrate your record-breaking trip, did you?" My uncle squeezed my shoulder, and I hugged him tightly. "Congratulations, kiddo."

"It was Daphne's idea," Mary said, matter-of-factly, smiling at Daphne. I turned to look at her, and she shrugged. "She was so proud of you. You should have seen her when you were coming back home last month. A bundle of excitement."

I couldn't help but smile at Daphne, who smiled softly back. She took my hand in her own and kissed it, before letting me go again so I could go say hello to the other guests that had arrived. The first of which had been Daniel, who was accompanied by his wife and children.

"Finn, Piper...This is the astronaut friend I told you about. The one who just broke the record for longest in space," Daniel explained, looking down at his children. "Remember Ruby? You met her a long time ago." He'd been right. They'd been so much younger the last time they'd seen me, I doubted they remembered much.

"You're a *girl!*" Piper, Daniel's youngest daughter, said excitedly.

I couldn't help but laugh. "I am." I squatted down so I was looking her in the eyes, my smile widening at her genuine excitement of the idea. "I know your dad probably tells you this all the time, but don't forget... Girls can do anything boys can do. Okay?" Piper nodded, her eyes still wide with fascination.

When I stood back up, Mason Evans had come to join us. He was sporting a very fashionable Star Wars button down, with little storm trooper heads all over it. It was marvelous. "Way to go, Ruby." I couldn't help but hug him in gratitude, and he hugged me back gently. "Always knew you had it in you."

"Thanks, Mason," I replied.

Mason turned his attention to Daphne then, a smile on his face, underneath all that thick beard of his. "You know, this party isn't just for Ruby, Daph."

Daphne had a curious look to her face, raising a brow. "Hm?"

"We all heard you just got your grant funding for the drug trial," he said, nodding. I watched him walk away from us, and Daphne and I followed curiously. On a table on the other side of the room was a large sheet cake. Sure enough, decorated in beautiful cursive writing on the top read the words "Congratulations Ruby and Daphne!"

When I looked at Daphne, she was smiling graciously. "You didn't really need to do that, Mason."

"Of course, I did," Mason replied, matter-of-factly.

Mary had appeared next to me, her hand on my shoulder. "Come on then, lets eat! I'm starving, and Ruby needs a little meat on her bones!" And I couldn't help but laugh.

ON A STEEL grey wall of the National Air and Space Museum in Washington D.C., there was a plaque hanging, with a small piece of the United States flag attached. Recovered from vehicle debris on the ocean floor. One of the very few things that they'd retrieved from the explosion of the space shuttle *Eclipse*. A tiny reminder of a man that I never got to know, but who would always be a part of me. I'd seen this plaque a handful of times now, when I had visited this museum in the past, and every time it took the air right from me.

"Rubs. Are you ready to head out?" I felt a tug on my arm that brought me back to reality. When I turned my attention back, I met the eyes of one of my best friends, Commander Daniel Richards, who had recently been promoted.

I gave one last look at the plaque on the wall, focused on one of the seven names etched into the metal. *Commander James Peters.* Husband of Elizabeth Peters. Father of Ruby Peters.

I'd gotten my love of space from my father, dreaming of it before I could even say the word itself. It was "in my blood," as my uncle Eric would say. I had only one goal in my life. To follow in my father's footsteps. But on my own merit. Not because I was the prodigy of a well-known astronaut, but because I'd worked tirelessly to get where

I was. And I had done just that. Accomplished what many astronauts only dreamed about. And somehow, it felt enough. Like I had done what I'd set out to do, and proudly.

Which was why I had traveled to Washington D.C. for the *Annual Space Symposium,* a few months after my return from my record-breaking trip to space. Dr. Daphne Carter would be speaking that day, about the next phases of her research, and I hadn't wanted to miss it, for more reasons than one.

Daniel and I weaved our way through the crowded museum, to a large conference room where Daphne would be speaking in a short while. While he took a seat out in the audience, I made my way up to the stage, where Daphne was busy setting up her presentation. I came to meet her, placing a hand on her shoulder.

"I was wondering where you went off to," Daphne said, smiling when she looked at me, those hazel eyes glistening under her black framed glasses. I leaned forward, planting our lips together, and it felt as wonderful and new as it had every time since the first time. When we parted, Daphne seemed to be at loss for words. Finally, she cleared her throat and spoke again. "I believe I'm almost ready." The room had nearly filled with people.

"I have something I want to say, before you get started," I said, meeting her gaze. "If you don't mind, that is."

Daphne looked curiously at me, and then shrugged. "By all means." She nodded to the podium and the microphone attached to it. I gave her a small smile, and then made my way over, tapping lightly on the mic. It let out a small bit of feedback, signaling that it was on. The entire room turned their attention on me, and the chatter that had been happening silenced.

"Good morning," I said, looking out into the crowd of people watching. "I'm glad you all are here today and have come to watch Dr. Carter's presentation. I realize I am not her, but I wanted to say a little something before she spoke."

I looked out into the crowd, finding Daniel a few rows back. He gave me a small thumbs up, which made a smile break on m face.

"For those of you who don't know, my name is Commander Ruby Peters. I'm Daphne's fiancée and have been a NASA astronaut for nearly the past decade. I worked with Daphne when she first came to the International Space Station a little over a year and a half ago, and have been assisting her since, watching her research grow and change the face of space travel as we know it."

"A few months ago, I got back from my record-breaking trip to the International Space Station and can proudly say that I'm the astronaut with the longest track record in space." There was a small round of applause that broke out in the room, and I waved a gracious thank you. "It was an incredible moment for me in my career, and a moment I know my father, Commander Jeffery Peters, would be very proud of, if he was still here."

I paused a moment, thinking about that plaque on the wall outside that I'd been staring at. Thinking of if my father had been here to see this moment, what it would have been like. How my life might have possibly been different. But I realized then, that I knew exactly what he would have said.

"Daphne told me about the first time she met my father, many years ago," I started speaking again, looking at Daphne briefly, and then back to the crowd. "She watched him speak at a conference once, and told me that she remembered something he said, very profoundly. That "curiosity is the essence of our existence." Daphne told me that my dad made her realize something. That whether you were an astronaut, or a scientist, or an engineer, or even just a human living on our beautiful planet Earth—we were all in this journey for the same reason. The joy of discovery. And that in and of itself is a grand adventure, regardless of what path you chose to take, or what life you live."

I paused a second, looking to Daphne again. She was smiling softly, and I assumed she remembered that conversation we had had now, years ago. I was surprised that it had stuck with me so much, but it had. Once I cleared my throat, I looked back again, taking a long deep breath before speaking.

"And with that being said, I'd like to announce that I will be officially retiring from the astronaut program to assist Dr. Carter with her research, full time."

There was a rush of murmurs in the audience. When I looked at Daphne yet again, she looked shocked, to say the least.

"I know this may come as a surprise to some. That I'd give up a life of adventure like I've had over the last handful of years. But I did what I set out to do. I accomplished the things I wanted to accomplish. And now, I just want to help Daphne, so that hopefully we can see a future ahead that's full of possibilities and set a frontier for young women to pursue dreams like ours. Because, if anyone can say it's possible, Dr. Carter and I can."

The End

THANK YOU FOR READING! If you enjoyed *The Space Between*, you should check out a few other of my longer bestselling novels *Forbidden Melody* and *Homespun*.

A NOTE FROM MAGGIE

I really hope you enjoyed my novel *The Space Between*. This was my favorite book out of all the ones I've written over my publishing career, which is saying a lot because of *Forbidden Melody*. I wanted to dedicate this book to all the women out there in STEM fields, the mothers who have little girls wanting to grow up to be astronauts and doctors and scientists.

When I was little, there was a commercial that used to run for "Space Camp." I saw it so many times that I remembered memorizing the number. I wanted to go so bad and remember working up the nerve to ask my mom about it. Instead, I ended up going to acting camp, which wasn't bad, but it wasn't what I really wanted to do. It happened again in high school, when I wanted to attend a special school for STEM, and instead I ended up studying musical theatre. Sometimes I wonder what my life would have been like had I pursued that path.

But then I might not have written this book. So, all in all, I'm happy the way things worked out. My hope is though, that there are more and more women encouraged to pursue STEM careers. It's still a male dominated career path, but it's slowly getting better. And I can't wait until the day that NASA is a 50% women workforce.

Thank you for reading my novel.

And remember that Marie Curie quote:

"Nothing in life is to be feared, it is only to be understood. Now is the time to understand more, so that we may fear less."

KEEP IN TOUCH

If you enjoyed *The Space Between*, I always really like it when people shoot me an email and let me know. It gives me a little confidence boost and I love knowing you read my book.

Email Me Here

For information about me, my books, my upcoming releases, ordering signed copies, and more, you can visit my website that I'm super proud of.

Visit My Website

If you're a social media fan, I am all about Twitter, but can also be found on Facebook and Instagram.

Here I am on Twitter
Also, on Facebook
Last, but not least, Instagram

And, of course, if you want to stay up to date on all the latest Maggie happenings, and get a free novella of mine to boot, you should sign up to my new newsletter!

Sign Up Hereh

OTHER BOOKS BY MAGGIE ROBBINS

Forbidden Melody

While the Music Lasts

Homespun

Stay

Nerd Love

Wildsky

Safe Words

Lightkeeper

Printed in Great Britain
by Amazon